The Mid
an
Mourning Man

David Anthony

First Edition: 1969
Current eBook Edition: 2013

Published in the United States of America
By James Mace and Legionary Books
http://www.legionarybooks.net

To Jacqueline, a lady around the clock

Forward by Elinor Jewett

Before light slipped through the curtains, before traffic rumbled down the streets, before our beagle whined to be fed, my brother and I woke to the *rat-a-tat-tat* of my father's Smith Corona typewriter. It was our morning lullaby. The tune said that my father was writing a mystery. And so it was every morning of every day for 30 years.

My father published nine novels that were printed in many languages and enjoyed by readers all over the world. He was nominated for the coveted Edgar Allen Poe award for mystery writing. And he even received fan mail. The theme of his adorers was always the same; they wanted more. More time in the gritty world he conjured, but, most of all, more time with heroes like Morgan Butler, a lone wolf with skill, smarts, humor and a no nonsense sense of justice. The reprinting of *The Midnight Lady and the Mourning Man* means that new readers will meet Morgan Butler, and, through him, my father.

My father's mysteries were not flights of fancy. Like his heroes, he walked with integrity and held himself accountable. He invented a personal "mystery writer's code of ethics," to ensure a fair and honest relationship with his reader. Rule number one, weave the plot and lay out the clues in such a way that the smart reader has a chance to solve the mystery on his own. No surprise look-a-like second cousins or twins switched at birth here. Number two, no matter what kind of hot water a hero got himself into, he had to get himself out on his own steam with his wits and his will. No rescues by sympathetic babes. That would be a betrayal. And three, every story must have a provocative and believable villain or it just isn't a good story.

His sense of fairness ran deep. That's why, in the end it was always all about justice. With his background as a farm boy during the depression, and a Marine in the front lines of Korea, I know he saw a lot of senseless killing and hurt in this world. But in a mystery novel, murder, greed and mayhem suddenly make perfect sense, or at least they do by the time the hero has solved the crime and brought the killer to justice.

The power of one man—one, lone, former marine turned security guard with a failed marriage can deduce the truth behind the facade the killer has created. Just one good guy could save the world. That's my kind of justice. No wonder his fans wanted more.

Preface

The rites of spring are well underway on the small Midwestern campus of Jordan City College when Morgan Butler reluctantly agrees to pinch hit for his ailing Marine buddy, the town constable. For Butler, a former detective turned gentleman farmer, it all seems fairly routine until he stumbles on the brutally murdered body of the beautiful, frosty coed Natalie Clayborne.

In search for the girl's killer he plunges into a thick web of intrigue that turns up two more murders and begins to uncover shocking relationships between notable members of the academic community.

The closer Butler gets to the situation, the more it appears that a disreputable member of the faculty still carries a torch for Natalie's mother; that the relationship between Natalie and her father was more than a little out of the ordinary; and that the distinguished editor of the local newspaper knows more about the secrets Natalie shared with her hippy boyfriend than he is letting on.

This is a powerful story about the explosive forces lurking beneath the staid veneer of the academic environment, and about the men and women forced to live behind this mask of respectability. The murder is the catalyst which unleashes a flood of pent-up furies and finally forces into the open the hidden secrets that have affected the very foundation of the community.

March, 1962

Chapter 1
***

It was too hot for March in Ohio, the kind of balmy day that makes you think nostalgically of the South Seas. Even if you have never been there. Or even if you were there only in the war, as was the case with me.

That Sunday morning the Jordan College campus looked deserted. As I got out of my car at the edge of the campus, I was aware of a sensation tourists must feel when they approach old cathedrals in Europe. Stately trees presided over a rolling, immaculate lawn, and the Gothic spires and towers of the oldest buildings (three had been built when Lincoln was President) promised dignity and stability. The sight inspired the reverence most Americans feel toward that mythical adventure called Higher Education.

But my college had been the South Pacific twenty years ago. Maybe that was why I felt like a tourist, my memories of that time and place revived by the fact that I was wearing an old set of Marine Corps khaki. Of course the insignia had been changed. In place of the division patch on the shoulder, I sported a constable's star with "JORDAN CITY" sewn in a circle around it. On my cap I wore a badge instead of the globe and anchor. I had resurrected the uniform and taken on the job three weeks before, as a favor to a friend.

Then I turned and mounted the steps of a building so new compared with those I had been admiring that it suggested the dawn of a new age. At least half the front was glass and copper, and that part which was brick gleamed in the sunlight as if it had been lacquered. This was the Forbes Institute of Research and Study. I tapped the thick glass door with a key, and at that moment a chime from one of the college towers announced the hour: nine o'clock.

Soon a face peered defiantly at me through the glass, then the door swung open. The man who stood there had a white shaggy hair and a pink complexion. He wore a wilted gray uniform and a .38 revolver in an open holster.

"I'm Morgan Butler," I said. "Dr. Pritchett called me about the burglary."

"So old Quartz is still laid up," he said in a piping voice. "I'm Cappy Chambers, the night watchman. I was due to go off at eight, but this damn—" Only then did the word penetrate to his mind. "Burglary!" he snorted. "Some burglary. To my mind, it was vandalism, pure and simple. Likely one of the screwball kids they let have the run of this joint. Hey, you're not even wearing a gun. Some cop."

"I'll borrow yours if the bad guys jump us," I said. "You think they're still on the premises?"

"I know for a fact they're not. Listen, I went over this place from top to—Aw, the heck with it. You talk to the doctor."

I followed the old man's arthritic gait down two long corridors. He halted before a wooden door with a mail slot in it and the words "CLINICAL PSYCHOLOGY" printed on it. There were deep gashes in the wood near the lock.

"A tire tool did that," Cappy said. "I found grease in the wood. Save you a little detective work." He chuckled, then took me in and introduced me to Dr. Pritchett. Cappy stopped chuckling when the doctor dismissed him.

Pritchett was about forty, tall, with a crew cut and a face that tapered gracefully to a narrow chin. He wore a tweed jacket that needed a pipe to set it off. Stronger than any feature was the overall impression of poise he conveyed, as if nothing you said would shock him in the least. The best of them develop it early, for it reassures. It disarms. It cauterizes the raw nerve ends and invites you to reveal the secrets no man should have to reveal to another. I had been there and back, but Pritchett would never know it.

"I'm sorry to drag you out on Sunday morning," he said. "But this sort of thing has to be reported. Say, you're not the regular constable."

"No, I'm a temporary replacement. Quartz Willinger is the constable. But he was injured in the line of duty a few weeks ago."

"Yes, I vaguely recall reading about it," Pritchett said. "It was a robbery at the Stagecoach Inn. Wasn't he shot?"

"No, just busted up. Three hardcases worked him over."

All this time the doctor watched me as if gauging my ability. He said, "Mr. Butler, I wonder if you're aware that the college has an arrangement with the Jordan City constable, and—"

"Quartz briefed me about the arrangement. Any dirty linen we can wash in the college laundry, that's the way we handle it."

"Bluntly put, but accurate." His smile was a little less gracious now. "Tell me, are you a law officer by profession?"

"No, I'm a farmer by profession," I said. "But I've had considerable experience in police work. I'm sure Constable Willinger would be glad to reassure you on my qualifications, if you care to call him."

"Not necessary, believe me," he said. He produced the pipe at last, a black briar, and began to fill it. "I raised the question only because we had an unusual theft here last night. And while we'd like it investigated, the whole business will require considerable tact, and ah…delicacy."

He deliberately made me wait while he packed the pipe, while he burned one match over it, tamped the result with a fancy pipe tool, then sucked the flame from a second match into the bowl. He thought he had piqued my curiosity. Now I was supposed to ask about the unusual theft. I just waited.

Finally he broke the silence. "First, you should know that one service the Institute performs for the college is to provide psychological counseling for those students who need it. This counseling isn't as complicated as psychotherapy, of course, but it requires the same tools. The experience of college can be traumatic for certain individuals. Some of them get into an emotional bind, and we try to help them get out. It's as simple as that. Tell me, do you have any idea how this kind of analysis is conducted?"

"Only what a layman would know," I said. "I understand that the patient talks, and the doctor picks out what's relevant and helps him put it together."

Now I had Pritchett's full attention. He clicked his pipe against his teeth, watching my face. "A farmer, you said?"

"That's right." But his scrutiny did not reveal a farmer to him. Nor did he see a small-town cop, now that he had taken the trouble to look beyond the camouflage of the uniform.

Physically he saw a man six feet tall who (because the farm did exist) looked considerably leaner than the hundred and ninety pounds he carried. He saw a head of thick hair salted with gray, as if every tenth hair had been painted, dark hazel eyes, a scar like a wayward dimple in the left cheek where I had got cut one night on Jap wire,

11

and a mouth that would be judged too wide if not for the extra bone in the jaw.

What Pritchett saw beyond that was anybody's guess. He merely gave me an amused look, to show that he wasn't fooled, and said, "Well, that description will serve our purpose. Yes, the patient talks. And not long ago we decided to allow certain students to talk to us even when they didn't have a scheduled hour. We thought it might help if they could get something off their chest when the mood seized them, rather than wait for a formal session."

"Tape recorders," I said.

"Yes, they have access to recording machines in the record library. And they can deposit the tape through the slot in the door out there."

"How do they get into the building at night?" I asked.

"We lock every door but the main entrance at six P.M. Between six and midnight a watchman sits at a desk in the lobby, and anyone who enters has to sign in with him. When the night watchman comes on at midnight, the front doors are locked. Of course, the regular personnel can get in at any hour, but they have to notify the watchman in advance if they plan to arrive after midnight."

"Does the same schedule hold true for Saturdays?"

"Yes. Many of the staff come in on Saturdays to continue experiments."

"So what did happen here last night?"

Pritchett's face showed displeasure that I had finally asked the question. "There were three tapes deposited in the slot between six and midnight. And at roughly five this morning, someone broke into my office and stole them."

"How do you know there were exactly three tapes?"

"Mr. Butler, I even know who deposited them," he said. "The watchman at the desk has a list of the students who have this privilege. His records show that three of them left tapes last night. And get this: there was nothing else touched in the office. Not the petty-cash box, not the typewriters, nor any of a number of things that could be sold."

He must have detected my flagging interest. It was a bizarre crime, but it was also trivial and a little silly. For the sake of Quartz, I put on a more professional demeanor and asked the pertinent questions. How did the thief get into the building? Was any of the staff on the premises after midnight? Did the watchman hear anything?

Apparently the thief entered the building with a passkey, of which there were at least fifty in circulation, in the hands of secretaries, clerks, professors, and even a student who fed the animals kept for experiments.

No, none of the staff checked in last night.

The watchman, who has a cubbyhole in the basement, heard nothing. When he discovered the broken door on his five-o'clock round, he searched the building and then called Pritchett.

"What about the three who deposited the tapes?" I asked. "Maybe one of them changed his mind and didn't want you to hear his tape."

"Not even remotely possible," Pritchett said. "They know that all they have to do is call, and we would honor the request. We'd destroy the tape."

"Blackmail," I said quickly in a low voice. But the good doctor didn't even interrupt the drag he was taking on his pipe.

"That occurred to me, too," he said. "It's tempting, but altogether fanciful. You haven't heard the tapes, Butler." He leaned back in his chair and smiled as if he would like to divulge some of the grubby secrets he had heard in this room. "Their problems are terribly important to them, of course. But I can't recall a single instance where blackmail would be possible."

"Then how about a lover who found out he was being discussed? I imagine it's safe to say that sex is one topic you get an earful of. Think about the three who deposited tapes last night. Was any of them on the verge of some earthshaking revelation on that score?"

He concealed his reaction, but not before I saw that flicker in his eyes like a shark fin in deep water.

"Tell it, Doctor. I'll respect the confidence."

"For a farmer, you're pretty sharp. Yes, one of the three has been very reticent about a love affair. But it's only a hunch. I'd hate to mislead you."

I nodded. "Well if I'm going to investigate this burglary, the first step is to learn which of the three had something worth stealing on his tape. So I'd better talk with them. I don't relish the task, but I'll do it."

"Don't you think I should contact them first? I don't mean to be protective, but it might be easier if I told them their tapes had been stolen."

"I'd rather watch their reactions when I tell them. It could be enlightening. I promise to exercise tact and—what was it?—yes, delicacy."

"That *was* patronizing of me," he said. "But then, how did I know I was dealing with a farmer?" That little mystery appealed to his fancy. He couldn't leave it alone. "Don't you want me to brief you about them?"

"I'd prefer you didn't. If I need any information, I'll call you."

"All right. Here's a list of their names and dormitory addresses."

I tucked the slip of paper into my shirt pocket, and stopped just long enough at the door to confirm the watchman's theory that a tire tool had done the damage. Any third-rate thief could have opened that door with a hangnail as fast as anyone could with a key. That, plus the fact that he didn't even have the grace to lift the petty-cash box, meant that I was dealing with an amateur, possibly even a prankster.

Outside, it was hotter, sultry. The air had a faint odor of sorghum molasses, as if the earth sweated beneath the grass. It was time to plow. My partner and friend, Johnny Bass, was no doubt at work right now in the field we planned to plant with alfalfa. It was rich bottomland. The soil spinning off the plow would be as black as all corruption. We owned a matched team of blacks that could plow from six to six with never a limp singletree.

Bat is was Johnny who plowed behind the blacks, while I set off across the campus to find three students of dubious stability in order to discuss, with delicacy, the cruel theft of their innermost secrets. Anything for an old friend. Especially if he has bled for you, as Quartz once bled for me.

14

Chapter 2
***

The first name on my list was Elaine French, sophomore, aged nineteen. She lived in Jefferson Hall, an old building that looked as if a growth of ivy held one of the faded brick walls together. In the lobby there was an intercom system with a handset. I rang Elaine French, and when she answered I identified myself and asked if I might have a few words with her in private.

"Did you say *Constable* Butler? You must be joking. Oh, all right. Why don't you wait in the parlor, just off the lobby? I'll be right down."

It was a room crowded with sofas, easychairs and lamps, all of it a little frayed and musty, as if too many generations had wrung the juices from their dreams and passions into the fabric. The place was empty, so I selected a chair and lit one of the short black stogies I enjoy.

Before long, a big girl in blue jeans and a man's shirt entered the room. She stopped abruptly. "You *are* a *gendarme*. I thought it was a gag."

"You're Elaine French?"

"Yes." She took the chair beside mine, slouching to tug a pack of cigarettes from her jeans. She wasn't a homely girl, but her nose was crooked and there was a gap between her two front teeth you could pass a matchstick through. "Hey, shouldn't I be warned that all I say can be used against me?"

I guessed that she used the flip manner to overcome a natural shyness. I said, "No, it's not like that. In this case, you're the victim."

"That's hardly a novelty. Tell me more."

I told her about the tapes being stolen. When I finished, she was sitting erect with her hands on her knees.

"That's only the second time I've put anything on tape," she said. "I thought it was safe. Who would take it?" Her voice was low, embarrassed.

"That's what I hope to find out, Miss French. Tell me, did you mention to anyone that you had made the tape?"

She gave a low, jerky laugh. "I haven't even told anyone I'm taking psych-counseling. I'm not proud of it."

15

"Not even your roommate?"

"Especially not her."

"How about a boyfriend who might have learned about it?"

Again the laugh, harsh, self-deprecating. "No boyfriend. No lover. Oh, there was a boy, but we broke up last fall. Now I suppose you'll say I took up psych-counseling to get over that." She lit another cigarette.

"Did you happen to mention his name on the tape you made last night?"

She was silent, smoking.

"Miss French, you understand that everything you tell me is confidential."

"That's what they said about the tapes. Now it'll be all over campus."

"No, that won't happen. I think your tape's already been destroyed."

"How can you be sure of that?"

"I think they were stolen to be destroyed. Someone learned that he was mentioned on one of the tapes in a way that would damage him. He had to take all three tapes to be sure he had the right one. Assuming yours wasn't the one in question, he wouldn't leave it around as evidence. So it's destroyed."

"That's only a theory." But her tone really didn't doubt it.

"Yes, but a theory based on the facts. And Dr. Pritchett agrees with them."

This cheered her up. Pritchett's name was the magic. She gave me a sheepish smile. "I didn't mean to panic on you. I guess I'm ashamed of the counseling. That boy whose name I wouldn't tell you. He's Sam Maxwell, a senior. We went together for a year. It was like being married, and I guess I couldn't take the divorce." Her eyes glistened over, her mouth was big and soft, and I knew she would confide the whole dreary story if I let her.

"I don't think Sam's our man," I said.

"No, he wouldn't break down a door to steal my tape." She said it with regret, a mournful epitaph to the whole affair.

I rose, thanked her, and told her I would call if I needed her for any reason. She waved vaguely in farewell, that rapt expression still on her face.

Lester Pearlman was the second name on my list. He had a room off campus, in a house located on a narrow macadam road called Constitution Avenue. The house was as gray as ashes, with rusty streaks down the side from leaks in the drain. The place looked abandoned, but I knew Pearlman was there. I had called from the campus, and he had said he would wait for me.

He didn't come to the door until I had knocked three times, and even then he hovered behind the screen, his eyes gleaming in the shadows. His voice was belligerent. "I can't imagine why you would want to see me."

"I'd rather talk about it inside."

"Oh, sorry." He opened the door suddenly, an exaggerated grin on his face. He had about an inch of forehead between the thick black hair hanging low in front and the eyebrows that grew together above the nose. His face looked oily with sweat. He wore a T-shirt, khaki shorts and a pair of soiled sneakers.

"Let's use my room," he said. "I thought Mrs. Watson would answer the door, but she's probably still at church. She owns the place."

He led me up a pair of creaky stairs and into a cluttered room where tiny balls of dust scurried like mice when he closed the door. There were clothes and shoes everywhere, but mostly there were books—books on shelves, stacks of books in every corner, boxes of books under the bed. He cleared the only chair for me, seated himself on the bed, and said, "I suppose this is about the poker games." He kept flashing that exaggerated grin.

"No. Do you play poker?"

"It relaxes me," he said. "I usually win and I thought one of the heavy losers had filed a complaint. Why else would you want to see me?"

Instinct told me to be cagey. "Dr. Pritchett gave me your name."

His laugh was like a cough. "Pritchett? That second-rate custodian of the cross? What's his complaint?"

"Why do you call him that?"

"Because that's what he is. A minister of morality. A guardian of the gospel according to St. Luce of *Time* magazine."

"Have you told Pritchett that?"

"Constantly. I tell him he's in a lucrative business only because every age needs its guardians of morality. Religion is defunct, so we have the flourishing mystique of psychiatry. The words are different, but these boys make the same judgments about your conduct. Of course, they're sophisticated. They call you 'disturbed' instead of 'sinner'." His voice was hoarse with loathing.

During my tenure as a patient on the psychiatric ward of the naval hospital in San Diego, I had listened to essentially the same speech every day for months. The orator on those occasions was a marine corporal who had killed his first sergeant with a bayonet one morning at guard inspection.

I said to Lester, "If you feel that way about Pritchett, then—"

"—why do I go to him? That's easy. I go to humor my faculty advisor and my mother. They say I'm too much of a recluse, too withdrawn, antisocial."

"Are you?"

"Hell yes! But I'm content, why shouldn't I be? Oh, those sessions with Pritchett aren't so bad. Most of the time I bait him with symbols I manufacture. I've read those books."

"Is that what you put on the tape you deposited last night? Just stories you made up?"

The bedsprings squealed, and his grin was so lethal I thought the noise had come from him. "So that's the story, is it?" he said.

"What do you mean?"

"That prig Pritchett reneged. He swore that everything on the tapes would be privileged information. But he had to call in the law."

"No, you don't understand." My protest was deliberately feeble. I wanted him to talk, and talk is what he did.

"How did *you* like the story? How do you know it isn't one I invented to snow Pritchett? Do I look like the type to follow a dopey little virgin *shiksa* around at night, scheming about how to stop this Neanderthal Veteran of the Foreign Wars from adding her to his scoreboard in the back seat of his car?" He waved at his books, as if they proved he was above such petty pursuits.

"Yes, Pearlman, you strike me as exactly the type of martyred timid soul who would do exactly that." I wanted to break through his façade, that structure of bookish self-contempt behind which he smirked and postured.

"Hah, so you believed the grotesque tale. You're as gullible as Pritchett."

18

"I didn't say I believed it. I've never even heard it, except for that version you gave me just now."

"You're lying! Why else would you come here?"

So I told him, in simple language, about the theft of the tapes.

At once he seized upon the most obvious explanation of the theft, which sounded like a conspiracy that had plagued him all his life. "It's somebody's idea of a practical joke. Some character with a warped sense of humor stole the tapes for entertainment at the next frat party. That's your big crime. It'll be a great show. The intimate confessions of three adolescents fascinated with their own neuroses—what could be more hilarious?"

It could have been bravado, but his grin was sickly, his sneakers twisted together, and he dug fingernails into his naked thigh as if her were going for blood. He was taking it worse than Elaine French.

So I tried to reassure him with the same argument I had given her, that the tapes were stolen to be destroyed. He didn't even listen. He was obviously happier with his theory he had concocted. So I got up to leave, and he bolted to his feet. "If you get the tape back, you'll let me know?"

"Yes." I went down the stairs and out of the gloomy house quickly.

I came very close to skipping the third one. After the first two, I was convinced that no matter how genuine their suffering, their experience was too limited to turn into the stuff of crimes. The bad taste left in my mouth by the first two persuaded me that the third would be another emotional cripple.

But the third one proved to be altogether different. This one had ridden to hounds. This one had known at eight how to speak with that little silken whip in her voice that raised welts on a headwaiter's ego at forty paces.

Her name was Natalie Clayborne, and my tip sheet gave her age, twenty, and her status, a junior. She lived in a white frame house that had been converted into a dormitory by the college. Located less than a block off the main campus, it had a gravel drive that curved between bright maple trees. I went there without calling, on the off chance that she had returned from lunch. This lobby didn't boast an intercom, just a panel with neatly typed names in slots and a buzzer beside each. I buzzed.

She appeared almost at once, and she gleamed with such a brilliant mixture of pastels that it was like seeing a mirage. She was tall, with green eyes like pale hothouse grapes and the kind of blonde hair, worn to her shoulders, that appears to give off showers of pollen in the sunlight. She wore a lounging outfit of light blue velvet that made her look sleek and glamorous. She gave no sign that she was surprised to see me, but that might have been poise.

I identified myself and told her I wished to speak with her briefly about a confidential matter.

"Then let's use my room," she said. "On Sundays it's permitted."

I followed her down the hall and into a spacious room where you could instantly distinguish between what belonged to her and what was furnished by the college. The Indian blanket that served as a bedspread was hers, as well as the woven Colonial rug on the floor, the framed charcoal drawing of a faceless nude (which might have been her) and, what seemed a harsh note, an obviously expensive reproduction of *The Old King* by Rouault. The room was almost painfully neat, the shelves of books above the desk the stack of paper beside the typewriter, the precise handwriting in a notebook open on the bed. She invited me to sit down. Her tone was that of the lady of the manor dealing with a chauffeur who had come to ask for a raise. To her, people who wore uniforms were tradesmen.

I knew the breed. Once I had been married to one, a delectable, graceful and immaculate girl, more spirited and riper than this one. Deliberately I lit a stogie and watched the lady until she asked me to state my business.

"Dr. Pritchett asked me to see you," I said. "And I'm supposed to exercise tact, as much as I can muster under the circumstances."

This amused her. Her mouth was wide, expressive. "It's not very tactful to say so, is it? Exactly what are these mysterious circumstances?"

"You deposited a tape last night through the slot in Pritchett's door. Then early this morning someone broke in and stole it."

She seemed merely puzzled. "You mean they broke in just to steal my tape?"

"Three tapes were stolen, but nothing else was touched."

"Isn't that peculiar? What value would the tapes have to anyone?"

"That's what I'm trying to find out. It's my hunch that someone was described on one of the tapes in a way that threatened him. He learned about it, and was worried enough to make sure no one else heard the story."

"But that hardly makes sense. What's to prevent the one who made the tape from telling the same thing to Pritchett in person?"

She had ignited my interest in the problem. "That's easy. The tape burglar is someone close to the student. He knew he would be able to persuade her not to repeat the story." I gave her a ring of stogie smoke to watch, then applied the kind of pressure she wouldn't like. "He probably convinced her that this feeling they have for each other is too sacred to be shared with strangers."

Her nostril wings flared. "Why would she listen to such nonsense?"

Now I decided that my thief was not only a neophyte at burglary, but also an amateur at intrigue. Or he would have coached her better. She should have been less rational, less curious about how much Pritchett and I knew.

I got a little rougher. "She's flattered. Her vanity feeds on the thrilling discovery that his jealousy would drive him to commit this violent act. Oh, he knew how easy she would be before he went after the tape.

Pink spots the size of quarters began to glow in her cheeks. Then I had a hunch about her. When these rich ones are young, sensitive enough to grow ashamed of the affluence, skeptical of the power Daddy wields, some of them want to rub the gilt from their lives with an abrasive. This one seemed to have all the symptoms, and I was beginning to get an image of my thief.

She said, "If you're insinuating that I'm this creature who's so easily manipulated, you're not being very diplomatic about it, are you?"

"Unless you are this creature, how could any of this offend you?"

"I'm not offended. Just bored."

"And I thought you were hanging on to every word. You're a good actress."

She was sharp enough to detect the sarcasm, and she decided to try a different tactic. She leaned back, clasping her hands around one knee. "I guess you expected me to go into a dead faint about the stolen tape. But there's nothing on it that would embarrass me. Most if was poetry, my own. Not very good poetry, I'm afraid, but I thought Pritchett should hear some of it."

Now she was basking in her own cleverness. She reminded me that three tapes had been stolen, and asked if she was the first one I had interrogated.

She used the word deliberately. I smiled, "No, you're the last."

"I'll bet the others laughed at this mythical Machiavelli you've invented."

"He's not entirely invented," I said. "He could be something like that drawing over there." I pointed my stogie at the faceless nude. I had been intrigued by the drawing from the moment I entered the room. If Natalie had posed for it, for her to display it seemed a subtle form of exhibitionism. Except for the blank oval where the features should have been, it was rendered in meticulous detail, complete to the triangle at the juncture of her thighs, a neat appendectomy scar, and a mole situated at five o'clock from the navel. The picture was tantalizing because the posture and lines of the figure conspired to suggest a lewdness that was negated by the blank face.

Natalie regarded the drawing with a quaint smile. "I don't understand the connection," she said.

"Well, suppose our thief cut himself breaking in," I said. "Suppose he left us a little blood, a few threads from his coat, fingerprints. With the lab equipment at Pritchett's disposal, it would be easy to make a picture of him. Everything but the face."

"Oh? And what have you deduced from all these clues, Sherlock?"

Her jauntiness probably meant that she had seen him since last night and knew he wasn't cut. But I went on. "He would be a rebel of some kind, a man of uncompromising ideals. He scorns wealth, despises the Establishment, and stimulates this girl with the gemlike purity of his motives and his dedication."

She laughed, catching on. "What, no place of birth? No religion?"

"There is one more thing," I said soberly. "He went after the tape because it frightened him. For all his charm—and it would have to be considerable—it would probably not be wise for the young lady to threaten to expose him."

"Kind sir, I'll bet you give all your suspects the same advice. You are a nice policeman, so considerate."

It was not act, merely pleasure she couldn't conceal, and I decided that I was wrong about her. Oh, her tape was the valuable one, and she knew who had stolen it. But the situation that had inspired the theft was unclear to me, except for the possibility that it included a fierce romantic attachment.

"I wish I could have been more helpful," she said, rising, playing the charade to the end.

"That's all right," I said. "Our files are full of unsolved cases."

"You're a funny cop," she said. "If I ever need a cop, I'll call you."

Chapter 3
***

I got into the dusty black Ford with the faded star on its side and drove down to the constable's headquarters on Pine Street. It was a small building, containing two battered desks, extra traffic signs stacked in a corner, an ancient sofa with broken springs, and a coal stove for winter. We didn't have a jail. We used the jail in Spencer's Falls, the county seat, eight miles down the pike. Quartz's old deputy, Frank Ferby, was dozing on the sofa when I entered. He was a little man of sixty, with phlegmatic eyes and a spry walk. I surmised that he had just returned from handling the church traffic.

I let him sleep and walked the block to Quartz's place, a sturdy four-room cottage that came with the job. Quartz had come home from the hospital the day before, wearing a black harness around his torso to immobilize a broken collarbone, a corset of tape where the ribs had been smashed, and a cast on his right leg. He was a stocky man in his early fifties, with the energy of a man ten years younger. His hair was walnut brown, worn in a crew cut, and his eyes were cobalt blue. He had served a thirty-year hitch in the Corps, and had been constable of Jordan City since his retirement three years before.

When I entered the cottage, I heard Quartz talking with a woman in his bedroom. I recognized her voice instantly. It was as melodious and husky as a torch singer's, and I had heard it last in a setting designed for it. The voice belonged to Linda Thorpe, who worked as a glorified hostess in the part of the Stagecoach Inn used as a private club. She had been on duty the night Quartz got stomped, and I had gone out there and talked with her the day after I hit town. We had talked in a small room walled with frosted glass behind which pink and lavender fluorescent light floated like smoke. The motif of the club was the Old American West, the wicked, gaudy and elegant version Hollywood loves to show in Technicolor, and Linda had worn a costume appropriate to the décor, complete with gleaming black stockings and a red garter on her thigh. Her hair was rakishly styled, and her earrings were Aztec sunbursts.

I called a greeting to Quartz, and he asked me to join them. I entered the room, and for the second time that day I was dazzled by the appearance of a woman. This time it was my fault, for erecting a false image. Now her hair—the dark burgundy shade usually seen only in a goblet—was beautifully groomed and tied in back with a ribbon. It framed the most unique face I had ever seen. That night at the Stagecoach I had given her credit for a clever makeup job. I'd been wrong. Her face was even more striking in the light of day. The planes and shapes of eyes, cheekbones and mouth gave an impression that was regal and Oriental. She was tall, slender of waist, with the kind of full figure you would call buxom if she added another pound. She looked sedate in a white blouse and slacks that matched the shade of her hair. She might have been thirty-five.

We exchanged greetings, and Quartz showed me a gift Linda had brought, a basket containing a ham and a fifth of Jack Daniels.

"It's really not much of a gift, considering what Quartz is going through," Linda said. "But Eddie wanted to express our gratitude, and since I was the damsel in distress that night, it's only fitting that I should deliver it. You met Eddie, Mr. Butler, the manager of the Stagecoach Inn."

It would take a while to get used to that voice. "I don't suppose you've seen Quartz's three playmates since our last talk?" I said.

She shook her head. "No, and I never saw them before the robbery. I'm convinced that they just stopped for a drink and robbed us on impulse."

"I don't agree," Quartz said. "This is a dry county, and how would they know they could get a drink there if they didn't know about the club in the back? They weren't as drunk as they acted. They came there to rob the place."

"But why did they make such a production of it?" Linda asked. "Would robbers raise all that fuss about getting a drink, and before witnesses?"

"Maybe they had to," I said. "After all, not being members, they could hardly case the place ahead of time. So maybe they played it by ear. They put on their act, three drunk hillbillies in cheap suits. But when Eddie told them he called the law, they couldn't make their move until they saw how much law they had to buck. Once the disposed of Quartz, they robbed at their leisure."

"Yes, it happened that way," Linda said. "I remember how surprised I was when they started hitting Quartz. When they took my bracelet, I was petrified."

"I didn't know they robbed you," I said.

25

"I reported it to Sheriff Casey. Oh, it wasn't a valuable bracelet, except to me. They won't get twenty dollars for it."

Quartz reached for a cigarette, winced with pain, and growled at me, "Hey, weren't you supposed to be investigating a big crime wave up at the college?"

"It's investigated, I said. "But I'm not sure you want it solved."

"Why not?"

I gave him a carefully edited version of the crime and my findings, including my theory about the Clayborne girl's romantic entanglement.

Quartz thought about it for a moment. "I'll have to get back to Pritchett on this. He'll probably want to get the whole story from the girl himself."

"Not this story, not this girl," I said. "Personally, I wouldn't be surprised if she told her friend about the tape to see if he would steal it."

"You're only guessing," Quartz said. "You can't tell that much about a girl from just one conversation with her. What do you think, Linda?"

She gave an amused smile. "I'm hardly an authority. But if she's having an affair, yes, it's possible. Maybe she's worried about how secure her position is. She might have been testing her man with the tape."

"My God, no wonder I never got married," Quartz said. "All right, that enough crime. Why don't you two go swimming or something? I'm for a nap."

His face looked strained. "Should I get one of your pills?" I asked.

"No, I quit taking them. They don't do much good."

He thanked Linda again for the gift, and she and I walked out to the porch.

"What a glorious day," she said, stretching with a sinuous movement that made me go a little dry in the mouth. "That wasn't a bad idea about the swimming. Too bad I have plans for this afternoon."

"That is too bad." I fished a stogie from my pocket. I felt like striking the match on my jaw to impress her. "Can I drive you home?"

26

"I have my car, thank you. But let's sit on Quartz's glid while. You know, he impresses me as quite the guy. It was you to drop everything and come down to help after he got admire that kind of loyalty."

"He plans to run for county sheriff this fall," I said. "That's why he wanted me to ride shotgun on his town while he's laid up. Sheriff Casey offered to have one of his deputies fill in, but Quartz has a low opinion of Casey."

"He said you owned a farm," Linda said. "He also made a cryptic remark about you that intrigues me. Maybe I shouldn't repeat it."

"Go ahead."

"Well, he said if he paid you your regular fee, it would cost him a thousand a week. Either you do very dangerous work, or it must require a special talent."

"You left out a third possibility. It might be criminal work."

Her eyes conducted an artful little inquest. "You look capable of it. You're not what you seem, are you, Mr. Butler?"

"No, and neither are you. That act you put on at the Stagecoach, like an elegant den mother in a high-class bordello, I suppose that's authentic."

She hoisted the Jolly Roger with a jerk of her chin. "Was that necessary? I thought you expressed your disgust thoroughly the night you were out there."

"Maybe I have an aversion to joints like the Stagecoach. No matter how you dress it up, it's still a cheap carnival. Where the local businessman plays out his lewd fantasies while you serve him his own liquor at a buck a throw."

The frost in her voice would have withered green corn. "So they have the trappings of sin without its sting. Is that so bad? But that's not the only reason you were rough on me that night. You thought I was John Sutro's girl."

She was right. I had gone out there angry because none of the hired help had lifted a finger when Quartz got his beating. I wasn't particularly cheered by John Sutro, a bald man of sixty who fancied himself a tycoon because he owned a plastics firm that produced everything from toys to TV cabinets. He didn't drool on Linda's naked shoulders, but he called her his "living doll" and hovered while we talked like an Armenian rug merchant exhibiting his most prized possession.

27

"All right, you're not John Sutro's girl. Whose girl are you?"

Something congealed in her face, and now she did look Oriental, inscrutable. "That's none of your business. Next question? No, let me tell you what the next question is. They all ask it sooner or later. Usually they wait until three A.M., when their gray matter is saturated with booze and they are truly virile and gallant sons of the Old West. Then they ask how a woman with my charm and—my assets, let's call them—ever got trapped in a town like this, a job like that. It's such a waste. Isn't that the question you had in mind?"

"Approximately. Look, what the hell are we fighting about?" I said. "All right, so I was in a foul mood that night and judged you wrong. I made a mistake, and I apologize for it. Why fight about it?"

"I don't know." She gave me a rueful little smile. "Maybe seeing Quartz reminded me of how much brutality there is in the world. Maybe I just wanted you to have a good opinion of me. What difference does it make?"

She got up, poised quickly with an exquisite tension, and moved to the yellow Chevy convertible parked at the curb. The tires squealed, and she was gone.

I decided that I really couldn't' blame those boys who sidled up to her at three A.M. in a lewd sweat and made their pitch. Apart from her beauty, she possessed a quality that made you want to dress her in a sunsuit, walk her bare-legged through sweet grass, and read poetry to her beneath a willow tree. I got up and went in to take a shower. Sunday is supposed to be my day off.

It came to me as I lathered up that I was the one who had really started the quarrel. It began when I had grown nasty with her over her curiosity about my avocation.

Not that my avocation is that much of a secret. When the Old Fox pronounced me fit for active duty in 1957, I resigned my commission and took a job in a high-class detective agency in San Francisco. The man who hired me had been my battalion commander in the South Pacific. He was still called the Colonel, a title that fitted him like his skin. He ran his office strictly by the book. We specialized in corporation work, checking into the private lives of executives being groomed for promotion, investigating suspected company spies, and setting up security systems in plants and offices. We also handled private cases and divorce work, but only if you had the proper credentials and could afford us. The Colonel refused all cases that

28

looked complicated, especially those that led down dark alleys. He had his record with the company to consider, and he despised failure.

I stuck it out for two years. The salary was good, and I was banking a good chunk of mine for a very private reason. For many years I had nursed a secret craving to sweat into my own land, to own a farm I could work by hand.

The Old Fox in San Diego had been skeptical about this obsession. The day I told him about it, he said, "Butler, how do you know this is not just another romantic cop-out, such as your marriage proved to be? Oh, I can see the appeal a farm would have, where you plant and grow, giving life instead of taking it. Especially to a man who spent six years out of eleven in war, mostly on the lines, destroying, burning, maiming. Remember the arithmetic, 1942 to 1953—six years of combat in two wars. Do you think the farm will be an antidote for that carnage? I would think twice about it were I you, Captain Butler. Yes, indeed."

He was a tough old fox, suspicious of phony schemes for salvation, and he had reason to be skeptical about the farm. Of course, neither of us knew at the time that I would have the avocation. It supports the farm in more ways than one.

I acquired the avocation on the day I quit the agency to accept a job the Colonel had rejected, a case involving a wealthy widow who fell for a suave young man who turned out to be a con artist. Her Casanova took her to Hawaii, where he and four associates bilked her of $120,000 with a real estate deal just legal enough to make the cops shrug. I soon understood the Colonel's aversion to the case. The lady wanted her money back, and she wanted the nasty men punished. Maybe it was the fee she offered me; twenty percent of all money I recovered. It took me just a month to separate the nasty men from their money. It wasn't painless surgery. Two of the five con men were dead, and a third, the Casanova, lacked both the profile and the confidence to ply his trade again. This last bit of news cheered the widow up considerably.

I still didn't know I had found an avocation. With my share of the money I returned to Ohio and bought the farm. Then I decided to build a new house on the old foundation, which led to my next job. It was referred to me by my ex-boss, the Colonel, which struck me as odd because I thought he was sore about my defection. But he assured me that he was all for a bright young man's striking out on his own. Besides, it was good for business for the agency to be able to refer certain clients to a troubleshooter who would take on an unsavory chore.

The Colonel's offer was spiced with just enough venom to put me on my guard, and in three years I had accepted only eight of the two dozen jobs he offered me. I had no doubt that the Colonel was waiting patiently for me to make a mistake and choose a job with one too many dark alleys. Yet there were times when I wondered if I didn't need him and his jobs as much as I needed the farm.

Of course, I didn't consider this constable work in Jordan City as part of my avocation. This was a holiday from both the farm and the other work, the first vacation I had taken in five years. As I emerged from the bathroom in the cottage, a fresh stogie in my jaw, Quartz called me from his room.

I padded down the hall. "I thought you were going to sleep," I said.

"I gave it up as a bad job. I just talked with Dr. Pritchett on the phone. He's not surprised that it was the Clayborne girl with the spicy tape. He asked me to give the farmer his regards. You playing games with the doctor?"

"He's the playful type," I said. "Which reminds me, I gather from Linda Thorpe that you were chatting with her about my business sideline."

"Why not? You didn't swear me to secrecy about that work you do."

"No, but I don't think it's smart to advertise it around here. You know small towns. It will be easier for me if I can pass myself off as the amiable, competent substitute for the amiable, competent constable."

He nodded slowly, but he had something else on his mind. "Tell me, Morgan, do you do it just for the money?"

I gave that a little thought. "No, the money's only part of it. The small part. If you're worrying about my losing money working for you, don't. I don't always get a thousand a week. Once I even took a charity case."

"I'm not worried about that," he said. "I just wonder why you do it."

"Because I have a talent for the work," I said. "And because I need a piece of action from time to time to keep me in good health."

"In other words, you enjoy it. At least that's an honest answer."

"As honest as an old reprobate like you deserves," I said. "Now, what's the final word on the Clayborne girl and her shady lovelife?"

"Lay off is the word. Pritchett wants to feel her out about it."

"Good. I have a handball date this afternoon with the local champ."

"So you couldn't land a date with the glamorous Widow Thorpe?" he said. "Tough luck. I tried to set you up with her."

"I didn't know she was a widow. Tell me about it."

"You're the boy with all the talent for detection. Do your own homework."

Chapter 4
***

During the week that followed, my job as constable of Jordan City lost its vacation status. It seemed my fate that week to encounter beautiful women in bizarre circumstances during the wee hours of the morning. I saw Natalie Clayborne three times and Linda Thorpe once, but these meetings were not what turned my job into work. If anything, they were respites from the demands made upon me by a spectacle I had never witnessed before.

The hot weather had persisted, stirring the sap in the trees and firing the blood of a thousand college students who had studied hard through the bleak winter. I soon found myself caught up in the Rites of Spring as practiced by the students of Jordan College. It began with a series of spectacular pranks on the campus on Monday (the most daring of these was performed by a gang who took all the toilet seats from a girls' dorm and hung them between two of the Gothic towers on the main building), reached a climax with an impromptu midnight parade through the village on Thursday, and ended when a thunderstorm moved in on Friday to cool everyone off.

Before the week was over I had rescued a hysterical girl who was being thrown high into the air from a blanket by the wrestling team; broke up, reluctantly, a Dixieland jam session held at four A.M. on the lawn of the Baptist church; interrupted a striptease performed by two coeds on the bar at the Tug and Maul; routed a passionate couple who were making love on a garage roof next door to a spinster who saw them in the moonlight; stopped any number of fistfights and several midnight serenades; and each night picked up a platoon of drunks off curbs and lawns and hauled them back to campus.

It was three o'clock on Wednesday morning when I had my first encounter with Natalie Clayborne. I was giving Main Street one last tour of inspection when my headlights caught the gleam of chrome from a place where no car should be, a narrow walkway between the hardware store and the nursery school. The walkway intersected the street at an angle, so that anyone staked out there had a view of half the storefronts on Main Street. Suspecting more shenanigans, I parked around the next corner, picked my way through the playground, and entered the walkway from the rear. Silhouetted

32

against the streetlights was a white MG with a girl behind the wheel. I waited, a flashlight ready. Each time a car passed on the street, she ducked her head. Finally I turned the flash on.

"Who's there?" She shielded her face, but I recognized the voice.

As I approached the car, she made a quick movement, but I seized her wrist and plucked the key from the ignition. "We meet again, Miss Clayborne."

"Give me back my key. I haven't broken any law."

"All in good time. I'd like to know what you're doing here."

"I had a late date, if it's any of your business."

"It looks like you got stood up." I sat in the bucket seat beside her.

"Still the funny cop, aren't you? Well, I did have a date, but I changed my mind and parked up here to avoid the guy." She lit a cigarette, and her face in the yellow flame looked strained, sulky.

"You're a poor liar, Miss Clayborne. You need more practice at it."

"Brother, that's all you know!" Her laugh was like the sound of dice in an echo chamber. "Look, why don't you go solve a crime or something? Did you ever find those tapes you were looking for on Sunday?"

"No, sweetheart, but you did," I said. It was partly hunch, partly bluff.

"What makes you say that?"

The sharpness of her reaction made it less a bluff. "Because obviously you'd like to get it back in the worst way. I see that I was wrong about the tape. You didn't incriminate someone else. The tape was damaging to you."

"Damn you!" She got out of the car fast and slammed the door. "All right, keep the car. I'll walk home."

"No, but you can have your key." I slipped it back into the switch. "But hear me out for a moment. There are all kinds of trouble, and some of it can be dangerous. If you're in that kind, don't hesitate to ask for help."

She got back into the car and her grip on the wheel seemed to restore her confidence. "Don't make me laugh. If I were in trouble, I wouldn't be fool enough to ask a hick cop for help. Get out of my car!"

33

I got out, and she started the car instantly. It drifted down across the curb, and then she gunned it, clashing the gears twice before she cornered.

Late the next night, just when I thought the Rites of Spring had subsided, I got a call about the jazz band that had taken up residence on the lawn of the Baptist church. When I reached the scene, they were filling the night with the sins of Bill Bailey before an audience of several dozen.

My appearance was greeted by catcalls and a sour raspberry from one of the trumpets, but the group dispersed without incident. I was walking towards my car when a husky voice called my name. A yellow convertible was parked across the street, and she was sitting with her head back against the seat.

"I was looking for you," Linda Thorpe said. "And when I heard the band, I naturally assumed you would show up here to break it up."

"Clever deduction," I said. "You're up late."

"Not for me. The Stagecoach doesn't close until two-thirty, and I seldom get to bed before four. One of the night people."

"Why were you looking for me?"

"Do we have to talk here in the street?" she asked.

"There's always headquarters. But I couldn't offer you a cool drink there."

"Then why don't you follow me home? It's only a few blocks, and you can make me a drink there. I have something to tell you that you ought to know."

She made a U-turn and led me through a maze of backstreets, cornering expertly, until we reached a bungalow surrounded by a lot of shrubbery. She ushered me into a cozy room with a fireplace, a black leather sofa that must have been eight feet long, and at least eight pieces of sculpture that looked like second-rate Modigliani. Cast in black metal, most of them depicted a woman in a frenzied posture, emaciated, grotesque, breasts like bitter thorns.

"I'm leasing the house from an art professor who's on sabbatical," Linda said. "You ought to see the ones I put in storage."

"I'd rather meet the model. Didn't he leave her hanging in a closet?"

Linda laughed. "No, she's very much alive."

"Would I recognize her from the work?" I asked.

She thought about it, her gaze moving from one statue to another. "You might, if you got to know her. Now make yourself comfortable while I get ice."

She returned with a leather-covered ice bucket, and I mixed gin and tonics in tall glasses. She was wearing a white dress with a narrow golden belt, and when she sat down in a black leather chair, mate to the sofa, I saw how perfectly she contradicted the room. The heavy masculine furniture and bleak statuary might have been designed to emphasize her graceful movements, her fine coloring, her sedately voluptuous figure. I served her drink and sat on the sofa.

"First, I want to apologize for losing my temper on Sunday," she said.

"Do we have to be so formal about it? I made a rude remark about you and your work, and got just about what I deserved."

"But you apologized, and I still couldn't behave decently about it."

I took a drink from my glass. After the day I had put in, it tasted like ambrosia. "While I'm still sober, is it fair to ask the dreadful question?"

"What question? Oh, how did I get trapped in this town?" I'd hoped you'd forgotten that. All right, you deserve an answer. Originally I'm from Mill Valley, California, a town just across the Golden Gate from San Francisco. I was married there ten years ago, to a brilliant, gentle man, Howard Thorpe. He was teaching at Berkley, supporting his mother, but he was a very talented writer. He had a good start on a big novel, an important book, and after his mother died we took the plunge. We had a little money saved, he got an advance from a publisher, and we went to Mexico, Cuernavaca. He worked on the novel for two years, and one day he got bitten by a tsetse fly, got encephalitis and died."

"I'm sorry." She didn't hear me. She appeared to be in a trance.

"That was a little over three years ago. For eight months I stayed on alone in Mexico, and I was in a bad way. I must have been a little crazy. I walked a lot. I burned Howard's manuscripts. I wrecked the car. It was Madge and Eddie Bell who pulled me out of it. Eddie, you know, manages the Stagecoach. They vacation in Cuernavaca each summer, and we had become close friends, the four of us. When they came down that summer, they took me in, and since I had very little family to go home to, they persuaded me to come home with them.

35

Well, finally I needed a job, and John Sutro offered me the one at the Stagecoach. So that's my pathetic little story. I'm afraid it lacks all the glamor the members at the Stagecoach expect. Which is probably why I've never told it to any of them." Her smile was crooked, and she seemed to have shriveled a little into the depths of the chair. "Now, aren't you sorry you asked the question?"

"No." I put my glass down carefully, crossed the space between us and kissed her gently on the forehead.

Then she astonished me. She bolted from the chair savagely against me, seized my face so hard her fingernails burned my scalp, crushed her mouth against mine, scraping my teeth with hers, her tongue darting like a viper. It lasted fully a minute. Then she put her head against my shoulder and said, "Don't you ever kiss me like that again. You'll destroy me. I'm neither a saint nor a mystic. I've got to get over it." We stood like that for a few minutes.

Finally she stepped back and lifted her face. "I'm sorry. I overreact to you. I don't know why. You're not even remotely like Howard. Let me go."

"Wait. I'm not medicine." I pulled her close and this time I kissed her. Soon I felt a deep combustion in her and she moved luxuriously against me.

"Yes, that's better," she said. "That salvages my pride, more or less intact. Mr. Morgan Butler, farmer and constable. My, my. Now please let me go."

She left the room, and I took our tepid drinks into the kitchen, poured them into the sink and returned to the bar. I was still stunned with her, like any man who has been in a collision. So I poured two fingers of bourbon and drank it neat, in the hope that it would cure my intoxication.

I was reaching sobriety when she returned. A hint of mischief in her eyes was the only sign she gave of what had occurred. "Butler, we've both forgotten that I asked you to come here for a reason."

"Why don't you call me Morgan?" I said.

"No, I like Butler. Hi, Butler. Do I have a drink?"

I made her one, and this time we both sat on the sofa. She sipped her drink, eased off her shoes with nimble movements, then watched me soberly.

"Remember that bracelet I told you about, the one stolen from me during the Stagecoach robbery? Well, I saw it today in Spencer's Falls."

"Just eight miles away," I said. "Tell me about it."

"I stopped at DePaul's over there on my way to work, to buy an air conditioner for the bedroom. While I was there, a woman came in and began looking at TV sets. She was a big woman in a gaudy red dress. She was wearing it."

"You're sure it was the same bracelet?" I said.

"Yes, it's very distinctive. Turquoise and silver. Howard had it made for me in Mexico. It was a foolish gift, because we couldn't afford it."

"What happened then?"

Linda made a wry face. "I blundered. She caught me looking at the bracelet and ran out the store before I could stop her. By the time I got outside, she was gone. I think she had a car. You couldn't miss that red dress."

"Did you report it to Sheriff Casey? You were in his back yard."

She shook her head. "He wasn't in, and maybe it's just as well. One of them called me later, at the Stagecoach. It was about ten o'clock."

"You mean one of Quartz's country boys?"

"Yes. He said that if I mentioned seeing the bracelet to anyone, I would get the same treatment they gave Quartz. He said I would be watched. He made a filthy remark about what else they would do to me, laughed and hung up."

"Did it scare you?"

"And how! Remember, I was there when they beat Quartz up."

"I think they're bluffing about watching you," I said. "They wouldn't dare hang around here. What say to another drink?"

I made two, and we discussed the wisdom of Linda's telling her story to Sheriff Jack Casey. I had met him when he drove over to see me a few days after I took over for Quartz. He'd heard that I'd been asking questions at the Stagecoach, and he didn't like it. He was a tall man in his fifties, as lean and limber as a buggy whip, and that morning he carried a burden of disgust. He was disgusted with Eddie Bell for having called Quartz that night instead of Casey's office. He was disgusted with Quartz for answering a call outside his jurisdiction. He was disgusted with me because I was an amateur.

37

Linda and I decided that she had better report both the business of the bracelet and the threatening phone call to the sheriff anyway. By then it was six in the morning, and I got up to go. At the door Linda held herself stiffly, but I palmed her cheek and kissed her softly on the mouth.

She smiled. "Please call me, Butler. I'm off on Sunday and Monday."

"I want you to lock your doors at night."

"If you say so, Butler. Goodnight, Butler."

I didn't think she was in any real danger, but to be on the safe side I drove up her neighborhood the next night just before she was due home. I parked several blocks from her house and cased the area on foot. It took me thirty minutes to satisfy myself that there was no one staked out near Linda's house. I had parked my car on a side street, and just as I was about to kick it over, the Clayborne girl passed beneath a streetlight not sixty feet in front of me. She moved at a trot, wearing dark slacks and sweater, a bandana on her head.

I gave her a head start, then eased around the corner without lights. She was a hundred yards away, making good time, and when a car approached her she darted behind a tree. I followed in low gear, but that part of town is full of quaint, winding streets that intersect at odd angles, and before long I lost her. There was little chance of locating her again, so I drove to the campus and parked across the street from her dorm. It was just three A.M.

She appeared fifty minutes later, alighting from a battered Ford station wagon with weak lights and sticky valves. From habit, I jotted down the license number. Natalie had started up the walk when the man in the car called to her. She kept moving, but he jumped out of the car, caught her arm, and they quarreled for a while. Presently he released her and returned to his car, a tall young man with good shoulders. The motor in the Ford clattered like an old washing machine.

I was tempted to follow, but then I had a dreary thought about Natalie Clayborne. Beneath the veneer of good breeding she might be just a neurotic girl absorbed with the excruciating pain of a messy love affair. It was plausible, given Dr. Pritchett and the purloined tape. Anyway, I was too tired, and I had had a skinful of antics of Jordan College students. I went home and to bed.

38

The thunderstorm hit about six o'clock Friday evening. It came like the granddaddy of all storms. The sky turned from blue to yellow to black in minutes. The wind came down Main Street like the cannonball express, and half the lightning bolts sounded as if they landed in your vest pocket. First, we had hailstones the size of marbles, then a rain that made the gutters foam.

At midnight, while Quartz and I were playing cards and eating some of the Stagecoach ham, I had a call from Frank Ferby about a tree that had blown down on Main Street. Frank had already called the street commissioner, a local druggist, who was rounding up an emergency crew. I told Frank to dig out some flares, and I donned boots and slicker and went out. Fortunately, the crew had a chain saw that hooked up to a power unit in the truck, and we had it cleaned up in an hour. I decided to cruise the village before turning in.

I wasn't looking for her, but as soon as my beams flashed over a figure huddled in the doorway of Musmano's grocery I know it was Natalie Clayborne. She was wearing a black plastic raincoat with white polka dots, which glistened in the light like snowflake obsidian. I was in no mood to be coy. Parking in front of the store, I put the spotlight on her and mounted the steps. When I lifted her chin, her face looked white with bone and will.

"The poor man's Dick Tracy," she said. "It's about time. I was close to giving you up. Take me home. Please."

"Where's your car?"

"I walked. It seemed like a good night for it."

I hauled her to her feet and took a better look. Her green eyes were as glazed as they smooth, mossy stones you find on the bed of a stream. Her mouth smirked. She darted a hand under my slicker and shook the gun in my holster, like a frisky kid. I got her into the car. From the glove compartment I took a flask of brandy, and she took a stiff shot without choking.

"That's good and hot," she said. "I must have taken a chill."

My guess was that she was in some kind of emotional shock. "You keep odd hours, and you find your amusement in the strangest places," I said.

"Oh, don't start that! Take me home. Spare me the lectures. Comfort me with apples. Slug me with brandy. But don't preach to me."

I drove slowly in the rain, occasionally crunching through water up to my fenders, and finally parked in front of her dorm. She made no move to get out.

"How about another shot?" she said. "One for the road. One to make merry. Or even Natalie. You could take advantage of me. You'd be in good company. I wouldn't even resist if you knew the password, the name of my predecessor. I'm a pushover when it's a case of the understudy replacing the star for a night."

I handed over the flask. It clicked against her teeth. I kept my voice low, casual. "Have you seen Pritchett this week?"

"He couldn't stomach this brew. A concoction of greed and lust."

"I have a cast-iron stomach," I said. "People compliment me on it."

"You're the funny cop. You keep making that offer and someday I might take you up on it." She laid her head on my shoulder. "Lord, I'm tired."

After a few minutes I thought she had dozed off. "Natalie? Why don't you take the flask with you. Get a good night's sleep."

"Now you're the sweet cop," she murmured, sitting up. "No, I don't need it. I'm better now. Sorry about all the nonsense. Must screw my courage to the sticking point. We Claybornes come from sturdy stock, or so they tell me." She squeezed my arm and got out. I waited until she was inside before I left.

On Saturday it rained sporadically all day long. After the turmoil of the Rites of Spring, the village looked as bleak and abandoned as a resort town in the off season. I made two calls that day. First, I tried to get Dr. Pritchett, to try and persuade him to take some action about Natalie Clayborne. He was attending a convention in Columbus.

The second call was to Linda Thorpe. I asked her for a date on Sunday, preferably something that might end with the two of us perched on that long black sofa before a cozy fire. I offered to bring my own logs. She was tied up Sunday, but invited me to a party in town on Monday night. No, she hadn't received any more threatening phone calls. But she hoped that wouldn't stop the very pleasant attention she was getting from the local police. I assured her that it wouldn't.

Chapter 5
***

When the phone rang on Sunday morning, I answered it on the extension beside my bed.

"Is this Constable Willinger?" It was a man's voice.

"This is his replacement, Constable Butler."

"This is Dean Collins, from the college. I have something terrible to report. One of our students is dead. I think she's been murdered." His voice faded to a whisper on the last word, as if he might be overheard.

"Who was it?" That wasn't the proper question, but I wanted him to deny the grotesque image rising in my mind like something from a swamp. Instead, he confirmed it.

"Her name is Natalie Clayborne. She's in her dormitory. The address—"

"I know the address," I said. "Don't touch anything in the room. Keep the door closed and keep everyone out. I'll be there in ten minutes."

I drank a cup of cold coffee from the previous night's pot, took two minutes of a cold shower, and climbed into my uniform. Then I woke Quartz and told him.

He was all business. "You go up there, Morgan, and do what you can. I'll have to call Jack Casey. There's no way out of it. I guess I should call Paul McIntosh, too." He saw my frown. "You met Paul, editor of the *News*. He earns extra money as a stringer for one of the wire services, and I'm sure the college would rather have him report this than some vulture who would play it up for sensation. I have to worry about that sort of thing."

It was a gray morning, sodden with rain, and as I drove to the campus the church bells tolling in the village sounded as mournful as a dirge. Apparently news of the murder hadn't yet spread, for the street in front of Natalie's dormitory was deserted. As I got out of my car, a portly man in a gray suit came down the walk. His mouth and eyes conveyed great embarrassment.

"I'm Dean Collins," he said, offering his hand.

"Let's go inside."

"Yes, of course."

We entered the vestibule, and he stopped me with his arm. "I've kept the other girls on the premises. Some of them have gathered in the parlor." He indicated a pair of glass doors with curtains on them.

I looked at my watch. It was just nine-fifteen. "Who called you?"

"Ah yes. That was Betty Childress, one of the students. She's an older girl, very reliable. She was the one who discovered...Miss Clayborne."

"Where is the Childress girl now?"

"I asked her to stand watch outside the door to Miss Clayborne's room."

"I want to talk with her first. Why don't you join the girls in the parlor? I think they'll appreciate having a man with them right now. You might ask if any of them heard any unusual noises last night or this morning."

"All right. I'll do it. Yes."

I went through the other door and found a girl in her early twenties sitting in a chair in front of Natalie Clayborne's room. She looked sensible, sturdy in a feminine way, with a pretty oval face, brown eyes widely spaced and an expression of concern on her face. "You're Betty Childress?" I said.

She rose to her feet. "Yes, officer."

"I understand you were the one who found Natalie. I'd like to examine the room for a minute, then talk with you about it."

"Why don't you come to my room when you're finished," she said. "It's number three, just across the hall and down a little."

"That's fine." She looked at me steadily for a moment, as if to determine whether I could be trusted to look upon Natalie dead. The she walked calmly down the hall. I entered Natalie's room and flicked on the light.

She was on the bed, lying on her stomach with her face turned towards the wall, covered to her neck with the Indian blanket. I lifted the blanket from her and draped it on a chair. She was wearing blue flannel pajamas and a quilted rayon robe of a much lighter blue. One foot was naked, and on the other she wore a dainty blue slipper. I spotted the other slipper under the desk about ten feet away. I left it there.

She had been strangled with the belt from her robe, but she had been unconscious when it happened. There was a stain of blood like a bright red rose on the pillow beneath her head, and the hair on that side was matted with it. The blood came from a wound on the top of her head. The bone was soft and indented there, as if she had received a tremendous blow from a piece of pipe.

The blanket and sheet on the bed beneath her hadn't been turned down, and I saw an ashtray and a pack of cigarettes on the window ledge above her head. She might have been stretching out on the bed reading when she had a caller. The chair facing the bed was a wire and canvas contraption called a butterfly chair. A patch of black mud was trapped in the weave of the Colonial rug in front of the chair. The rest of the room looked as neat and immaculate as it had the week before. Every book was in its place on the shelves, and her closet looked as if the maid had just finished arranging it for inspection.

She had been a fastidious girl with her possessions and her person, but apparently she had been slovenly in her choice of companions. From all the nonsense she had jabbered at me that night in the rain, I recalled the phrase *A concoction of greed and lust*. For a moment the cold, dead girl seemed to lend the words a profound significance. But they were useless words without names and faces, and I knew I'd better learn what I could before Sheriff Jack Casey arrived to remind me of my amateur standing.

I left the room and walked down the hall to the one occupied by Betty Childress. She was sitting erect on a small chair with her hands folded neatly in her lap, as if she had been arranging her thoughts for meditation.

"Betty, tell me about this morning. Take your time."

She nodded. "I went to Natalie's room at eight-thirty this morning to wake her for breakfast. She didn't answer when I called, and then I noticed that she was turned wrong in the bed. She always sleeps with her head towards the corner of the room. So I touched her, and I knew she was dead."

"Does she usually get up at eight-thirty on Sunday morning?"

"Hardly ever. But she came to my room last night before I went out and asked me to call her for breakfast. She planned to study today. She's been neglecting her courses lately, and wanted to catch up."

"Did she tell you she's been neglecting her courses?"

"Yes, but I knew it anyway. She's in two of my classes this year, and she's hardly shown up this past week."

"Now back to last night. Did she have a date?"

"No, I don't think so. She was in her pajamas and robe when she came to see me. She said she was going to stay in and read American history. That's one of the courses we have in common, and she asked me for the reading assignment."

"How well do you know Natalie, Betty? Did she confide in you?"

She gave this a little though. "I think it's accurate to say that I knew her better than anyone else in the dorm. We were roommates last year. This year she wanted to live alone, and paid double for the room. As to the other question, no, she didn't confide in me. This year we haven't been close."

"Betty, let me confide in you a little. Natalie and I talked several times last week. She was in trouble of some kind, and I think it involved a man she was dating. Do you know who it was?"

"The only man I know that she saw regularly is Arthur King. I think they were engaged for a while last year, but this year he's more like a friend. He's a student, but he's several years older than most of the seniors."

"How much older?"

"He must be twenty-five."

"How about someone she might have been meeting on the sly, a secret love affair? Maybe she was romantically involved with a faculty member. Did she ever hint about anything like that?"

"No!" she said emphatically.

"All right, let's change the subject. Do you know if all the girls except Natalie were gone from this floor of the dorm last night?"

"It was Saturday night," she said. "There were parties all over campus, and a dance at the gym. It's a good bet that she was here alone. I left at ten, and I think I was the last."

"How many entrances are there to the house, Betty?"

"Just three. The front door, a side door through the parlor which is always locked, and a door in the basement for the janitor. He can enter to fix the furnace without coming through the house. There's a stairway to the basement, but we keep that door locked. We store trunks and things down there."

"Show me the basement door you keep locked."

Her eyes signaled relief that the interview had ended. She led me down the hall to the kitchen, and pointed to a door beside a refrigerator. The key to the door was hanging on a nail beside it. The door was locked, but it could easily be opened with a skeleton key. Betty seemed to drift toward the stove.

"Can I pour you a cup of coffee?" she asked.

"No, but you can have one."

She put the heels of her hands on the sink. "I think it just hit me. If I had the coffee, I'd get sick."

"Wait here. I'll get one of the girls."

"No, I'll be all right. Just leave me alone. Please."

I started down the hall toward the parlor, but halted outside the murder room with a sensation as if a knotted thread had been jerked through my heart. There was a discrepancy in the image of the room I carried in my mind, something so trivial I couldn't place it. Stepping back into the room, I put the light on and just stood there. Again, I imagined the scene as it must have been last night, with Natalie reading on the bed, the house quiet. The murderer knocks on the door, identifies himself. She lets him in, returns to the bed, he to the chair. They talk. Suddenly he hits her, then turns her over and strangles her. He departs. The piece was still missing.

Shifting my position, I inspected the room again, impressed anew with her neatness. Then the knotted thread jerked again, and I had it. Where was the book she'd been reading? It seemed unlikely that she would cross the room and return it to the bookshelves before opening the door. Nobody was that compulsive. I went to the shelves, found Beard's *American Civilization* and two other books on American history, but I still wasn't satisfied. A minute later I found the book wedged down between the bed and the wall. It wasn't American history. It was Dostoyevsky's *The Brothers Karamazov*, a handsome edition bound in red leather, with the title and author lettered in gold. I held it with the spine on the palm of my hand, and it fell open as if she had left a bookmarker in it.

But it wasn't a bookmarker. She had apparently folded a page of the book double into the binding, then folded the bottom double again, like a paper airplane. Excited, I sat at her desk and riffled the pages until I found two others folded in exactly the same way. In each case the folded page had been mutilated with sharp fingernails along the fold. The numbers of the pages were four, thirty, and thirty-nine. It looked like a date. There was an inscription on the flyleaf of the book. *For Betty—Who has the soul to endure the suffering and the heart to appreciate the passion and truth revealed in this book.—*

Your sometimes Dimitri. It was written in a bold, flamboyant style, with long tails on the *y's* and tiny circles as dots for the *i's*.

I walked swiftly back to the kitchen. Betty was sitting at the table, staring at her folded hands. I placed the book on the table, and when her eyes focused on it she jumped as if I'd slapped her.

"That's my book," she said. "Where did you find it?"

"In Natalie's room, behind the bed. I thought you said she was reading history."

"But she finished *The Brothers* a month ago. She was supposed to give it back."

"If you knew she had it, why did you ask where I'd found it? Did you look for it this morning?"

She hesitated. "Yes, I'm ashamed to say. I remembered that she had it and I imagined they would seal up her room or pack all her things, so I saw no harm in taking it off her shelf. But it wasn't there."

"Who's your 'sometimes Dimitri'?"

She moistened her lips. "An old friend from home. He gave me the book as a Christmas gift. May I have it now?"

"Sorry, I have to borrow it for a while." I was tempted to ask her to keep quiet about the book, but the risk was slight that she would mention it unless the sheriff did, and I had already decided that he wouldn't.

I went outside and put the book in the glove compartment of my Ford, exchanging it for a flask of brandy, which I put on my hip. I had just made it back to the porch when Sheriff Jack Casey and his crew arrived from Spencer's Falls. They came in two cars and an ambulance, sirens wailing, dome lights spinning, tires squealing as they turned into the street. It looked like the entire county government. You don't get a murder in Parson County every day.

Jack Casey got out of the lead car before it stopped bouncing on its springs. He came up the walk with long strides, tall, lean and tough, as supple as seasoned hickory. The hat to his uniform had a brim all the way around, like a World War I campaign hat, and the eyes beneath the brim glistened like polished acorns. Behind him five other men debouched from the vehicles. Three were uniformed deputies, and the two in civilian clothes carried bags of equipment. A pair of attendants in white jackets stayed in the ambulance. One of the deputies looked as big as a bulldozer. He must have weighed

46

close to three hundred pounds. The gun and belt he wore resembled toy replicas of the real thing.

"I understand we got ourselves a killing, Butler," Jack Casey said.

I told him that was true. He nodded as if I had informed him that the fish were biting today.

"Before I go inside, let's you and me have an understanding, Butler. A crime of this magnitude [he pronounced it *mag-ni-tood*] falls under the sole jurisdiction of the county. You can look on, if you want, and see how it's done, but I will personally have your hide if you get in my way. You got the message?"

"I think it's kind of you to let me watch, Sheriff. I'd like to see you catch a real live murderer."

The sheriff detected a flaw in my answer. "You like to clown, don't you? That's what I call a happy coincidence. My deputy Humpty likes to clown, too." Without taking his eyes off my face, he raised his voice to speak to the big deputy. "Humpty, this fellow likes to clown. Think you could accommodate him?"

"Sure, Jack," Humpty said. "I know a few jokes he likely hasn't heard yet. Rough as a cob, some of them." Humpty grinned from one side of his mouth. In the other cheek he had a chew of tobacco the size of a doorknob.

"See, Butler, we can accommodate you with all the clowning you have the stomach for. Now show me the killing."

Apparently his staff knew their assignments. Two of the deputies remained outside, while Humpty and the two civilians followed us through the lobby and down the hall to the room. The sheriff had me wait in the hall with Humpty while he and the civilians entered.

Five minutes later Jack opened the door, beckoned me inside, and offered me the seat behind the desk. The coroner, a solemn young man with spectacles, was working over the body. The other man was dusting furniture with a soft brush. "Give me the layout," Casey said. "Who called it in? Who found it?"

I gave him a summary of what I had learned before he arrived. I didn't mention the book I had found, nor did I tell him about the stolen tapes and Natalie Clayborne's penchant for prowling at night. It was no that I minded the silly threat he made to put me in my place. His enmity I attributed to the fact that he and Quartz were political enemies. Jack Casey had been sheriff of Parson County for

47

twenty years, and Quartz apparently had a good chance of beating him in the fall. So I wasn't offended by Casey's antagonism. I just hadn't decided yet to trust him.

When I finished, Casey said, "So a good-looking snail like this stays home on Saturday night, all alone in her room. Some bucko drops in for a chat, and when she says something that makes him sore, he ups and kills her. Pretty neat, wouldn't you say?"

"It's neat, all right."

"It's so neat it stinks," he said. "If she didn't have a date, how did out bucko know she was here? We're assuming she knew him and let him in because of the mud on the rug in front of the chair. 'Course it's possible he busted in and killed her, then sat down to admire his handiwork. But I lean toward the friendly chat. Now what could a snail like this say that would get her killed?"

"Maybe he proposed and she turned it down," I said.

"Yeah, she's got the hardware to get under a man's skin, especially if she'd been giving out samples. What was the name of that student she was engaged to?"

"Arthur King," I said.

Casey walked to the door, said something to his deputy in a low voice, and strolled back to the desk. "We might as well begin with him. Just between us men, Butler, I think it's going to be that simple. I been expecting something like this at this college for a long time. They let these kids run wild. Hell, a batch of students stirred up a near riot over to the Falls last year, just because Jim Caldwell wouldn't cut a nigger's hair in his barber shop. Half of them looked like New York Jews to me. I'll lay ten dollars to your one that this snail is knocked up." He raised his voice, "Doc, you check that out, you hear?"

"That's S.O.P., Jack, in a situation like this. Say, you want an estimate on the time of death?"

"I'd dearly love it."

"Between midnight and two A.M. One o'clock's a pretty good bet."

"All right, let's go talk to that college dean and his brood of nervous little chicks," the sheriff said.

When we entered the hallway, the big deputy named Humpty was talking with the editor of the *Jordan City News*, Paul McIntosh. I knew him slightly. He had interviewed me for an item in his paper a few days after I moved in as Quartz's replacement. A man of about fifty, McIntosh had the kind of dark wavy hair women envy and the kind of rugged homely face men admire. The clothes he wore were dated, suits with vests and wide lapels and too much material in the trousers, but they somehow seemed right for him. They were part of the impression he created of shabby gentility, a small-town patriarch, calm, judicious.

Jack Casey said, "My, if it isn't the crusading editor himself. I didn't think you'd have the stomach for this story, editor. But I guess you can't afford a reporter to do your dirty work, not on a rag with a circulation like yours."

McIntosh looked at him soberly. "Jack, this is hardly the occasion to air our old feud. To you this may be just another job, but to some of us it's a tragic business and should be treated that way."

Jack Casey curled his lower lip. "What you mean is that these college jokers would dearly love to hush the whole thing up. They had their way, you'd write it as if that girl in there slipped in the shower and broke her neck."

"That's not true an you know it!"

"Get off my back, editor. How many parents will want their brats in a school where a bum can wander in off the street and murder them in bed?"

"Is that what happened?" McIntosh asked.

"Naw, that's just the story the parents will read no matter how you sugarcoat it. We don't know who killed her yet. But I intend to find this killer, editor. And when I do, he will burn for it. I don't care if he has a New York accent and a suitcase full of degrees. You can quote me on that."

"Is that what you want me to tell your constituents? That you've appointed yourself judge and jury, as well as sheriff? Maybe I will quote you."

"Go ahead, editor. Most of my constituents don't read your rag anyway. If you want the facts in this case so far, you can get them from Quartz's boy, Constable Butler. Humpty, I don't want either of them in the murder room." Casey went down the hall with his limber stride, and Humpty moved in front of the door. He all but hid it from view.

"Where's he going now?" McIntosh asked. He looked ruffled and angry from the encounter.

49

"He's on his way to the front parlor, to interview Dean Collins and the girls," I said. "I don't think we're invited."

"I've already talked with Collins," McIntosh said. "He gave me a message for you. He said none of the girls heard anything suspicious last night."

"I'm surprised he remembered. When I saw him, he looked as if he were about to go into shock."

"Poor Collins, who can blame him? To have a murder here is incredible. It's unreal." He fumbled a notebook from his pocket and looked at what he had scribbled there, as if his notes might give him a grip on reality. "I wish Casey had been more cooperative. As you probably observed, we are not on the best of terms. He knows I'm going to back your friend Willinger in the election next fall. Not that I'm all that eager to look at the dead girl."

"No sweat, editor. You ain't going to look at her." This came from Humpty, who watched us implacably from his post near the door.

"We're not doing any good here," I said to McIntosh. "Let's go into the kitchen, and I'll fill you in on the facts as I know them."

"That's decent of you, Butler. I should file a story for the wire service."

The kitchen was empty when we entered, and I closed the door for privacy. The coffee was still hot, so I plucked cups from a wire rack on the sink and poured us each a cupful. I laced mine with brandy, then handed the flask to McIntosh. "Bite into this. You look as if you could use a straight shot."

He drank, choked, took a deep breath and drank again. "Wow. Thanks, Butler. I needed that." His eyes had teared, and he wiped them with the heel of one hand. Then he took out his notebook and pen. "I'm ready when you are."

"First, I want to ask you something off the record." I lit my first stogie of the day. "Is this Casey as good as he wants everyone to believe he is?"

McIntosh shrugged. "He's probably as *tough* as he acts. I know he got his start in the Harlan County union warfare back in the thirties."

"On which side?"

This drew a smile from the editor. "A legitimate question. But it was the right side, helping organize the miners against the owners.

They say he was one of the boys who went in to help arm the miners. Of course, the union always denied that, but more than once I've heard Jack refer to his revolver as a 'John L. Lewis Peacemaker.' I can't say how competent he'll be on a case like this. Why do you ask?"

"I've had a fair amount of experience dealing with cops. I've found that the more a cop throws his weight around without cause, the less competent he proves to be. Casey read me the riot act before you got here."

"I don't get the point," McIntosh said.

"The point is this. I don't trust him. I've decided to conduct my own investigation of this case, behind Casey's back if necessary."

"Do you think that's really necessary? Butler, I know you're a close friend of Quartz's and I wonder if your reasons are political. I'd hate to think you'd compete with Jack just to try to discredit him."

"Spoken like the good citizen you are, editor. I admit I wouldn't mind having egg on Casey's face as a fringe benefit. But my reasons are a lot cleaner than that. I want to deliver the killer. I don't think Jack will.

McIntosh still looked dubious. "Isn't that a pretty ambitious boast? Considering the advantages Casey has, experience, facilities, manpower?"

I couldn't very well tell him that I had worked successfully without (and even against) those advantages in the past. So I decided to play my trump. "I happen to have a few advantages of my own. And I think you'll agree that they more than offset Mr. Casey's. First of all, I had a few talks with the Clayborne girl last week, and I've got some facts that the sheriff doesn't have."

"So you actually knew the girl? How well?"

"Well enough to know that she was in serious trouble. If I'd been a little more curious about it, I might have prevented her death. Maybe not. But I feel uneasy enough about it to want to deliver the killer. Besides, as the old cop says, it happened on my beat." I told him briefly about the stolen tapes and the girl's apparent anxiety to recover hers. "It has the smell of blackmail about it, although I admit that's only a hunch."

"All this does make a difference," Paul said. "But why tell me?"

"Two reasons. Because your sentiments happen to be in the right place, and because you're in a position to know the people in both

51

the town and the college better than anyone else around. From time to time, I'll need fast, accurate information from someone I can trust. What do you say?"

Now the editor's face looked robust, his eyes zestful. "I'm your man," he said. "But only because I have the college's interests at heart."

"All right, here's your first chore. I took a book out of the murder room before Casey arrived. It could be that the girl left it behind as a message about her killer. It's a copy of *The Brothers Karamazov* with three pages marked in a certain way."

"But if she had time to do that, why didn't she just write a message?"

"No, she did this right under the murderer's nose. If I'm right, she took the book off the shelf as soon as she knew who was at the door. No doubt this was an unscheduled meeting, and she was frightened. And while they talked she fiddled with the book and folded a few pages. There wasn't time to write a message, and no guarantee that he wouldn't see it and take it with him. Actually, using the book was a clever move, assuming we can unravel the message."

"You think you can do that?"

"It would help if you'd give me a summary of the novel. Have you read it?"

"*The Brothers Karamazov?* Yes, several times. Of course, it's been some years since the last time, but you don't forget a story like that."

"Was there a murder in it?"

"Yes!" Then his expression changed from excitement to dejection. "But it was the father who was killed in the book. There's no comparison."

"Never mind that. Just tell me the story. As briefly as you can."

"You mean right now?"

"Yes. Just the details about the crime and who committed it."

He thought about it. Finally he opened his mouth to speak, then shook his head gently. "It's not as simple as you might think. First, let me point out that there were four Karamazov brothers. And if you interpret the story the way the author intended, three of them were involved in the murder."

He clasped his hands under his chin, concentrating. "Here's what you want. Old man Karamazov was killed. The eldest son, Dimitri, was tried and found guilty of the murder. Bear in mind that he had reason to kill his father and had threatened to do it. Ivan, the next son, brooded over the possibility that he might have been a conspirator in the murder. He hated the old man, too, and finally convinces himself that he is guilty because he tacitly urged the killer on. But the son who actually killed the old man was Smerdyakov, a half-brother to the others." He paused, an intense, abstract expression on his face. "Here, I'll write it down for you. We have Dimitri, who was punished for the crime; Ivan, who went mad out of guilt; and Smerdyakov, who did it and hanged himself." He handed me the sheet from his notebook.

I looked at the three names and the brief descriptions he had written. "Can't you identify them better than this?"

"That's a good point," he said. "Dimitri was a man of violent passion, erratic, dissipated. Ivan was a student, a philosopher, a cynic, you might even say a poet. Smerdyakov was a meek and sly devil, a servant for the old man."

"And how was the old man killed?"

"Smerdyakov crushed his skull with an iron paperweight."

The words jolted me, because she had died the same way. But they also made this clue of the book seem suddenly suspect, a terrible mockery. She couldn't have known how she was going to die when she selected the book. The ugly suspicion seeped into my mind that the murderer himself had planted the book as a red herring.

The same notion occurred to McIntosh a few minutes later, as I was giving him the details of how she died for his story. He jerked his face toward me, the ball-point pen poised over the notebook. "But that's grotesque! You said—"

"I know. There's always the chance that the killer left the book."

"Then he must be mad. What a demented thing to do."

"Let's get out of here," I said. "I've got to check in with Quartz and bring him up to date. He'll be climbing the walls."

McIntosh rose slowly, jamming notes into his pockets, his expression skeptical, discouraged. "I hope you know what you're doing, Butler. God knows I don't."

Apparently his faith in my ability was shaken. But I reacted differently to this image of the killer's planting the book. For a moment I experienced the sensation that the phantom who had killed her was leering and cackling at me from some corner of the jungle he had created between us by the act of murder. It was the first time I had felt his presence.

Chapter 6
***

"The fact that the girl and old man Karamazov both had their skulls cracked in is pure coincidence," Quartz Willinger said. "We'd be fools not to believe that the girl left us the book. The big question is, why did she choose this particular book? Was it because of the story it tells? Or because it was the only book that was certain to be taken out of the room? Apparently it's a prized possession. So she knew the Childress girl would claim it."

"I'll check the other books in Natalie's room," I said. "To make sure they all belong to her."

"Yes, but even if they do, we can't rule out the Karamazov story yet." Quartz riffled the pages in the book. "And one more thing. We have to know the name of this 'sometimes Dimitri' character. It's a good bet the Clayborne girl knew it, and that's another fact that makes the book special."

"That may be tough, but I'll have a go at it," I said.

"Now let's get to these folded pages," Quartz said. "That's the nugget in the mattress. You say this girl struck you as clever?"

"She was clever. But not clever enough to keep herself from getting killed by someone she trusted."

Quartz merely grunted. It was noon, and we were in his room in the cottage. I had given him a detailed resume of what had occurred that morning, and his eyes had glittered over the part of the story about how the Clayborne girl switched books before she let the murderer in. As a piece of speculation it was merely plausible if you ignored the folded pages. But these pages were what excited Quartz the most.

He had me roll over to his bed the narrow table that he normally used for meals, so that he could make notes on a pad as he examined the book. We both read the first forty pages, and we were satisfied that the information given on the pages themselves did not make up any part of the girl's message. There was no common denominator over which the three folded pages fitted. "We'll forget that part of it, Morgan," Quartz said. "The numbers are the puzzle, the key, the combination to the safe."

His enthusiasm was contagious. I realized that the book was one part of the case that Quartz could focus his energies on. It was a challenge to his ingenuity, and after weeks of inactivity he was starved for significant work.

"Here's what we've got so far," he said, reading from his pad. "Three numbers, four/thirty/thirty-nine. A date is the most obvious possibility, but that would take us back twenty-three years. It could be a phone number, since the local exchange has five. Or it might be an address in code. Anything else?"

"How about a license number?" I said. "That's identification."

"Good." He scribbled that on the pad.

Recalling the night last week when I had watched her get out of the battered station wagon, I took out my notebook and found the license number I had taken. It wasn't even close. It occurred to Quartz to substitute letters for the numbers, using a zero as an *o*. We got *d/co/ci*. We tried other combinations with the alphabet, and with the title of the book, but none made sense. Also, she didn't have time to be that clever.

"There's not one of these I can't check out by telephone, from this bed," Quartz said. "That'll free you to dig around. You'll have to talk to this ex-boyfriend, Arthur King, and any other boyfriends you can turn up."

"The simplest way to solve this case would be to find the tape," I said.

"Assuming it still exists," Quartz said. "Whatever purpose the tape was to serve, it probably ended with the girl's death. Blackmail, for example. And the killer would destroy that piece of incriminating evidence first thing. So I don't think you'll find our man by looking for the tape."

"I'm not going to find him anyway, if I don't get some chow inside me. You work on the numbers while I scramble some eggs."

I was halfway to the door when the phone rang. It was Paul McIntosh.

"Brace yourself, Butler. Jack Casey just called me with the news that he's already arrested the killer."

"He can't be that good," I said. "Who is it?"

"Butler, that's the incredible part. You and I should have known who it was this morning. That clue the girl left was perfect. We had

56

the murderer's identity practically spelled out for us, and we ignored it."

"Are you going to tell me who it is?"

"Yes, of course. It's Smerdyakov, the servant. It's the man from the college maintenance department, the janitor who takes care of the furnace in the Clayborne girl's dorm. His name is Dicky Bill Ewing."

"How did the sheriff get a lead on this janitor?"

"It seems the other girls in the dorm raised Ewing's name as a suspect. Two of them accused him of swiping certain dainty undergarments they had hung in the basement to dry. Another caught him peeking in her window."

"So Ewing's a dirty old man," I said. "Is that the whole case?"

"No. The old guy's already admitted he was in the dorm basement last night. He stopped to fire the furnace, or so he says."

"I'd like to see this murderer," I said. "Think Casey would object?"

"He practically insists upon it. Casey wants me over at the old geezer's place for the story, and he thought you might appreciate a lesson in police work."

"That's right neighborly of him. All right, I'll pick you up."

"Right. I'm at my office. I'll wait for you out front. There's something eerie about it, wouldn't you say? Smerdyakov, and the way she was killed?"

" 'Eerie' a kind word for it."

Quartz listened to the tale and shook his head. "If this janitor turns out to be the killer, I'm the Queen of Sheba. But I wouldn't give Casey an argument about it. You'd have to tell him about the book and the tape, and it would be just his speed to run you in for withholding evidence."

"I'm a spectator getting a lesson in police work, remember?"

I went out into the chilly, overcast day and drove up Main Street until I spotted McIntosh in his shabby trenchcoat. He got into the car with alacrity, his face flushed. After giving me directions, he said, "Listen, Butler. I've got to use that angle about the Dostoyevsky novel in this arrest story. I don't mean to sound ghoulish, but that's the meat of his story."

"No," I said.

"But why keep it a secret? It's a dandy little twist, the kind you dream about in this business. Every paper on the wire service will pick it up."

"I said no. Maybe you can tell it later."

"But there won't be any story later. I've already filed the murder story. This is the arrest, the end. The trial won't be big enough to get any space."

We were almost there. The janitor lived in one of five small trailers on a lot four blocks from the campus. The trailers had been used for married-student housing during the great influx of veterans after World War II, but they had been abandoned by the college years before. Now they were empty except for the one Ewing occupied. Surrounded by weeds, it looked like a dirty cardboard box with a metal roof.

"I'll make you a deal, editor." I deliberately used Casey's word for him. "If I'm convinced that this janitor killed the girl, you can use the angle of the book in your hot little story. If I don't believe it, then you won't use it."

"What's to prevent me, either way?" he asked. "We don't have a contract."

"Something called 'integrity,' a quality I thought you had a fair share of when I took you into my confidence this morning. That talk was off the record."

He lapsed into silence as we pulled up behind Sheriff Casey's car and parked. One of the small deputies, meaning he was only six feet tall, was sitting with his feet out of the car. The other one was at the door of the trailer. The first one waved us toward the trailer, and the second one opened the door as we approached. The inside of the trailer smelled like a cave where a bear had hibernated for the winter.

The first person I saw was the deputy Humpty. He was sitting on a bed at the end of the trailer, the buttons and harness of his uniform gleaming with such luster in the drab surroundings that he seemed to fill the entire wall. Jack Casey was leaning indolently against a small refrigerator, switching a flyswatter in the palm of his hand like a riding crop. A gaunt man with a huge Adam's apple and hair the color of butterscotch sat at a small table beside Casey. The gaunt man wore a blue work shirt buttoned at the neck and brown corduroy trousers. His eyes were pale and squinted, and his mouth was as plump and pink as a shrimp.

58

"Welcome to the working press, and to you, Constable Butler," Casey said. "I want you to meet Mr. Dicky Bill Ewing." He flicked the flyswatter over Ewing's head, just nipping the scalp. Ewing winced as if it were a red-hot poker, and mumbled something.

"What did you say?" Casey asked him. "Speak up!"

"I said you got no right to do that!" Ewing said. "You had no right to go through my private belongings, neither." His voice had the cadence of a sideshow barker's, but it was corrupted by a whining quality as offensive as a scratch on a record.

"Humpty, you hear that?" Casey said. "This janitor is accusing you of pawing through his private belongings. Is that right?"

"Not me, Jack. I was just admiring this fellow's collection of panties and them cute little slingshots girls tuck their goodies into."

This time Casey stung Ewing smartly on the back of the neck with the swatter. "Now you tell us about that collection, boy. And tell it straight."

"Them's just rags," Ewing said. "Nothing but rags I picked out of the trash barrel to clean up with."

"Show that collection to Butler and the editor," Casey said to Humpty. "We'll get another opinion."

Humpty turned a little, picked up a good-sized drawer from the bed with one hand, and held it towards McIntosh. The editor took it in both hands, brought it into the light, and placed it on a hot-water tank between us. It was full of lingerie, panties and brassieres of every imaginable style and color, red with black lace, blue with pink rosebuds, some as sheer as gauze. The clothes looked soiled, as if they had been handled a lot. As McIntosh looked at me across the drawer, his expression became grim, resolute.

"What do you think now, Butler?" he said. "It makes your flesh crawl."

"It's inflammatory stuff," I said. "It might sell a jury of little old ladies in high-button shoes. It doesn't prove murder."

"You're a cautious man, Butler, and I respect that," Casey said. "Humpty, show him that other fancy rag you found in the janitor's collection."

Humpty grinned and tossed it over. It was a pantie girdle, pale blue and dainty, with little buckles suspended from the bottom. It had a name on it: *"Natalie Clayborne."* Across the back of the girdle someone had written a single word with red paint: "HARLOT!"

59

"What about that piece of evidence, Butler?" Casey said. "Why would our janitor choose this particular rag to write on if he didn't itch for that girl?"

"Maybe he knew something about her we don't know," I said.

"That's a filthy thing to say!" Paul McIntosh said. "You can't defend this scum by vilifying that dead girl. It's disgusting."

"Now calm down, editor," Casey said. "I'm as sorry as the next man for the murder victim, but none of us are going to make her out to be a virgin choir girl with the dew still on her. Not that snail."

McIntosh's mouth sagged a little with distress. "It isn't enough that she's dead," he said. "But you can't even conduct an investigation without smearing her good name. You all make me sick."

Suddenly Dicky Bill Ewing bolted from his chair and shouted at McIntosh. "What about my good name? I read the Good Book and I preach the gospel when the spirit moves me, and I am innocent of this crime in the eyes of the Lord."

Jack Casey cracked him hard in the mouth with the flyswatter.

"Sit down and shut up!"

Ewing glared at each of us in turn, then dropped back into his chair.

Casey began talking to the back of his head. "Yes, the janitor told us he was a lay preacher in the Nazarene church. We found a bundle of religious pamphlets in his junk. We also found some other reading material. Give it, Humpty."

Humpty gave it, plucking the sheaf of magazines from the bed behind him and turning them over to Casey. The sheriff handed them to me. It was cheap erotica, magazines with names *like High-Heeled Capers, Silk Stocking Show* and *Mankillers on Parade*. Most of the photos depicted bare-breasted women, generously endowed, striking provocative poses as they smiled coyly into the camera.

"That's the filth they use to corrupt the minds of American youth," Ewing said mechanically. "I'm not ashamed to have it. I show it to the congregation and denounce the purveyors of such filth."

"I'll bet you do," Casey said. "I'll bet you boys sit around and cluck your tongues and get bug-eyed and work yourselves up into a good holy sweat."

60

"As God is my witness," Ewing said, but he sounded a trifle sheepish.

"Okay, let him be your witness while you tell us that story again, about how you spent your time last night. Now tell it!" Casey stung him hard on each ear for emphasis.

McIntosh winced a little with the sound of the swatter. It was a technique I had seen used successfully before. You shove a grown man around with an innocuous implement, like a flyswatter, and it can demoralize him more quickly than the brutality of a rubber hose. Some men resist pain better than ridicule. Once I saw a husky man break down after a shrewd cop had struck him in the face at crucial moments with a soda straw.

Ewing pumped his Adam's apple a few times, and said, "Okay, I'll tell it. At eleven o'clock I was sitting on a stool at Conway's tavern watching the wrestling matches. I had a few beers and a plate of pigs' knuckles. The wresting was over at midnight, and then I watched the late news."

"What time did you leave?" Casey asked.

"Twelve-thirty," Ewing said. "On the way home I decided to run over to that dorm on Madison and fire the furnace. It had turned cold again, and you can't let that furnace go from Friday to Monday. Them girls'd freeze. So I hiked over there and fired it up. It didn't take ten minutes. I banked the fire, turned the draft low and got out. I was here in my trailer by one A.M."

"And you never went out again?"

"No, and that's the gospel truth."

"And did you get your fancy rags out and play with them after you got home? Did you take them to bed with you?" Casey tickled Ewing's scalp with the swatter.

"That's a rotten lie!"

"Okay, janitor. Let's go back to the dorm for a minute. Now, I got your ring keys right here." He jangled them beside Ewing's ear. "I want to know which key fits that door at the head of the stairs. Don't lie, now."

Ewing squirmed, peered cautiously at the keys, then massaged his hands together. "So I have a key to that door. Sometimes I got to go up there to make repairs. Them girls is always misplacing their key to that door, and I carry a spare. They keep me hopping on that job. I got to work fast."

61

"Yeah, and you worked fast last night, didn't you?" Casey said. "You hiked over to that dorm, all right. Then you did a little window snooping. There was only the one light burning on the first floor, and you knew whose room it was. That was the harlot's room. You've had your eye on that girl. Oh, she looks all honey and innocent on the outside, but you know her mind's as full of sin as Satan's black heart. So you went into the basement, and you pussyfooted up the stairs and unlocked that door. You made sure the rest of the dorm was empty, then you pecked on the harlot's door. Maybe you told her you had fixed her radiator. You probably had a wrench in your hand, to make it convincing. So the harlot let you in, and you made your pitch. Maybe she threatened to call the law, or called you a raunchy pervert and not the Lord's good right hand. So you cold-cocked her with that wrench. Then you ripped her belt off and strangled the life out of that worthless harlot. You gave her the punishment the good Lord intended. Now why not tell the truth, janitor?"

Ewing denied it. First he whispered it, shaking his head, then he shouted it, pounding a fist on the table, and then he threw his head into his arms on the table and slobbered it out. Casey just stood there waving his flyswatter like a wand. Finally he said to Humpty, "I give him twelve hours in the cage."

Humpty snorted. "I figure on six, eight at the most."

"Handcuff him and take him in," Casey said.

Humpty did it with the air of a man taking out his laundry.

"That's the story, gents," Casey said. "All we need is the wrench, or whatever he sapped her with. We'll find it, either around this trailer or in that basement. Then we'll have a nice neat package for the county prosecutor."

McIntosh had been scribbling notes furiously during the sheriff's speech. He gave me a triumphant look and said, "Jack, it looks entirely plausible to me. Solid as a rock. Especially if you find that wrench."

"He'll find it," I said. "And it'll have the girl's blood on it and a full set of Ewing's fingerprints on the handle."

Casey's eyes narrowed, but he was too full of good humor to let it offend him. "No, we don't need any plants on this janitor. He'll tell us where the wrench is. I expect this boy to open up like a lanced boil before noon tomorrow."

"He'll confess to Lincoln's assassination if you have Humpty sit on him while you gag him with that flyswatter," I said.

Again, Casey took it as a joke. "You can tell old Quartz he can stop sweating this one," he said. "His little college is safe again. Maybe you ought to write it up that way, editor. Ease everyone's mind a little."

"And give credit where credit is due," I said.

"Why not?" McIntosh said. "If this janitor is guilty, certainly Jack will get the credit. Maybe your nose is a little out of joint, Butler."

He went out of the trailer fast, full of dignity and purpose. He was sitting stiffly in the front seat of the car when I got behind the wheel. I drove slowly through the quiet streets until I reached his office. As he started to get out, I reached an arm across his belly and held the door.

"What are you trying to do?" he asked.

"I want a word with you."

He nodded with mock weariness, and I took my time lighting a stogie.

"Smerdyakov didn't kill Natalie Clayborne," I said.

"Why not?" he said.

"Several reasons. The stolen tape, the trouble she was in last week, even the book. You don't throw out all the pieces that don't fit just to make one man look guilty."

"Butler, don't try to double-talk me. There doesn't have to be a connection between the stolen tape and her death."

"The janitor didn't kill her," I said. "His type don't kill. He gets his thrills in his fantasies, and he would never confront her like that."

"Now you're a psychiatrist, too. In other words, Butler, you don't want me to reveal the business of the Dostoyevsky novel. Isn't that it?"

"That's part of it," I said.

"Don't you realize the sheriff's case would be even better if he knew about the clue she left? You're asking me to withhold valuable evidence."

"Listen, if Ewing had killed her on impulse, the way Casey told it, she wouldn't have known it was coming until it was too late. She wouldn't have had time to mark the book."

"Neither of us will ever know what went on in that room, Butler," he said. Paul fidgeted a little, shaking his head. "All right, I'll agree to this much. I'll write the arrest story for the wire service without the book. But my own paper comes out on Wednesday, and I'll release the clue of the book then. By that time Jack will probably have a confession, so he won't be too sore. Now that's as far as I'll go. Is it a deal?"

"It'll have to do, editor," I said.

He got out of the car, then stood on the sidewalk and leaned back inside. "You have to understand my position, Butler." I happen to think Casey has solved the case. Maybe it's wishful thinking on my part. Maybe I want to see the college get off this easily. But I honestly believe we've got the man."

His face was as sincere and homespun as Lincoln's stovepipe hat. "You're right, Paul. I'm grateful for three days. I'll keep you posted."

He slammed the door, and I drove down to Quartz's cottage to report the big arrest of Smerdyakov Ewing, with his harlot's girdle and his trusty wrench, with thwarted lust in his gospel-ridden soul. Wait until the Sunday feature boys got their hooks into it. Ewing would be convicted in this county before the week was out.

But even I had to admit the truth of what McIntosh had said over the phone a few hours earlier. There was something eerie about the accuracy of the killer in the novel, Smerdyakov, and the janitor named Ewing.

Chapter 7
***

As if Smerdyakov were not enough of a problem, on Monday I had my Ivan and Dimitri. No doubt any given community will give you a full set without much effort: three men who resemble roughly the three Karamazov brothers implicated in their father's murder. But in this case all the pieces in the set had something in common, a connection with Natalie Clayborne. You would think that would be enough. It wasn't.

Even before I had Ivan and Dimitri, I had the father.

In the Dostoyevsky novel, of course, it is the father who is killed, so there is no comparison intended here. For Philip Clayborne was very much alive. It was Jack Casey who first informed me of how vigorously alive this Clayborne was. I had tried to call Casey that morning on another matter, and he got back to me a little after noon.

"Good to talk to you, Butler. Say, I just spent half the morning trading insults with that blonde snail's daddy. He blew into town before dawn this morning with blood in his eye and fire in his nostrils."

"You could always sic Humpty on him, Jack, if he gets in your hair."

Casey chuckled. "Not this boy. He keeps a gilt-edged lawyer at one elbow to light his cigars, and a bodyguard at the other to haul the ashes away."

"Didn't you tell him you had the killer in jail before the body was cold?"

"Yes, but that didn't impress him as much as I thought it would," Casey said. "He did change his tune a little when I flung that blue girdle on his lap. That gagged him."

"I'll bet." I could imagine Casey doing it. "But I don't understand. What's Clayborne's complaint?"

Casey's voice became less folksy. "Well, you know the type. They want action. They want the evidence all in, the forms filled out, and the man hung with a clean rope just after lunch. This Clayborne fellow is a big boy in his neck of the woods, and he didn't like me telling him he was just another suit of clothes in Parson County. He threatened to bring a brace of Pinkertons in to double-check me."

"I gather this means you haven't got the confession yet," I said.

"Not yet." He chuckled with less mirth. "That janitor's stubborn."

"How about the wrench? Did you find that yet?"

"We found a dozen, but none of them any good."

I gave him a few words of sympathy on that score, and then I tried to be clever. "Jack, I called earlier about another item you might have found in Ewing's trailer when you searched it. Something he might have lifted from the dormitory along with his collection of rags."

"And what might that be?"

"It's a spool of tape from a tape recorder. It was stolen a week ago from one of the girls in the dorm. I thought Ewing might have picked it up."

The silence in my ear dragged on for more than a minute, punctuated by the tapping of a fingernail on the mouthpiece. Finally Casey spoke. "It's a funny thing you should ask about that tape, Butler."

"Why is it funny? I could use a laugh."

"That spool of tape is what the snail's daddy was so fired up about. He raised such a stink about it, I sent a deputy back to Jordan City with him so he could ransack the trailer again."

"How did Clayborne know about the tape?"

"How did *you* know about it? And suppose you tell me what it's all about. I hope you weren't holding out on me, Butler. I get mean when I get sore."

"It's not like that at all, Jack. I'm not sure there's any connection between the tape and the murder. She told me herself that it was only a recording of her own poetry." I gave him a brief summary of my investigation of the stolen tapes, but said nothing about Natalie Clayborne's frantic excursions into the night. "I just saw it as a loose end we might tie up."

"Yeah, but you were pussyfooting me. I don't like that."

"Get off my back, Casey! You're not sore at me. You're sore at Clayborne for beating you over the head with his money and his lawyers and his Pinkertons."

I hung up fast, pleased at this proof that the spool of tape was still the prize in this case. Natalie's father wouldn't be that anxious to recover the tape if he didn't know what was on it, and the fact that he was searching for it meant that he had reason to know that it hadn't been destroyed. I was eager to meet this father.

I got my wish two hours later, although it was Quartz Willinger who arranged the meeting behind my back.

After my talk with Casey, I'd gone up to the college to check out the license number of the Ford station wagon that had brought Natalie home from one of her mysterious sojourns. A clerk in the main building told me the car was registered to a student named Arthur King. King's address turned out to be the second floor of an abandoned service station, located a half mile from campus on the Old Sawmill Road. They had long since ripped out the gas pumps and boarded up the part that had been used as a store. The other half of the ground floor had been the repair shop, and I gathered Arthur King used it as a garage, parking his car over the old grease pit. King wasn't home when I inspected the place, so I left a note on his door asking him to drive in to see me. Then I drove back to town for lunch at the Tug and Maul, a place that didn't become a student hangout until after six each evening. I ordered the steak sandwich, a salad, and a bottle of Tuborg beer.

I was working on my second beer when the Athlete entered the room. He moved like on, the stiffness of the shoulders and the subtle swagger with the pelvis, but he worked at it. His suit was an impeccable tan sharkskin with just a kiss of plaid, and he wore a tie so thin the knot was the size of your thumbnail. He had brown wavy hair, a dimple in the chin, and a set of caps that probably gleamed like neon in the dark.

He eased into the booth opposite me uninvited, sniffed at my stogie as if it were marijuana, and said, "You're a hard man to locate, Butler."

"I didn't think you'd need me," I said. "I thought you boys were smart enough to find the secret compartment beneath that janitor's refrigerator."

He couldn't quite conceal the quiver of anxiety. It trembled in his jaw muscles so that his dimple appeared to wink at me. Then he shook his head, smiling. "I guess it's true what they say about small towns, everybody knows your business. But that secret-compartment gag is strictly Hicksville. I wouldn't advise you springing it on the old man."

"Who's the old man?"

"Aw, don't play dumb on me. Philip Clayborne, the girl's father. He owns the Clayborne Construction Company in Philly, among other things. His money isn't quite as old as Rockefeller money, but it's older than the Kennedys'. By the way, my name's Swanson."

"What do you do for the old man, Swanson, besides helping him age his money?"

He liked that, for some reason, and smiled his expensive smile "I'm just a handyman, a glorified errand boy."

"I'll bet you're paid well, though," I said. "Tell me, do you get a bonus for carrying that .38 in the shoulder holster?"

"I'm licensed to carry it, if it's any of your business. Now, come on. The old man wants to see you. He cleared it with your boss, the Chief. We're at the Cavendish Hotel. Oh yes, Mr. Clayborne said to say please."

"That's the magic word. You don't mind if I make a phone call first?"

"Be my guest. I'll wait out front."

I went to the pay phone in the rear of the room and called Quartz. I told him about Swanson's invitation, and asked how much he had told Clayborne.

"I'm glad you called," Quartz said. "This Clayborne is big brass. He put me on the spot, old buddy, and I passed the buck to you."

"Exactly what do you mean, 'old buddy'?"

"Well, he already knew about the tape. Seems his daughter wrote him about it. He wants that tape, and the last time this guy didn't get what he wanted was the year Alf Landon lost. He has no confidence in Casey, incidentally."

"So he doesn't think the janitor is the killer?"

"Let's say he has reasonable doubt. Anyway, he was talking about bringing a platoon of private dicks to turn this town upside down. That's when I stuck my neck out and told him about your sideline business. I also explained that you knew his daughter and had found some evidence Casey overlooked. I think he wants to hire you. He seemed impressed when I quoted him your fee, a thousand per."

"All right. Maybe that was your best move. Any progress on the numbers in that book?"

"All strikeouts. It's not a local number or address. No word yet from the license bureau. Looks like we're stuck with the date."

"I'll try it on Daddy," I said. "Maybe she left the message for him."

I hung up and walked out to the street. Swanson was standing beside a black Cadillac, flexing his charm at a group of coeds who were passing. When I started toward my car, he intercepted me. "Hey, old man prefers you come in his car. He wants to keep this meeting on the Q.T."

"Maybe I should wear a disguise."

"I thought you were," he said.

We got into his Cadillac and drove a mile out the Carthage Pike to the Cavendish Hotel. A replica of a Southern mansion, the place had been a local spa back in the days when hot springs and mineral baths were in vogue. Then it became a white elephant until an enterprising couple had it renovated, installed an antique shop and a tea room on the first floor, and made a subsidy deal with the college.

Swanson parked the Caddy on the gravel in front of the Doric pillars, left the door on his side hanging open, and led me through the lobby with the air of a man traipsing through his private beach house. The self-service elevator was about the size of a phone booth, and on the way up Swanson checked his tie, hairdo and cufflinks in the small mirror mounted on one wall. I was tempted to ask him if my nose was shiny, but I had wearied of the sport. There is a special insolence that develops in people who work for millionaires. No matter how banal their duties, they become accustomed to the way people genuflect before the mystique of the money. It is heady stuff, and after a while they learn to exercise this power with relish.

We emerged from the elevator and approached a pair of doors that gave entrance to the entire east wing, the suite of rooms the hotel kept in reserve for Nobel prizewinners and other royalty. Swanson pushed a button that ran an electric chime within the suite, nodded at the command to enter and ushered me inside. The room was decorated with early American Colonial pieces, a Virginia sofa, a set of wing-back chairs with Queen Anne legs, a desk and sideboard that glowed with the deep luster of expensive wood. Silhouetted against the bay windows was a tall man with the kind of profile they loved to mint on old Roman coins. His brow and nose were prominent, even formidable, and the lower half of his face was saved from burliness by a mouth like his daughter's, expressive and a shade delicate. He wore his thin black hair combed tight against his scalp, and his

69

tanned complexion looked as if it had been buffed to a high gloss. His eyes were dark and deep-set. They looked melancholy, but maybe that was just the mood we caught him in. His suit was black mohair.

"I'm Philip Clayborne," he said, crossing the room. "You're Morgan Butler. I suppose you had to wear that uniform. Well, no harm done. Thank you, Swanson, I'll call you if I need you." His voice had the resonant timbre of healthy self-confidence. And the eyes were truly melancholy. The grief smoldering in them reminded me of the eyes of the walking wounded.

Swanson departed through one of two doorways in the back of the room, and Mr. Clayborne offered me a chair across from the Virginia sofa. He produced a cigar case and held it open toward me, but I declined and took out one of my black stogies. He plucked a cigar from the case, but made no move to light it. He said, "My lawyer, John Reynolds, is in another room. He wanted to be present at this meeting, but I thought it should be completely confidential."

He paused as if waiting for me to confirm this. I nodded.

He said, "I understand you were present when this janitor was arrested for Natalie's murder. Did he kill her?" He didn't stumble over the tough words.

"No," I said.

"That's refreshing," he said. "A man who doesn't equivocate. Now before we start letting our back hair down, Mr. Butler, I have to know more about you. Your friend Willinger gave you quite the buildup. I only hope you can live up to it. If you do, you can save me a lot of time. I'd much rather employ a man already involved in the case, assuming he's the right man."

"Exactly what do you want to know?" I said.

He smiled, and it made his face astonishingly handsome. "You're friend said that you've had considerable experience as a private investigator. He claims that you're extremely capable, the soul of discretion, and that you don't scare easily. It's a rare combination. You don't mind if I'm a wee bit skeptical?"

"Not at all."

"Fine. Then, what kind of references can you give that will impress me?"

70

After a little thought, I gave him three names in three different cities. He wrote two of them down on a pad he had picked up from the coffee table.

"This Hammersmith in Philadelphia," he said, "is that the judge's brother?"

"Yes, and the son of the old judge," I said.

"If you'll excuse me for a moment." He went into one of the rooms in the back, and returned in a few minutes. "Reynolds is checking it out. I don't know Alex Hammersmith personally, but I know his brother quite well and Reynolds happens to belong to the same club. May I ask what kind of work you did for him?"

"It was a confidential matter. And if that was meant as a test, Mr. Clayborne, it was pretty clumsy."

"Yes, it was." But he wasn't in the least embarrassed. He strolled to the window and seemed to fall into a trance. At least he didn't move for fifteen minutes, after which the same door opened slightly and a voice called his name. Clayborne talked in a low voice at the door for a few minutes, then returned to the sofa. A subtle exuberance controlled his movements.

"Even Reynolds was impressed," he said. "It appears that you did a very delicate and ugly piece of work for Alex. And you did it so cleverly that no one will ever connect him with it. Now my curiosity is aroused."

"If we're on speaking terms now, Mr. Clayborne, I'd like to give you my position on this. I waited for you to go through the rigamarole of checking me out because I need your confidence. That doesn't mean I need your money. Eight days ago someone stole a tape your daughter made. Then yesterday she was killed. I happen to believe the two crimes are related. I've already decided to find the murderer. Money isn't going to make me do this any faster or any better. So why should you pay for something you're going to get free of charge?"

He was a good listener. All his senses seemed to focus on you with an intensity that made you feel special. Finally he nodded. "Very commendable of you. But you'll see that I do have sound reasons for hiring you. First, I want to employ you exclusively. You'll get rid of that uniform and your other duties, and devote yourself to this job. Secondly, and I can't stress this enough, you must find the tape above all. I'm sure it hasn't been destroyed. You

71

are not to listen to it. You bring me the tape intact, and I take it from there."

His voice fairly cracked with an emotional current I had heard before. It was a combination of iron will and wealth that has become an expression of personality. No wonder Jack Casey hard smarted from its sting. "Let me get this straight," I said. "You want me to find the tape, which is probably in the hands of your daughter's murderer. I'm to lift it from him and deliver it to you, and you'll take it from there. I don't think we can make that kind of a deal. I had seriously considered arresting the man. I may even have to kill him."

"Obviously I haven't made myself clear," he said. Clayborne massaged the bridge of his nose between a thumb and finger. "If you have to kill the man to get the tape, I would be grateful. The desire for blood vengeance is something I never thought I'd experience. But maybe I'm not as civilized as I like to believe. My daughter and I were very close, Mr. Butler. She was my only child. She was my princess." He paused for a moment, swallowed hard, then continued in a lower voice. "Of course, if you have to arrest this man, I suppose we'll get justice. But bear in mind that the tape must never be made public. It comes to me."

We waited. The room was absolutely quiet, but it was the kind of hushed atmosphere that made you feel that a hundred people were listening breathlessly behind the walls. We both knew I had to ask the question.

"What's on the tape that makes it so important, Mr. Clayborne?"

"You don't need that information. Believe me when I tell you that you won't be handicapped in any way by not knowing what's on the tape."

"You can't be certain of that. That information could help me identify the murderer. The least you can do is give me a general idea."

He finished his drink, massaged his nose again, then took out a white handkerchief and wiped his palms. His gaze went a little abstract. "Maybe you're right. First, you should know that I'm particularly vulnerable right now to any kind of scandal. If all goes well, I'll be offered an important position in our government very soon. And a few years hence I may be asked to run for the Senate. You understand, I hope, that all of this is in the strictest confidence?"

"And the scandal is on the tape," I said.

72

"Yes. Oh it's not merely my good name and reputation I am trying to protect. It's Natalie's, too, even though the crime was hers. I use the word 'crime' advisedly. You see, when she was sixteen she got involved with some very disreputable people, unbeknownst to me. She didn't come to me until something rather serious had happened. I had the choice of either letting her pay the penalty or buying her out of it. So I bought her off. It's the sort of dirty business I would have no defense against if my enemies learned about it. Natalie was old enough to appreciate that fact, and to be trusted to keep it secret."

"Is that a fact? Then doesn't it strike you as odd that she should recite the whole sordid story into a tape recorder for her psychological counselor?"

Ne nodded stiffly. "Yes, that puzzled me until I talked with Dr. Pritchett. I didn't even know she was seeing a psychiatrist. But the doctor said she was under stress. He called it the fervent self-investigation of a young girl who fancies herself in true love. He suspects that she felt uneasy about this sin of hers and wanted to purge herself of it. All for the benefit of her true love. Unfortunately, she never mentioned the man's name."

"I understand she wrote you a letter about the tape," I said.

"Yes, postmarked last Monday. But I didn't get it until yesterday, an hour before I learned that she was dead. I was in Florida on business, and only my office mail was forwarded to me. As you might suspect, I was already making preparations to come out here when I got the call from the dean."

"May I see the letter she wrote?"

"I destroyed it immediately. Believe me, there was nothing in it to suggest that her life was in danger."

"Can you give me the gist of it? It might help."

"Well, she said that she had exposed our evil deeds on a tape for her doctor, and someone had stolen it. She suspected foul play. That was her phrase."

"Do you think she meant blackmail?"

"Naturally that occurred to me, but I honestly don't know. My impulse was to get out here and recover the tape. But then she was dead."

"I'm surprised she didn't try to call you on the phone."

"Yes, but maybe she was too embarrassed. She must have felt as if she had betrayed me a little. As if that matters now." His expression was bleak, his eyes hot. "I wish she had never come to this school. I was opposed to it, but Natalie wanted to come because her mother graduated from Jordan."

"Then you didn't attend Jordan College?"

"No, no. Harvard, thirty-five."

That reminded me of something. "Let me ask you an important question, Mr. Clayborne. Does the date April thirtieth, nineteen thirty-nine have any special significance to you? Think about it."

He shook his head. "No, but I was married in September of that year."

A quick, nervous thrill passed through me. "Does that mean your wife graduated from Jordan in June of thirty-nine?"

"Natalie's mother, yes. We were divorced when Natalie was ten. That would be fifty-two. I've since remarried."

"How long ago?"

"That's hardly relevant. Two years ago."

"Was Natalie on friendly terms with your first wife?"

"No, Natalie hasn't seen her since the divorce. That was one of the terms of the settlement. You see, I won the decree. Oh, if you're wondering if my first wife knew of this scandal, the answer is no. *Had* she known, she would have used it against me long before this. Ours wasn't an amicable parting. I proved adultery."

"May I ask her name?"

"Eleanor Sheridan was her maiden name. It might be Eleanor Baxter now. The last I heard, she had gone to Chicago with a man named Baxter."

"All right, let's get back to our deal, Mr. Clayborne. There's a detail we have to iron out. It would be wrong for me to give up the constable's job. Not only does the job give me a good cover, a reason for nosing around, it also gives me the authority to question people. That's an advantage I sorely need."

He shrugged. "I'll trust your judgment about that. As long as there is no conflict of interests, such as your thinking you need the tape for evidence. Now as to salary. You have a lot of nerve charging a thousand a week."

"My nerve is what you're paying for. Along with my discretion."

"Well, I won't quibble." He took a check from his pocket and handed it to me. It was for a thousand dollars. "I'll pay you the thousand a week for three weeks. That's a guarantee. But if you deliver the tape to me before that time, I'll pay you a flat five thousand."

"Is that what you gentlemen call an 'incentive bonus'?"

"Your levity doesn't amuse me, Mr. Butler. Now here's a Philadelphia number where you can always reach me. I have to take my daughter home tonight. I'll have Swanson drive you back to town."

Clayborne went to the desk, rang a buzzer at the base of the telephone, then pulled a sheaf of papers from a briefcase and began reading the top one. I felt a grudging twinge of admiration for the man's ability to function.

"Ready to roll, officer?" It was Swanson, who had entered the room quietly behind me. He looked as if he had shaved and changed shirts.

He must have called down about the Caddy from the other room, because it was parked just where we had left it, with a tall colored boy in the blue livery of the Cavendish wiping imaginary specks of dust off the windshield. Swanson flipped a coin toward him and we started back to town. Swanson was the type who liked to spray fenders with gravel as he turned onto the highway.

"You had quite a session with the old man," he said. "You on the payroll?"

"I'm sure Mr. Clayborne will tell you all about it when you get back."

"Cagey fellow, aren't you? But hell, I know he hired you and I know why. To find the spool of tape his snooty daughter made as a last will and testament."

"What's the matter, didn't the girl like your brand of charm?"

"Do I look like an Eskimo? That girl was the original Snow Queen. Frigid and rigid, a libido like an igloo. It was all I could do to keep a straight face this morning when that hick sheriff told us she wasn't pregnant."

"Casey must have been disappointed. He predicted she would be."

Swanson snorted softly into the steering wheel. "That cornball. He thinks he's got the killer locked up, too. What do you think?"

"What I think doesn't carry much weight. It's his case."

"Not very sociable, are you? Hell, we're on the same team. The old man confides in me and relies on me. Personally, I think he's worried that somebody's going to hold him up for this tape, and for a fancy price."

"Suppose you prove he confides in you by telling me what's on the tape," I said. "Then we'll socialize all you want."

"Oh, you're a shrewd operator, Butler," Swanson said, grinning. "Shame on you, trying to pry the old man's secrets from me. He wouldn't tell you what's on that tape for all the kale in Fort Knox."

He said it with a breezy confidence, but I doubted that he knew what was on the tape. I doubted if the lawyer, Reynolds, knew either. We were in Jordan City now, and Swanson wheeled the Caddy expertly to the curb a few doors up from the Tug and Maul.

"Good hunting, Butler," he said. "Maybe I'll read about you in the obituaries."

It was just bad timing on his part. I had been too humble for too many hours to too many men with an exaggerated sense of their own importance. I flicked him across the eyes with the back of my hand. Sudden pain in unexpected places shocks a man out of all proportion to the impact of the blow. His arms jerked up far enough for me to snake the .38 from under his left arm. When he grabbed for it, I cracked him across the knuckles with the gun.

"Reach for it again, and I'll mount it to your dimple for you," I said.

He was breathing hard through his teeth. "So you can't take a joke. You are from Hicksville."

"You said you wanted to be sociable. This is one of the games we play out here in the sticks, taking guns away from snot-nosed punks just for the exercise."

"I told you I had a permit. Wait until Clayborne hears about this."

"Yes, you tell him. He'll feel very secure knowing he has a bodyguard with reflexes like yours. He'll replace you with a fat cop on his pension."

The venom was like crude oil in his eyes. "Give it back now."

"You know the word."

"Please."

I handed it to him and watched him put it away.

"I won't forget this," he said.

76

"Careful now. You say the wrong thing, and we'll have to do it again."

He wanted to tell me I couldn't, but he waited too long and the little gangrene of doubt began to eat at his confidence. He touched his eyes gingerly. "So I cracked wise out of turn. Hell, no hard feelings in the end."

"That's the spirit. So long, Swanson." I got out, watching his hands, and he drove away. It was a silly incident, but I felt as if I had gotten some of the poison out of my system. I walked down to my car, and there was a young man sitting in it on the passenger's side.

I wasn't quite ready to identify him as Ivan Karamazov.

Chapter 8
***

"I'm Arthur King," the young man said, getting out of the car. "Don't think I'm here just because of the message you left on my door. I was coming to see you anyway after I read this." He shoved a copy of the *Spencer's Falls Gazette* towards me. "Are you a party of the frameup of this idiot janitor? He didn't kill Natalie Clayborne."

He had the most intense blue eyes I had ever seen, like the bluing on a new rifle barrel. They were separated by a nose that had been broken and healed with a bone spur on one side. That, plus a broken front tooth, kept his face from being too handsome. His black hair was worn very long, but with his height and husky build the effect was graceful instead of feminine. He wore a faded plaid shirt, khaki pants, and a tweed jacket with elbow patches.

"What's the matter, do you think she was too refined to be killed by a man with such a low social rating?" The sneer in my voice was as thick as lard.

King made a savage little gesture, and for a moment I thought he was going to swat me with the newspaper.

"Go ahead," I said. "I'm just in the mood to wrestle with you. It's a course I run for the college on the hazards of making irresponsible accusations."

He retreated a step, and the belligerent lines around his mouth faded into a smile. "Sorry, that was stupid of me. That session I had with the county sheriff yesterday must have soured me on cops. I should have known better. Natalie told me you were no ordinary cop. She liked you."

"But not well enough to trust me when she was in trouble," I said.

"You're in good company." His voice had a rough edge to it. "I thought I was her closest friend, but she wouldn't confide in me, either."

"Let's get off the street," I said. "Why don't we go out to your apartment. This morning it struck me as a very private place."

"That's why I have it," he said. "Sure, I don't mind. I just put my car in the shop for a tune-up. I can use a lift home."

"Good. First, I want to make a quick stop at the office." I drove down to the constable's office, and asked King to wait in the car.

As soon as I entered, Frank Ferby got up from a chair and strutted toward me, a sly grin on his face. "I got that dope you wanted, Morgan. In fact, here's a little bonus you hadn't counted on." He dropped a brass key into my palm.

"I take it that's the key to the dead girl's room," I said.

He chortled. "That's it. They put a padlock on the door, but nobody's guarding it. I buddied up to that deputy Casey's got watching the trailer. Told him I wanted to sneak a look at the murder room, purely for professional reasons. He gave me the loan of this spare key."

"Good work. Listen, Frank, after I make a call I'll be gone for the rest of the day. You man the desk, and check in with Quartz before you leave."

"Yes, sir!" The murder had starched him with self-importance. Old cronies and strangers alike stopped him on the street and pumped him about the crime, or so he had complained that morning.

I went to my desk and called Dr. Pritchett at Forbes Institute. As soon as I identified myself, his voice took on a conspiratorial tone. Now we had a bond between us. Yes, he had talked with the father that morning, as a gesture of courtesy. After all, the man had suffered a grievous loss. No, he couldn't think of a solitary fact about the Clayborne girl that would be of any help to the police. Nevertheless, he would be willing to meet with me and answer any questions. We set a date for five o'clock.

Arthur King was so deep in thought when I returned to the car that he jumped with alarm when I opened the door. His expression was haggard, as if I had caught him exploring some distasteful memory. There is this about murder in a small community; it forces people to look to their secrets. They sweat about blunders long concealed, peccadilloes of every description, crimes and the lust to commit them. I got the impression that King was immersed in this morbid investigation. I drove slowly to his apartment.

"So Sheriff Casey gave you a bad time yesterday," I said. "How so?"

King responded sluggishly. "Maybe I just didn't like his style, all lewd suggestions and threats coated with his bucolic humor. I guess he considered me his number one suspect until he got his hands on that janitor."

"Tact is not Jack Casey's long suit," I said. "But I promise to mind my manners as long as I have you under suspicion. What kind of alibi did you give Jack for Saturday night?"

"Very funny. He, wait a minute. You're not joking. You mean it."

"We've decided the janitor didn't do it. That leaves the field wide open."

He looked at me intently for a moment, then shrugged. "I had no alibi. I was at home studying that night." He laughed, shaking his head. "If this isn't straight out of the theater of the absurd. I was the one who was going to bomb you with information, to persuade you to find the killer. How naïve."

"No, go ahead. Bomb me with information. Just make sure you include last Thursday night, when you met her in town and had the fight on the way home."

"So that's it." He gave a cynical laugh. "Okay. But first let me give you a little background. I've known Natalie since she was a freshman, but we didn't become friends until last year, when we took a poetry class together. At first I thought she was just another rich bitch trying to prove how democratic she was. You see, I kicked around for several years before college. Two years in the Army, one year of construction work in Alaska, another year in a steel mill. She seemed too impressed by all of that. Well, to make it short, we began dating and grew very fond of each other. She had her share of hang-ups, but beneath it all she was a sweet and complicated person. There was a time, late last spring, when we flirted with the idea of marriage."

"I have to ask the one tactless question," I said.

"I know. You probably won't believe me any more than the sheriff did. No, we were never lovers. In fact, that proved to be her worst hang-up. She could never make it, and she was bitter with herself about it. During the summer she wrote and told me that we ought to forget it. When she came back in the fall, we were just good friends. We met for lunch occasionally, and she would sometimes give me a few of her poems to read. We both enjoyed it that way. But even that relationship began to degenerate late in the fall. After the Christmas holidays, I didn't see much of her."

80

"Let's get back to last week," I said. "How did you know she was in trouble?"

"She told me, in so many words. But she never told me what it was. Last Monday night she came to my apartment and woke me up. It must have been four in the morning. She was upset, but it all seemed a little theatrical to me."

"But she must have had a reason for coming to see you."

"Oh, she gave me a reason. She said she came to tell me how lucky I was it hadn't worked out between us. She hinted that I would hate her if I knew the truth about her."

"That's a pretty flimsy excuse to wake a man up at four A.M."

"Exactly what I thought. I knew there was a lot more on her mind, but all she would say was that she suspected someone was going to betray her. Then in the next breath she insisted that she deserved it."

"Did she say anything about a tape that had been stolen from her?"

"No. Wait! She did say something about a tale being told by an idiot, meaning herself, that had fallen into the wrong hand. That's the way she was talking."

At that point I turned into the gravel driveway at the abandoned service station where King lived. On one side of the building an advertisement for Mail Pouch chewing tobacco was just legible. Beneath it the rusted hulk of an old car was overgrown with weeds.

"The poet's retreat," King said. "That's my trade, in case you hadn't noticed. That's the way I feel about poetry, it ought to be a trade. All the crudeness and sweat and stench of life has to be in it, along with the more fragile sentiments. Maybe I'll found a new school, the roughneck poets. Lately poetry has become so academic and sterile you can't breathe in the atmosphere. Well, all this is very much beside the point." He got out of the car.

I followed him up the flight of wooden stairs that led to the second floor of the building. "Is poetry your major?" I asked.

"No, I'm majoring in philosophy. I like to read the stuff." He said it gruffly, as if he regretted having exposed himself to me.

At that moment I made the association between Arthur King and Ivan Karamazov. I experienced an electric sensation, for the connection also plugged into that first conversation I had had with Natalie. I remember the description I had conjured up of the kind of man she would attach herself to in order to purge herself of the morality of wealth, a man who as at once idealistic, outside the Establishment, dedicated to his work. In short, a maverick who would scrub the tinsel from her illusions. The description fitted Arthur King like his skin.

King unlocked the door and ushered me into a room that covered the entire floor of the building. It was spartan in appearance, with a desk made of an old door mounted on legs, bookshelves made of bricks and boards, a bed that appeared to be little more than a piece of plywood covered with a thin mattress. A crude kitchen had been fashioned in one corner, with a chipped refrigerator, a two-burner gas hotplate, a small sink and a cardtable. The only decorative touch was an Indian rug on the floor, a red totem woven against a black and white background.

"How about a beer?" King said. "I've been dry in the mouth since this thing happened."

"A beer would be fine."

He got two cans from the refrigerator and punctured the tops. Like most people, King acquired an extra measure of poise in his own home.

We sat at the cardtable, and I said, "Let's get back to last week. What happened after her visit Monday night?"

"I began to worry about her," he said. "But she wouldn't even answer my calls. That meeting on Thursday night was an accident. I'd studied here until about two A.M., then drove down to Pike's diner for a snack. She stumbled into Pike's around three, looking like death warmed over. I drove her back to campus, and on the way I coaxed her to unload on me. We argued about it. She was in a rough mood, sexually aggressive, castigating herself with wild language."

"Yes, I had a sample of that the next night," I said. "Listen, did she ever discuss the fact that her mother was once a student here at Jordan?"

"She mentioned it once or twice." He started to drink, but halted with his can in midair. "I think you've hit paydirt. Waldo Mason."

"Who?"

"Waldo Mason. That's one of the names I was going to bomb you with. He's on the faculty, teaches American history and literature. And he was a student here in the same class as Natalie's mother."

I lit a stogie to conceal my excitement. "Why were you going to mention his name in relation to Natalie?"

"Once last fall she told me they had a long conversation about her mother, and it stimulated Natalie enormously. Later she told me he'd made a pass at her. She laughed about it, but I felt there was something between them."

"What kind of man is this Waldo Mason?"

King smiled. "A renegade and something of a rogue. He's pretty radical, even for this school. He sports a full beard and acts as if he's been appointed gadfly of this particular Athens. He's quite the scholar, though, and his classes are always jammed. Somehow he fits in with the life she began leading last fall."

"What kind of life?"

"Well, she began to hang out with what I call the beard-and-sandal set in Jordan City. In college towns like this there are always dilettantes and weekend Bohemians who like to patronize the arty crowd from school. There's a guy in town named Eddie Bell who holds regular soirees for this crowd, with poetry readings and folksinging washed down with cheap wine and cheaper innuendos. Bell tried to get me to read some of my stuff there, but I refused. He strikes me as an oily little voyeur. I know he had some influence with Natalie, enough to flatter her into reading some of her poetry to his audience of gushers."

"I've met Eddie Bell," I said. "He's manager of the Stagecoach. Was Natalie thick with anyone else in that crowd?"

"Just one other that I know about. Carl Metterman. He's the guy who runs that arts and crafts shop on Main Street. He also teaches a few classes at the college. He weaves on the loom, pots on the wheel, does portraits for tourists at the summer art shows. You name it. Anyway, Natalie was mixed up with him, too. They were taking in each other's emotional laundry, from what I gathered."

I said, "King, you seem to be awfully well informed about her private life. Considering that you two broke up last year."

"I've explained that! We were still friends, and she used to mention these people as if she wanted my reaction to them. Yes, and maybe she did it to torment me a little. She had this imperious, cruel streak in her. I told you she was a complicated person."

"And you were never offended or angered by that kind of treatment?"

83

His eyes slewed away from mine. "Of course I was. I was in love with her. But she was unattainable to me in every way, financially, spiritually and, to make the trinity complete, sexually. Maybe I helped erect the barriers. What difference does it make? She's dead. Some demented bastard killed her."

He had the stony look again, and I wondered a lot of things about him. But he seemed to have given all he could for the moment, and I snapped him out of it long enough to try the cryptic numbers on him, reminding him that Natalie's mother had graduated from the college in thirty-nine.

"Try Waldo Mason," he growled. "Maybe that was the date he seduced the mother, and he planned to lay the daughter on the anniversary next month."

At least he was an imaginative poet. I thanked him and took my leave. As I descended the wooden steps outside, a girl on a bicycle turned into the gravel drive and glided to the foot of the steps. She wasn't much more than five feet tall, dressed in soiled jeans and a man's shirt. She seemed composed of a delicious plumpness, of hips, breasts, arms and cheeks, but her large, soulful eyes and the way her long black hair draped over her face gave her an oddly ascetic look. Tilting her head, she gave me a shy smile.

"Is Arthur home?" she asked.

"Yes, but he's in a foul mood."

"What else is new?" she said, starting primly up the stairs past me.

I wheeled the car onto the macadam, and five minutes later parked across the street from the neat white house in which Natalie Clayborne had met a violent death. I hoped to have a talk with Betty Childress while I was here, but when I entered and rang her buzzer, a slender girl appeared and said that Betty was still in class. The girl agreed to clear the hall of young women in scanty attire, and soon I was inside the murder room, with the door closed.

At first glance the room appeared to be unchanged, except for the fact that the bed was stripped to the naked springs. But then I saw something that was conspicuously absent: the charcoal drawing of the faceless nude. It had been here yesterday morning. Assuming that Casey and his boys hadn't removed it, the theft made sense only if it had been, after all, a picture of Natalie, and the artist who drew it didn't want his connection to the girl revealed.

84

But I had come here for another purpose. I took the first book off the shelves behind her desk and flipped open the cover. This meticulous girl had pasted a bookplate on the flyleaf, an old woodcut with name neatly printed on the bottom. Every hardbound book on the shelves was decorated with one. It didn't prove anything, but it lent weight to the theory that she used the Dostoyevsky novel to send her message because it was the one book that would be taken from the room.

Then I devoted ten minutes to a thorough search of her desk. I found a flat box full of the bookplates, and on a hunch took on and stuck it in my wallet. In a deep drawer she had a file of manila folders, neatly labeled. There were term papers, book reports, class notes, and one folder called "POETRY BY N.C." I plucked this one from the file, opened it and read a few poems. One of them, dated a year ago, could have been written to Arthur King.

A blaze of sunlight in your smile
The depth of oceans in your eyes
The power of trees in your voice
The comfort of home in your arms.

A day wasted
Is a day without you
A day with you
Is a day worthwhile.

All the poems were dated, but none was more recent that the previous summer.

All the neatly typed dates reminded me of 4/30/39, and in the next instant I was paralyzed with the notion that the missing charcoal drawing had borne that date in the corner. Artists, like poets, have a habit of dating their work, and the thirty-nine could mean that it was a picture of her mother.

I thought about it until my mind felt like a clenched fist, then I went out to the lobby and called the county medical examiner in Spencer's Falls. I even remembered his name: Stackpole. I got through to him after a little fuss, and he remembered me from yesterday.

85

"Doctor, I understand you've already done an autopsy on the dead girl."

"Yes, and I have already given Sheriff Casey a full report," he said.

"I know, but this question just came up. Can you tell me if the girl had an appendectomy scar, and a black mole just southwest of her navel?"

"Nothing easier. Hang on while I grab the morgue shot." He was gone for a minute, then he said, "Here we are, nice front shot, full length. And the answer is negative. No scar, no mole."

"Thank you, Doctor." I hung up. So it wasn't a drawing of Natalie.

I went back to the room and completed my search of her bureau and closet. Maybe I hoped there would be a diary, or a package of love letters tied with a silken ribbon, or a locket with the face of the murderer in it. But she wasn't that kind of girl, and I was already late for my appointment with Dr. Pritchett. I left the room and the house no wiser than when I had entered it.

Dr. Pritchett greeted me in his office with the proper mixture of cordiality and regret. The gentleness didn't diminish that fine armor of poise he wore like an extra skin. "I've been reading through Natalie's file again," he said, tapping a blue cardboard folder on his desk. "I've found nothing concrete to offer you. After all, I've only been seeing her for two months."

"Doctor, she must have had a specific problem," I said. "She didn't impress me as the kind of girl who would enter into this sort of thing lightly."

"I agree, Mr. Butler. But whatever her problem was, we never opened that particular package. It often takes more than two months just to establish confidence between a doctor and a patient. In fact, Natalie often had great difficulty expressing her feelings to me. Which is why we decided to experiment with tapes. She was quite articulate in her first one."

I couldn't imagine Natalie inhibited, inarticulate. I had come here seeking clarity about Natalie Clayborne, and instead I was conscious that my own image of her was becoming more distorted. "You told her father she was in love," I said. "Didn't she give you any idea of what the man was like?"

"She refused to discuss him. Oh, she seemed proud of the love, and she wanted to be worthy of it. But she wouldn't talk about the man."

"How about her relationship with Arthur King? Surely she discussed that."

"Yes. At first she thought she had failed King, but she had rationalized this feeling with the belief that their attachment was really platonic."

"Then she must have told you whether the affair was ever...consummated."

He smiled. "Delicately put. Yes, she told me, and no, it wasn't. Of course, you understand that this crisis of sex is frequently the real test of a love relationship. The emotions can be quite ruthless in their judgment, and apparently Natalie rejected King when the chips were down."

"How about this new man? Was she sleeping with him?"

Pritchett hesitated. "I can only hazard a guess, but my answer would have to be in the affirmative." He began to fiddle with his pipe. "There is this, for what it's worth. Once or twice I got the impression that she was concerned about her father's approval of the match. After meeting Mr. Clayborne this morning, I'm not surprised. He didn't strike me as a father who would give his approval easily."

"I agree. Now let me ask you if she ever mentioned these people to you by name. Carl Metterman. Waldo Mason. Eddie Bell."

He reacted to one of the names with his eyes and nostrils. I repeated it, "Waldo Mason. What did she say about him?"

Pritchett shook his head, flushing slightly. "No, you misunderstand. It wasn't Natalie Clayborne who mentioned Waldo Mason."

"Then who did? Her name's connected with his, and I have to know about him."

"You put me in an embarrassing position, Butler. You must remember that I'm more than a doctor here. I teach two courses at the college. I socialize with the faculty, serve on committees." His professional demeanor was askew.

I leaned across the desk and bared my teeth. "Don't start shuffling your ethics at me, Doctor. This is murder we're talking about. A girl was bludgeoned and strangled in her bed yesterday, not two hundred yards from your front lawn. The other day you made

87

quite a fuss about protecting the college's sterling reputation. That was all well and good while we were talking about petty theft. But the picture's changed. If we have to stain the reputation to catch a murderer, it may even be worth it. So how about it?"

Pritchett got up and wandered around his office as if he were looking for a picture to straighten or a file to close. Then he settled down in his chair again and began diligently to scrape the bowl of his pipe.

"All right, I'll tell you what I know about Waldo Mason," he said. "He's a devoted scholar and teacher, and once you say that you have to say that he's an impulsive, ill-mannered and arrogant man. Two wives have left him over the years, and he's not very popular with the faculty. They consider him irresponsible, and with good reason. He's on probation right now because of an affair he had with a student last year. The girl wasn't the most stable material for a mistress. I know, because I had to pick up the pieces. Well, she finally exposed the whole thing to her parents and they took her out of school. It almost cost Waldo his tenure, but the school board hushed it up and put him on his good behavior. I don't consider myself a prig, but I think the college would be well advised to get rid of him. That's Waldo Mason. Now, is that all you wanted to know?"

"Not quite. Can you tell me where he lives?"

He glared at me. "He's in the phone book. Surely you can do that for yourself."

I found Waldo Mason setting out tomato plants in his garden. The garden was directly behind his house, a shingled bungalow that looked worn and middle-aged, like a woman who has raised too many children on too little money. It was located only a mile off campus, but it was adjacent to the state park, and the heavy stand of timber gave the impression that it was deep in the country.

Apparently Mason hadn't heard my car, so I stood for a moment with the sun at my back and watched him work. Clad only in a pair of old khaki shorts, he resembled a shaggy bear. The effect was created in part because he was a hairy man, with a chestnut-colored beard and a heavy growth on his arms and chest. But he was also stout, rotund, and his movements as he knelt in the garden were clumsy, like a bear fishing in a stream.

88

I walked to the edge of the garden and leaned on a clothesline pole. "You're planting them too close together," I said.

Mason didn't jump. He merely settled back on his legs and turned to look me over. There were three little frown lines in his forehead, and he had worked up a nice sweat. "Are you an expert on tomatoes?" he asked. It was a rich baritone which seemed to deserve a beard like his.

"I've planted a few in my time. You should leave five feet between plants for the vines. Unless you plan to stake them."

"I never stake," he said. "But some of these won't make it. About a third will die on me, and that will thin the patch out."

"Then you're probably using too much of that commercial fertilizer," I said, pointing to the bag. "That burns up the roots."

"Good God Almighty," he said. "A man can't even till his garden without getting unsolicited advice from the government. Yesterday the mailman criticized me for planting string beans with my corn. Next, the county agricultural agent will offer to pay me for rotating my crops." He climbed to his feet and brushed the dirt from his legs. "Now, officer, do you want to inspect my lettuce, or shall we retire to the porch for a bottle of home brew?"

"Home brew would be fine," I said.

"Take a seat on the porch. I'll put this stuff in the garage and join you."

On the screen porch were two wicker chairs with a low table between them. There was a book on the table, *The Varieties of Religious Experience* by William James, with a notebook wedged into it to mark the place. I picked up the whole package, tucked my thumb in as a bookmark, and began to read his notes. At once I recognized the flamboyant handwriting. I had seen it yesterday morning on the flyleaf of *The Brothers Karamazov* in Natalie Clayborne's room. Now I had my Dimitri. Nothing like a full set.

Presently Waldo emerged from the kitchen behind me, carrying two glasses in one hand and a quart of beer in the other. "I always decant and rebottle after it's aged a month," he said. "But you never get all the yeast. So it has to be poured with care." He performed the act meticulously, holding bottle and glass against the light. His eyes were dark and shiny as anthracite, and there was no gray in his beard. I judged him to be about forty-three.

He served me the beer with a nice head on it, and stretched out luxuriously in his chair, rubbing the sweat into his belly. "Now to the inquisition," he said. "It has to be about Natalie Clayborne, deceased. I suppose they've told you that she's taken two courses from me, that she fell under my sinister influence last fall when we had some rather intimate talks on such profound topics as the rarity of love in a materialistic society, and that I patted her delightful fanny once in sheer appreciation of her nubile beauty. No doubt they've told you a lot of things about me. I've never been celebrated as the most salubrious member of this deadly little society, but since last year, when I foolishly became romantically involved with a very unstable young lady, my reputation has reached a new low. I am Jack the Ripper, the Marquis de Sade, or Mephistopheles, depending on your literary bent. It never ceases to astonish me that people can base their moral codes on their warped sexual ethics. In communities like this, we are ruled by government of the libido. So I've become the evil power behind every unsavory development on campus, from the radical political groups to the shaggy beards some of the more virile young men are sporting." He stroked his own beard as he said this, and his expression was sly, mirthful. "But it's certainly a novelty to be suspected of murder, if that's the case. I suppose I'm talking too much. I yield the floor to your piercing questions."

It was quite a speech, but a little too rich with sarcasm for the mood I was in. I couldn't tell how much of it was anxiety on his part. I quaffed off an inch of his beer and watched the sunlight in the trees for a while. Finally I said, "The murder doesn't seem to disturb you very much."

His smile was wide, as gentle as a priest's. "My friend, do you really think that you have access to my personal feelings because you wear that uniform? Would you prefer that I weep copiously into my beer, rip my shorts to tatters, and moan the loss of that lovely girl? Would I then fit your image of what is normal and respectable? I'm sorry, I don't play those games." He drank from his glass, brushed the foam from his moustache with a fingertip, and said, "I had a rather paternal feeling of affection for Natalie Clayborne. She seemed to inspire it. She was a girl full of contradictions. She took a course in American history from me, and she seemed fascinated with every instance of rebellion, revolution, of underdogs struggling for their rights. I got the impression that she wished she could enjoy that

90

kind of dedication to a cause. Ah, this can't help you. It's all random impressions, speculation."

"I understand you knew her mother, Eleanor Sheridan," I said sharply. "That you and she were students together here at Jordan years ago."

The professor straightened a little, canting his head as if to get a better look at me. "That's true," he said. "Curious you should mention that. I knew Eleanor over twenty years ago, and had practically forgotten her. But the first time I saw Natalie I had the incredible sensation, just for a moment, that she was an illusion. The resemblance is amazing. No doubt that's why I felt fatherly towards the girl."

"Yes, this fatherly feeling interests me," I said. "Exactly how well did you know her mother?"

"Ah, *et tu*," Waldo said. "You're like the rest of these cocktail party Freudians. Sex is the great roaring beast that motivates us all. God, deliver me from such idiocies."

"Oh, cut it out, Mason! I'm sure your act is a big hit in the classroom, where a beard and an occasional dirty word make a man into a Bolshevik at the barricades. But you're wasting your talents on me. So why don't you drop the act and answer a few questions."

He looked as if I had hit him in the face with a dead fish. "Get out of here!" He got to his feet, his face flushed to the color of port wine. "I don't have to answer any of your obscene insinuations."

I got up slowly, grinning. "What scares you, Waldo? You were the one who boasted about having patted the girl's fanny. I'll bet you also patted her mother's fanny years ago. Maybe you were in love with her mother. But Eleanor Sheridan spurned you for the Harvard boy with the million bucks. Then along comes Natalie, Eleanor reincarnated, and you have a second chance. No, it's better than that. You can have your lady fair and get revenge on the Harvard boy at the same time. But maybe Natalie was going to spurn you too. You couldn't take it twice. The illusions you have at forty are a lot tougher to give up than those of twenty-one. So maybe you killed her, Mason."

He sagged back into his chair. "God, what an imagination you have. You can't believe that. I wasn't Natalie's lover."

"How about her mother?"

He wasn't looking at me. His gaze was on the sunset, and he seemed to be listening to music. "I won't talk about that," he said.

"Then talk about this. Where were you on Saturday night?"

"I was here, alone," he said. "If that makes me guilty of murder, then arrest me. But you're wrong. I didn't kill Natalie Clayborne."

He was too subdued. Men accused of murder usually deny it with more vigor, guilty or not. They bluster, fume with indignation, call a lawyer, aim a punch at your jaw. The do not withdraw into a shell of contemplation, indifferent to the accusation. But of course Waldo Mason was no ordinary man. This may have been his idea of a wise move, another pose. His beard concealed his expression too well for me to read it. I hadn't solved the problem of the tape yet, but I began to get a new idea about it.

Well, I had played a little chess in my time. I finished my beer, complimented Mason on its quality, and started down the steps.

"You mean you're leaving?" he said.

"Why not? You said you didn't kill her. That's the big question I came out here to ask."

I walked around the house, got into my car, and drove slowly back to town. When I unlocked the door to the constable's office, the phone was ringing. I answered it, and Linda Thorpe spoke my name in that marvelous husky voice.

"Butler, I've read about the murder. What an evil thing, especially to happen to someone so young and lovely."

"Did you know her?"

"I recognized her picture in the paper. I met her once at a party at Eddie Bell's. The same sort of party we were supposed to attend tonight. I called because I assumed you'd forgotten all about our date."

"Not at all. But do you think they'll have the party now?"

"Oh, it's still on. They wouldn't miss the opportunity to talk about this. But we don't have to go, Butler. Maybe you'd rather spend a quiet evening here."

"Tell me, will an artist named Metterman be there?"

"Carl? Yes, he wouldn't miss it."

"Let's go to the party," I said. "I want to meet some of these people. Apparently the Clayborne girl spent a lot of time with them."

"I don't understand. I thought they arrested the murderer, that janitor."

"He didn't do it, but that fact is not for publication. I'd rather the murderer thought he was off the hook. He might get careless."

"Butler, do you mean he might be one of the guests at Eddie's party?"

"It's possible, if our murderer is someone who would be conspicuous by his absence," I said. "What time shall I pick you up?"

We agreed upon nine o'clock.

Chapter 9
***

For the party that night I wore civilian clothes—a dark, summer-weight suit with just enough wool in it to give it character—and I drove my own car. My car did not come out of a dealer's showroom. I got it as payment in full for a job I did for a man in Las Vegas. He owned three just like it, cars he used to make long-distance deliveries of boxes full of cash that was never entered on anybody's bank statements. I took the car in lieu of a twenty-thousand-dollar fee because it seemed a sound investment in survival.

To the casual eye, it looked like a black, slightly battered 1960 Mercury. But the appearance is deceptive. You can safely drive this Merc at 150 mph, if you have the pavement and the nerve. The motor was made to specification by Mercedes, and mounted in a body reconstructed by a Las Vegas mechanic who was something of an artist. He installed a four-wheel brake system, welded an extra layer of high-carbon steel to the factory metal, and mounted four steel bars inside the roof. He also designed the rubber racing tires with metal strands woven through the nylon. He secreted a small compartment behind the glove compartment, and another one, the size of a suitcase, under the floor of the trunk.

The small compartment in the front holds a Luger with extra clips and a .25 Mauser. The box under the trunk contains other tools of my trade: a first-aid kit; extra clothes and shoes; a spare Luger; and a wallet with five hundred dollars and a complete set of identification papers for one Douglas Hollingsworth, business consultant, with an office address in Cleveland. It's a cover that will stand up under any but the most diligent investigation.

When I set out on a job behind the wheel of the Mercury, I'm aware of a sensation of security. I have slept in her, killed from her, bled on her, and on more than one occasion the Dark Lady's speed has helped me stay alive. She is the edge I give myself, the derringer in the gambler's hat, the dagger in the lady's garter, the trip flares wired to the underbrush at night.

Precisely at nine o'clock, I parked the Mercury in Linda Thorpe's driveway. She opened the door as I lifted my hand to ring the bell, and the sight of her gave me pleasure beyond mere sensual appreciation. It may have been because of that intimate moment we shared, or possibly because she was wearing a jade necklace of very small stones, matching earrings, and a black cocktail gown with those tiny corded straps that bite into the shoulders with a silken whisper of cruelty.

She appraised me with a smile. "So this is what the well-dressed farmer wears when he's not behind the plow. Come in, Butler, and fix us a drink."

"You'll mock that farm once too often," I said. "Then I'll take you up there for a visit, dress you in Levis and a denim shirt, and work you for eight hours in the hayfields. You would be cured of all skepticism. What will it be?"

"A Scotch with a beard. We'll need it if we're going to hobnob with a murderer." She said it with levity, started to laugh, and stifled it. "I'm sorry. I can't get that out of my mind. It was either turn it into a joke or become very grim. Nervous tension, I guess."

I remained silent until I carried the drinks to the long black sofa. She accepted hers demurely, as if she expected anger, and I sat down beside her.

"This won't do at all, Dr. Watson," I said. "How can you help me tonight if you're going to buttonhole all suspicious characters and frisk them for concealed weapons? That's considered bad form, even as a parlor game."

We laughed, and she said, "All right, I stand rebuked. How do you want me to behave tonight?"

"Exactly as you always do at these parties. Don't be self-conscious about me. Tonight I'm just a date. I'll mingle and make small talk."

"So you're using me as a decoy. No, that's not the word."

"As concealment, as a cover," I said. "But remember, we made this date before the murder. Consider it pleasure, with a little business on the side."

She feigned aloofness. "Nevertheless, I'm not sure I like being used in such a fashion. It's not very flattering to the lady's vanity."

It was all very coy, so I took her drink from her, put both glasses on the coffee table, and kissed her glistening mouth. At first we were clumsy, but it quickly became scalding and luxurious. We broke it off with smiles.

"You devil!" she said. "I didn't plan on that until later."

95

"You invited it."

"Yes, didn't I? Butler, don't mind if I act a little foolish with you. I never thought I'd be like this with a man again. Now, may I have my drink back?"

It had been a friendly kiss despite its carnal flavor, the kind of mutual caress that is sometimes necessary to get rid of surface tensions and establish a mood where conversation is possible.

Presently she said, "Butler, remember that Sunday in Quartz's room when you told us about the tape that had been stolen from the Clayborne girl? Was there any connection between that business and her death?"

"I think so, and I'm not alone. The girl's father is convinced that she was murdered because of the tape. Daddy wants it back."

"But how can he expect you to do that? If you find the tape, you'll have to use it as evidence, won't you? Or am I naïve about those things?"

I said nothing. Not that I distrusted her. It was merely habit with me never to reveal the details of my employment.

"Hey, Butler." She put a hand on my cheek and turned my face toward her. "He didn't try to bribe you, did he?"

"My dear lady, are you suggesting that a leading citizen of the sovereign state of Pennsylvania would stoop to such an act? You have a suspicious nature."

Her expression was grave. "I'm thinking of that on Sunday on Quartz's porch, when you hinted that you sometimes hired out for work that wasn't altogether legal. There is something sinister about you, Butler. Maybe I hope that's not what makes you attractive to me."

"Listen to who's worried about the purity of her emotions," I said. "The Stagecoach hostess, expert at fulfilling the fantasies of the tired businessman."

She nodded, her mouth swollen with feeling. "But only their fantasies. I'm the jolly girl, the vamp, the big sister, the soiled child, the hard-nosed wench, the good sport, the naughty divorcee. I'm a quick-change artist, girl of a thousand faces. But they're all disguises, Butler."

"I know that." I thought of my own fanciful urge to walk her bare-legged through sweet grass. "Let's go to the party, sweet lady."

She rose with a stately movement. "I'll get my wrap." In a few minutes she returned carrying a tiny jacket with a fur collar. She flicked on the porch light, locked the door and we got into the Mercury.

I had talked with Eddie Bell once about the robbery at the Stagecoach. He was a short, bald man with a plump mouth, a sharp dresser who moved quickly and talked slowly. Arthur King had called him an "oily little voyeur," but the description didn't fit the man I had met. Maybe that was poetic license. I said to Linda, "Tell me about your friend Eddie Bell."

She turned toward me on the seat. "Eddie's all right. He's a more complicated man than he appears to be. He started out as a gambler in a place called Steubenville, Ohio, which I gather is a pretty rough town."

"I know the place. A steel town up the panhandle. They used to call it Little Chicago."

"Well, he jokes about those days now. Speakeasies, Blind Pigs, a job he had booking shows for local nightclubs. People in show business and the arts fascinate Eddie. He regards them as special people, and he's quite touching about it. He admired Howard, and loved to talk with him about literature. Eddie's self-educated, but amazingly well read. Of course, he romanticizes the college Bohemians a little much for my taste, but it's all very harmless."

"What about his wife?"

"Madge? She's something of a character, a live wire. But she's good people. You'll see what I mean when you meet her."

The Bells lived in a renovated farmhouse not far from Jordan City. There were several cars parked on the shoulders of the road in front of the house, and the front lawn was decorated with bicycles and motor scooters. Apparently the Bells strived for the rustic effect. On the walk to the house we passed an old hooded well, complete with rope and oaken vines. We entered from the porch into a gigantic room with exposed beams and a stone fireplace you could have roasted an ox in. Light was furnished by four large candelabras judiciously spaced. The furniture was sturdy but not fancy – with the exception of the bar, a gorgeous creation in black and white leather.

A tall woman detached herself from a crowd and came to greet us. She wore stretch pants of a burnt-orange color that emphasized

97

her tall, sinuous figure. Her blouse was snug over neat, pointed breasts and showed an inch of midriff. She wore her blonde hair in a short ponytail, green eyeshade, and the largest pair of ceramic earrings I had ever seen, glittering disks like black African totems. Her sandals were gold, her toenails painted to match. Her eyes looked hot, her mouth bruised, and she bristled with energy. This, no doubt, was Madge.

"Linda, you doll, I'm glad you came, "Madge said. "And you're welcome, too, sir, although I haven't had the pleasure."

Linda introduced us.

"Ah yes," Madge said. She leaned toward me with a conspiratorial look and half-whispered, "I'm glad you didn't come in uniform. Most of this crowd don't cotton to fuzz." She laughed gaily at her own wit, and guided us toward the bar. "Let's concoct a drink. We have wine of various colors and vintage. Or you can have hard stuff, wrapped in just about anything."

"We're both on Scotch this evening," I said.

Just as she finished mixing them, another batch of guests arrived. Madge said, "You two circulate and make friends. Linda, you know most of the guests."

But I wasn't ready to circulate. Instead, I guided Linda to a pair of hassocks at one side of the room, from where we could watch the party for a while. In the most distant and dimly lighted corner, two couples glided slowly to the rhythm of Brubeck jazz in front of a hi-fi set. One girl with long hair and black tights danced alone, flinging her arms, hips and torso with spectacular abandon. She danced with her back to the room, as if enthralled with the contortions of her gigantic shadow on the wall.

There were at least thirty people in the room. More than half of them were between eighteen and twenty-two, and without exception these young ones wore variations of the accepted costume of rebellion. The boys affected long hair, beards and moustaches where the flesh was willing, Levis and denim shirts. The girls wore shapeless dark dresses and cotton stockings, and spurned makeup. I saw a Negro boy with a splendid physique and a golden earring in one ear, and a Negro girl wrapped in a soiled red sari. There was a lot of byplay and stylized gestures among this young crowd, but the dominant characteristic was the posture and expression of absolute detachment. This was most noticeable with the girls, whose smooth, set faces seemed to float through the candlelight like features painted on balloons, unmarked, unruffled, nerve less. They seemed too weary of the world at too tender an age, hardly experienced enough to have exhausted life's possibilities and passed judgment up on them.

But even more estranged than these young ones were the middle-aged Bohemians, of which there were at least a dozen examples in the Bell's living room. I encountered them as I began to make a slow tour of the room, and from time to time I paused to listen to them. Here was an earthy fellow who had found Truth in the potter's wheel and the loom. There was the Poet of Unrecognized Genius, who for years has been publishing his poems in obscure magazines, and editing one in which he printed the work of his counterparts. Here was the Happy Homosexual, his makeup barely showing in the soft light, extolling the virtues of his malady to a small circle. There, God help her, was the wiry little woman who believed that the evils of the world would vanish if everyone ate organically grown food. You can spot them by their belligerence, their bitterness, the sneer they turn on you if you so much as hint that theirs is not the only salvation.

When I stopped and stood beside the fireplace, conspicuous in my suit, one of the girls in sandals glided to my side. I recognized her only because I had looked into those large, delicate eyes that afternoon. The becoming plumpness was all but concealed by a brown burlap dress. "How's Arthur?" I asked.

"You shouldn't have accused him like that," she said. Her face was earnest, her voice as soft as musical chimes. "He wouldn't hurt Natalie Clayborne."

"So he told me. But he also told me that he was one of the roughneck poets. They express themselves pretty violently at times."

"Not Arthur. Oh, he can be harsh and even cruel. But that's just his temperament. He would never take life."

She seemed possessed of a quaint, nunlike devotion. "What's Arthur to you?" I asked. "And please tell me your name."

"I'm Nancy Brewer. I'm a good friend of Arthur's, that's all."

"I'll be you iron his shirts," I said.

"I beg your pardon?"

"I know you. You go out there to cook for him, scrub his floor, dust his typewriter and massage his ego. You're his devoted little peasant."

Her eyes glistened with reproach. "That's hardly any of your business."

"No, but you should be told that there's no future in it if you're going to make yourself all that available. Someone ought to tell you, Nancy Brewer, that you're a pretty nifty dish beneath all that camouflage."

She barely concealed one of her shy smiles. "I suppose you think I'm a timid little virgin, a masochist who enjoys being abused."

"No, you're not really timid. And as to being a virgin, I'm surer you sacrificed that article for some noble cause long before this."

"Hey, you are vulgar," she said, coloring a little. "No wonder Arthur was upset." Then she had an idea that took her breath. "Say, you don't include me among your suspects, do you?"

"You had a motive," I said. "The guy you love was hung up on this cold rich bitch, and she wouldn't quite let him go."

Her eyes narrowed as she scrutinized my face, but she saw something there that made her smile. "You're teasing. But you're right when you say I didn't like her. I tried to be fair, but 'cold rich bitch' is pretty close."

"I hope you're not this honest with everyone," I said. "I admit it's charming, but you ought to make us work a little."

Again I was rewarded with the smile. "Oh, stop it. 'Nifty dish' indeed. You're not careful, I might start to like you."

"Thanks, but I send my shirts to the laundry," I said.

Then she surprised me. She made a fist and jabbed me playfully in the stomach, winked, and walked away. I suppose it was a gesture of affection.

Then I noticed Eddie Bell was acting as bartender, and I crossed the room to get a fresh drink. He was no slouch at the trade. He lined six glasses on the bar and manipulated ice, bottles and stirring rods like a card shark dealing losing hands to everyone but the house. He served the drinks and returned, neat and dapper in blue sport shirt, tailored slacks and blue suede shoes. We exchanged greetings, and he made me a drink with a flourish.

"I'm glad you could make it, Butler," he said. "I guess you know that you're escorting a pretty special person. Madge and I are very fond of Linda."

I had to adjust to the slow articulation of his speech after the nimbleness of his hands. "So I understand," I said. "It just occurred t me, Mr. Bell, that you and I seem to get together only after a violent crime."

"Twice is hardly a pattern," he said. "And will you please call me Eddie." He wiped the bar slowly. "It's a nasty business about Natalie Clayborne. I've had her here as a guest several times, and she used to clash perfectly."

"I'm afraid I don't understand."

His gaze roamed the room. "It's not easy to explain. She didn't dress like these other girls. Natalie was always groomed to the teeth, and she wore bright, stylish dresses and heels. She cut a figure among these others. She didn't mind looking chic and expensive where it was least appreciated."

"I'm surprised they didn't resent it," I said.

He nodded. "I have a theory about that. Most of these people are eccentrics of one sort or another, although I'm sure they would resent being called that. But, they tolerate one another's hang-ups, and I finally decided that they looked on Natalie's money as her hang-up. They didn't condemn her for her conspicuous consumption. They didn't resent her loot because she was sincere about her poetry and the rest. I guess it sounds silly to you."

"No, it fits with what I know about her." This Eddie Bell was a neat little package of contradictions. His pate was bald, but he had a luxurious growth of hair on his forearms. His movements wee quick and his speech slow. The hardness of his eyes was neutralized by dainty lashes. Once he had associated with hoods, and now with this crowd in pursuit of the intangible pleasures of art. He was a city boy in a country house, a short man with a tall wife, and he could say "loot" and "conspicuous consumption" in the same breath.

At that moment I saw a crown bearing down on us with empty glasses. "Eddie, let's find some privacy. I've got a few more questions about Natalie."

He looked quizzical. "Sure, I don't mind. Let's use the patio."

He led me around the fringe of the party, opened a sliding glass door, and we were on a flagstone patio lighted with an amber coachman's lamp mounted on a post. Eddie removed the canvas from the glider and we sat down. He took his time lighting a long cigarette.

"I thought the case was closed," he said. "I thought they nailed this sexual freak, and they had the goods on him."

"Yes, but the girl's father is in town kicking up a fuss," I said. "We're humoring the man. He says that Natalie wrote to him faithfully, and that she mentioned you in one or two letters. It seemed worth a few questions."

"I can't imagine why she would mention me," Eddie said. He had arranged the seating so that the amber light was in my face and his features were in shadow. It might have been an accident.

I gave him my most affable smile. "I'm sure it wasn't anything incriminating. Something about you staging a reading for her poetry. Her old man thinks poetry is the bunk, so that makes you a suspicious character."

"For Eddie Bell to take a rap for poetry is some joke," he said. "Of course, I invited her to read her stuff here. I do that with a lot of the students. In fact, we're having a student playreading tonight. The author is too much influenced by Beckett, but it's a provocative piece of work."

Again I was struck with the paradox, like seeing a man strolling on the beach in bathing trunks and spats. "Eddie, it might help if you could tell me who she was close to in this group. She must have had boyfriends. You told me how she glittered among the rabble."

"Yes, but that was just the trouble. She intimidated most of these boys. She was too poised, too expensive, unapproachable. Of course, Carl Metterman was an exception. They were pretty thick for a while, and he's here tonight. But if you're looking for hanky-panky, I don't think he's your boy."

"Why not?"

"You put me on the spot. Tales out of school, and all that. But Madge is really my authority on this. She's convinced that Metterman doesn't really like women, if you dig my meaning. Of course he could be what they call ambidextrous, AC/DC, but Madge says no. Hearsay testimony, for what that's worth."

"Now I'm the one on the spot," I said. "I don't mean to be crude, Eddie, but isn't that a chance that it's just Madge that Metterman doesn't like?" You can often judge a man by his reaction to such a

102

question, and my hope was that I would get a look at Eddie Bell without the contradictions. I halfway expected a throwback to Little Chicago, but instead he became formal and stuffy.

Rising to his feet, Eddie sucked air into his chest and looked down at me. "Mr. Butler, I don't tolerate insults to my wife. Not from anyone."

"My apology, if you took it that way. I intended no insult."

He stood there for a long minute, the amber light gleaming like enamel on his pate, then turned on his heel and went into the house. I took out a stogie and winked at the match flame as I lit it. Either he had grabbed at the chance to end our conversation with his act of indignation, or he had uneasy feelings about his wife. Madge looked like a woman who could make a man uneasy. She wasn't beautiful, hardly even pretty, but she gave off the kind of neon glitter and frenzy that made you suspect she was never idle, never lonesome, never sated. Inevitably I began to compare her with Linda, and without warning the connection produced an image that fairly made me bite through my cigar. Madge had been the model for the little black statues in Linda's house. I had shortchanged the sculptor. He was better than I had thought. How clever to make her black and polished, with sharp, metallic edges like exposed nerves, and all the spasms frozen in space. If I were Eddie Bell, and if I had seen that exhibit of statuary, I would be uneasy, too.

I jettisoned the stogie into the barbecue pit and rejoined the party. The talk was more animated, the laughter more manic, and Brubeck had been replaced on the turntable by Coleman Hawkins. Exposed teeth and ceramic jewelry flashed like signal lights in the gloom. Linda Thorpe caught my attention from across the room and beckoned with her eyes. She was part of a group gathered around a low coffee table, most of them sitting on cushions. I maneuvered my way over and eased to the floor beside her.

They were talking about the murder. A young man with a yellow moustache was insisting that Natalie's death was a perfect example of how the brutal forces in our society tend to strike down what is pure and beautiful. A slender girl with brilliant black eyes debunked this as crass sentimentality. She had known Natalie personally, and in her opinion the real tragedy robbed her of life before she truly lived it. A third suggested that Natalie's poetry should be collected

103

and published in book form. I squeezed Linda's arm, and she followed me to an empty corner of the room.

"They discuss it with such relish," I said.

Her smile was gentle, sad. "They're young. They make philosophy out of it to protect themselves from the horror."

That wise statement enhanced all her charms for me. At times the memorable words of a woman can have more impact than a physical intimacy, and I felt that kind of thrill for her now. But she was focused on something else.

"I saw you go out with Eddie, and he looked angry when he came back. Surely you weren't accusing him. He worked at the Stagecoach that night until three in the morning."

"He thinks I insulted his wife. He should have waited. I was about to tell him that I had admired her naked form in various poses the other night."

Linda took a quick step from me. "You are sharp, Butler. Yes, Madge posed for Barrows the sculptor. She did it on the sly, and Eddie was furious when he saw the result. So I'm glad you didn't mention the statues."

I surveyed the room as well as I could in the bad light. "Waldo didn't make it tonight. Not very sporting of him."

"You mean Waldo Mason? Was he one of those you expected to see here?"

"Yes. Do you know him?"

She nodded. "As well as I want to know him. I've seen him here twice. He reminded me of some character in Shakespeare, a king holding court."

"Did you ever see him with the Clayborne girl?"

"Not that I recall. I'm afraid I don't attend many of Eddie's parties. Was she involved with a man that old, that—I almost said 'grotesque'."

"We'll talk about it later. Right now I want you to introduce me to Carl Metterman."

"All work and no play. Butler, I'm beginning to think that the only way I'm going to get any attention from you is to become a suspect."

"Be careful. You know what happened the last time you started that."

"The kiss? Maybe that's what I have in mind." Her mouth drooped at the corners, as if heavy with desire, and I was tempted to take her quickly to a place with more privacy. But she drew back from me. "I'm sorry. I shouldn't behave like this when you're working. There, that brawny fellow with the blond hair. That's Carl Metterman."

He was sitting in a semicircle with several of the young people, and as I watched, he finished a story that made them all laugh. Metterman was certainly brawny. He wore leather sandals, tight pants and a pullover shirt of some rough fabric he might have woven himself. His hair was golden, thick and long, so beautifully waved that you wondered if it had been set. He was a true Nordic, with pale blue eyes and a wonderful tan for so early in the spring. In this light I couldn't tell his age. He might have been anywhere between thirty and fifty. I had seen him on the street, but hadn't known that he owned the small arts and crafts store on Main Street until Arthur King told me.

"Lure him out to the patio," I said. "Then make some excuse to leave us."

"He may not be susceptible to my charms," she said. "Madge told me—"

"I know, but use your imagination. Tell him a man wants to meet him."

I strolled to the bar, which was deserted for the moment, and made myself a drink to carry out to the patio. Fortunately, the place was still empty, and this time I took the seat that put the light to my back. A pair of moths fluttered around the amber light, and crickets droned in the darkness.

Linda and Carl Metterman emerged from the house as I finished my drink. He was at least three inches taller than I was and was going to fat around the waist. I rose for the introduction. His handshake was sturdy.

"I understand you wanted to see me about something important," he said.

"Linda, you're exaggerating again," I said in my jolly tone. "No, Mr. Metterman, it's just that Natalie Clayborne mentioned you in a letter she wrote to her father. I thought you might be able to help us clear up a few details."

"She mentioned me in her letters? I don't know whether to be flattered or annoyed. In what way can I be of help?" He sat down beside me.

Linda said, "You two chat. It's too chilly for me out here without my wrap. I'll see you inside, Butler."

I waited until the door closed behind her, then took my plunge. "How long have you taught at the college, Mr. Metterman?"

"That's easy to answer. I came here in thirty-seven, so it's twenty-five years. I taught full time for a while, then opened my shop in town. Now I teach ceramics and weaving and an occasional class in sketching."

"You hardly look old enough to have been here that long," I said.

"If you want to know my age, Mr. Butler, you have only to ask. I'm forty-six. I came here when I was twenty-one."

"Then you must have known Natalie Clayborne's mother," I said. "She graduated from Jordan in thirty-nine."

His expression became neutral. There had been a mutual antagonism since the handshake, as if he had long steeled himself for this interview. Now he gave me a Continental shrug. "I might have known the woman, but that's so long ago."

I dropped the jolly act. "Her name was Eleanor Sheridan. And you possibly did a drawing of her in the nude. It was a very detailed sketch, of a woman on her side, but without a face. Natalie had the drawing hanging in her room. It was there yesterday, but now it's gone."

"Do I understand you? Are you accusing me of stealing this picture?"

"Not yet. First, I'm asking if you remember drawing it."

"That's just as ridiculous. Who could answer a question like that? I've done literally thousands of sketches over the years, and a lot of those were nudes. We have classes with live models all the time. And you're asking me to remember one lousy sketch done twenty years ago. You amuse me, Mr. Butler. You make me laugh." He gave a snort of contempt.

"You're something of a joker yourself, Metterman. I heard you inside earlier tonight, telling the cool little chicks how virile you are because you work with your hands. Is that the same line you used on Natalie?"

He stiffened with hauteur, an authentic Prussian. "You assume a man is beneath contempt because he chooses to earn his living in a unique way. I happen to enjoy working with my hands. Oh, I don't pretend to be an artist. But I'm a competent craftsman. I like to design in fabric and clay, and lead a simple life."

"Metterman, I'm impressed. Now tell me about you and Natalie."

Again he shrugged eloquently. "There's very little to tell. She was interested in my work, and she seemed to be able to relax in my presence. She said that I had a soothing influence on her. I've been told that by others."

"I'll bet." His expression was aloof, dreamy, as ascetic as such a smooth, well-fed face could become. I was convinced that he was a fourteen-carat, nickel-plated phony, but I couldn't challenge him until I had something on him. I got to my feet. "That's all for now, Mr. Metterman, and thanks."

" 'For now'? What does that mean? Surely we've exhausted the subject."

"You never know. I have a hunch that a common interest in art will bring us together again." I left him with that little thought, and returned to the party.

There was a bustle of activity around the big fireplace at the end of the room, and I realized that Eddie and his crew were arranging a stage for the playreading. The dance floor was deserted, but there was a record on the turntable that didn't seem to belong there, a song from the past that stirred memories. It was "Little White Lies," appropriate background music for my chat with Metterman. I spotted Linda alone near the bar, eased over and asked if she would like to dance.

"Love to, Butler."

She didn't say another word until the song ended. It was a very private dance. The small of her back was strong and pliant, like sinews of silk, and her breath on my neck as soft as the wings of a moth. The moment of enchantment separated us from the others in the room so definitely that, when the record ended, the party was over for us.

I said, "No insult to Madge and Eddie, but I'd rather skip his play."

"Yes! Come on. They're all busy now. I'll get my wrap."

I don't think anyone noticed our departure. Linda held my arm with a steady pressure down the path to the car, humming the song from the record under her breath. In the mercury she put her head on my shoulder and I kissed her. I could taste her vitality in the rich lining of her mouth.

When I raised my head, she smiled and said, "Butler, I don't care how sinister you are, or what kind of work you hire out for."

I made her sit up with I started the car. It didn't occur to me to open the hidden box behind the glove compartment and arm myself with the Luger. I didn't think I needed a gun just to take my girl home from a party.

Chapter 10
***

Only the amateur can take refuge in the excuse that his mind was so saturated with thoughts of love that he failed to react to the signals of danger. There were at least two I should have detected. One was the black pickup parked off the road halfway down the block, exposed briefly in the sweep of my headlights as I turned into Linda's driveway. The second was the comment she murmured lazily into my shoulder, "Looks like the porch light burned out." And besides, I should have smelled them.

But none of this is to criticize how well they staged it. There were three of them waiting for us in the dark house, each at an assigned post. I even helped them by blinding us with my stogie lighter while Linda unlocked the door. My first hint of trouble came after Linda had crossed the threshold and I had already committed myself to the step to follow her. Her form was suddenly jerked into the blackness out of my vision. I lunged to complete the step, and catapulted myself sideways into the room. Even so, a heavy weight ricocheted from the side of my skull, igniting a yellow flare behind my left eye, burned my ear and struck the top of my shoulder with an impact that seemed to shatter the nerves all the way to my fingertips.

I landed on my back and slid a few feet on sheer momentum. The door had slammed shut behind me, leaving the room in total darkness. My head felt cracked and my arm like a railroad tie strapped to me. There had been no sound from Linda since she was snatched off her feet, and I wondered if she had been sapped, too. I could feel blood on my neck.

Just then a hearty voice called out, "Hit the light, Charlie. I got him a good lick, but he was moving and he might be playing possum."

"Here you go, LeRoy," Charlie said, and the lights went on.

I feigned unconsciousness. It didn't take much acting. "Lordy, look at the blood." It was Charlie's voice. "You clobbered him sweet, LeRoy. Maybe you kilt him."

"Let's see," LeRoy grunted. He stepped forward and kicked me in the thigh.

I half expected a kick, but nothing that hard, and I couldn't restrain the groan that passed my lips.

"Naw, he's just stunned, is all. I'll fetch him over by the fireplace, and you bring the bitch over, Cash. Let's get cozy."

Then a third voice spoke. "I'll bring her, LeRoy, but I get to hold her. This is some juicy bundle to hold. Look at her squirm.

"Cut it out!" LeRoy commanded. "You behave yourself with her until I tell you different." He got a grip on the back of my belt with one hand, lifted me off the floor, and dropped me on a rug by the fireplace. It was a hundred and ninety pounds of dead weight, and only my hands dragged enroute.

"Find his gun, Charlie."

Hard hands turned me over and rummaged my body. "He ain't got a gun. I guess he don't tote one when he's courting. Here's his wallet."

"Give it here," LeRoy said. I heard the snap of plastic, and he said, "Yeah, this is the bird we want. Cash, keep your hands off that woman!"

"But she's fighting me," Cash said. "She's a pussy cat, damed if she ain't." His voice was nasal, shrill, and had a nervous, demented quality about it.

LeRoy said, "Lady, if you don't cut it out, I'm going to paste you. Don't make me bust that pretty face. It would be a pure shame."

I risked a look. The one named Cash had Linda on the black leather sofa. One of his arms pinned both of hers to her sides, and with the other hand he covered her mouth, the fingers and thumbs deep in her cheeks. One of the straps of her gown had broken, and the top of her breast looked glossy with sweat. Cash was a tall bony man with thick black hair, crooked yellow teeth and hairy hands. Half of his right earlobe was missing, as if it had been bitten off.

Charlie, who was standing with half a shotgun cradled in his left arm, looked enough like Cash to be his twin. Their complexions were swarthy, their cheekbones prominent in a way that suggested Indian blood.

LeRoy was an ox. He might have been five eight, but he was so wide he looked shorter. His shoulders were a yard wide, and he seemed to have neither wrists or neck. His yellow hair was shaggy and long, and his mouth hung low on one side as if an important

110

muscle had been cut by the knife that had left a three-inch scar in his cheek. He was gently slapping a homemade sap into his left palm. At least eight inches long and as thick as my wrist, it looked like a wool sock packed with double-O buckshot. It had a leather thong for a handle. In the hands of this character, it was as deadly a weapon as an ax.

They looked like Cumberland Mountain boys, descendants of those rugged mountaineers who had settled the Kentucky highlands and clung to the primitive life of the frontier with all the tenacity and superstition of the Indians they had exterminated. I'd known many of them in the Marine Corps. For generations they have lived off the land, and part of their heritage is to despise any effort to tame their lawless souls. They brawl with fists, guns and knives, eat hog fat and collard greens, drink their white lightening, and breed among themselves with impunity. They are as cynical, hardened and bitter a breed of men as I have ever encountered outside prison walls. In the Corps, they were hard to discipline, but in combat they were the most fearless and savage killers I have ever seen. Once on Tarawa I caught one of them taking Japanese scalps with his bayonet.

They were the same three hillbillies who had worked Quartz over that night at the Stagecoach.

My head throbbed, but my vision was good and I felt the blood moving in my left arm. The hand tingled as if it had been frostbitten.

Cash whispered into Linda's ear, and she jumped violently in his arms.

"Stop fussing with the bitch," LeRoy said. "Where's that roll of tape? Do I have to do everything in this lashup?"

"It's in the kitchen," Charlie said. "I'll fetch it. Don't forget John L. Law. He might take it in his mind to jump you."

"I hope he does," LeRoy said. "There's not much sport in stomping a sack of coal." LeRoy prodded me once with the sap and turned his attention back to Linda. "Lady, we're going to let go you mouth so's we can tape it. If you start yelping, I'm going to crack your skull. So be smart."

I took another furtive look around, searching for a weapon. I found one on a stand not five feet from me, one of the black metal statues of Madge Bell. It was about two feet tall, jagged steel, with the hands raised in front of the body like claws. I didn't have much time to plan.

111

I heard Cash return, and then the long rip of someone unwinding tape. "Mind what I said, lady," LeRoy said. Linda stifled a sob when Cash released her mouth. After a moment LeRoy said, "All right, turn her on her belly and we'll tape her arms, too. Boy, she is a piece, ain't she? Feel that Charlie. Plump and tender as the day is long. That never had a belt whomped on it."

None of it made me angry. Since the blow on my head, I had been charged with that cool, murderous vitality you develop only in combat. My plan was to eliminate first the man with the most lethal weapon. That would be Charlie and the shotgun. The shotgun worried me a lot. But if I was lucky enough to get my hands on it, I might have them cold. I waited, peering at them through slitted eyes, and they made their first mistake.

Charlie laid the shotgun down on the end table beside the sofa to join in the fun and games. "Maybe now's the time to strap her, LeRoy," he said. "We warned her to keep her mouth shut about seeing Nell and that bracelet, and she didn't do it. She's got it coming, ain't she, LeRoy?"

They had Linda face down on the sofa. Cash was sitting on her feet, grinning at LeRoy's antics. LeRoy was hunkered down in front of the sofa, working his hands. Charlie had moved in for a feel, about four feet from his shotgun. I couldn't hope to reach the shotgun, but I made a quick change in my plan of attack. The first target was LeRoy. And the time was now. I would never get a better one. I took a deep breath and went for the statue.

Cash let out a yell and LeRoy bolted to his feet. His back was still toward me when I hit him in the side of the head with the stature. I was the old bambino stroking for the centerfield bleachers. I was the slaughterhouse man hitting the thousand-pound bull with the twelve-pound sledge. The statue broke in half. LeRoy toppled sideways, but Charlie darted for the shotgun. I lunged after him, hampered a little by the bruise on the leg LeRoy had kicked. Just as he grabbed the gun in tow hands, I smashed him as hard as I could on the head with the butt of the statue. He went into the wall, shotgun and all, and I turned to see Cash frantically trying to claw a .45 automatic from his belt. He had just cleared it when I hit him with my shoulder.

The sofa toppled over backwards, spilling all three of us to the floor. Cash was a bobcat, snarling, gouging, clawing. He had lost

112

the pistol when we hit the floor, and I had lost the piece of statue. We rolled over three times, and then I kneed him good where it hurts, seized a bony wrist and levered his arm behind his back. He was going for my eyes with his free hand when I broke his shoulder. His scream seared my face with a smell like rotten meat.

I was kicking free of him when LeRoy called my name like a clap of thunder in the room. "Butler! I'm gonna kill you for that."

Apparently he was indestructible. He was standing at the end of the sofa, wiping blood from his face with one arm, brandishing the deadly sap in the other hand. I moved four feet and snatched Cash's .45 from the floor. I pumped the slide to put a round in the chamber and cock the weapon.

LeRoy threw his head back and laughed. "Go ahead, cowboy, gun me down. It ain't even loaded. We don't let Cash tote a live one. He's got screw loose. Here's the one with the bullets in it." He patted a .45 tucked in his wide leather belt. "You can have it if you can take it off me." He began to move toward me, grinning with the half of his mouth that worked.

Linda was lying where she had fallen when the sofa toppled, her hands taped behind her back. Her face was so white it looked artificial. Holding the gun as a club, I moved to maneuver LeRoy as far from her as possible.

He came crouching on the balls of his feet like a boxer, holding the sap high like a hatchet. Against his strength I couldn't gamble on catching his wrist and flipping him. So I decided to go for the sap itself. It was what he would least expect. After the violent exhibition I had staged, he would be focused on my going for his head with the gun. We faked and bobbed, circling like two crabs. Suddenly LeRoy bounced forward and chopped at my head. He almost caught me leaning. The tip of the sap burned my cheek going past. LeRoy flung his other arm up to protect his face, but I threw the gun at him and dove for the sap, hoping the thong was securely laced to his wrist. It was. Seizing the sap in both hands, I jumped away from him and jerked him off balance. As he fought to recover, I moved behind him and pulled his right arm over his shoulder with all my strength. He crashed to the floor on his back. Before he could recover, I snatched the .45 from his belt and smashed his mouth hard. I felt teeth go and maybe bone. Then I rammed the muzzle into his

113

mouth up to the trigger guard. I wasn't trying to scare him. I was going to blow the back of his head off.

Charlie saved his life. While we were fighting, Charlie had retrieved his shotgun, propped Linda up against the overturned couch, and rammed the muzzle between her breasts. "Don't kill him, bucko!" he shouted. "Or I'll spread the redheaded bitch all over this sofa."

My hand began to shake, and LeRoy started to gag from the blood in his mouth. I was afraid Charlie might risk a shot at me in spite of the danger of hitting LeRoy, but apparently whatever load he had in the shotgun wouldn't allow it. At such times you have to decide instantly. "All right, put your gun down and you all walk out of here."

"No, you first. I don't like the way you play. You're as coldblooded a son of a bitch as I've ever seen since LeRoy."

"If you believe that, friend, you better believe this," I said. "She's just what you called her, as far as I'm concerned, a bitch. I won't think about her five minutes after you cut her down. But before you can work that pump, I'll kill LeRoy and you, too. Now clear out. Or shoot. There's no third way."

The tone of my voice convinced him. He took the gun away from Linda and pointed it at me. It looked like the entrance to the Lincoln Tunnel. "How do you want to unlock it?" he said.

"Lay your gun on the floor and go bring your truck around. Back it into the driveway, and I'll deliver fat boy."

"No sale. You'd kill him as soon as I was outside. Or shoot me before I made it to the door."

LeRoy was going to choke to death anyway if I didn't do something fast. So I eased the gun from his mouth to the back of his neck and sat him up. He spit blood and teeth on the floor. "Tell him, LeRoy," I said.

LeRoy choked it out. "Take the chance, Charlie. I'm hurting."

"Let me clear the gun and take it along," Charlie said. "It cost fifty bucks."

It was a small concession, but I feared he had more shells in the truck. "You've got to leave the gun."

"Dirty rotten no-good bastard," he said tonelessly, putting it on the floor. He walked over to Cash, who was conscious but

114

whimpering. Charlie helped him to his feet, and they made it out the door with only a little moaning.

I peeled the sap from around LeRoy's wrist and prodded him to his feet. He shook himself like a bull and coughed up more blood, but he walked steadily to the door. When the pickup truck showed, I went out with him, then moved over behind my Mercury. But LeRoy walked straight to the truck and climbed in. I hated to see them go free, but I couldn't see any point in trying to raise an alarm. They had their choice of a dozen back roads out of Jordan City, and they could as easily be from West Virginia as Kentucky. But it was a terrible mistake to let them go. This breed never leaves a score unsettled, especially if blood has spilled, and they would be back if they weren't hunted down.

I should have killed them after Charlie put the shotgun down. Only two things had stopped me, and neither one of them was conscience. No, I was inhibited by Linda Thorpe's horrified eyes, and by the possibility that even my constable's badge wasn't license enough to explain it satisfactorily to Sheriff Casey. For when it comes to killers I do not subscribe to the quaint fantasy of the shoot down in the dusty street, the American hero's code of fair play as manufactured by Hollywood and TV. If LeRoy's first blow had caught me flatfooted, he would have driven part of my skull into my brain. I couldn't excuse it as overzealousness. Anyone who sets out to maim or kill me I will kill with impunity, and I won't hand him a pistol to defend himself before I do.

By then they were gone, and I hobbled back into the house, hurting in a dozen places. Linda had somehow gotten to her feet during my absence, and she stood leaning against the upturned sofa, her legs spread in an unnatural stance. Her hair was disheveled, her eyes wild, and one cheek was soiled or bruised above the black electrician's tape plastered over her mouth. At the sight of me she began to sway, a muffled sound coming from her flared nostrils. I hurried forward the caught her in a dead faint, easing her to the floor. Then I ripped the tape from her mouth and wrists.

This slight exertion unleashed another jagged flash of lightening behind my left eye. The bolt needled the top of my spine like an electric shock. It hurt like hell, and it scared me. I half-suspected that LeRoy had chipped off a splinter of bone and it was gouging something very precious and irreparable. I went to the bar, uncorked

115

a bottle of bourbon, carried it with me to a chair and quaffed a good two ounces. When that shot had settled down, I took another. Soon I felt the seductive influence of sleep, which is one of the reactions to violence and injury. If not for Linda, I would have put my head back and let it take me under. But I got up, and it took all my strength to lift her and carry her into the bedroom.

Her breathing was shallow and jerky, but her pulse was strong and I couldn't discover any broken bones. I covered her with a blanket, hiked out to the Mercury, and got my first-aid kit from the compartment in the trunk. While I was there I picked up a Luger, for ballast if nothing else at this stage in the game. On the way back I locked the front door and gathered up the weapons we had scattered around the room, the shotgun, two .45's, and the sap. Even Casey might be impressed with such a collection. I hid them in the record cabinet. I wasn't up to wrestling the sofa upright.

Linda hadn't moved. Her breathing was still a little spastic, as if her lungs were constricted with tension. I gave her a whiff of smelling salts. She rolled her head to avoid the sting, moaned some gibberish, then her eyes and mouth opened wide. She clutched my arm with the panic of someone about to go down for the third time. "Easy, lady," I said. "It's all over. They're gone."

She was working for that one deep breath that aids stability. She got it, and then another, and slowly she released my arm and eased back into the pillow. "Oh, Butler, they were brutal with their hands. I thought they'd killed you. I almost went crazy with fear. I'm such a coward."

"Just relax and take a drink of this bourbon. We have plenty of time to talk about it." Lifting her head in my best bedside manner, I held the flask while she drank. After two slugs, the color came back into her cheeks.

She shuddered and the bourbon made her voice even more husky than usual. "What if I had come home alone? What if they *had* killed you? Where would—"

"Don't go hysterical on me!" I gave her a shake. "I need your help. I'm afraid I might pass out on you. You can't go to pieces now."

That sobered her. "They did hurt you! There's blood all over your neck and shirt."

116

"It's not all mine. Now listen. I don't think I'm badly hurt, but I want a doctor to check me out. Do you know one who will come over here at this hour? One who won't ask a lot of stupid questions?"

"Yes. Dr. Fisher would be perfect. He lives nearby, and he's a Stagecoach member. I'll go call him, and…"

"Wait a minute." I had another of the lightning flashes, but it was only a flicker and the sting felt much less lethal. "Let's scheme a little. We need a plausible story for the doctor. Then we have to tidy up a little. I'll get clean clothes from my car, and put this head under a shower. You'd better shower and chance first."

She was sitting up now, her expression solicitous. "But can you do all that? Can you hold out?"

"I've got some pills in my case here that'll stiffen the sinews," I said. "Now let's scheme."

Our story was simple but credible. We had come home from the party and surprised a burglar. He had slugged me and scared Linda into a faint. After we came out of it, I began to worry about my head and we called him. It didn't occur to Linda to ask why we had to distort the facts, but I had my reasons. I had formed a black suspicion about these hillbillies while I was bleeding on the hearth, and I didn't want to advertise their visit until I had sorted it out.

After Linda had gone to the shower, I took one of the milder painkillers from my kit. The morphine tempted me, but I didn't want to get that doped up. Then I limped out to the Mercury again. I traded the medicine chest for a clean suit and shirt, and this time on the way back I found the strength to tilt the sofa back into place. I sat on it and lifted each foot to untie my shoes. As long as I held my head level I didn't get any jolts. By the time I had stripped down to my shorts, Linda entered the room wearing slacks and a sweater. She sucked in her breath at the sight of my bloody ear and the bruise on my shoulder, which was the size and color of an eggplant. But her face was full of purpose, and she went to the phone and called the doctor. While I showered, she was supposed to clean up the room and perform some other minor chores.

By this time I was giddy with the effect of the pill, and that was the fuel that got me into the bathroom. First, I set the shower as cold as I could take it and stood beneath the spray with one hand on the pipe above the nozzle. Next, I turned it on fairly hot and soaked my

117

shoulder and leg. Only then did I stand before the mirror and inspect damage. The side of my head was swollen and the scalp split a good two inches, but it felt hard and not mushy. Back in Linda's bedroom I dressed slowly in clean clothes, foregoing the tie and jacket, and wrapped the soiled clothes in a bundle. Now I was getting a little jumpy with the soreness, and I took another pill before going into the kitchen.

"Perfect timing," Linda said. She poured hot black coffee into bit mugs. "How do you feel now?"

"Ninety-eight years old," I said.

She had an ice bag ready, wrapped in a towel, and I eased it into place with my left hand. We sat facing each other at the small table and drank our coffee. She held her cup with both hands and watched me over the rim.

"Butler, why do I feel so burned up emotionally? So numb and apathetic? I have to force myself to do the simplest thing."

"You were in shock," I said. "You're just working your way out of it."

She nodded. "You know, I can never repay you for what you did tonight. Those crazy men meant to punish e for telling Casey about the bracelet. God knows what they would have done to me once they got started."

"We'll talk about it later," I said.

Just then the doorbell rang, and we went into the living room to greet the doctor. Fisher was a chipper little man with a gray moustache and a belly, both of which seemed to please him. He squeezed Linda's hand and gave her a courtly little bow, conveying the impression that she, too, pleased him. He listened to our story as he examined my head, grunting with sympathy, but even his concern couldn't dent that spirit of merriment which seemed to be his natural disposition. He spent a long time peering into my eyes and ears with a tiny light, and he probed the bruise on my shoulder with nimble fingers. I didn't show him the one on my thigh because it didn't fit the story.

"Yes, you've got a nasty rap there," Fisher said. "I'm ninety-nine percent certain that it's a concussion and no fracture. I hold out one percent until I get a picture. Sneaky of me, I know, but professional as all hell. Now, why don't we move into the kitchen while I tinker with your head. Maybe you'll stop by tomorrow for an X ray, at

118

your convenience. You should have told me about that medication you took. Fooled me for about ten seconds."

We moved into the kitchen, and Fisher went to work in his shirt sleeves. He pricked my scalp with a needle, and drank a cup of coffee while the anesthetic took effect. Then he took out a pair of surgical scissors and began cutting my hair around the wound. When it was exposed to his satisfaction, he cleaned it, inserted the clamps, applied some kind of ointment, then a bandage that ran from the top of my forehead to the back of my head. "That should do it. Nothing I can do for the shoulder except admire the way you discolor. You really should spend two days in bed out of respect for the head. Here I'm leaving a few more pills in case your own supply is limited. Ha, ha. Merely a jest."

Fisher then gave Linda a swift examination, using that light in her eyes, pronounced her fit, and gave her a mild sedative to help her sleep. Before he left, he drank a shot of Jack Daniels neat, smacked his lips, and wished us well.

"You pick good doctors," I said to Linda.

"Isn't he something? I told you he would be perfect."

"He's shrewd. He knows there was more to the story than we told him."

"But with him it doesn't matter. Butler, do you want the ice bag again?"

"No, thanks. The anesthetic is still at work. My head feels like it's full of helium. How do you feel?"

She was watching me with an odd expression. "Very tense, shamelessly hungry, and a little frightened of you."

"Why? Because of what I said to Charlie when he had the shotgun on you?"

"Yes! You said you would forget me in minutes. You were very convincing."

"I called his bluff with one of my own," I said. "All he really wanted was to trade you for LeRoy, and that's what we did."

"Maybe, but when you were fighting them you were a different man. Even your voice changed. It was full of—" She hesitated. "It was full of murder."

"Why not? Sure, if things had gone a little differently, I would have killed at least one of them. And not just on your behalf. Because they didn't come here just to punish you. They came to put

119

me out of commission, the same way that put Quartz out. And I think they were hired to do both jobs by the same man for the same reason."

"Wait, that's too fast for me," she said. Then her eyes widened. "God, you're not suggesting that they're the ones who killed the Clayborne girl?"

"No, they didn't kill her. But they are insurance agents for whoever did. Our killer doesn't like a cop in residence close to the scene of his crimes. When he eliminated Quartz, he had no way of knowing that I would enter the picture. But I did, and he had to do it all over again."

"I can't believe it, Butler. It's too sinister. Don't you see? That means someone planned to kill the girl weeks before it happened."

"Not necessarily. Remember, the first crime was the stolen tape. And at first I think that was the only crime planned. Here's the sequence of events: On Saturday night they stole the tape from Pritchett's office. On Sunday when I talked with Natalie, she was calm and even a little smug about the theft. Either that night or the next day she mailed a letter to her father, telling him about the tape. That letter was dynamite, and she knew it. As busy a man as he is, she knew he would come running out here as soon as he got the letter. Any scandal now would jeopardize his political ambitions. Clayborne didn't get the letter on schedule because he had taken an impromptu vacation. But later his reaction was the one they had counted on."

"Wait a minute, Butler. You make it sound as if Natalie were part of some conspiracy against her own father."

"Yes, I think she helped rig the whole thing. She couldn't very well make a tape and just had it over to someone. So she did it for her psych-counselor and arranged to have it stolen. But at some point after she mailed the letter, she had a change of heart. She spied on her partner in the conspiracy, discovered something that made her renege, and possibly she threatened to denounce the partner. So he had to kill her. And if I'm not mistaken, the original crime will still bear fruit. Philip Clayborne will be blackmailed with the tape."

Linda shook her head in wonderment, her lower lip between her teeth. "Dear Lord, it does sound accurate when you tell it like that, with all the pieces. And I thought those hoodlums were after me.

120

When all the while they wanted to get you because you knew too much."

"My God!" I bolted to me feet and nearly fell on my face from dizziness. "Quartz is alone, and he knows practically everything I know about the case. They may have gotten to him first." I went to the phone and dialed Quartz's number. I had a disturbing vision of Quartz lying in a tangle of broken casts and tape. But he lifted the receiver and spoke in a sleepy voice.

"Quartz, Morgan here. Are you all right?"

"Wait a minute." He went away from the phone and came back. "Christ, Morgan, it's three A.M. Did you call at this hour to inquire about my health?"

"No, I thought you might have had a visit from your hillbilly friends. Linda and I tangled with them tonight, and we're still picking up the pieces."

Now his voice became crisp. "Tell it, Buddy."

I told it, play by play, rounding it off with my theory that these country boys were hired to disable us by the Clayborne girl's killer. Quartz was dubious at first, but after I had summarized it as I had for Linda, he began to believe it. "Boy, you have been doing your homework," he said. "Those three characters come and go with too much freedom for my taste. You can't persuade me that Jack Casey couldn't put his hands on them if he wanted to."

"I plan to chat with Casey about that tomorrow," I said.

"Fine. You coming home tonight?" No, I'd better hang around here. I'll be down late in the afternoon."

"All right. I'm going to make sure this place is locked up. With those boys, you never know. Good night, Morgan."

Linda had waited until she was certain Quartz was unharmed, then she had squeezed my arm and left the room. The relief about Quartz eroded all the tension from me, and I was almost out on my feet. Just then Linda reappeared, carrying a blanket folded over one arm and holding my Luger awkwardly in the other hand. She looked strained, and her color was high.

"The spare bedroom is ready," she said. "I thought you'd want this near you. Do you want one of the pills Fisher left for you?"

"I'll take them with me in case I want one later," I said. "Just show me to that bed."

She led me down the hall to a small room with a double bed. I slipped the Luger under a pillow, and Linda suddenly cupped my face between her hands and gave me a chaste kiss on the mouth. "Sleep and heal, Butler. Your pills are on the table there." She was gone. I kicked my shoes off, shucked out of my trousers, and felt sleep wrapping me like a cocoon.

I slept soundly, but always after a violent encounter there is a part of my mind that remains vigilant, tuned for unnatural noises, the whisper of menace, the return of the intruder in the night. It's the chemistry of survival at work, and primitive man must have experienced it every night of his life. So when the noise awakened me in the dark, my hand was already on the Luger and I knew exactly where I was. I felt as thorny as a porcupine with alertness. At once I detected the immobile white figure in the doorway. "Linda?"

"Yes, Butler, it's me. I'm sorry I woke you. I was just looking in."

"What time is it?"

"Six in the morning. Butler, I'm such a coward. I haven't slept at all. Oh, I've tried. I took the sedative. I took a drink. Even a warm bath. But every time I get into bed, strange sounds pluck my nerves like banjo strings."

She had moved to the bed as she talked, a stately apparition in white, ice tinkling in the glass in her hand.

"What have you got in the glass?" I asked.

"More bourbon."

"Give it here. My mouth's dry." I took a drink, put the glass on the table and whipped down the covers. "Get in with me." With a sigh she slid her head to the pillow and tucked her long legs under the bedclothes.

I slipped a hand to the small of her back and she trembled. She was naked under the flimsy gown, silent, warm, abundant. My leg and shoulder were stiff and the lump on my head was hot, faintly throbbing, but I found her mouth with mine and none of my injuries hampered me. Nor was I troubled by thoughts that she was tendering me this gift as payment, or that she needed sex to relieve the terrible tension that reigned in her. She was too much the woman, too sweet, too voluptuous, her tongue, nipples and thighs quivering and swelling at my touch. It was all so effortless and natural, I

122

experienced a sensation that we were performing a rite that had sketched itself in our minds and only waited for the right moment. I felt the superb heat, the richness of her movements in ecstasy, the husky, moaning laughter in my ear. We were silent, slippery with the bath of love, and after a while we began again. It was the most intimate contact possible, with every nerve bared for plunder, and we didn't stop until we slept.

Chapter 11
***

I woke up at two in the afternoon, feeling hungry, mildly erotic, and more than a little dissipated. I was alone in the bed, but Linda's scent seemed to rise above the sheets, a mixture of honey and oil, the mildew of love. I sat up gingerly, but my head felt no worse than a bad hangover, and my leg and shoulder merely sore. The door to the room was ajar, the aroma of coffee and ham hung in the air, and I could hear Linda humming in the kitchen. All my rough edges were blunted.

With an effort and an oath, I got to my feet and into the bathroom. I used one of Linda's shower caps to protect my bandage, took a shot shower and a brief cold one, then shaved with the razor Linda doubtless used on her legs. Dressed in the clothes I had taken from the Mercury the night before, I felt human enough to walk into the kitchen.

Linda turned from the stove, spatula in hand. She wore a pale green dress with a pleated skirt, a dainty apron, and her hair was tied in the back with a ribbon. "Good morning, Butler. You can have juice, coffee, and a kiss, not necessarily in that order, then all the ham and eggs you want." There was no coyness, no false humility, no self-deprecating wit. Just an expression of pride on that unique face, and a faint, secretive smile. I had the kiss first, and not for reasons of diplomacy. She whispered in my ear, "Butler, darling, all my vital organs are alive again. Now, sit down. Let me feed you."

I feasted on ham, eggs and rolls, and drank four cups of coffee. She sat across the table from me, smoking, sipping coffee from a cup, that odd smile flirting at the corners of her mouth. "I've been up since one," she said. "Quartz called, and the phone woke me. I told him to let you sleep. I knew you wouldn't follow Fisher's advice about staying bed. Lord, I haven't even asked how you feel."

"Rejuvenated," I said.

"Don't grin at me like that, you rogue. You'll get me all flustered. I thought I was doing very well, for one with such limited experience."

"As an amateur, you're spectacular," I said.

"Will you please stop? Tell me what you're going to do today."

"There's not much of the day left," I said. "The big item is a session with the honorable Sheriff Casey. I want him to pick those country boys up."

"Even mentioning those three doesn't upset me," she said. "I'm more than rejuvenated. I'm intoxicated. Butler, I want you to promise me one thing—that you'll stop at the clinic today for the X-ray."

"I promise. Now I'd better go."

She had made a neat bundle of the clothes I had worn in the fight. I opened the bundle on the sofa, took the collection of weapons from the record cabinet, and rolled them up inside it. At the door she lifted her face for a kiss.

"If you work tonight, call me before you leave the Stagecoach," I said. "I want to check the neighborhood out before you get home."

"No, Butler. Tonight I want you in bed early. I'll have Eddie bring me home. He has a gun. Now remember the X ray."

I went out to the Mercury. The sunlight stung my eyes and I began to sweat instantly. I wasn't in the best of shape. I drove slowly to Quartz's cottage, and he was waiting for me in his livingroom, ensconced in his wheelchair.

Quartz grinned when he saw my head. "Say, you do look like you've been in combat. Let's have the details. Wait, before you start, get my clipboard from the bedroom. It's hard to navigate these halls in this buggy."

I went for the clipboard. Quartz had been taking notes on the case since the murder, writing down every incident I reported to him in neat black script. In the margin he jotted down pertinent questions in red ink. The top sheet on the board was a summary of the theory I had given him on the phone the night before, about how the Clayborne girl had conspired against her father, and the possibility that the hillbilly hoods were working for the killer. A not in the margin read: "How to trace connection between Waldo Mason and mt. boys. Waldo has lived in J.C. for 15-plus years. What does he do in summers?"

Handing the clipboard I said, "Looks like the professor is your chief candidate."

"Yes, I like the professor," Quartz said.

"You may change your mind when I tell you about Carl Metterman. I think he's the artist who drew the nude that hung in Natalie's room."

"Tell me about him," Quartz said, sliding a clean sheet to the top of the clipboard. "Start at the beginning."

I gave him a summary of my evening. When I was finished, Quartz said, "Yes, Metter man has a stench about him. Do you think he's queer, as Eddie suggested? That would be a flaw."

"I don't know, but I can find out. I'll get a rundown on Metterman from Paul McIntosh. I owe Paul a visit, anyway. I'm going to give Sheriff Casey the clue we hid from him, the book, and Paul and I ought to have our stories straight."

"Do you think it's smart to give up that sample of Mason's handwriting? It helps tie him in."

"I didn't say I was going to give jack the original," I said. "I'll make a duplicate for him, with everything the same except the inscription."

Quartz thumbed through his notes. "How about this character Eddie Bell?"

"Yes, he deserves checking out. He might have a record in Steubenville."

"That's easy. I'll send a wire to the law up there."

"And I'd better call the local branch of the law right now." I moved to the phone and put a call through to Sheriff Casey. His greeting was affable.

"Constable Butler, I'm glad you called. I wanted to give you an invite to the inquest, scheduled for Thursday at eleven in the morning."

"So you got the confession."

"Oh, we got it, all right. I told you that boy was ripe."

"And not a mark on him, I'll bet."

"Nary a mark. The good Lord in his wisdom told the boy to sing, and he made like a choir. 'Course, he'll plead insanity, and a lawyer worth his salt might save him from the juicebox. But it's all out of my hands now."

"Yea, let's give him a fair trial and then hang him," I said.

"You are one for clowning, aren't you, boy?" He was a little testy now.

"Jack, to show you I bear no grudges, I'm going to drive over right now and give you a piece of evidence that will help you pull the switch on that janitor."

"And what might that be? You been holding out on me?"

"No, this is something I just figured out. I'd rather show it to you than try to explain it over the phone. Oh, yes, another reason I called. You remember those three corncobs who held up the Stagecoach a while back?"

"I remember. Why, you seen 'em?"

"Last night. We brawled a little, and then I took three guns and a sap off of them and sent them home."

"Why didn't you bring "em in? You got a badge."

"If you're serious, boy, you'd better come over now."

"I'm on my way, Jack."

I changed into fresh khakis, strapped on my .38 and picked up the package I'd made of the hillbillies' weapons. First, I stopped at the bookstore on Main Street and bought a copy of *The Brothers Karamazov.* I took it out to the car and doctored it up, folding the same three pages Natalie Clayborne had folded. I took out my wallet, found the bookplate I had lifted from her room, and pasted it on the flyleaf.

Then I drove to Spencer's Falls. It's the county seat of Parson County, and Casey's office was in the courthouse. This was a square building with columns in front, the same replica of Greek architecture you find in all the county seats in the Midwest. There was a park around it, with a fountain that didn't work, a dozen old gents on benches sunning brittle bones, and the usual Civil War statue. Jack Casey's office was on the second floor, a big square room with windows on two sides and two overhead fans lazily spinning. I interrupted a conversation between the sheriff and his deputy, Humpty. Casey was behind his desk, his booted feet propped on a drawer, and Humpty sat on the edge of a table against the wall.

At the sight of me, Casey straightened up in the swivel chair with a snap. "Welcome, brother Butler. Hey, you have been in a scrap. I was just telling Hump here that you tangled with them bad hombres. Hump's what you call a skeptic. He don't see how one man could whip three hardcases like that."

Humpty bore the title of skeptic with his usual phlegmatic expression. I laid the package of weapons on the desk and unwrapped it. Even the skeptic was interested enough to shuffle over for a look. "The outsides of the guns are pretty well smudged," I said. "But you may find some prints on the shells and magazines. These boys may have records. Their first names are LeRoy, Cash and Charlie. I'll match the names with descriptions if you want to take them down."

Casey ordered Humpty to sit down with a pad and pencil. Then Jack looked me straight in the eye. "Tell your story, Butler."

I told it with only a little distortion, slanting it so that I appeared to believe that the three had come to Linda's house to punish her for having reported seeing the woman with the bracelet. "But I don't see how they could have known that, unless they had a pipeline into your office," I said.

You could have shaved with the edge in Casey's voice. "Let's not go off half-cocked, Constable." He turned to Humpty. "They sound like Kentucky white trash to me. What do you think?"

"Yeah, they likely live up some hollow across the river," Humpty said. "They do their dirty work here, then sneak home like the scum they are."

Casey looked at me. "Damn shame you didn't bring one of them in."

"As I told you, it was a standoff," I said.

"Yeah, I know, you told me," he growled. "Well, I guess I got egg on my faced. I was wrong about them three being transients. I'll get the work out to all the neighboring counties. We'll pick "em up. Now, what about this fancy clue that's going to sew up my case on this janitor?"

I gave him the phony book and a story to match, explaining that I found the book on the floor beside the bed on the morning of the murder, and had returned it to the bookcase without knowing it was important. It was only when I mentioned it to Paul McIntosh yesterday that the significance of the story came out, the fact that Smerdyakov, the murderer in the book, was also a janitor of sorts. So I got the book from the room and discovered the mutilated pages. I had no idea what the numbers meant.

My negligence about the book gave Casey a fine opportunity to chew me out, but all his irritation was focused on the book itself. It seemed that the county prosecutor had a nice simple case to present, and the presiding judge liked his cases simple. But this so-called clue was just the sort of thing a sharp defense attorney might use to confuse the issues and distort the facts.

"That's up to you," I said. "But you better show it to your prosecutor. Paul McIntosh is going to write that book up in his story, which comes out tomorrow."

"Yeah, I'll let the prosecutor sort it out," Jack said. "He's an educated man. Maybe he's even read the damn thing. But let's get our stories straight. I don't want to have to put you on the stand, Butler, so you can tell how you bungled this. Let's say that I found the book Sunday morning, and that I was the one who got the story from McIntosh just today. That'll help keep it simple."

"Fine. I think Paul will be willing to write it that way."

"He damn well better. Okay, thanks for nothing, Butler."

I started to leave, and then came back and asked Casey if he had removed the nude drawing from Natalie's room. He gave a sigh of exasperation and said no, but it didn't matter because he already told her daddy that he could pack her things and take them home.

A quarter of an hour later I parked in front of the office of the *Jordan City News*. When I stepped from the car, my head began to throb in tune with my pulse. Dots like tiny gnats danced in my field of vision. I entered the newspaper office, tinkling a small bell on the door as I closed it.

I stood before a counter on which there were several pads for writing classified ads. A piece of machinery creaked and rattled in the background. The place smelled like the inside of the books you find in the old trunk in the attic. I reached back and rang the bell some more, and the machinery stopped making the racket. Paul McIntosh appeared from behind a partition, wearing a blue bib apron over shirt sleeves. His broad, homely face was beaded with sweat. "Constable Butler," he said, smiling. "I'm glad you stopped by. Say, you've been in a fight!"

"I could use a drink. If you've got a bottle stashed away behind your editorials."

"As a matter of fact, I have," he said. "Come back to my office. You caught me setting type, but I can finish it later."

I followed him down a passageway, past a tall machine with metal arms and a huge keyboard. "I hope you weren't setting the murder story," I said. "I've just come from Casey's office. I gave him the book, and he wants your story to read as if he found it."

"How typical of Casey!" Paul said. "This election next fall must really have him worried. Well, I can easily revise the story to read that way. But who'll believe that he read the book and saw the significance of Smerdyakov?"

As we entered his office, I explained that Casey wanted Paul to retain credit for that discovery. Paul's office looked more like a study. Mounted on one wall were several framed scrolls announcing awards made to his paper by journalism societies. Another wall supported shelves of books. There was a huge roll-top desk, an ancient Underwood on a typing table, an easychair, a studio couch, and a water cooler that held two trays of ice cubes. Paul took glasses and a bottle from his desk and a tray of ice from the cooler.

"Bourbon on ice, that suit you?" he asked.

"That's perfect," I said, lowering myself into the easychair.

Paul served me, then took a cigar from a humidor on his desk. "There's nothing like bourbon and a good weed to relax a man," he said. He offered me a cigar, but I declined. He got his going and looked at the bandage on my head.

"Is there a story in that for me?"

"There may be later. There's no point in telling it until I have an ending."

He studied his cigar as if there were a melancholy message written on it. "I don't blame you for not trusting me. On Sunday I behaved badly. I jumped to the conclusion that you were out to discredit Casey for political reasons. I was wrong. I apologize." He raised his gaze to my face. "Now I'm convinced that you were right about the janitor. He isn't the murderer."

"What changed your mind, Paul?"

"Fair question. The answer is, several things. As a newspaperman, I have a healthy respect for facts. That business about the stolen tape intrigues me enough to give Dr. Pritchett a call. He verified your story. Then, yesterday I had an interview with Philip Clayborne, the dead girl's father. He acted as if he had proof that the janitor didn't do it."

I cut in sharply. "Did he discuss the tape with you?"

"He was annoyed that I even knew about it."

"He's worried about that tape," I said. "What else convinced you?"

130

"Well, now it gets more complicated. Yesterday evening I had a visit from one Arthur King, student and poet. He said you suspect him of the murder."

"He's just a name on a list," I said.

"Yes, but he's pretty upset about it."

"Why, did he come to you about that?" I asked.

"The boy's seen too many movies," Paul said, smiling. "With my reputation as defender of the underdog, crusading editor, he wanted to team up with me and find the murderer. He got angry when I turned him down. But he did sell me the idea that the girl was in trouble. So I put it all together and decided that the janitor is probably innocent."

I thought about it for a moment. "Paul, does this mean that you want to change your story about the janitor?"

"Not necessarily. I can run it the way I wrote it. But, if you prefer, I'll use this new information to raise doubts about his guilt. You see, I'm offering the cooperation I more or less withdrew on Sunday. In fact, I have something that might help you. King mentioned that the dead girl's mother graduated from Jordan in thirty-nine. That happens to be the same year my wife graduated. So we looked Eleanor Sheridan up in Judy's yearbook last night. There are several pictures of her in it, and I thought you might be interested."

"Hell, yes," I said. "Why didn't I think of that?"

"The book is over at the house," Paul said, rising. "Come on, it's only a five-minute drive. It's time to lock up here, anyway."

The drink had given me temporary stability. Paul locked up, and I followed his station wagon down wide, shady streets to a white house with a spacious lawn. Two boys, ages about twelve and fourteen, were catching baseball on the lawn. The house needed a coat of paint, but it had bright awnings over the windows and well-kept flower beds on either side of the porch. Paul waved to the boys as we went up the walk.

The living room was as neat as the flower beds, with shabby but comfortable furniture. Paul waved me to a chair, and a tall, handsome woman entered the room. She wore an apron, and her complexion was rosy, as if she had been cooking.

"Paul, I didn't expect you for hours," she said. "Isn't this press night?"

"Something came up," Paul said. "Judy, meet Morgan Butler, Jordan City constable while Willinger is on the inactive list." He began rummaging in a magazine rack. "Where's that yearbook we were reading last night?"

"I put it back on the shelf." She crossed the room to the bookcase and got it for him. It was a flat book, bound in faded maroon leather, with "JORDAN COLLEGE, CLASS OF 1939" embossed on the cover.

Judy McIntosh had greeted me with a cool nod. She was stately, a trifle wide at the hips, with black hair hacked off short as if she had done it herself with garden shears. She had beautifully shaped hands.

"Join us for a minute," Paul said. "Mr. Butler wants to know more about Eleanor Sheridan, and you might be able to help."

She seemed reluctant. "Well, let me turn the oven down."

Paul had thumbed the pages in the book until he found the one he wanted, then handed it to me. The page showed several portraits of seniors. One of them was Eleanor Ruth Sheridan, and there was a quotation under her name: "A witty woman is a treasure, a witty beauty is a power—Meredith." Aside from the quaint hairstyle and a black mole at the corner of her mouth, she did bear a marked resemblance to Natalie. The expression in the picture was at once mischievous, shrewd, vivacious, conveying an impression of a blonde vixen. Under the quotation was a list of her extracurricular activities, including dramatics, tennis, the French club, and several committees. Then there was a prophecy: "Eleanor (known to her intimate friends as Chérie) is a blithe spirit who will always triumph over any obstacles life dares to put in her path. She will someday reign over beautiful parties in a mansion, will be a source of inspiration to her husband's success, and will raise beautiful children endowed with her cleverness and wit."

"Purple prose," Paul said, smiling at my grimace. "Now if you'll turn to the other bookmark, you'll find several pages of snapshots taken while she was a student. I've marked the ones where she appears."

My palms were sweating. I was positive I would see one photograph with the date in April under it. First, I saw her in tennis clothes with two other girls. Next there were a few snaps of her as Nora in a production of Ibsen's *A Doll's House.* There were two shots of her with groups on the campus, and one of her alone with

132

Waldo Mason. I wouldn't have known him if the caption hadn't identified him: "Eleanor Sheridan and Waldo Mason, Beauty and the Brain." He was just another husky young man with his arm around a lovely, slender girl. I was disappointed to read that the picture was taken in thirty-eight.

I closed the book just as Paul's wife came back into the room.

"How do you know Eleanor Sheridan, Mrs. McIntosh?"

Judy sat on a hassock, her legs folded neatly to one side, her graceful hands in her lap. "We lived in the same dorm during our senior year," she said. "We certainly didn't move in the same social circles. She was an extremely popular girl. I guess you could call her the campus queen that year."

"What was she like? You must have an opinion of her."

She lifted a corner of her mouth in amusement. "Well, I can only repeat what I told Paul last night. This opinion is highly personal, and I'll tell you why. I'm British. Or was. I came to Jordan as an exchange student for my last two years of college. England, you may recall, was taking a terrible beating in thirty-nine. I lost my parents that year in the Blitz. But Eleanor Sheridan was what the yearbook calls her, a blithe spirit. She still acted as if she were living in the twenties, part of flaming youth. No doubt that added to her appeal as far as the boys were concerned. Most of us were pretty grim in those days, full of social consciousness and all that. So, looking back, I would have to say that she was essentially a vain and frivolous girl."

"What about her and Waldo Mason? Was it serious between them?"

"I honestly can't remember the details of that. It's been over twenty years. Of course Waldo would probably remember."

"Waldo refuses to talk about it," I said. "Especially in light of the fact that he was involved with the daughter."

"My God, are you sure?" Paul asked.

"Waldo doesn't deny it."

"Then it's only a coincidence," Paul said. "I know Waldo. It's true that he has an erratic personality, but he's incapable of violence. Why, he's been working for years on the definitive history of slavery in America. I've read parts of it, and it's an impeccable work of scholarship. This history is an obsession with him and doesn't leave him time for the social amenities."

133

"Let's get back to Eleanor Sheridan," I said. "Mrs. McIntosh, did you ever hear anything about her posing for a nude portrait?"

"Odd that you should bring that up," she said. "I mentioned it to Paul last night. There was a scandalous incident that last year, about someone showing a nude painting in an art show with her face on it. But as I recall, it was all a hoax. Someone had painted her face on another painting. Something like that."

"Are you sure it was a painting?"

"Yes, and Carl Metterman was the artist involved. I recall that because Carl and I joked about the incident at a party not long ago."

So Mr. Metterman was another one with a bad case of forgetfulness.

"Well, I'd better go," I said. "Paul, I'd like to borrow this yearbook, if you don't mind. And, on the subject of your story on the janitor, I'd prefer you ran it as Casey tells it, with the janitor guilty as sin."

Paul nodded. "Fair enough. A little strategy on your part, I take it."

I started to rise, experienced a white flash inside my skull, and nearly blacked out. Through a mist I saw Judy McIntosh kneeling beside my chair.

"Are you all right?" she said. "Maybe you should see a doctor."

"I've seen one," I said. "Just let me sit here for a moment."

She rose, and I could hear them whispering in the background. I let my head fall back on the chair and dozed. When I came out of it, Judy was on the sofa, quietly sewing. The patterns of sunlight on the rug had shifted noticeably.

"Hello," she said. "Did you have a good nap?"

"How long was I out?"

"No more than an hour. Paul had to go back to the office. We thought it best to let you sleep. You looked done in. How about coffee now?"

"I'd like that," I said.

She left the room and returned presently with two cups of coffee on a tray. "I've long since given up on tea," she said. "I'll have a cup with you."

I sipped mine. It scalded, and I took more. "Good," I said.

She was staring at me intently. "I have a confession to make. I didn't like you before I met you."

134

"Why not?"

"Because of the spot you put Paul in the other day, making him conceal evidence from Jack Casey. You don't know Paul. He hates anything underhanded, especially when it smacks of politics."

"Didn't he tell you that I gave Casey the evidence in question today?"

"Yes, but now you've enlisted him in another scheme. I don't like it."

"Mrs. McIntosh, Paul happens to believe, as I do, that the man who killed the Clayborne girl is still on the loose. He's offered to cooperate in my investigation. I got the impression it was a matter of principle with him."

"Oh, that's rich!" she said. "Maybe you don't know that he might soon go to prison because of his principles."

"I don't understand."

"It's an old story. He's been hauled up before one of your Congressional committees, just because he belonged to a Marxist discussion group back in the thirties. They want him to tell the names of others who were in the group. He won't do it, and he won't take the Fifth, so there's a chance he'll be indicted for contempt of Congress, or some such asinine charge."

"That's rough. I'm sorry, I didn't know."

"How could you?" She dipped her head over her cup, but she didn't drink. Finally she said, "No, I'm the one who should apologize. I detest interfering women, and I'd be grateful if you didn't mention this to Paul. It's just that he's been under a lot of pressure lately, with this committee business, and I get burned up when people take advantage of him. He's too easy, too good."

The intensity of her devotion put timbre in her voice, and I admired her for it. Paul had chosen wisely. I got to my feet. "I'd better go now."

Judy accompanied me to the door, leaving me with an impression of shabby elegance, of a gracious woman a little strained and fatigues by her circumstances.

The episode with my head worried me enough to send me to the college infirmary, where Dr. Fisher had told me to report for an X ray. I was expected. The X-ray technician was an elfin woman with a caustic wit. She turned my head for several poses, calling them mug shots, and was finished in five minutes.

As I started to leave the building, I heard quick steps behind me in the waxed corridor. "Officer Butler, may I speak with you, please?"

It was Betty Childress, Natalie Clayborne's ex-roommate. Her white nurse's uniform made her oval face look even more angelic, serene.

"I thought you were a student," I said.

"I am. But I work here three evenings a week as an aide. Listen, I heard you were here, and I'm on my break. Can you spare me a few minutes?"

"Of course. Where can we talk?"

"In the solarium. It's empty now. This way." Her walk was graceful. The uniform and her slender calves emphasized the fullness of her hips, that sturdiness of her body which seemed also a quality of her character. She led me into a room with windows on two sides, and we sat down in adjacent chairs.

"What did you want to see me about?" I asked.

She moistened her lips daintily. "My book, *The Brothers*. You said you would give it back soon, and I wondered if you were finished with it."

"Sorry, things have changed since Sunday. Besides, you lied to me."

Her eyes expressed a gentle incredulity. "How did I lie?"

"You told me Waldo Mason, your 'sometimes Dimitri,' wasn't involved with Natalie."

She stiffened, swaying a little from the waist. "If it's true, I didn't like to you knowingly. But I don't believe it. You're wrong about him."

"How do you know?" I said, gravel in my voice. "Are you privy to his secrets? Are you his mistress?"

She gave a brazen little laugh, brazen for her anyway. "Obviously you haven't done much research on me. I'm notorious for my chastity. Can you imagine me having a cheap affair with someone like Waldo Mason?"

I shook my head slowly. "Betty, no affair involving you would be cheap. But that's not the point. The point is that Waldo knew Natalie much better than he'll admit. He was also thick with her mother years ago, when they were both students. Here, look at this."

136

I had the yearbook under my arm, and I opened it to the snapshot of Waldo and Eleanor Sheridan.

Betty paled, as if this piece of physical evidence confirmed everything I had implied. "Dear God, he's so young." It was a term of endearment.

"Betty, did Waldo ask you to get that book back from me?"

She wouldn't answer. She seemed incapable of it.

"All right, listen. You tell him that I wouldn't give it to you because Natalie left it as a clue to her murderer. Tell him that."

"Why don't you arrest him, if you're so positive?" she said defiantly.

"All in good time. If he murdered Natalie Clayborne, I'll arrest him when I have the evidence I need to make the charge stick."

"But you're absolutely wrong!" she said. "He didn't leave his house that night. I was with him until five A.M. Do you understand? I *am* his mistress. I love him." Her pink face looked as exposed as her reputation.

"And you stayed awake all night to make sure he stayed put?" I said. "Even if you swore to it, Betty, it wouldn't be enough to clear him."

"Oh, that's very funny. Not to be believed about that. It's ludicrous."

I left her there. Outside, I got behind the wheel of the Mercury and sat for a while in the early twilight. Now the throbbing in my head seemed a punishment, just desserts for using Betty to send that message to Waldo. Oh, it was a shrewd move. Smoke him out. Inform him that you know about his latest conquest, to make him sweat about his job. Insinuate that you have other evidence. Apply the pressure that produces anxiety. The he might panic and commit the blunder.

I drove to Quartz's cottage, took one of Fisher's pills, and went to sleep.

Chapter 12
***

The next day the murder story was on the front page of the Jordan City News. Jack Casey was the hero of the piece, as Paul McIntosh had promised, and the clue of the book was cleverly inserted to make the case against Ewing damning. There even appeared to be a physical resemblance between Ewing and Smerdyakov, and the story surmised plausibly that the victim had held the janitor at bay with words while she prepared the book as a message.

Quartz read the story to me over a breakfast of hotcakes and sausage, which he began to serve when I came out of the shower at one o'clock.

"That's a pretty good piece," I said when he was finished. "It may even get Casey elected instead of you in the fall."

"Not if you bring me the real killer, tied in a red ribbon," Quartz said. "Then Paul will write us a story, and Casey will have to find another sinecure."

We were chatting in this vein when the telephone rang. The caller was Waldo Mason, and as soon as I identified myself, he ripped into me.

"God damn you, Butler! I don't care if you are an officer of the law. You had no right to break into my house and tear the place apart. You ruined the work of months when you scattered my notes all over the floor. Why didn't you complete the barbaric act and burn them? I swear to God—"

I interrupted his tirade and informed him, in a calm voice, that I hadn't been near his house. He called me a liar and began to roar again. I broke in with the same speech uttered in the same tone. I added, "If you want to report a crime, I'll listen. Otherwise, you can take your business elsewhere."

"Naturally you deny it," he said. "But this has your touch about it, Butler. Especially after what you said to Betty yesterday. I suppose you'll deny that."

"No, I admit to that, and I admit that it was on the brutal side. But listen to me, Professor. I'm getting sick of being lied to by you scholarly chaps who have such a high regard for the truth."

138

"That's just another tactic, Butler. You attack when you're accused. Don't you think I know what you're trying to do?"

"Suppose you enlighten me," I said.

He breathed harshly into the mouthpiece for a moment. "Never mind. You'll get no cooperation from me in the future."

"How does that differ from the way it was in the past?"

But he hung up before I finished the sentence. Quartz had wheeled into the living room to listen on the extension, and when I joined him he was still holding the phone, looking at me reproachfully. "You didn't tell me you'd gone gunning for the tape. You must want that bonus awfully bad."

I missed the levity of our earlier conversation. Quartz nursed a cyst of irritableness about my avocation that made him suspicious. I shook my head. "You're mighty quick on the draw, Constable. When I'm ready to go for the tape, you'll know about it."

He lowered his eyes. "My mistake. Then who is looking for it?"

"I don't know, but I don't like it. I've got one idea: Arthur Kind, boy detective. He was eager to get something on Waldo."

"That's all we need," Quartz said.

"I'd better run out to King's place," I said. "He hasn't got a phone."

I finished dressing and drove out in the Ford. Elderberry bushes along the Old Sawmill Road were in full bloom, and the weeds around the gas station looked as if they would overrun it by midsummer. King's car wasn't in the garage, but his apartment door was ajar. After I got out of the car, I could see that the ring of steel to which his padlock was fastened had been ripped off the doorframe. The white chip of broken wood hung on the weathered door like a flag. I went up the stairs as quietly as possible.

The place was empty, but it looked as if every movable item in the room had been torn from its place: cans and boxes of food, books, bedding, even the porcelain top off the toilet, and everything was on the floor where it had landed. I nosed around a little, but I couldn't determine if the searcher had found what he was looking for. I decided to wait for King downstairs. I would give him thirty minutes.

He arrived in twenty, glaring at me from his station wagon as he wheeled into the garage. He came out with a scowl on his face and

139

several books under his arm. "To what do I owe the dubious pleasure of this visit?" he asked.

"You've been burglarized," I said.

His jaw tightened, and he went up the steps three at a time. I followed at a more leisurely pace, entering in time to see the triumph on his face as he returned to the center of the room.

"So they didn't get it," I said.

"Get what?"

"Whatever it was you ran up here to check on. You must have a good hiding place." He had come from the corner where the bed was, and I examined that part of the room again. It baffled me until I saw the khaki laundry bag tied to the head of the bed, army style. No one likes to handle dirty laundry, and if you are the least bit fastidious, you don't even see it.

King, who had been watching my face, began to back toward the bed as if to defend it. In his eyes I could see the combative glint.

"Relax, roughneck poet," I said. "I'm not going to fight you for it."

He snorted as if I had misunderstood his movement, but he threw the mattress back on the bed and sat on it. I moved a chair close to the bed and straddled it. "You want to know why I'm not going to fight you for it?"

"I'm sure you're going to tell me."

"Because I don't believe you have the tape in the laundry bag."

"What tape? Oh, the tape they stole from Natalie?" He laughed. "No, you're right. No tape in the laundry bag."

I lit a stogie, watching his face. He had a curl in his lip I could have hung my hat on. "Let me tell you a story, poet. Once I knew a young newspaperman in San Francisco. He was sent out to cover a killing one night, and he happened to see something that nobody else saw. It had to do with his being Catholic, but the details aren't important. Anyway, he stuck this clue in his pocket and began rummaging around in people's lives. He smelled a scoop. A couple of days later he turned up missing, and a few days after that he washed up on Stinson Beach in Marin County, wearing a piece of wire for a scarf."

"Do you think I scare that easy?" King said. Then he realized what he had admitted. "Besides, I don't see how your story applies to me. I'm not after a scoop."

140

"No, but I understand you're after a killer."

"That's a little ridiculous, isn't it? Considering that I'm your chief suspect? Who told you I was playing detective?"

"I deduced it," I said.

"Like hell. It was Paul McIntosh. All right, so I am rummaging around. But I'm not so ambitious that I would try to bring the man in. I'll leave that to you. All I want is to name him for you, with evidence to back it up."

"That's still a lot of ambition. What have you got to work with?"

"That's my business." This amused him, and he laughed with genuine mirth. "But you can rest assured I'm not Catholic."

Bright young people have a tendency to hole the intelligence of their elders in contempt. It took me all of five seconds to recall that being a poet was his business, that Natalie Clayborne often gave him poetry to read, and that I hadn't found any of her recent poetry when I searched her room. I said, "Just because she wrote a sonnet to the guy docsn't mean he killed her."

His eyes slewed as if I had trapped him in a corner. He jumped to his feet with the savage look on his face I had seen there the first day I talked with him. "Get out of here!"

I got up from my chair. "One more word of advice—"

"No! No more lectures. No more snide remarks. Nancy Brewer told me how you grilled her the other night. You made her feel cheap and dirty."

"My, it sounds like your little slave has revolted. All I told her was that she had nothing to lose but her chains. Poetically speaking, of course."

I picked my way through the debris and down the rickety stairs to my Ford.

Driving back to town, I felt uneasy about the aggressiveness of this marauder. No more did I enjoy the sensation that he was blundering along behind me, pillaging the houses of suspects I uncovered. If this were true, Eddie Bell's domicile would be next on his list. So I skirted Jordan City, operating purely on a hunch, and took the country road that led to Bell's renovated farmhouse.

An old green MG was parked in the driveway, but that meant nothing to me. I walked up on the porch and knocked. No one stirred. The door was open, but the screen was latched, and the

141

hallway inside looked as cool as a cave. I knocked louder, with the same results, so I left eh porch and followed a flagstone path that led around the house. At the rear corner the path passed through a grape arbor. Thick old vines and new leaves made substantial walls and a snug roof overhead. Halfway through the arbor, I was immobilized by a laugh that cut like a jagged silver knife through the fabric of the afternoon. Parting the vines, I had a clear view of Eddie Bell's patio forty feet down the slope. I was witness to a spectacle.

It was Madge Bell who had laughed, Carl Metterman who had provoked it, and the reason the laugh had sounded so alien to the day was because it was an expression of pure erotic feeling. The two of them were entwined on a chaise longue in the sun, naked to the waist, both of them blonde, tan, oiled, their limbs writing. Madge was wearing the bottom half of a bikini, and Carl was in slacks. Compared with her tanned body, her breasts wee like white tennis balls. Carl was feasting on them, and she had both hands buried in his hair, murmuring to him. No wonder they hadn't heard my knock. Now I knew why it behooved Madge to label Carl a queer to her husband. For a moment I stood entranced, an unwitting voyeur to the lascivious scene. His hands prowled over her, caressing her rump. Her thighs coiled around one of his.

Aware that I was beginning to feel a little goatish, I turned away and retraced my steps back through the arbor and around to the front porch. I had no qualms about interrupting their sticky embrace. Using the butt of my gun, I knocked on the door with a vigor that must have raised dust in the attic. I paused, giving them time to emerge from the carnal depths, then knocked again. Presently I heard the sliding glass doors, bare feet patting across the living room, and Madge appeared behind the screen. She had popped her breasts into a flimsy little halter composed of two cups and some cord, and she wore sunglasses.

"My, if it isn't Officer Butler. And so handsome in his uniform. I'm sorry to report that Eddie isn't in. He's already gone to work."

"That's all right," I said. "I'd just as soon talk with you, anyway. Assuming I'm not intruding."

"No, no." Her gaze flicked to the MG and back. "I was just sitting on the patio with a friend. You probably met him at the party the other night. Carl Metterman? He's making some drapes for me, and we were going over the fabrics." She unlocked the screen.

"Come in. I'll bet you could use a cold gin and tonic. Or are you one of those sticklers about duty?"

"No, I'd like a drink," I said.

I followed her tall, sinuous figure back through the living room. I had never seen a woman so slender who managed to come off so voluptuous. I saw the tracks of Metterman's hands through the oil on her back, and the smudges on the tight fabric over her bottom where he had wiped them. When we reached the patio, Metterman was wearing his net T-shirt and sandals and was hold a neat package of swatches on his lap. Their drinks, the ice long since melted, were on a little metal table with an umbrella mounted over it.

"Carl, I believe you know Constable Butler," Madge said.

Carl grunted, making no effort to hide his distaste. His mouth looked bloated, his eyes a little out of focus, like a man just awakened from sleep. Madge took their glasses over to a little cart and made us all fresh drinks. Then she perched on the chaise longue, her knees primly together.

Apparently I had the floor. "Mr. Metterman, it's a stroke of luck my finding you here. I had planned to pay you a visit today anyway."

"For what reason?" he asked.

"Surely you remember," I said. "Didn't I tell you the other night that a common interest in art would bring us together again? Well, since our little chat I've learned on good authority that you once did an oil painting of the woman we talked about, Eleanor Sheridan. I understand the painting was a very lifelike nude and created quite an uproar when it was exhibited while the girl was still a student here. I'm very much interested in this painting."

Metterman worked hard to act indifferent, but I had caught him with his guard down, and he couldn't quite conceal his distress. After a long drink from his glass, he said, "Listen, I don't know why you're hounding me, but I told you the other night that I couldn't possibly remember work I did twenty years ago. I don't care who your so-called authority is." He turned to Madge. "This jerk is trying to involve me in the Clayborne girl's murder. Can you imagine anything so absurd?"

To my surprise, Madge wasn't at all sympathetic. "Carl, it sounded to me as if he's just trying to track down a painting. Why

143

don't you help him? Didn't you tell me once that you might forget a face, but never a naked figure you'd painted? Help the man, Carl."

Incredulity bloomed in his eyes. He wiped his mouth rudely with the back of his hand, as if to eradicate her taste. "Say, you are a bitch!"

She threw her head back and laughed. "Didn't I warn you I was a bitch? That didn't bother you earlier. Now, answer the man's questions, Carl."

"I will not!" He got to his feet so abruptly the bundle of swatches fell to the ground. Now his anger turned on me. "You're way out of line, Butler. I happen to know this murder case is closed. I read today's paper. They're indicting that crazy janitor tomorrow. So get off my back."

"You intrigue me more and more, Mr. Metterman," I said. "Why would a few questions about a painting get you so upset?"

"That's not the point," he said, trying to look calm. "I have my rights. I'm not required by law to answer your questions. I resent your Gestapo tactics, your arrogant invasion of my privacy."

"My God," Madge said. "Next he'll claim he spent the war in a concentration camp. Where's your tattoo, Carl?"

He turned and flicked his arm in one motion, knocking the glass out of her hand. It smashed on a flat rock. "You're a cheap slut with a viper's tongue!" he said. "No wonder your bald runt of a husband needs a stand-in."

Putting my glass down, I stepped behind him and took both his arms in a grip just about the elbows and turned them in sharply. He yelled and started to struggle, so I screwed them a little tighter. Before I could prevent it, Madge pounced to her feet and hit him a hell of a clout on the jaw with her fist.

"That's your ban for the day, you fat-headed Dutchman," she said. "You think you're a man. Compared with that man you call a runt, you're a cap pistol. You better stick to your giddy schoolgirls." The exertion has dislodged one of her halter cups, and the exposed red nipple looked as hard as a ruby.

Turning him away from her, I said, "Looks like you've worn out your welcome, Carl. You better run along." I released him, stepping back quickly, but he seemed to have exhausted his belligerence. Her attack upon his manhood may have been more painful than the physical punishment. His expression was sullen as he rubbed his

144

shoulders, picked up his swatches, and trudged up the slope. Neither Madge nor I spoke until the sound of his MG had faded.

Then she said, "That was fun. I've been looking for an excuse to send that lout packing. What say we have that drink inside?" She adjuster halter as casually as if she were putting on a hat.

"Yes, it is hot," I said.

She wheeled the bar cart into the living room, where she made herself a tall drink, arranged the cushions on a low sofa to her taste, and draped herself among them. I sat in a chair across the coffee table from her. She puzzled me. She hardly acted the part of a wife who has just had a scrap with her lover before a stranger. It was possible that Carl was merely the latest in a long line of playmates, a stud who hadn't measured up, and yet I had an impression that she was not so dim-witted as her behavior seemed to indicate.

"You still haven't told me why you dropped in today," she said. "Or did you actually come looking for Carl?"

"No, but I'm glad he was here," I said. "I wouldn't have missed that show for anything. You were pretty rough on him."

"Was I?" She lifted a hand and preened her hair. "Do you think I bruised his libido? Wouldn't it be funny if the next time he coaxed one of his virginal little art students to the couch he couldn't make it? That would be the worst thing that could happen to Carl."

"If that happens, he may come back for revenge," I said.

She considered it, then rejected it with a gay little laugh. "Not Carl. He's afraid of Eddie. Which is one reason he came calling in the first place. To demonstrate that he was the better man."

"That's interesting," I said. "Do you think they were competing in the same way for the Clayborne girl's affections?"

"Oh, that's sneaky of you. Just like a cop. No, Eddie doesn't go for these tender little chicks. I would know. That's not Eddie's style, Eddie's taste."

I thought that over while Madge twinkled her red toenails at me, sipped her drink, and reminded me that I hadn't yet explained the purpose of my visit.

"I have reason to believe that someone may try to break in to search your house," I said. "Two other people who knew the Clayborne girl had their houses ransacked this morning, and I thought Eddie might be on the list."

145

She sat up on the sofa, her face sharp with curiosity. "I don't understand. Whose houses were broken into?"

I told her, and I emphasized the violence of the searches.

She had to wet her lips before she spoke. "I wonder what they're looking for? Hey, you're not making this up to scare a girl?"

"You don't scare that easy, Madge. Who are you kidding?"

"You'd be surprised," she said. "Just because I slugged Carl like that doesn't mean I'm tough. I'm alone here a lot, and sometimes I get the blues." She touched her naked stomach as if she listened to the blues with her fingers. "Why don't you sit over here, so we don't have to shout?"

"I'd love to, Madge, but I'm already late for an appointment." I got up.

She rose slowly, holding her eyes on mine, and glided around the table. "You're cruel. You chase away the only guy around, tell me a robber might come calling, then abandon me." She blew a little puff of air on my cheek.

So I kissed her, and suddenly I was grappling with a sexual athlete. Her sinewy tongue lashed the inside of my mouth, her talons tracked my spine, and she caressed me with a knee. It was like getting jolted with a hot wire, and I realized she was still in rut from her dalliance with Metterman. She hissed in my ear, "I know I'm not as juicy as Linda, but neither is she as talented as me."

"That's not the point," I said, extricating myself. "Once we start, we won't stop until we're burned out. That would be a long night."

She took it as a compliment. "The nights are out. But you call me after two in the afternoon. If the coast is clear, we can have eight hours."

"That might do it. Now, if you see anyone prowling around, you call me."

She laughed in her throat. "You've just given me an idea."

I was still in a lewd mood when I reached the office in the old schoolhouse. Ferby was out making rounds, but he had scrawled a message for me on our blackboard: "Morgan: Call op. 17 in Philly. Urgent!"

After I had opened some windows, turned on the fan and fired up a stogie, I settled down at the big desk and placed the call. A moment later I had Philip Clayborne on the line. "I've been trying to get you for two hours," he snapped. "Where have you been?"

"I'm working on a case, remember? Did you think I was going to solve it from behind a desk?"

"All right, let's not go into that. Have you any progress to report?"

"A lot has happened, Mr. Clayborne, But if you're asking if I've picked up that item we discussed, the answer is no."

"I thought that buildup your friend gave you was too good to be true. You told me you had all kinds of evidence to work with, that you would produce results. I'm beginning to have serious doubts about you, Butler."

I took a drag on my stogie. "So he's made contact. And it's blackmail."

"Not over the phone, you ass!" His breath was as harsh as static in my ear. Then suspicion triumphed over his caution. "How did you know?"

"It's the one thing that could shake you up," I said. "Even though we suspected it would come, it still jolts. Now you're certain they have it."

"Yes! I suppose I thought that by now—"

"—I would have performed the small miracle of locating the item in question. Sorry, no such luck."

"But are you close to it? You don't realize the implications of—"

"Maybe I realize more than you know. For example, I hope you don't think I believed that cock-and-bull story about the wayward daughter and doting daddy."

Anger made his voice sound as if he were talking through wool. "Butler, if you've betrayed me, I swear to God I'll destroy you for it. There's only one possible way you could know that story was false."

"Oh, stop acting like a hysterical old woman!" I said, giving vent to my spleen. "That's the trouble with you third-generation robber barons. You inherit so much guilt with the money, you see a jackal behind every copy of the *Wall Street Journal*. I knew that story was phony because I'm not stupid. You told me your daughter did something naughty when she was sixteen, and you bought her out of it. Clayborne, there's nothing you could have bought, murder included, that wouldn't stay bought. Because your high-priced legal help would have made sure that you bought a fix at the same time. A

147

fix means police, and police keep records. Their version would assign guilt, if that were essential, and they would have placed your daughter in Timbuktu when this trouble occurred. You can't change those police records with dynamite, because that would mean that the cops who made them were either incompetent or corrupt. So they would be very hard on anyone who came to them with a story told to a tape recorder by a love-sick, hysterical girl, and no one would dare publish the story without police clearance. Need I go on?"

He sighed as if resigned, but his voice was irritable, rough. "No, you're right. I invented the story. The real facts are more complicated, and you can take my word that the tape is a danger to me. Which is why I want you to intensify your efforts. Put pressure on these people. I've found that people under pressure tend to panic if they have something to fear. So if you throw a good scare into the right man, he might give himself away."

It sounded like something his daddy might have told him over a glass of sherry at the Harvard Club. "I'll bear that in mind. Now, do you want to give me the details about the message from your friends?"

"No, I'll give you that information tomorrow. I'm flying over and should get there about three in the afternoon. I have to bury my daughter at noon."

"When is payment due?"

"Friday night, and in your neighborhood."

"That's a tight schedule. I assume you'll pay, barring a miracle."

"Yes. Certainly."

"All right, talk to you tomorrow. Wait. Answer me a question, Mr. Clayborne. Did you call in those Pinkertons, after all?"

"Certainly not! Surely you realize that the fewer people involved in this, the better. Why do you ask?"

"No reason. Just idle curiosity."

My first thought after hanging up was that the killer had won the first round. Nothing I had done had interfered with his original plan: blackmail. I dug out a bottle and glass from the desk, took a neat shot of Old Taylor, and thought about it some more.

Obviously the killer felt very secure to have made his contact on schedule. I couldn't believe he meant to collect the money and run, for that would brand him a murderer. No, he meant to salt the money away and go about his business, until his departure occurred as a

148

normal event. So he was smug. He even planned to make his collection under my nose. Nothing personal in that, of course. It was just good strategy to stage the pickup here on the killer's terrain, far from Clayborne's home ground and a big-city police force.

That earned me another drink, a double. This one seemed to peel away the varnish on my own confidence, for suddenly I wondered if the killer's name was even on my list. It was possible that I had missed him completely, and that he knew it. I poured a third drink. I had just enough in the bottle to help me brood my way through this mild sensation of defeat.

Chapter 13
***

At eleven the next morning I attended the inquest on Natalie Clayborne's murder in the Parson County courthouse. The presiding judge was a feisty old character with the demeanor of a church elder – and Law was his holy scripture. The county prosecutor more resembled a Shakespearean actor in his favorite role. A tall, slender man, he had a gift for the telling gesture and a voice that vibrated like a French horn. When he lowered it to whisper for effect, you could hear every word distinctly in the back row, and when he aimed a piece of bombast at the rafters, it echoed like the clap of doom.

The inquest was a cut-and-dried affair. Jack Casey, in polished boots and brass, was the star witness. The six members of the coroner's jury were as enthralled as choir members listening to their favorite hymn. They swayed in unison when the prosecutor exhibited the dresser drawer full of lingerie and the girly magazines. He didn't introduce the Dostoyevsky novel as evidence, which didn't surprise me.

The defendant never took the stand, but his gaunt face bore a rapt expression throughout the proceedings, and when his confession was read into the record, he smirked over his shoulder as if to see if everyone was listening. The confession sounded exactly like the one Jack Casey had invented in the janitor's trailer on the day of the arrest. Ewing's attorney was a chubby man, appointed by the court. The judge sustained only one of his objections.

The jury never left the box. The judge indicted Ewing for first-degree murder and set a date for the trial with the air of a man announcing the text for next week's sermon. You got the impression that all unrepentant sinners had better attend.

My seat in the back row was near the exit, so I ducked out ahead of the crowd and lit a stogie on the way down to the courthouse park. I found a bench in the shade, and soon I saw Paul McIntosh emerge, deep in conversation with a reporter from the *Spencer's Falls Gazette*. Paul waved, and when the two parted, he walked over and sat down beside me.

"Bible-belt justice," he said, and you could have sanded barnacles from a ship with the scorn in his voice. "Did you see the audience licking their chops? If that janitor hanged at noon tomorrow, those people would turn out in their Sunday clothes, with a picnic basket and the young'uns."

I gave him a cigar and lit it for him. "Ewing's the perfect villain," I said. "A sexual cripple who killed a young girl in a fit of perverted lust."

"No, it's more than that," Paul said. "Most of those hicks in there wrestle with the same fantasies they accused Ewing of having. They ogle the naughty magazines on the sly, have hot flashes when pretty young girls prance down the street. And did you see their women? Sticks of wood and straitlaced bags of laundry. They're all sexually deprived, thwarted. They all share a horror of the flesh and morbid fascination with it. They want Ewing destroyed, because he represents urges that terrify them."

"Is that the way you're going to write the story for your wire service?"

He smiled sheepishly. "No. I'll just write the facts. The papers that pick it up with give it one paragraph next to the obit page."

"Don't let it get you down. You may have a better story before long. One that will feature a murderer with a lot more class than Ewing."

Paul looked at his cigar as if I had given him a sour one. "You mean Waldo Mason. I gave you my opinion on that score the other day. Waldo would let himself be crucified publicly before he'd kill a girl to save his reputation."

"But that wasn't the motive for this murder, Paul."

His face sharpened with interest. "What is it, then?"

"It could be a combination of motives. Revenge, greed, and one I haven't figured out yet."

"Hey, that reminds me." He put a hand on my arm and looked around as if we might be overheard. Stragglers from the courthouse were moving past us on the walk. "I've got something to tell you. Why don't you give me a ride back to Jordan. Judy needed the car today, and I came over on the bus."

"Sure, I'll give you a lift. Wait here until I have a word with your friend Jack Casey."

Casey had just come out of the courthouse and was standing on the steps, accompanied, as always, by the big deputy Humpty. Jack looked a little more dapper than usual, but he was still the buggy whip, lean, limber and hard. Humpty nudged him as I approached the steps, and Casey grinned.

"Mr. Butler, how did you like our little show?" Casey asked.

"Very impressive. You had the janitor so well trained, I thought he would slit his throat for an encore. Just to save the county the expense of a trial."

Humpty turned a deep shade of pink and snarled, "You watch your tongue, hotshot, or by God—"

"Easy does it, Hump," Casey said. "You've got to learn to be generous when you win. After all, we plucked this murder right from under the constable's nose. That same nose is bound to be a little out of joint."

"Very magnanimous of you, Jack," I said. "Actually, it's the efficiency of your department that brought me over here. Have you got a lead on those three hillbillies we talked about the other day?"

"Humpty's working on that personally," Casey said. "He's right on it."

Humpty was packing his jaw with tobacco. He merely nodded.

"We'll keep you posted," Casey said. "Since those three are probably holed up outside our jurisdiction, it means playing politics with some other county sheriffs. Some of these old boys are temperamental."

Humpty spoke abruptly around his cud, "Them three's probably got the word the heat's on, and taken off clear out of this part of the country."

"Not those three, deputy," I said. "They'll be back. My only concern is that the next time I might have to kill them. Then the sheriff here would get sore at me for giving his county a bad name."

"Yea, I would at that," Casey said.

We were both watching Humpty. He snorted gently, shifted his cud, hefted his shoulders, and spat a brown stain against one of the courthouse pillars. So I bade them good day, turned on my heel, and walked back down the steps.

Paul McIntosh rose from his bench as I approached him, and we walked to where I had parked the Mercury. When we reached the city limits, I said, "Now, what is this information you have for me?"

152

"I'm half embarrassed to tell it," Paul said. "I'm hardly the one to play amateur cop, after the way I criticized Arthur King the other day. But Kind did mention one man as a potential suspect who strikes me as an unsavory character. I've always been curious about his past, and this seemed a good time to check into it."

"You must mean Eddie Bell," I said.

"That's the character. When he moved to Jordan to manage the Stagecoach, oh, about three years ago, I interviewed him for a piece in the *News*. All I learned was that Eddie had managed a nightclub in Steubenville, Ohio, and his wife worked there as a dancer. Well, after I talked with King on Monday, I called a reporter I know on the *Herald-Star* in Steubenville. That's a wild town."

"I've been there," I said. "I gather your friend got back to you."

"Just this morning," Paul said.

"And he dug up some dirt on Madge and Eddie Bell for you."

"Yes, my friend says that during the war and for a few years afterward Bell was Steubenville's most notorious pimp, and Madge was the star performer in his stable. Later he got into trouble with the head of the rackets up there, and got demoted to the status of nightclub manager, a real dive, according to my friend. Then the two of them lived in Mexico for a while, and when Eddie's old enemy died, they went back to Steubenville. But he couldn't work his way back into the rackets. So he took this job in Jordan."

My mind drifted to the neat package of contradictions, Mr. Eddie Bell. "Maybe they've reformed," I said. "I've known a few from the fleshpots who have. All it takes is a little character."

"Do you sincerely believe that?" Paul asked.

"Paul, you're beginning to sound as sanctimonious as that crowd back in the courtroom. Remember? The ones you caught drooling over Ewing's corpse?"

"That's not very funny," he said. "I thought you'd appreciate having this information." His voice was thick with ruffled feathers, and he lapsed into silence. After another mile he surprised me by chuckling. Then he said, "The hell of it is, the analogy isn't altogether inaccurate. It must the old Puritan twitch working in me, to condemn Bell because he was once a pimp, his wife a Jezebel." Again he chuckled to himself. "I guess I don't have much future as an amateur cop."

153

"Don't resign yet," I said. "The fact is, I may have to ask you to take on an assignment tomorrow night. If it comes to that, you have my word that there won't be any risk involved. It'll be tame work, but necessary."

Paul sighed and watched the ornament on the hood for a full minute. "I suppose it's childish of me, but I wish you hadn't added that remark about no risk involved. Oh, I know why you did it. Because Judy denounced you in her own sweet way for taking advantage of me. She told me about it last night."

"I hope you weren't angry with her," I said.

"Angry with Judy? No. Actually I was touched by her concern. She's a rare woman, a thoroughbred. She's a little bitter about this Congressional committee business, but there's still a fair chance that I won't be indicted. I'm pretty small potatoes for those boys. My lawyer tells me that they were really sore because of some of the editorials I wrote about them a while back, proving how un-American they are. They hate to be criticized by the ink-stained wretches of the fourth estate, even one with the little influence I have."

We were in Jordan City at last, and Paul asked me to let him out at his office. After he had stepped to the pavement, he held the car door open and looked me in the eye. "You'll call on me for that assignment, right? In spite of Judy?"

"I'll call you, Paul."

He closed the door, and I drove down to Quartz's cottage, where I just had time to grab a sandwich and change into civvies before my meeting with Philip Clayborne. Quartz was dozing in his wheelchair, and I didn't wake him.

Promptly at three I entered the lobby of the Cavendish Hotel. The desk clerk all but genuflected when I asked for Philip Clayborne, murmuring the room number in such a low voice that I had to lean to hear it.

Clayborne's suite was more modest than the one he had occupied on Monday. He opened the door as soon as I knocked, and ushered me into a small sitting room. Somehow I had expected him to look different, drawn with grief, fatigued with the ordeal of the funeral, tense with the anxiety of paying the blackmailers. But, if anything, he looked healthier, alert, confident, as if he had buried his grief with his daughter and approached the task at hand with zest.

154

"I didn't mean to be all that testy with you on the phone last night, Butler," he said.

"I'm used to that. Besides, when you hired me on Monday, you hoped I would fix it so you wouldn't have to make this trip."

"Yes, I guess I expected you to perform what you called a 'small miracle' on the phone. All right, I'm resigned to the fact that you haven't recovered the tape. I've come prepared to pay the money they've asked for, and I'm sophisticated enough to know that this is only the first installment, in spite of what they say in their note. But that doesn't mean we're giving up the hunt, Butler. Quite the contrary. So before we get on to new business, what kind of progress have you made? Who are your suspects? Surely you've got something."

I hesitated.

"Come on, man. For a thousand a week, I'm entitled to a report."

"All right. I've got four names on my list so far. Three are older men, and two of them knew your fist wife when she was a student at Jordan."

"I fail to see the relevancy of that," he said. "But tell me their names. It's possible Natalie mentioned them to me in some significant context."

"Waldo Mason," I said. "Carl Metterman."

Clayborne shook his head. "Neither rings a bell. You said there were four names. Who are the other two?"

"One's a student named Arthur King. The other is an ex-gambler who is now a local patron of the arts, Eddie Bell."

"Seems to me she mentioned this fellow King. I'm not sure. Is that all you've got? Just the names, no evidence? No motive for killing my daughter?" He was the chairman of the board criticizing a chintzy stock dividend.

I said, "Didn't you bring a sackful of motive to buy back the tape your daughter made? How much did they ask for?"

"A hundred thousand." He murmured the sum indifferently, his attention on something else. "But how does the blackmail explain the murder?"

"I thought you would have figured that out by now," I said. I took a stogie and inspected its length and texture.

"No, I haven't figured it out. You'll have to give me the benefit of your wisdom." He spoke precisely, but his concealed fury made the room seem smaller.

"I can tell it, if you can live with it," I said. "Your daughter conspired with someone to blackmail you. She didn't need a psych-counselor. But she signed up with Pritchett and acted the part so she could put that piece of scandal on tape for her partner to steal. It was the only way she could furnish her partner with the scandal and still appear to be innocent. So apparently you and your princess weren't quite as close as you led me to believe."

His face looked like a wood carving. "Why would she do that?"

I shrugged by moving my stogie an inch. The tension in the room made every gesture that expressive. "Maybe she was in love with the guy, and they needed a nest egg," I said.

He had to wet his lips before he asked the next question. "But that still doesn't explain why he killed her."

"One of two reasons," I said. "Either he meant to kill her from the beginning, as soon as he had the tape. Which I doubt. Or she discovered that there was a third person in the conspiracy, a silent partner. That would mean betrayal, and she might have threatened to expose them. I like this theory."

"So it's only a theory," he said. "You have nothing to substantiate it."

"I have you to thank for that," I said. "If I knew what was on the tape, Mr. Clayborne, I could substantiate it without much sweat."

Now his will seemed to have become tangled with mine, as if we were two stags who had locked antlers. I was aware of the gloss in his high forehead, the hair in his nostrils, a blemish on his cheek. He broke the spell.

"No, that won't do. My original rules about the tape have to stand." He produced a handkerchief and dabbed the sweat from his forehead. Then he was silent for quite a while, his gaze abstract. "Maybe Natalie did have cause to resent me that much."

" 'Resent' strikes me as a tame word for what she did," I said.

Clayborne seemed not to hear. He said, "Well, let's move on to new business." He took an envelope from his pocket, removed a paper from it, and handed it to me. It was a letter typed on cheap bond paper.

Philip Clayborne:

The attached transcript from a tape recording made by your daughter should convince you that I have the original tape in my possession. As you can tell from this sample, the tape pulls no punches in describing certain events that occurred in the summer of 1957. The other document enclosed shows that I can support your daughter's testimony with that of an eyewitness.

I will sell you the tape and the other paper for one hundred thousand dollars.

You know that this tape will destroy you if it is made public. Believe me, I intend to publicize this material if you do not follow my instructions to the letter.

    1)   The currency must be in used bills, with no consecutive serial numbers. No more than half in fifties, balance in tens and twenties.

    2)   You will deliver the money next Friday night.

    3)   Leave Jordan City exactly at 11:15, alone in a convertible with the top down. Travel east on Carthage Pike at 40 mph. You should reach the town of Aldenburg at roughly 11:45. Turn right at the traffic light (only one in Aldenburg), and drive south at the same speed for ten minutes. Watch for an Esso station on the right side of the road. Make sure you reach the station at midnight. Stop for gas, and you will receive further instructions.

    4)   *WARNING*: You will be watched constantly until the money is delivered. You must come alone, and no one is allowed to follow you. If you violate these conditions, the deal is off and the tape will be made public. There will be no second chance.

    5)   If payment is made, you will receive the tape in the mail in Philadelphia. *And you will never hear from me again.*

The letter was unsigned. I read it through twice before raising my eyes.

"What do you think?" Clayborne asked.

"The convertible's a nice professional touch," I said. "He wants to make sure you don't carry a passenger. There is one thing that troubles me about this. Our friend should have warned you to get me off his back, but he didn't."

157

"There's a perfectly simple explanation for that," Clayborne said. "The man doesn't know you're working for me."

"Maybe he doesn't know I'm hunting him as a blackmailer. But he must know I'm after him as a murderer."

"Then he must feel awfully secure," Clayborne said with scorn creeping into his voice. "Maybe you haven't even gotten close."

"That's a possibility." Another reason for the omission occurred to me, but I didn't care to discuss it with Clayborne. "Now let's get to this other item of proof our friend enclosed. What was it exactly?"

"I can't reveal that to you," Clayborne said. "You can take my word that it's authentic, and very persuasive."

Intuition is a strange thing. As Clayborne uttered these words, some trick of light combined with the lines in his face to remind me of the Rouault portrait of *The Old King* that had hung in his daughter's room. I don't mean that he resembled the portrait in any way, but he awakened my memory of it, along with the fact that across the room from the mask of greed and corruption hung the charcoal drawing of the pagan nude with no face – Clayborne's wife – and on the bed between them a young girl lay dead. The wound on my head, nearly healed, now throbbed with what felt like revulsion.

"No, Mr. Clayborne," I said. "I'm not going to take your word for that one." Slipping my wallet out, I took from it the check he had given me on Monday and threw it on his lap. "You better get yourself another boy, one who's willing to work with the restrictions you impose." I got up and started for the door.

"Wait, for God's sake!" He came out of the chair and seized me by the arm. "You can't leave me at such a crucial time. Please, Butler. Let's talk it over like civilized men."

"No, you're too tricky and secretive for my taste. I don't mind working against house odds, but you don't even give me that percentage. Maybe it's your reputation that's at stake, but it's my life, buddy."

"All right, tell me what you want. This is all new to me. Maybe I expect too much. Just sit down. Five minutes one way or the other won't matter."

I looked at his face for a moment, then returned to my chair. "I'll invest five minutes."

Clayborne went to the desk, opened one of those spiffy traveling bar kits, and brought a bottle and two glasses to the table between us. "Shall I call for ice, or will you have it warm like the English?"

"None for me, thanks," I said.

He poured one for himself, lifted it and took it neat. He looked around for a napkin, smiled, and wiped his mouth roughly with the back of his hand. "So I impose too many restrictions," he said, his voice a little hoarse.

I told it without preliminaries. "On Monday you lied to me about what Natalie put on the tape. I explained what a silly lie it was over the phone yesterday, but today you tell me that the tape is still top secret. That's one. Number two is the fact that apparently you lied about the relationship between you and Natalie. On Monday you were close friends, but today you were hardly surprised to learn that she schemed to bilk you. Then we have number three, this mysterious document the blackmailer enclosed, which you want me to accept on faith as authentic. My faith in you has worn too thin, Mr. Clayborne."

Clayborne's head was tilted a little, and his expression was, for him, oddly humble. His voice matched. "You speak of faith. Did it every occur to you that if I reveal what is on the tape that you might have neither faith in me nor respect for me? Suppose it's *my* crime that's on the tape?"

"I'd already assumed that," I said. "How bad?"

He poured himself another drink, savored it on his tongue, swallowed. This time he didn't bother to wipe his mouth. "The word 'crime' is not really accurate," he said. "No one was harmed, and I can honestly say I felt no guilt."

"You're stalling."

"I suppose I am. I feel like a man about to throw himself on the mercy of the court. It doesn't come easy for me."

"I'm not here to judge you."

"But you will. Everyone does on this subject. All right, let's put your sophistication to the test. I only hope that Alex Hammersmith was right about you. That summer of 1957 we spent at my house on Cape Cod. We have our own private stretch of beach, our own wharf, and that year we had a new boat, a twenty-three-foot cabin cruiser. Natalie was fifteen. She'd had a bad year at school, academically, and I hired a young man from Yale to tutor her. We

159

had our share of visitors in July, but in August there were just the four of us in the house, Natalie, the Yale boy, myself, and housekeeper, Mrs. McPherson." He paused.

"I'm with you so far," I said.

He nodded and went on. "This isn't meant as an apology for myself, but you have to understand that I was in a strange mood that summer. I'd been divorced five years, remember, from a woman who behaved like a bitch in heat. Twice in those five years I became interested in a woman, and both times it ended badly. One was a conniving little gold digger. I was soured on women. That summer I began to read a lot of philosophy and poetry, stuff I'd hardly touched in college. The Yale boy and I would often sit on the beach and talk about the books. I read several that he recommended. He was very bright and had a certain charm. He practically venerated the ancient Greeks."

Clayborne stopped to pour himself another drink. He spilled a little because he was watching my face. I could have stopped him at that point, but I had to be sure. He drank and scoured his mouth with his knuckles.

"I'll make it short, Mr. Butler. I kept refreshments on the cruiser, wine, food, and ice, and we used it as a cabana of sorts. One afternoon the Yale boy and I drank a bottle of champagne on the boat, and we ended up imitating the Greeks' idea of the purest form of love. That was the first of three times. Natalie happened to walk in on us the third time. Of course she was upset at first. But I sent the boy away, and she and I talked it out until I felt that she understood that nothing really terrible had happened. She even seemed sympathetic in the end. If anything, the experience seemed to draw us closer. So you see, I didn't really lie to you about that."

Clayborne sat down deep in his chair, his arms on the rests, his face sweated.

It was one hell of a thing to have admitted, and that impressed me.

"Obviously Natalie changed her mind about it later," I said. "Maybe she decided that this bent of yours was what alienated your wife."

"That occurred to me," he said. "The irony of it is that there was no bent, no proclivity on my part. I'd never been tempted before that summer, and certainly not since. I think Natalie believed that. No, she wouldn't have turned against me if she hadn't fallen under some vicious influence."

"This still doesn't explain that the other document the blackmailer sent you."

He took a deep breath. "That was a letter from the housekeeper, Mrs. McPherson. Apparently she saw us the one night we used the house. She wrote it all down for someone, and she mentioned the Yale boy's name. They blacked out parts of the Photostat, so I couldn't tell who the letter was for."

"Could the Yale boy be involved in this?" I asked.

"Not a chance. He's married now and has a job in government. This would destroy him, too. No, I think it was Natalie the old woman wrote the letter to. Maybe she thought that Natalie was finally old enough to learn the truth about her father. The old hag couldn't have known that Natalie already knew about it."

"That fits," I said.

"Are you still working for me?" Clayborne asked.

"Why not? You're still the victim here, and that's what I go by. The peccadilloes of the idle rich have long since ceased to shock me, Mr. Clayborne. I'll have that drink now, if you'll join me."

He poured, and we both sipped from the glasses. He grew cheerful. "How about tomorrow night? Will you try to trap the man, or is that too risky?"

"I'll have to think about it," I said. "Let me borrow this letter from the blackmailer, and we'll talk about it tomorrow." I got to my feet.

Clayborne rose quickly and thrust the check into my hand. "You'd better take this." Then his fingers tightened on my arm. "Butler, I think I know why the blackmailer didn't insist that I force you off this case."

"What's that?"

"You'll think I'm melodramatic, by maybe he already has plans to eliminate you as a threat."

"I'd already thought of that," I said. "I'm surprised you did."

"You'd better be careful."

"I'm always careful," I said.

I left the Cavendish burdened with the weight of Clayborne's secret, as if I carried a huge dead fish under my arm. I felt the temptation to share it, but even Quartz would sneer at this dead fish. His attitude toward homosexuals was one of salty masculine contempt, seasoned by thirty years in the Corps.

So when Quartz and I went over the blackmailer's instructions that evening, we discussed only the delicate problem of how to tail Clayborne without detection when we made the payoff. Every play we invented was flawed by the fact that we didn't know where Clayborne would be sent after the Esso station. So we shelved all plans until I could inspect the station. After dinner I changed into dark sport clothes and blue canvas shoes with rubber soles. I wore the Luger under my arm. I was keyed up. Until now I hadn't realized how much the uniform hampered me. I was accustomed to getting information in nefarious ways, with money, with the leverage of a sordid bit of knowledge leaned on the fulcrum of guilt, by showing someone the thing he feared. Now, spurred by that warning of omission in the blackmail note, I thought it might be a good time to prowl, Butler style.

First, I drove up to the constable's office and made some phone calls. I couldn't raise Carl Metterman, either at his business or his home. So I dialed Waldo Mason. He answered, and I identified myself.

"Ah, yes, the constable who can't stand to be lied to by us scholarly chaps," he said. "Have you solved your crime yet< Constable? Have you nabbed the culprit? Made the pinch? Which reminds me, ever hear this bit of verse by Wilde? "The vilest deeds like poison-weeds/Bloom well in prison air."'

He was drunk. A woman's voice called sharply ato him in the background, but his answer was muffled. I heard his breath on the mouthpiece again.

"I want to talk with you" I said.

"Why not? I knew that dialogue we began on Monday wasn't really finished. Maybe that's why I was so nasty to you on the phone yesterday, over a little thing like your breaking into my house. I realize you have your job to do. A violent line of work like yours requires violent tactics. So let's get together by all means. When would you like to resume the inquisition?"

"Right now," I said. "I can be there in ten minutes."

"No, that won't do. I have company, a lady. Give me an hour. Let's say nine-thirty. No, let's say ten. To be on the safe side."

"Ten o'clock it is." I hung up.

I poured a drink from Quartz's desk bottle and brooded about the change in Waldo's attitude. Yesterday he had been hostile, tonight he was downright jovial, eager to cooperate. Considering the circumstances, drunkenness was not an adequate justification. This was no night for me to observe the social amenities, such as giving Waldo time to prepare a special greeting for me. Besides, I was curious about his visitor. I decided to be early for the appointment.

I lifted the receiver again and dialed Linda Thorpe's number at the Stagecoach. After we had exchanged greetings, she said "Butler, you'll make me a confirmed believer in mental telepathy. I was thinking about you when the phone rang."

"Chastising me for neglecting you, no doubt."

"Don't tease, I know you're busy. No, I was thinking of how nice it would be to spend a few days on that farm of yours. Maybe we can once this ugly business is over. I guess I need a vacation from this perfumed atmosphere, from all the hearty American Legion types. You've spoiled it for me, you rat."

"The spoiler, that seems to be my role in life," I said. "Listen, I called for a reason. I want to double-check Eddie Bell's alibi for Saturday night. You told me he worked at the Stagecoach until three A.M. Could he have ducked out for an hour without your knowing it?"

"Not even remotely possible, Butler. Speaking of Legion types, that was the night the Elks held their annual clambake. Eddie was the toastmaster, host to at least forty people. Why have you got something on him?"

"Just a reputation. That reminds me, I've got a story to tell about your friend Madge."

"That's a coincidence. She's here how. She drove out for dinner, which she often does, and she's hanging around to see if any lively groups show up. But Thursday's our slowest night. There aren't a dozen people in the place."

"Then why don't you get out of there early and buy me a drink." As I said it, I realized that the business about Eddie's alibi had been self-deception. I wanted to see her to eradicate that stench y employer Clayborne had left with me.

"My, how impetuous," Linda said. "Yes, I can get away early. Say midnight at my place. That gives me time to get out of this masquerade."

"Midnight at your place is perfect," I said.

I turned the lamp off and sat in the dark until it was time to visit Waldo Mason. I had plenty to occupy my thoughts. Before I left I check the clip in the Luger and called Quartz to tell him where I was going.

Chapter 14
***

I witnessed the departure of Waldo's visitor from a thicket across the road from his house. She did not leave gracefully. First, the front door opened with a bang. She yelled some angry words, slammed the door, fumbled with the latch on the screen door at the top of the steps, jerked it open with a sharp twang, and hurried down the steps.

By this time Waldo had lurched onto the porch. Grabbing the screen door before it closed, he called out in his rich baritone, "You have to learn that love can't be nourished with pious commandments and spaghetti sauce. Love is amoral, or it is nothing!"

This stopped her as if she had hit an invisible wire. She turned to face him in bright moonlight. It was Betty Childress. "Don't lecture me about love. All you know about love is how to destroy it. You don't want someone to love you. You want shipping girls to punish because that woman betrayed you. No wonder you drove two wives crazy."

"How trite to throw that in my face!" he roared. "I thought you were a woman, but I was wrong. You're just another girl who wants to trade her favors for security."

"Whatever I am, Professor, I value myself too much to go on serving as a tranquilizer for your neurotic outbursts." With that, she turned and walked into the shadow beneath a tree, emerging almost at once with a bicycle. Pausing only to flick on the headlight, she mounted it on the run and floated away. Waldo slammed the screen door and was in the house before the sound finished echoing from the timbered hills.

After five minutes I crossed the road and made a complete circuit of the house. Nothing stirred except a new batch of home brew percolating on the back porch. At the side of the house I skirted the splash of light from a window, drifted beneath an elm tree, and moved to where I had a view of Waldo inside.

He was peeling off his T-shirt. Gathering it in one hand, he wiped sweat from under each arm, gave a swipe at his chest, and flung the shirt aside. Then he left my field of vision. A needle scratched a record, amplified by the speaker, and then loud discordant music filled the night. Presently Waldo returned with a tall drink in his hand and eased himself into a big chair. During the next fifteen minutes he moved only to lift his glass and drink.

Satisfied, I left the yard and hiked up the road to where I had parked my Mercury behind a state road shack. A minute later I mounted Mason's front steps and pounded on the screen. Waldo turned the music off and opened the door.

"Ah, the constabulary. I didn't recognize you out of uniform. Come in. Ignore the filth of my bachelor digs."

I followed his naked back into the room, where he waved me to a chair. He offered me a drink, but I declined. The room was furnished in the most haphazard fashion, as if each piece of furniture had been bought at a different rummage sale. The aroma of a spicy sauce hung in the air, and on the dining-room table in an alcove I saw the debris of a spaghetti dinner.

Waldo followed my gaze. He said, "My lady friend insisted upon cooking me a meal. She found me in the cups and thought she should sober me up. I tried to eat, but I have no stomach for food tonight. So we quarreled, and I behaved like a barbarian. I think I've alienated the fair lady for good. And I have you to thank for it."

"So now I'm the heavy in your love life," I said.

"Yes! You're the one who planted in Betty's fertile imagination the fact that I knew Eleanor Sheridan, and the suspicion that I was her daughter's lover. So Betty began to interrogate me, and very astutely, I might add."

"You must have given some answers," I said.

"I gave her too many answers. I don't want to make the same mistake with you. I'm an incompetent drunk. Dipsomania is not my refuge."

"What is your refuge, Waldo?"

He gave me a sly look. "No, forget that. In all conscience, I must withdraw my accusation. I can't blame you for my fight with Betty. Actually I planned early in the week to break up with her. It wasn't so easy to do. Ergo, the bottle. When I'm drunk I can be repulsive without much effort."

The question seemed to immobilize him. He pulled absently at his beard. "Listen, Butler, I believe you're a sincere man. I think you're making a genuine effort to track down this murder. You're questioning the people who knew Natalie, searching for a motive,

166

and so on. But has it occurred to you that she may have been killed by a stranger? Just as a hypothesis, let's imagine a man, half mad with hatred, who comes to Natalie for a certain piece of information. He won't be denied. A man can be driven, tormented."

"What man, Waldo? You're still too abstract for my simple mind."

He bobbed his head like a wrestler squaring off with an opponent. "What if I told you a little tale about just such a man? A man tormented with hatred because he loved a girl desperately, only to have her mock his love viciously."

"Even Hollywood has stopped using that mossback." His coyness invited crude treatment. "But I might listen to your soap opera if you cast it for me."

He looked at me with a pained expression. "All right. I was the fool in love, over twenty years ago. Eleanor Sheridan was the girl. She was the kind of girl you invent in your dreams, a goddess. Or so I thought at the time. I was totally in love, gorged with fantastic energy, sensitive to every blade of grass. She led me to believe that she loved me. She even let me take her to bed, as if to seal some unearthly pact between us." He raised his face. Sweat was running into his beard. "But in the end she dumped me with terrible cruelty. She couldn't just withdraw from the dream. She had to defile it, mock it."

"So you were tormented," I said. "And you decided to kill her."

"Not her." He had to wet his lips. "It was the man she married, Clayborne."

"Why him?"

"You didn't know her. One night just before graduation I caught her alone. I must have looked like a maniac. She was scared. So she told me a story of how she was forced to marry Clayborne because he had a terrible hold over her father. He could send the old gent to prison because of a stock-fraud deal he got sucked into."

"And you believed her? Lord, that's a plot out of the eighteenth century."

"But she was brilliant. She wept on me and made love to me. It seemed a terrible tragedy, our love destroyed by this cruel tyrant. I wanted to kill him." He looked as if he were bloated with the memory of that night, sitting erect with his fists clenched on his thighs.

167

"But Mr. Clayborne survived your murderous impulse," I said. "Why?"

"A few days later I got a newspaper clipping anonymously in the mail. It told how Eleanor's father had committed suicide during the crash in twenty-nine."

"Did you ever learn who sent the clipping?"

"It had to be Eleanor. She didn't want her bridegroom bludgeoned before she got him to the altar. Not with all that money."

From his behavior, I decided that everything he had told me so far had been merely preface to something important. I said, "We seem to have covered the past. Now let's move on to the present. Let's talk about Natalie."

"So you won't listen!" he said harshly. "You won't even entertain the possibility that a man deranged like that might kill just because someone tried to thwart his murderous impulse."

I leaned forward. "Let's get something straight, Waldo. The man who killed Natalie Clayborne is now blackmailing her father for one hundred thousand dollars. That was his motive from the beginning. It was Natalie who gave him the material to sell to Clayborne, and once he had it, he killed her."

"I don't believe you!" he said. "How could you know such a thing?"

"Because I've read the blackmail note," I said.

"My God, if that's true, then it is evil." He shook his head violently. His teeth were clenched, very white against the beard.

"Whatever you know, Waldo, now's the time to tell it," I said.

Just then the phone rang. Neither of us moved. It continued to ring, three, four, five times. I picked up the receiver.

It was Madge Bell. "Butler, I'm glad I caught you. Quartz said I could reach you here. Remember yesterday you warned me about a burglar on the rampage? He's in my house right now. Or he was five minutes ago."

"Give it to me fast."

"All right. I was on my way home from the Stagecoach when I saw a light moving behind my upstairs windows. I know I loved the house up tight before I left. So I turned and drove back to Turley's service station on the highway. I'm calling from there."

"Stay there. Watch for a black Mercury. I'll blink my lights when I pass the station. Give me ten minutes, then follow me in."

168

I hung up and turned to Waldo. "I've got to leave, but I'll be back."

Speech seemed to require great effort for him. "Not tonight. No more tonight." He was the picture of dejection. Even his beard looked wilted.

I went to the Mercury, fully aware that this might be the trap Clayborne had warned me against. Five minutes later I passed Madge Bell, pink and tall in high heels and a sheath dress, standing in the glare of the service-station lights. I turned into the narrow macadam road, hit seventy-five on the long straightaway, going uphill, then cut the lights before I cleared the crest. The moonlight made it easy to navigate the last quarter mile downhill to the Bell's driveway.

The house was absolutely dark. I left the Mercury and circled behind the garage to the patio. One of the doors was open, cracked where the latch had been forced. That made it look less like a trap. I moved to the door, the Luger in my hand, and waited, listening. Then I stepped into the room and listened again. I was convinced that he had gone. Probably he had seen Madge's car lights when she turned earlier.

But I played it safe. I inspected the downstairs with my pencil flash, then went up the old staircase. The master bedroom was torn up a little, although it appeared that our friend had lacked either the ability or the time to open the safe he had exposed on the wall. Just as I started down the stairs, Madge's headlights swept the windows below me. He heels clattered on the porch, her keys jangled, and she opened the door. She made a nervous gesture before she recognized me.

"He's long gone," I said. "But you were right. He was here."

She mad a catlike sound, already in motion, and darted past me on the stairs. I followed quickly. In the master bedroom she went straight to a closet, dove to her knees and vanished except for her feet. She shouted a very unladylike obscenity, emerging with an empty metal box in her hand.

"What did he get?" I asked.

She threw the box back into the closet and got to her feet. "Nothing of value, except to me, the lousy bastard. Who was it? You seemed to know a lot about him yesterday." Her face, lean enough at best, was gaunt with fury.

169

"I don't know. But I intend to find out. Where does Metterman live?"

"Do you think it was Carl? You said he might come back for revenge. This is the way that spineless Dutchman would go about it."

"Where does he live?"

"I'll tell you downstairs. I need a drink."

When we reached the living room, Madge went directly to the bar and poured herself a shot. "Have a snort," she said. "I'm all unglued, and I could use the company. The Dutchman will keep."

I took the telephone book off the stand and began thumbing the pages.

She said, "Hell, he lives a mile out the Old Sawmill Road, in the old mill house, where he does his painting, his potting and other smeary things."

"Is it right on the highway?"

"No, a few hundred yards off on a dirt road. But you can't miss the mailbox at the entrance. It's a big white birdhouse, one of his own creations."

I went out and climbed into the Mercury. Soon after I reached the Old Sawmill Road I passed Arthur King's place. His apartment was dark. After a mile I slowed down, but trust a woman to judge distance. It was another mile before I spotted the mailbox. The lane led downhill, so I cut my lights and engine and rolled down the smooth dirt road. When I saw a clearing in the trees to my left, I turned into it and stopped in deep grass. I went back to the road and began to jog.

Soon I rounded a long turn in the road and saw a stream with a wooden bridge over it. The moonlight was brilliant. Hard against a hill on the other side of the bridge was a stone house. A dim light glowed on the first floor. Then it went out, and a minute later the lights on the second floor came on. I crossed the bridge with my silhouette lower than the guard rail, drifting to the right into a growth of trees. Metterman's MG was parked in a carport beside the house. Everything looked so peaceful, I wondered if I had been mistaken about the prowler's next victim. But then I heard a noise like a dish breaking, and a shadow moved swiftly past the upstairs window. So I circled to the back of the house, and behind the carport I found another car, and brand new Oldsmobile. The engine was warm. I

170

moved on to the back of the house, where I found a window wide open. Someone in the room was breathing steadily, harshly, as if he had run uphill until he collapsed. I risked a look, but couldn't see a thing. So I went over the ledge fast and lay flat on the floor, the Luger in my hand. There was no change in the breathing, and the man upstairs didn't stop moving.

Easing my pencil flash from a pocket, I shot the beam toward the breathing. Carl Metterman was lying face down on his bed, his hands tied behind him and his feet wired to the spokes at the bottom of the bed. He was unconscious, but I didn't see any blood. Flashing a light across the room, I saw a spiral staircase of black metal. A panel of light splashed the wall at the top of the stairs from an open door. I was moving toward the stairway when that light went out. I fell behind an easy chair just as the first hard footfall hit the metal. The light from his flash, much larger than mine, danced over the room in bizarre patterns as he descended noisily. When the beam came to rest on Metterman, I knew he was down. The light on Metterman grew larger, and the man whispered, "Sweet dreams, Blondie." The whisper sounded as if the man suffered from asthma.

There was a lamp on a small table beside my easy chair, and as I ran my hand up to the switch I rested my gun on the arm of the chair. I snapped the light just as he turned to leave.

"You're a dead man if you move," I said.

It's the unexpected that hurts you. Except for his eyes, the man seemed to have no face. My astonishment must have shown, for he flicked off his flashlight at my head and kicked the side of the chair violently. Even so, I could have shot him at least once. But we weren't well enough acquainted.

I ducked to avoid the flashlight and spun off the impact of the chair. But the chair knocked the lamp over and the bulb smashed against the wall. I leaped away from there like a frog, expecting him to jump me. But his gun went off instead, a brilliant flash that blinded me momentarily. The bullet snickered into soft wood not a foot from my head. I fired to the right of the flash, but he wasn't there. I didn't hear him move, but suddenly the door opened thirty feet away and he was outside. I went over the window ledge and reached the corner of the house as he was running for the carport.

Again I could have shot him. Instead, I fired a round into the corner of the building about twenty feet ahead of him. The bullet

171

cracked as if it hit a nail. Scarcely breaking stride, he shied toward the trees near the bridge. I jogged to the carport. From the woods he fired twice, one round plunking into Metterman's MG, then he darted for the bridge. A leg shot was tempting, but moonlight is deceptive. The flagrant way he exposed himself suggested either panic or his confidence that I wouldn't kill him.

I reached the bridge in time to see him duck into a grove of poplars on the other side. He fired two more rounds from there, then another from a position farther up the road. I gave him a minute, then crossed the bridge tight against the guard rail. My big worry now was that I would lose him in the woods. I wasn't sure I could trace him through the Oldsmobile.

I expected another shot when I left the bridge, but none came. I scrambled into a gully at the side of the road, good cover if he was waiting for me in the trees. As I started up the ditch I realized what his plan was. Since he hadn't heard me arrive, he surmised that I had parked up the land, and his hope was that I had left the ignition key in the car. I grinned to myself. The key was in my pocket, and he wouldn't have time to jump the ignition. Just then I heard two more shots. I went flat before my mind informed me that the noise they made wasn't right. They sounded muffled, yet the gun was a heavier caliber than my intruder had been using. I heard no bullets.

When the gully grew too shallow to afford cover, I left it and moved into the trees. After a moment I saw moonlight reflected from the Mercury. Nothing stirred, but the door of the Mercury was open on the driver's side. The overhead light wasn't on because I don't have the light wired to work with the door. Then I thought I heard a car start up on the highway, but it might have been on passing. I circled to my right for a better look at the Mercury, in case my man was hiding in the back seat, and I saw a black object in the weeds beside the car. It looked suspiciously like the body of a man.

I crossed the clearing in a crouch, alert for any movement. The object in the weeds was a body, all right, the man I had been chasing. My flash revealed the flesh-colored nylon stocking he wore over his head, and two holes in his chest from which the blood still oozed. They looked like holes from a .45. My guess was that someone had been waiting in the car, lying on the front seat. My prowler had jerked open the door and the slugs had slammed him back on the grass. Then the killer had trotted up to his own car parked on the highway.

I asked myself the obvious question: How did the killer know the prowler would come to my car? He didn't, of course. It was Morgan Butler he expected to open the car door. The killer had come down the lane of foot, spotted the Merc, recognized it as mine, and had taken up his vigil. I was sweating from all the exertion, but in my gut there was a cube of ice the size of my fist.

The man at my feet wasn't going anyplace, so I got the brandy flask from the glove compartment and took a throat burner. The block of ice began to thaw.

Then I turned on the overhead light, dragged the dead man into the yellow square it threw on the ground, and peeled the stocking from his head. It was Swanson, the arrogant pup with the dimple in his chin, Philip Clayborne's stooge.

So Clayborne had taken out insurance. He had sent this boy to raid the premises of suspects I lined up to get the tape. No doubt he had offered Swanson a bonus, too. I began to unravel the mechanics of it. On Monday Swanson had followed me after I got out of his car, first to King's and then to Waldo Masons's. He had knocked off their houses on Tuesday, but then he was stymied. He couldn't know that I went to the party on business. But no doubt he had received the other names late this afternoon, not long after I so stupidly recited them to Philip Clayborne. So Golden Boy had blundered on, smelling that bonus, full of arrogance and images of movie tough guys. And all he got was two pieces of lead like sledgehammers in the chest. Well, I would have the dubious privilege of telling Clayborne that his insurance policy had lapsed.

No, that was not the way to handle it. If I told Clayborne, I would have to report the killing now, and that meant jack Casey and trouble. The whole story would have to come out, including the blackmail scheme and the fact that Clayborne had hired me. There was no way I could sell this to Casey as another killing by the author of the Clayborne murder, not with his janitor so beautifully indicted. So not only was I robbed of the chance to rip into Clayborne. I had to work like hell to keep him from being implicated in this mess.

It was Swanson himself who showed me how to do it. I knelt on the grass, emptied his pockets, and returned the car to inspect my plunder. First, I unfolded the drawing of the faceless nude that had once hung Natalie's room. This went into the glove compartment. His wallet, along with the usual identification, contained two hundred and twelve dollars and five credit cards. I found a switchblade knife, a gold cigarette case and lighter, a pair of cotton gloves, a key to the Olds with a Hertz tag, a pocket sap and a motel key chained to a piece of plastic with the words "SLUMBER HAVEN" embossed on it.

I knew the Slumber Haven, a collection of cheap pine cabins located fifteen miles north of Jordan City. It was across the county line, and that pleased me. My watch said five minutes after midnight. I stashed Swanson's belongs in my glove compartment, went to the trunk and got a piece of tarp six feet square. Spreading it out, I rolled Swanson up in it. My foot collided with his gun in the grass, and I put that with his other stuff.

Then I got into the Mercury, drove back to Meterman's house, transferred to the Oldsmobile and drove back to the body. When I opened the trunk of the Olds, I discovered an attaché case. I put it on the front seat, returned, and heaved Swanson into the trunk. He fit with only a little folding. Then I trotted back to the house.

Metterman moaned in his sleep when I entered. Not wishing to awaken him yet, I located the telephone with my flash and carried it into the kitchen. I dialed, and Linda answered at once.

"This is Butler. I want to offer you a more exciting date than the one we had planned. If you're willing to help me out of a jam".

"Nothing as exciting as our last date, I hope," she said.

"Dull by comparison. There's some risk involved, but only with the law."

"Since you're the law, that shouldn't be hard to handle. Well, it's better than being stood up. What do you want me to do?"

I liked that. No questions, just a request for orders. "Drive two miles out the Old Sawmill Road. You'll see a big white mailbox. Park there and wait."

"When should I expect you?"

"Say fifteen minutes from now. You should be there in ten."

"All right, Butler." She hung up.

I carried the phone back into the main room and turned on several lamps. The place was so over decorated it resembled a curio shop, with framed paintings, tapestries, old chairs and stools, pieces of pottery and statuettes, and a giant mobile with a thousand moving

174

parts. I cut the rope on Metterman's wrists, unwired his ankles, and turned him over. He sported a nasty bruise on the left side of his forehead, and there was a raw place on his chest where hair and skin had been scraped off. I gave him some brandy from a cut-glass decanter that might have come over on the Mayflower. He spluttered, groaned, and came out of it.

"You're Butler, the cop," Metterman said, as if that proved something. "Where's the other one? The one who slugged me?"

"He must have taken off," I said. "I just arrived. Did you get a good look at him?"

Metterman started to sit up, but his head advised against it. "Oh, I saw him. But he wore a mask over his whole face. It was hideous." He touched the raw place on his chest. "See what he did? At first I thought it was you in disguise."

"Why did you think that?"

"I don't know." He closed his eyes, using all the muscles in his face. "I remember. He wanted to know how well I knew Eleanor Sheridan. That's what you were harping on, so I thought it was you for a minute."

"So you told him about the oil painting you did of Eleanor," I said.

"Yes. Jesus, he held the point of a knife against my eyelid."

"What else did he ask you?"

"He wanted to know about Natalie Clayborne and me."

"What did you tell him?"

"The truth. All right, so I lied to you. But I didn't kill her. All I did was steal back the drawing of her mother. When I showed it to Natalie last fall, she wanted it so badly I gave it to her as a gift."

"I'll bet you sold it to her." He said nothing. "Don't tell me it has sentimental value for you," I said.

He flushed, and for a second I thought he might bluster with indignation as he had on Madge Bell's patio. But instead, his eyes watered, diluting the blue, and he covered them with his hand. Swanson had done his work well. Carl seemed to lack the stamina for resistance for even deception. Finally he said in a low, murderous voice, "She was a slut!"

"Which do you mean? The mother?"

"Yes, Eleanor, or Chérie, as she liked to be called. I was her lover, along with half the senior class. That was how she paid for the painting. And when it was finished, so were we. She wanted it as a parting gift for someone. No, I didn't steal the drawing for sentimental reasons. I was afraid someone would spot my signature under the frame and involve me in the murder."

"Did Eleanor tell you who she meant to give the painting to?"

"No, but I got the impression that she meant to shock someone with it. She was a malicious bitch. That's one of the qualities I got into the painting, the malice, along with the scarlet lust beneath all that milk and honey. That painting was the best thing I've ever done."

"When did you finish it?" I asked. "I want the exact date."

He thought about it. "Late in the winter of her senior year. I know it was cold, because she complained about posing in the nude."

"Could it have been April?"

"No. Because I exhibited the painting at an art show in March of that year. My idea of revenge because she didn't know it was finished."

"All right, let's get back to Natalie," I said. "She looked a lot like her mother. Maybe you got the two of them mixed up, and had to take revenge again."

"No, nothing like that." His voice was weary. "I'm afraid she wasn't susceptible to my fading charm. The Madge Bells are more my speed these days. No, Natalie came to me to learn about her mother. She seemed to be conducting an investigation about her. That's why I dug out the sketch. I didn't have the heart to tell Natalie the whole truth about Chérie, especially after—"

"—after what? Tell it all, Metterman."

His mouth drooped sheepishly. "This may strike you as incredible. I know it did me. One night last fall Natalie practically accused me of being her father."

"That would mean quite a discrepancy in her age," I said.

"No, her age is accurate. She actually checked that out with the hospital. But somehow she found out that I taught a summer session at Temple in Philly in the summer of forty-one. You see? Anyway, it was a strange thing to be charged with. I denied it, of course. But it made me feel more spiritual toward her."

"I'll bet." The idea of Natalie searching for her father excited me. It fit the story Clayborne had told me, but it also suggested that Natalie had found evidence to prove that Clayborne wasn't her father. If that were true – and if she had finally located her real father – that might be the bond I was searching for.

Suddenly Metterman said hoarsely, "I'm going to get away from this place! Give up the shop, the teaching job. I might go to the Coast, San Francisco."

"How about the tape, Metterman?"

He had to turn his head to look at me. "He asked me the same question. That's when he cut me. I swear I don't know what tape you're talking about."

"Good night, Metterman."

"Wait! What if this guy's still around? Maybe he hid when you drove up. Upstairs, maybe." His anxiety, and the way he was sprawled on the bed, made him look like an invalid of long standing.

I went out and got into my car and drove up the lane to the clearing. Backing the Merc well into the brush, I transferred to the Olds and drove up to the highway. I saw Linda's car under a tree well off the road. I parked behind her, and eased into the seat beside her.

"Hello, Butler." She squeezed my hand. "You do arrange unique dates for a girl. May I ask what trouble we're in tonight?"

Her profile, her scent, and touch of her hand made me want to caress her violently. It was my reaction to having just missed a one-way journey with the old gent with the scythe. Embarrassed by the weakness, I began to talk rough with her. "The less you know about his, the better. I'm going to deliver a car to a place, and I want you to give me a lift back."

"Is that all? I thought you wanted me to do something dangerous."

"Next time I'll arrange a scavenger hunt," I said.

"That's a nasty thing to say. I'm not after cheap thrills. I just want to do something to make up for the way I behaved the other night."

I slipped a hand under her arm and lifted her a little closer. "You behaved fine the other night. I told you how good you were."

"I don't mean about sex, damn you," she hissed. "I'm talking about how cowardly I was. The way I came apart when those hoodlums touched me. I guess I wanted to show you that I have courage, that I can be resourceful."

177

There was something about the way she was holding herself, the tilt of her head, I think, that made kissing her a necessity, almost an act of mercy. I found her mouth. Then abruptly I began to plunder her with my hands.

"Butler! You hurt." She seized my wrists. "What happened tonight?"

Her astuteness was more effective than a reprimand.

I went back to Swanson's car, smarting with cynical thoughts about myself, and began the journey. Twice at intersections I stopped to read road signs. Soon I was on the Carthage Pike, cruising just under the speed limit. The Slumber Haven was located on a fairly deserted stretch of highway, the entrance marked by a blue neon sign. I dimmed my lights before turning into the drive, relieved to see that the cabin numbers were clearly marked with red reflectors nailed into trees. Six was my number, and I parked in the slot close to the cabin. Killing the engine and lights, I sat there for a minute.

Country music drifted through the trees from a cabin I couldn't see. Otherwise the residents of Slumber Haven seemed to be tucked in for the night. I got out of the car quickly and unlocked the cabin door. Using my small flash, I pulled the blinds and drew the curtains. The cabin smelled of freshly cut pine and shellac. It was furnished with a double bed, a couple of chairs, a throw rug, and a writing table. I turned down the bed and went out to the Olds.

I opened the trunk and, stooping, heaved Swanson onto my shoulder. He was heavy, but I mounted the steps, closed the door, and dumped him on the bed. With the light on, I performed the grisly task of stripping the tarp from him and getting him covered with a blanket. Then I went out and got the attaché case.

I opened the case on the writing table. It contained the booty from his searches. The sight of three rolls of recording tapes in flat boxes excited me until I read the labels. They were lectures given my Waldo Mason on different subjects in American history. Next I found a packet of letters written by Natalie Clayborne to Arthur King, all dated the previous summer. A sampling showed them to be one long dissertation on the theme that the love between them was really a beautiful friendship. Then I picked up one of those long flat filing envelopes that open like an accordion. In it I found five hundred dollars in fifties, and at least two dozen photographs of

178

Madge Bell, naked, engaged in sexual acts with different men. Most of the men appeared to be drunk or anxious. But Madge posed with the aplomb of a show girl, her back arched, her eyes coy, her smile professional. No wonder she had been upset.

The final item surprised me. It was a flat metal box with the lock sprung, and it belonged to Paul McIntosh. It contained his army discharge papers and dogtags, a tarnished cigarette lighter, a dog-eared collection of naughty limericks, and a handful of foreign coins in a chamois bag. Either Swanson had uncovered something on his own, or he had mistakenly assumed that my visit to Paul's office marked him as a suspect.

I closed the attaché case, parked it near the door with the tarp, and inspected the room. The bureau contained the usual haberdashery, shirts, socks, and underclothing. In the closet were two expensive suitcases, three suits, a trench coat, and a brand-new tape recorder.

The last item altered radically the picture I had formed of Swanson as the obedient young lion. The tape recorder could only mean that Swanson was after the Grand Prize. Once he had the tape he could name his own bonus. So greed rather than zeal was his fatal flaw.

While this was going through my mind I was cutting the Philadelphia labels from the suits in the closet. The police would identify him eventually, but a few days' grace might be to my advantage. Slipping one of Swanson's socks on like a glove, I wiped everything in the room I had touched. On the way out of the cabin, I turned out the light and hung a "DO NOT DISTURB" sign on the doorknob. Parking the tarp and attaché case on the steps, I gave the Olds the same going over with the sock.

With my bundle under my arm, I hiked up the lane to the highway. Linda was parked exactly where she was supposed to be. She started the motor before I reached the car, and jumped on the accelerator before I closed the door. The rear end shimmied as it lurched from sod to pavement, and one tire gave a yelp.

"Take it easy!" I said. "All we need is for you to sideswipe someone."

"Sorry." She slowed down to fifty. "Nerves, I guess. I thought you'd gotten into trouble. Shouldn't you tell me about this? I wouldn't know what to say if anyone asked me about it."

179

"Say nothing. There's not a chance in a thousand you'll ever be asked."

"All right, if you say so." She sat erect, both hands on the wheel.

"Turn around and go back the way we came. I have to pick up my car."

She nodded stiffly, punishing the car as she braked for the turn, reversed, and slammed back on the highway. She was chewing her lower lip.

"Linda, it's not that I don't trust you. It's just that I don't want you implicated. You're the only person I could call on for help tonight, the only one I could trust. Can't you do it on faith? Believe me, it isn't worth the risk..."

"Risk? What did I do tonight that was as risky as what I did on Monday night? Do you think I slept with you to pay you for saving me from those thugs?"

"I considered the possibility, but decided against it."

"Oh, how magnanimous of you. How very generous." She was silent for a while, then the car slowed perceptibly. "Ah, Butler. I didn't mean to sound like a spoiled virgin trying to whine you into marriage. Is that how I sounded?"

"Or a reasonable facsimile thereof," I said.

"I'm terrible. What I want to say is that whatever we started on Monday, I want it to run its course. I want it to have adolescence, youth, maturity, and to end with dignity. Even if its lifespan is only a year. So I'm in love with you, with those conditions, and I can't stand it when you cut me out. It's as if you've given me back my joy and vitality, and then threaten to take them away again. Maybe I'm too sensitive about it." She gave a rich, self-conscious laugh. "It's still in its adolescence. We've only had the one time."

"Stop the car," I said.

"Right here?"

"Yes, stop it."

She pulled off the road into high weeds, jerking the emergency brake, scrambling to meet me. She kissed me as if every nerve and muscle in her body had concentrated on the act. I dipped my hands into her hair and kissed her eyes.

"Your gun hurts me, darling."

180

I shifted on the seat. "You're right," I said. "We've only had the one time. So let's get my car and go to your place. To hell with the conditions."

We did it just that way. When we reached Linda's house, she said she wanted to put on something appropriate to the occasion, so I went to the shower and scrubbed off what seemed like several layers of sweat: one from exertion, one from fear, and the oil that leaks out in the presence of violent death.

Her room was lighted by a miniature lamp with a pink shade, and her hair was like flame on the pillow. As I approached the bed she rose to her knees. Her breasts looked swollen and tender beneath the sheer pink gown. As soon as I touched her, she jerked the towel from my hips and we entered the smoldering climate we had created in the car. It was tropical, pagan, a place where conscience was as remote as the Arctic Circle. Never have I been so perfectly mated. Her beauty was enhanced by desire, by the tribute she paid to pleasure with husky phrases. Her body was both heavy with sensuality and astonishingly nimble. She was active without being aggressive, submissive without humility, lusty without greed.

I was mad for her. That night was a banquet of lovemaking. If her description of the life-span of our affair was accurate, that night we disposed of both the adolescence and the youth and entered maturity.

Chapter 15
***

At ten o'clock the next morning I pulled into the Esso station south of Aldenburg where the blackmailer had instructed Clayborne to be at midnight. It was a tidy station, with a gravel apron, two sets of pumps, a garage, and a public phone booth attached to the outside of the building. I was in civvies, driving the Mercury, and when the attendant appeared I asked him to fill it with high-test. While he was shaking out the hose, I got out and looked him over.

He was in his late twenties, wearing grease-stained army fatigues and a ball cap. His face was lean, with large teeth and freckles, and his hands moved as if they knew how to work. I strolled over to the phone booth, quickly made a note of the number, and strolled back. The attendant was soon finished.

"What's the damage?"

"Four eighty," he said.

I handed him a ten-dollar bill. "Keep the change."

He moved a quick step back from me, his expression wary. "That's a big tip for this neck of the woods, mister. No offense, but I've heard of guys tipping fancy like that to fake a guy out before they rob him."

I still had my wallet in my hand. "Look here." I showed him the corners of several twenties and fifties. "What have you got in your till, thirty bucks?"

"Just about." He smiled sheepishly, looking at the ten now as if he recognized Hamilton as an old friend. "Sorry, I wouldn't be so leery if I hadn't noticed them racing tires and that extra metal you carry."

"Just safety precautions," I said. "I'm a bum driver."

He put the ten in his pocket. "This is a big tip. What does it buy you?"

"The answers to a few questions, I hope," I said. "I might as well come clean. I work for a rival oil company, the name of which I can't disclose. They're thinking of putting in a station a few miles down the road. They've run traffic surveys, checked out local property values, future expansion, the works."

"Shell Oil, I'll bet," he said.

I gave him a wink. "You said it, I didn't. But the fact is, the report on this site is pretty negative. Not enough traffic to warrant two stations."

"I can testify to that," he said fervently.

"Exactly. Part of my job is to verify the statistical findings by asking a few questions of you men already working the area. Believe me, there's no danger of your helping the competition. Tell me, are you the owner?"

"Half owner. My cousin and I have had the franchise for three years."

"You mentioned robbery. Have you had any?"

He spat into the gravel. "The night man got hit just a year ago. We weren't insured, neither."

"That can hurt," I said. "I guess your night man's reliable and wouldn't fake a robbery. We get some of that with my company."

"Charlie?" He snorted at the suggestion. "He's my cousin, the other owner. Honest as the day is long. They had to knock him cold to get the money."

I nodded, then asked, "Do you get much trade from midnight on?"

"Just the shift change from the pottery, a few trucks. We close at two A.M."

Just then a pickup truck pulled into the station behind me, then a car drifted in from the opposite direction. I thanked the man, fairly confident that neither he nor his cousin knew anything about the blackmail. Climbing into the Mercury, I idled along for another mile until I spotted a diner. I stopped for coffee, too the number from the pay phone, and returned to town.

Quartz had prepared a surprise for me during my absence. When I entered the cottage, he was standing in the middle of the living room with a brace on his leg in place of the cast, a cane in his hand, and a sling for his arm instead of the harness he had worn for the broken collarbone.

"Jumping the gun, aren't you?" I asked.

"I leaned on the doc a little. He was grinning from back molar to back molar. "But the cast was due off Monday anyway. It was only a simple fracture. This sling is only for show. He'd got the collarbone taped."

183

"Can't you get around dragging that steel?

"A cinch." Turning smartly, he moved at a good clip into the hall and back. "Not only that, I can drive, too. Oh, I couldn't fight a clutch. But with and automatic shift and power steering, I can manage."

"So you want to tail Clayborne tonight," I said.

"Yes! They'd spot you in a minute. But no one will be looking for me. I'll wear farmer's clothes, glasses and a corncob pipe. I'll be invisible."

It was the blue fire in his eyes that decided me. "I'd like that."

"I only wish this had happened yesterday," he said. "Then I could have helped you out of that jam last night. Not that I don't trust Linda, but when the story breaks, she may feel that you duped her. Women can be very strange animals. After all, she could be charged as an accessory after the fact."

I smiled in spite of myself. "That's what she wants to be charged with."

"So it's like that, is it? Okay, buddy, it's your funeral."

I had left her at first light, in a tangle of hair and sheets, dressing in the bathroom with a heady sensation of perfect equilibrium. I let myself out of the house and drove to Pike's diner, where I ate a big breakfast and checked the morning papers to see if they had discovered Swanson's body. They hadn't. I turned to Quartz's cottage for a long, luxurious shower. By then he was awake, and I recounted the nights adventures (excepting the last one), and gave him Swanson's plunder. Now it was neatly arranged on the dining-room table."

"What's the score Constable?" I asked, walking over there.

"All ciphers," he said. "I've played the professor's tapes, and am now an authority on the Populist /Revolt, the Dred Scott decision, and the Muckrakers. I've read the girl's letters, one long Dear John in ten chapters. If you study the pictures of Madge, you get the impression that her playmates didn't know they were being photographed. "Looks like she kept a few souvenirs."

"How about Paul McIntosh's collection of souvenirs?" I said, tapping the metal box. "I'd love to know why Swanson raided him."

"Easy, he saw you visit Paul. That's all he needed to raid King and Mason."

184

"I don't convince that easy," I said. "Paul went to a lot of trouble yesterday to suggest that Eddy Bell was the killer. Not only that, he married a girl from the same graduating class as Eleanor Sheridan. He might have known Chérie. She was a very popular girl. How long has he owned the paper?"

"Twenty-five years", Quartz said without hesitation. "The Town and Gown society had a party for him in February to celebrate the anniversary. I can also tell you how he happed to marry Judy." Quartz sat down and propped his game leg on a stool. "Paul had been running the paper about two years when Judy graduated in thirty-nine. She's English, you know, and lost her family in the Blitz. With the war on in thirty-nine, she stayed on here and took a job in the college news bureau. Early in forty-one she went to work for Paul on the paper. She ran it practically single-handed while he was overseas, and a year after he came back, he married her. Nothing strange about any of it."

"Maybe not. But I won't be satisfied until Mr. McIntosh tells me that he was burglarized. I'll give him the chance right now. If he's going to help me watch our rogue's gallery tonight, I'd like to know I can trust him."

"You're a hard-nosed, suspicious man, Morgan Butler," Quartz said. "All right, but if I'm going to tail Clayborne tonight, shouldn't we make a plan?"

"Get the map."

It was really a modified version of one of the plans we had discussed the night before. Quartz was to station himself in the diner south of the Esso station, and when Clayborne received this midnight instructions, he would relay his destination to Quartz by phone. Quartz's job was to reach the site first and stake it out. Our scheming had the flavor of a military operation.

"But no heroics, Captain," Quartz said. He felt the tension of combat, too.

I went out and drove up to Paul McIntosh's office. I found him at his desk, typing on and old Underwood. He looked up and the clacking stopped. "Oh, it's you." His mouth was grim, his eyes sad. "Have a seat, Constable."

I did so. "I've come to talk about that assignment I promised you."

185

"Maybe I've changed my mind," he said. "Of course, if I'd been here when you called last night, we might have worked it out. But you didn't want to be greeted last night, did you? You just wanted to snoop."

I listened to the tone as well as the words. I said, "I can only tell you what I told Waldo Mason the other day. I'm not your burglar."

"Yes, Waldo told me on the phone this morning how you tore his place up."

"Easy, editor. Did Waldo also tell you that the same man burglarized Arthur King and Eddie Bell? Did he tell you that the guy sapped Carl Metterman last night, then tickled him with a knife to make him talk about Natalie Clayborne?"

This hit him. He had worked up a fine head of righteous wrath, and it pained him to be wrong. "No, Waldo didn't mention any of that. Who was it?"

I shrugged. "Man of mystery. Metterman said he wore a mask."

Paul produced a handkerchief and wiped his brow. "Again I had to go off half-cocked. You do inspire it in me, Mr. Butler."

"Before you waste an apology, I have one cop question to ask," I said. "Where were you around midnight last night?"

Slowly his features formed a sheepish expression. "That puts me in an embarrassing position. I was playing amateur detective. You didn't exactly whoop with glee when I gave you that dirt on Eddie Bell yesterday. So last night I decided to drive out and beard him in his lair, with the pretext that I wanted to do a feature on the Stagecoach. I had the wild idea that I might trap Bell into some kind of incriminating remark. Needless to say, I didn't."

"You were at the Stagecoach? What time?"

"I got there around eleven, and left about midnight."

"Good enough," I said. "Now back to Waldo. Why did you call him?"

"No, he called me. He placed an ad to rent his house. He's going on a sabbatical in June. He was in a foul mood."

"He was drunk last night. But I think he'll be well enough to imbibe a few beers with you tonight at the Tug and Maul."

He was quick. "So that's the assignment?"

"That's it. Believe me, it will be to Waldo's advantage to be in good hands between midnight and one tonight."

"Do you expect something to happen tonight?" Paul asked.

186

"Let's just say I'm conducting an experiment," I said, rising.

"Wait! There's no guarantee that Waldo will accept the invitation."

"Prevail upon him," I said. "Tell him you want to discuss the case with him. Mention Eleanor Sheridan's name. That should put him on his soap box. I'll check with you later to see if he's accepted."

"All right," Paul said. "I think I can swing it."

I went outside and strolled a few blocks to the drugstore. The village was tranquil beneath a blue sky and a breeze that stirred the limbs of the shade trees, sweeping the pavement with sunlight. But I was the intruder, the alien, soldier of fortune master-minding a pseudo-military operation, concealer of dead bodies in cheap cabins, exchequer of tawdry secrets pried from troubled minds. All of this was true, but none of it altered the splendid sensation of equilibrium with which I had started the day. A woman works her magic in wondrous ways. I entered the drugstore and called Linda.

"So there you are," she said in that memorable voice. "An hour ago I reached over to touch you, and you were gone. I missed you. I've just limped out of the bath. I'm bruised and sore in the most peculiar places."

"That's why I called, to compliment you on your natural resources. Didn't you say last night that you wanted to show me how resourceful you could be?"

"Beast! That's not what I meant. But who am I to quibble? Natural resources are nothing if they're not exploited. Right? That makes you an imperialist, a robber baron. For all I care, you can exploit me again tonight."

"Don't you have to work?"

"I'm supposed to, but I don't care whether I ever go back to the Stagecoach. You're responsible. Before I met you, I didn't mind exhibiting myself for the jolly Rotarians. But you've made me value myself again. Now I can't stand their smutty jokes, their oily hands. Am I making sense?"

"Yes. Maybe you should quit. Don't worry about money."

"Was that an invitation for me to become a kept woman? Mr. Butler!"

"Stop the clowning and answer me a question. Did you happen to see Paul McIntosh at the Stagecoach last night?"

187

"You mean the editor? The quaint character who wears the funny suits? Yes, he was there. He was talking to Eddie when I saw him."

"What time was that?"

"A little after eleven-thirty. I remember because I interrupted them to tell Eddie I was leaving early."

Eleven-thirty was alibi enough. Unless he was a magician, Paul couldn't have been lying on the front seat of the Mercury at a quarter of twelve.

"Don't tell me he's become a suspect," Linda said.

"No questions about the case until it's over, remember? Which reminds me, I'd love to exploit you tonight, but I can't make it. Maybe tomorrow night."

"All right, I'll go to work like a good girl. But my heart won't be in it."

My plan now called for a visit with Arthur King, but I decided to have lunch first at the Tug and Maul. As if to prove how neatly the plan was falling into place, I found King ensconced in a booth in the back room, holding an intense conversation with, of all people, Betty Childress. They hadn't seen me, so I chose a booth behind a rough-hewn beam and watched them. I wondered if she was unloading all her suspicions about Waldo.

Presently Betty got up and left. I went over to King's booth. He was scraping a label from a beer bottle, watching it as if it were a crystal ball.

"Can I buy you another beer?" I asked.

He snapped out of the trance. "Why not? Have a seat, Constable."

I ordered two beers. "How's the sleuthing coming along?"

"Not bad," he said warily. "At least I haven't given up yet."

"Did Betty have anything to contribute? Besides the fact that she and Waldo had a lover's spat?"

He fielded that one neatly. "Is that why you came over? To pump me?"

"As a matter of fact, I came to ask a favor. Do you own a suit and tie?"

"I might. What's the favor?"

"I'd like for you to go out to the Stagecoach Inn tonight and keep an eye on Eddie Bell for an hour or so."

188

"Why should I? Do you expect some kind of trouble tonight?"

"I'd just like to know if Bell slips out on any errands, say between eleven-thirty and one. You shouldn't mind. Isn't Bell one of your suspects?"

"That was last Monday. Eddie Bell's not your man."

"What makes you so sure?"

King said harshly, "Bell doesn't qualify. The man who killed Natalie was her lover. Tell me, have you learned that her mother was a strumpet?"

It seemed an odd word for him to use. "Yes, did Natalie tell you that?"

"It's something I figured out," he said.

"From the poetry she gave you?"

He raised his beer glass in a mock toast and drank. "Who's watching Waldo for you tonight?" he asked abruptly.

"Who says he needs watching?"

"Don't try to snow me. Did you know that Waldo hasn't worked on his slavery book since the murder? Someone broke into his house, or so he claims, and threw his notes all over his study. He hasn't even picked them up."

"What does that prove?"

"It worries Betty Childress. That book on slavery is Waldo's passion. Isn't it possible that he tore up his own room in a fit of rage or madness?"

"Anything's possible," I said. "Let's get back to this favor I asked for. Even a poet ought to go watch the Babbitts at play once in a while."

"I'm not sure I can afford it," he said. "My G.I. check is over-due."

I slipped a twenty under his beer. "For expenses. Take your own bottle and pay corkage. The lady at the door is named Linda Thorpe. Tell her I sent you."

He watched me for a minute. "All right, what the hell. That party I was going to hit on campus sounded dull, anyway. Will I see you out there?"

"I may drop in. After all, someone has to cover Waldo."

He left, and I ordered lunch. My mood was one of detachment. I was like the battalion commander who has deployed his forces, marked every position on the acetate overlay with a grease pencil,

189

and now sits beneath the map waiting. There was work that I could do. I could visit Madge Bell and ask is she had sent the killer after me last night. There was the germ of suspicion about Philip Clayborne that had taken root with the news that he wasn't Natalie's father. But the hunt was suspended for today. The blackmailer had scheduled the action for tonight, and it seemed wise not to spook him.

After lunch, I drove out to the Cavendish Hotel and explained the plan to Philip Clayborne. He was jumpy and irritable, no doubt because he couldn't get in touch with Swanson, but I ignored that. I gave him two numbers to call in case of emergency. On the way out of the Cavendish, I stopped in the lobby and called Paul McIntosh. His date with Waldo was set for eleven-thirty.

Then I drove down to the cottage, where Quartz and I discussed the setup from every possible angle. We ate a light meal, and I relieved Ferby for dinner.

At ten-thirty that night Quartz slipped out of town in an unmarked car. The costume he wore was a good disguise if you weren't looking for him – a worn felt hat, overalls, steel-rimmed glasses and a corncob pipe. At eleven-fifteen I was parked across the highway from the Cavendish Hotel when Clayborne left to keep his rendezvous. Then I drove into town and parked across the street from the Tug and Maul. Paul and Waldo showed up at twelve and entered the café. I started the Mercury, eased through town, and drove south to the Stagecoach Inn.

Linda was sitting behind her desk in the small reception room. In the smoky pastel light floating in the glass panels around her she looked artificial for an instant. When she saw me, she came from behind the desk quickly.

"You told me you had to work tonight," she said. She gave one covert look over her shoulder, then shamelessly raised her face for a kiss.

"I am working. I can stay for a short while."

"Hmm. So mysterious. Your young man arrived, if that's who you're checking on. Very intense, and very scornful of our little playhouse."

"He's a poet," I said. "Scorn is his stock in traded. Is Eddie around?"

"In the card room. There's a poker game on tonight, and Eddie's playing for the house. Our regular tinhorn gambler is sick."

"How long will the game last?"

"They're usually good until two A.M. Oh, Madge is here. So watch out."

I had told Linda last night about Madge's crude invitation. At first it had angered her, but later she said it fitted the frantic, vengeful behavior Madge displayed when she and Eddie were engaged in their annual domestic battle. Apparently it was almost a family rite. The previous year Mage had packed up and gone to Chicago, only to return after a week, contrite and weary. Eddie had taken her back without a word of recrimination. Considering their past, I wasn't surprised, although I hadn't revealed their fleshpot history to Linda.

"I'll be on my guard" I said. "I'll see you later."

Entering the main room of the club was like walking into a movie set of an elegant Western saloon. In one corner, a man in cowboy garb played honkytonk piano. Red drapes and mirrors lined the walls, and waitresses minced around in scanty dancehall costumes. The bar was genuine mahogany, and above it hung antlers, powder horns, and a painting of George Armstrong Custer giving his all at the Little Big Horn. The place was about half full. I saw Madge Bell at a table with three middle-aged men who were snickering at some sally she'd uttered. I drifted past the card room, where Eddie was one of seven men around a table studiously engaged with their cards. He wore a green eyeshade, a white bandana, and a cowboy shirt with stars over the pockets. Across from this doorway Arthur King sat alone at a table, a bored expression on his face. I went to the bar, ordered a beer, and looked at my watch. It was just midnight. Suddenly Arthur King was at my elbow.

"Butler, this is the most surrealistic scene I've made since I worked in the open hearth. Are you relieving me?"

"No, you're on duty until one-thirty. Now scram. You shouldn't know me."

"All right. But I may have to drink that fifth I brought in self-defense."

He left, and a minute later the phone behind the bar rang. I had stationed myself near it, and when the bartender began scanning the customers, I raised my hand. He placed the phone in front of me. It was Quartz.

"Morgan? It's the Greyhound bus station in Brandywine."

"Be sure you get there first," I said.

"I'm on my way." He hung up.

I sat there for fifteen minutes. A few more customers arrived. Eddie Bell kept playing poker. Madge circulated. At twenty after twelve I went back through the reception room and out to the parking lot. Linda was greeting several members when I passed her, but we managed a nod.

I put the Mercury through its paces on the way back to Jordan City, and at twelve-thirty-five I parked in front of the Tug and Maul. The bar in front was lively with students, and I lingered near the doorway to the back room only long enough to see that Paul and Waldo were there. I took a small table practically under the pay phone near the bar and sat there with another beer.

Then, for no accountable reason, I was stricken with a sensation of futility. I don't mean that I merely had doubts about the surveillance I had set up. This was an upheaval, a spasm of the ego, what the Old Fox in San Diego used to call a form of "psychic epilepsy." My mind was feverish and my bones like wax. In the grip of this convulsion, I had a hallucination so vivid it seemed absolutely true. This was no dry run. The killer was going to make his collection tonight, and he would do it without detection.

It couldn't have lasted more than a minute or two. I came out of it to the sound of laughter from a pretty girl at the bar. My throat was dry and I had an iron grip on my beer bottle. I wondered cynically if I had ignored a number of relevant cues and impressions which the dark side of my mind had absorbed and arranged into a significant message.

Whatever had inspired the seizure, when the phone rang at twelve-fifty and Quartz told me he had lost Clayborne, I felt neither surprise nor annoyance.

"How did it happen?" I asked.

"I was waiting when he came into the bus station. First, he went to a locker and opened it with a key he had in his pocket. He took out an envelope, read the message, and bought a ticket for Pittsburgh on the twelve-forty-five. I waited a while before I bought a ticket, and waited until they announced the bus before I went out to the platform. Clayborne was first in line. He took a seat near the driver, and I sat in back. Just as the driver started to close the door,

192

Clayborne jumped up and got off. The bus was moving before I got the driver's attention. I had to fight this bad leg getting off. Clayborne was gone."

"All right. Come on home."

I stayed put until one-thirty. Paul and Waldo were still in the back room. I called Arthur Kind. He said Eddie hadn't budged from the poker table.

"You can call it a night," I said. "And I appreciate the help."

"That's all right, Constable. Actually, you did me a big favor tonight."

"What's that supposed to mean?"

"It means I am ninety-eight percent certain that I know the killer. Remember those numbers you recited to me on Monday?" He gave a wild laugh. "Tonight, with the help of Jack Daniels, I matched them to one of Natalie's poems."

"You'd better tell me about it," I said.

"Oh, no! First I have to be absolutely certain. I may even produce that tape everybody seems to want so badly."

"Listen, Arthur! You're a little drunk. You don't realize the danger. Remember the story I told you about the reporter in San Francisco?"

"Don't worry. I don't have to go near the killer to convict him." He hung up.

The fool! I was tempted to try to intercept him, but my first concern was Philip Clayborne. I could only hope that either King was wrong, or he knew what he was doing. But the exuberance in his voice echoed in my mind as I drove to the Cavendish Hotel and took up residence in the deserted lobby.

I didn't have long to wait. At two o'clock Philip Clayborne entered. I joined him in the elevator, and as soon as it started I asked the question.

His face was sharp with tension. "I delivered the money," he said. "But now they want something else. They ordered me to get you off the case."

When we reached Clayborne's room I said, "Let's talk about it."

He peeled off his jacket and flung it aside enroute to the whisky bottle on the desk. The first shot he put down neat, then he fixed a second drink with soda and turned to me. His expression was as chiseled as the faces on Mount Rushmore. "There's nothing to talk

193

about. You're off the case. Of course you'll keep the check. You've earned it."

I let that pass for the moment. "How did they tell you to fire me?"

"Read the two letters in my coat, the short one first."

I took the letters from the side pocket of his coat and read the short one:

Philip Clayborne:
The enclosed key fits locker 30 in the Greyhound bus depot in Brandywine. There you will find further instructions. To reach Brandywine, drive south for five miles to a traffic circle. Take the first right turn off the circle, and drive eleven miles west. The bus depot is on your right just after you enter town. Park in the lot beside the depot, and open the locker. Carry the money with you at all times. Remember, you are being watched.

IMPORTANT: I know you have hired Morgan Butler to track me down. Get him off the case immediately, or the tape will be publicized in spite of the money you pay.

"Did you have the gas-station attendant make the call to Quartz?" I asked.

"Yes, I slipped him a note and ten dollars when I paid for my gas."

"Did you ask him how the instructions were delivered?"

Clayborne nodded. "He found an envelope under his door when he opened this morning at seven, along with twenty dollars and instructions to deliver it to me."

I read the second letter:

Philip Clayborne:
Go to the ticket window and buy a ticket on the 12:45 bus to Pittsburg. Then go to the platform and wait in line. Get a seat as far forward in the bus as possible. Wait until the driver has loaded all passengers and starts to close the door. Then get off the bus, move as fast as you can to your car, and drive west out of Brandywine. Go ten miles at the speed limit, and you will see a roadside park on the right. Park there. The time should be 1:00 A.M.

Get out with the money, walk up the path to your right, fifty yards uphill to a stone fireplace on a knoll. Slip the money into the fireplace, return to your car and drive back to Jordan City by the same route you used to reach this destination.

NOTE: If there are any cars at the park when you arrive, do not deliver the money tonight. You will be observed at the bus depot and at the park.

"Pretty slick," I said. "Our man didn't have to meet you to get the money. He could pick it up any time before dawn. So my surveillance was a waste of time."

"No, he was there," Clayborne said. "There's a wooden toilet on that knoll, back in a grove of trees. I saw it when a car passed while I was at the fireplace. He closed the door as the light flashed over it."

"Maybe it was the wind," I said.

"There wasn't any wind." Scorn put a rasp in his voice. "Let's face it, Butler. You don't have the remotest idea who this blackmailer is. Hell, you should be glad I'm taking you off the case. None of us likes to fail."

"I don't fire that easy, Mr. Clayborne," I said. "You seem to forget that I was on this case before you started throwing money around."

His smile didn't contain an ounce of humor. "My dear fellow, with one phone call I can have you taken off this case in a very painful way."

"For a job like that, I'll bet you plan to call Swanson. He's still in the neighborhood, isn't he?"

He shifted his weight but not his expression. "Why do you say that?"

"Hell, he's been following me around all week, busting up furniture looking for that tape. It wasn't very bright of you to send a boy like him on a man's errand. Suppose he blunders into the killer. Have you heard from him lately?"

"God damn you," he said. "You know a lot more than you're saying."

Now it was my turn to get tough. "So do you, friend. And look how tolerant I've been with your lies and evasions. Up until now."

"How can you say that? After I all but bared my soul to you yesterday."

195

"Yes, that was quite a tale. It impressed me. But I'm a skeptical man, Clayborne. Later I began to wonder if that tale wasn't meant to impress me."

"You fool! Would I invent a story like that just to impress you?"

"You might." I got ready to move quickly. "If you killed Natalie."

He took a wild step toward me, and some of the whiskey in his glass shot out in an amber arc. I was up, feeling nimble and loose. But he gained control of himself. He put the glass down on the desk and wiped his hand. "You are a fool." His voice was strained through the dregs of his rage. "My own daughter."

"Even that's open to question," I said. "Natalie had good reason to believe she wasn't your daughter."

He gave me a sharp look. "That's more nonsense. How can you accuse me, the man who hired you to find her killer? Does that make sense?"

"Sit down, Mr. Clayborne, and I'll tell you why it makes sense. You'll either have to throw me out or hear me out. It's that simple."

"My God, you're serious." He took a deep breath and exhaled slowly. "All right, I'll listen. If only to learn how big a fool you really are." He sprawled in a chair beside the desk, his very posture conveying contempt.

I lit a stogie with great deliberation. I didn't have complete faith in what I was about to do, but it had to be done. I said, "The most puzzling thing about this case from the beginning was the motive for Natalie's murder. Even if she had had a change of heart after she gave the blackmailer the tape, he didn't have to kill her to silence her. She wouldn't have told the police – or you either – because of her own part in the conspiracy."

Clayborne straightened a little. "But you said yesterday you thought she might have learned about a third person in on the blackmail."

"That theory gives us a motive," I said. "But it leaves one important question unanswered. If the discovery of a third person meant that she had to die, why didn't Natalie fear for her life? I talked with her Friday night, and she didn't expect to be murdered. We'll set that aside for now. There were two other things that puzzled me from the start. I didn't know why you were being blackmailed, and I couldn't justify Natalie's part in it."

196

Either I had snared Clayborne's interest, or he was a good actor. "But the story I told you yesterday answered those questions," he said.

"Oh, it satisfied the blackmail question. But the way you told it, Natalie wasn't alienated enough for my taste. What really made the story work for me was when I learned last night that Natalie was convinced you weren't her father. She wasn't a fanciful girl. She must have had some evidence to support that."

"I told you that was nonsense!" Clayborne said.

"Hear me out. Let's suppose for the sake of argument that you aren't her father. Suddenly most of the pieces in this case come into focus. I know for a fact that Natalie was looking for her real father here at Jordan, among her mother's old lovers. Suppose she found him. That's the bond I need to justify her part in the conspiracy. Your romance with the Yale boy would make you fair game in their eyes. Now remember that letter you sent you about the tape? Suppose you got it on schedule. You might have seen through her little scheme right away. You might have come out here on the Q.T. to find out who she was mixed up with. You could have stopped by her dorm on Saturday night to force her to reveal his name. Her crime against you might have been forgiven if she were your daughter. But if she were another man's child, you might have killed her."

Clayborne had paled, and his mouth looked crumpled. "I told you I was in Florida when my daughter was killed. I can prove it with witnesses."

"Mr. Clayborne, a man in your position can buy anything. Let me tell you something else that fits. Our killer has had all week to get rid of me. Why did he wait until last night to try it, a few hours after you hit town?"

"I didn't know an attempt had been made on your life," he said.

"Two shots at close range. Where's your gun?"

"What gun?"

"The one you wanted to take along on your payoff tonight."

"Oh, I'd forgotten. It's in my suitcase in the bedroom."

"Let's go get it."

He got up slowly and staged into the first step. He was too subdued for my taste. It was either an act or he was mush inside, and mush didn't fit his character. But he led me into the bedroom and

197

stood there while I opened the suitcase. The gun was a flat pearl-handled derringer with two barrels, a woman's bedroom gun. It was the only gun I could find. Back in the living room, Clayborne sagged into his chair. Just to be doing something, I took the two rounds out of the derringer, peered down the barrel, then reloaded it.

"This isn't the gun," I said, slipping it into my pocket.

Clayborne had nothing to say. His face looked bloated with emotion.

"What's the matter with you?" I asked.

He spoke with effort, "Yesterday I said that no one was harmed by what happened that summer. I was wrong. Natalie died because of it. Oh, I didn't kill her, but look at me. All your life you operate from strength, then you succumb to one temptation, and that deed is what you are judged for."

"Oh, stop feeling sorry for yourself," I said. "You make me sick."

He snapped upright, breathing hard. "What happened to Swanson?" he asked.

I felt reckless, unsettled by his histrionics. "He's dead. He stopped those slugs last night that were meant for me."

Clayborne shook his head. "I didn't see anything in the papers about it."

"No, I stripped him of his identification and put him in his motel room back across the county line. I wanted to keep you out of it."

"You mean you didn't report it? Isn't that against the law?"

"Yeah, now you've got something on me."

"I didn't mean it that way," he said. "You stuck your neck out for me. Thanks." Then his voice rose an octave. "God, that's two who have died."

"If it'll make you feel any better, Swanson planned to hold you up for the tape when he found it. So don't mourn him too deeply."

Suddenly Clayborne emitted a brutal, self-deprecating laugh. "Jesus. First my loving daughter. Then my trusted bodyguard. Not to mention my sluttish first wife. What was it you called me yesterday, a victim? You were kind. I'm more like a dupe, a chump, and easy mark. Let's drink to that, Butler."

This self-castigation struck me as a healthier sign than the despair he had begun to wallow in. He poured the drinks with a certain zest, gave the brutal laugh again, and sat down beside me on the couch.

198

"I'm in no mood to trust anyone," he said. "Why do I trust you, Butler?"

"Maybe it's because I accuse you of murder."

"Do you still believe it? Come on, no equivocating."

"Let's say I have my doubts. But you stay on my list."

"Fair enough. Does that mean you'll go on working for me? I mean it. To hell with their threat. I want to get this man."

"That threat in the note was bluff", I said. "They wouldn't give away the tape just to punish you for not firing me. That tape is probably worth half million dollars to them. They can get rid of me a lot cheaper than that."

He digested this. "You knew that a while ago, when you refused to quit. You make me feel like a louse, Butler."

"Don't start that again," I said, rising.

"Wait, I want to give you more money, "he said. "We'll call it hazardous-duty pay. Say five thousand."

"No, thanks. If I recover that tape, and all goes well, I'll hold you to that original bonus you offered." I bade him goodnight.

Chapter 16
***

It wasn't until I had gone down in the elevator and out to the parking lot that I found Clayborne's derringer still in my pocket. I turned to go back, then decided against it. It was already three A.M., and throughout my conversation with Clayborne ganglia of anxiety about Arthur King had crawled my spine like hairy spiders. I wouldn't sleep until I had seen him.

King's apartment was dark when I reached it, and the garage where he parked over the old grease pit was empty. I told myself that he could be snuggled on a couch with Nancy Brewer in the parlor of her dorm. But I got out of the Mercury, took a short crowbar from the trunk, and mounted the stairs. I sprung the lock on the second try, stepped inside, and bolted the door. Whether or not King's hunch tonight had been accurate, whether or not he had run into trouble, I wanted to find the poem of Natalie's that had identified the killer for him. King had cleaned up the mess Swanson had made, restoring the big room to its Spartan bleakness.

Naturally I went first to his laundry bag, but all it contained was dirty clothes. He had changed his hiding place. I spent twenty minutes going through his desk, including a box full of King's own poetry, suspecting the old purloined-letter trick. I didn't relish the idea of leafing through all the books on his shelves, but as I looked them over I saw a volume that made me suspect I wouldn't have to. It was a tall, slender book bound in faded maroon leather, another copy of the Jordan College yearbook for the class of thirty-nine. Plucking it off the shelf, I thumbed pages until I found the envelope, used as a bookmark on the page that showed the snapshot of Eleanor Sheridan and Waldo Mason as Beauty and the Brain. The poem was in the envelope. The postmark showed that Natalie had mailed it to King last Saturday, not many hours before she died. He had probably received it on Monday. Why hadn't the jerk shown me the poem?

I sat down at King's desk and examined the poem carefully. It was neatly typed, with the date 2/10/62 at the top and Natalie's name at the bottom. This was a carbon, so no doubt the original had been given to the hero of the poem.

CORONATION

At certain times you stand like Vulcan at the hearth,
Though steel be not your broth; you stir man's fate and luck,
The lies he tells about himself from birth to death,
The masks he wears, to wed, to vote, to make a buck.

And from this mawkish stew you forge still other tales,
The pap man swills with zest, as Britons swill their tea,
So you are chained, Prometheus-like, a slave for sale,
And I, with gift as frail as love, can set you free.
For you are fit to bed the wives of ruthless kings,

And I shall reign with love where once a strumpet spoiled.
Let tyrants fall. We'll applaud while angels sing.
If there be justice, let it be poetic, royal.

It was hardly the sort of poem a girl would write to her daddy. After reading it through twice, I could sympathize with King's conclusion that Vulcan was Waldo, forging history from his research. But one line baffled me completely: "For you are fit to bed the wives of ruthless kings." The plural didn't make sense.

I copied the poem quickly on a sheet of paper filched from King's desk, returned the typed version to the yearbook, and replaced the book on the shelf. Then I shut the place up and went in search of Arthur King.

Forty minutes later I was satisfied that he wasn't at any of the all-night lunchrooms in town, and that his car wasn't parked at any of the lateral parking slots on campus, including the ones adjacent to Nancy Brewer's dorm. Now I was worried. I drove straight to Waldo Mason's house, and this time I wheeled into his driveway with the beams on, stopping about twenty feet from his garage. His car wasn't there. I got out and pounded on the door, but no one stirred. Where would Waldo be at a quarter of five in the morning?

One window on the porch had a screen in it that slid out with only a little effort. I raised the window with my shoulder, stepped inside, and turned on the overhead light. I prowled the house. His kitchen stank of spoiled meat and home brew. His bed looked as if it hadn't been made in a month. Then I entered his study. The floor was littered with shoeboxes, reams of five-by-seven file cards, and yellow manuscript pages.

Back in the living room I found a college phone directory and dialed Nancy Brewer's dorm. The phone rang at least twenty times before someone answered.

"Please call Nancy Brewer to the phone. It's very important."

The phone was banged down and there was a clatter down the hall.

Presently a breathy voice said, "Hello? This is Nancy Brewer."

"Nancy, this is Constable Butler. Remember me?"

"Yes, I remember. Why did you call? What's the matter?"

I played it cheerful. "Nothing that I know of. I wanted to have a chat with Arthur King and thought he might be with you. I realize it's almost five A.M. and I apologize for the hour. But something came up I thought Arthur should know about."

"You're lying! He's in trouble, isn't he?"

"Why do you say that?"

"Well, someone broke into his apartment the other day, and he's convinced it was Natalie's murderer. He has a theory about who it is. Then tonight he broke a date to go on some mysterious errand."

"I wouldn't worry about it," I said. "He's probably at home right now. That wreck he drives around might have broken down on him. Goodnight."

I broke the connection and went out to the Mercury, trying to orient myself so that I could drive to King's place over the back roads in spite of my scanty knowledge of local geography. I made one wrong turn that took me to a barrier guarding the entrance to the state park, but I reached King's place at the first hint of dawn.

King's car still wasn't in the garage, but his light was on and I knew I had turned it off. Snaking my Luger from under my arm, I went up the stairs and waited for a moment with my ear against the doorframe. Nothing moved inside, so I kicked the door open and entered. The place was empty, but it had been ransacked. Papers from King's desk were strewn around, and even the vegetable bin from his refrigerator had been dumped. The maroon yearbook was open on the floor, and the poem was gone.

It made me want to kick myself down the stairs for my blunder. I should have known that he would have to find whatever had led King to him. If I had waited here instead of giving him an hour to search, I could have welcomed him when he came calling. But I had refused to believe King was that clever.

I wasn't nearly so eager to find King now, but that was the next item on the agenda. Turning off the light, I went down the stairs, climbed into the Mercury, and started my turn through the gravel. I stopped when my headlights revealed the glossy black shoe just at the entrance to King's garage, as out of place there as a pearl in a bucket of coal. Then I detected the two furrows in the gravel that ended where the shoe sat. So I took my flashlight from the glove compartment and got out, walking past the shoe and into the garage, and flashed my light down into the old grease pit.

Arthur King was lying in the filth of the pit on his back, his eyes and teeth reflecting light. He was fully dressed except for his right shoe, even to his tie. His eyes seemed to gaze at me with reproach. I didn't want to go down there, but I saw something that made it necessary, a book jammed under his belt in front.

I went to the end of the pit and descended the steps, hunkering down on the bottom step to tug the book from under King's belt. It was slender volume, a copy of Shakespeare's *Hamlet.* I knew that story. The big murder in that one was Hamlet's father, the king, and I felt a chill at the association.

Gripping the flashlight under my arm, I used both hands to riffle the pages of the book. None were folded or marked. The flyleaf bot Arthur King's name, so obviously the killer had grabbed it from King's library during his search for the poem. I tucked the book back into King's belt, closed his eyes gently, and turned him enough to see that the back of his head had been bashed in.

I climbed out of the pit and lit a stogie in the pale light, punishing my lungs with the bitter smoke. As I turned the Mercury onto the macadam, I wondered why the killer had dumped King and kept his station wagon. Only one answer made sense. The killer was working alone and had no one to haul him home. But he would have to ditch the wagon somewhere.

The sky in the east was flushed with pink when I parked in front of Quartz's cottage. I found him asleep in an armchair, his game leg braced on a footstool. Only then did I remember that he was to wait up for a debriefing after my talk with Clayborne. I shook him gently. He opened his eyes, smiled.

"Hi, Morgan. I must have dozed off. I was bushed after that trip." Then he noticed the light at the windows. "Hey, it's morning. Where've you been?"

"There's been another murder," I said.

He cursed once sharply. "Clayborne?"

I shook my head. "Arthur King." Then I told him the full story, from my last conversation with King to how I found the body in the pit.

"I'll better call Jack Casey," Quartz's said. His voice was sour, dejected.

"Let me call Clayborne first," I said. "He'd better know about this." I dialed the Hotel Cavendish. Clayborne answered in a sluggish voice.

"This is Butler. You'd better wake up. I've got bad news."

He muttered something, then put the phone down and, from the sounds, went to the bathroom and doused his face. I heard his return. "Now, let's have it."

I told him about the murder and warned him that there was a chance that he would be questioned about it. "Unless you want the blackmail business exposed, we'd better get our stories straight, "I said. "Let's say you were never satisfied that the janitor killed Natalie, and you came back to talk with me about it. That would explain my visits to the hotel."

"Agreed," Clayborne said. "But don't hang up. I've got questions. Why—?"

"Not now. I've got to go welcome the sheriff." I hung up.

Quartz limped out of the kitchen, rubbing his face with a towel. "I've got last night's coffee heating," he said, taking the phone.

While he called Casey, I got out cups, listened for the hiss of the pot, and poured the coffee. Quartz was replacing the receiver as I entered the room.

"The news didn't set well with Jack," Quartz said.

We drank our coffee, and on the way out to King's apartment I filled Quartz in on Clayborne's story of the blackmail payoff. Then I gave him Natalie's poem.

It seemed to depress him. "I suppose it could be addressed to Waldo," he said. "But it's all gobbledygook to me."

204

When we reached King's apartment, I parked well off the gravel and we stood at the edge of the pit for a while. "Why would the killer bring him here, rather than ditch him in the woods someplace?" Quartz asked.

"That's easy. He had to search King's apartment, and he had to get the body away from the scene of the crime. Since he couldn't know how long the search might take, he solved both problems at once. Anyway, if you consider the copy of *Hamlet*, he wanted us to find the body right away."

"That's a cold-blooded touch," Quartz said. "I saw the movie they made of that play. The king is killed, and now King is killed. It makes you wonder if the killer left that first book, too."

"That's what he wants us to think," I said.

"She mentioned some king in that poem you showed me," Quartz said. "I don't suppose there's any connection there. No, the killer's not that crazy. If he's the man she wrote the poem to, he wouldn't leave a clue referring to it."

He uttered the words listlessly, merely thinking aloud, as we passed from the gloomy garage back into the sunlight. But the words electrified me. I snatched the poem from my pocket and read it again. My expression must have looked peculiar to Quartz. He said something to me.

"Not now!" I crossed the gravel to the wooden steps, sat down, and lit a stogie. Yes, the key to the whole case had been handed to me in different forms during the week, but each time I had rejected it because of the stench it gave off. Apparently I still lugged around a dog-eared morality that caused me to recoil each time the idea tapped at my consciousness. It had taken another murder – along with that copy of *Hamlet* – to shock me out of my ignorance. Oh, the killer had selected *Hamlet* as a prop contrived to dupe and confuse, but the logic of his madness had also guided his choice.

Now I knew why Natalie Clayborne had to die. I didn't know the killer's name yet, but I was very close to it. I was halfway to the Mercury when Quartz grabbed my arm.

"Morgan, where are you going? What the hell's the matter with you?"

"I've got to see Waldo Mason."

"That can wait. You have to be here to tell your story to Casey."

"You tell it. Or stall him. Quartz, I can crack this case now, today. But I've got to see Waldo immediately, if he's still alive."

"My God, do you think he's dead?"

"If he's not, he could be our man," I said. "But I have to find out now. Tell Casey I'll be right back. I'll fill you in later." We were both frozen in place by the distant sound of a siren.

But I got into the Mercury and drove off in the opposite direction from town, taking the route to Mason's house that I had figured out earlier that morning. This time I made no mistakes, and I parked around the bend from the house not ten minutes after leaving Quartz. I climbed a wooden fence and approached the house from the rear. Just as I reached the back porch I heard a car on the road. I stayed out of sight as the car lurched into the driveway and stalled there. I heard the starter grind a few times, then the slam of the car door and footsteps on the front porch. I trotted around the house and braced Waldo just as he got the door unlocked.

I didn't use my gun. I merely seized him high on the muscle of his right arm, jerked him off balance, and turned him while I frisked him for weapons. What I had thought was a gun in his coat pocket turned out to be a flat pint whiskey bottle with a few ounces left in it. One whiff of his breath told me where the rest of the pint had gone.

"Get your hands off me!" he said in a hoarse voice. His beard was matted on one side, and his suit had sweat stains under the arms.

I released my grip and he would have fallen if the wall hadn't been there to support him. His sluggishness suited my purpose.

"Where's Eleanor Sheridan, Waldo?" I said. "You might as well tell me. I know she's in Jordan City, or nearby, and I know she's implicated in her daughter's murder. I know you've been seeing her. In fact, you were with her last night, weren't you?"

His face clenched and opened like a fist. He wet his lips and sighed deeply. "She didn't show up. She was supposed to meet me at three this morning, but she never came. I only hope she's all right. She's never failed to show up before." Then his eyes focused on me with a tormented expression. "It could mean that the killer has found her at last."

"Let's get inside, where we can talk," I said.

Waldo was shaky on the way into the house, but once he was ensconced in his favorite easychair, his spine seemed to stiffen. "I was tempted to tell you about Eleanor the other night," he said. "I've

206

been distressed ever since that janitor was indicted for a crime I know he didn't commit. But I was afraid you'd expose Eleanor's hiding place to the murderer. You see, she's the one he really wants to kill." He gave me a moment to digest this, then he asked sharply, "How did you know she was here?"

"From something Natalie told me, a message I didn't unravel until this morning." I was cagey because what he had told me so far didn't fit the picture I had been building. But my explanation seemed to relieve Waldo.

He said, "Before I tell you about her, you have to swear to leave her alone until you've worked out a plan to protect her from this maniac."

"She'll have all the protection she needs," I said. "Now tell it, Waldo."

"All right." He settled back into his chair. "It began early last fall, when she called me on the phone one night out of the blue. You can imagine how it affected me, not having seen her for over twenty years. She sounded so old and frail, I didn't believe it was her at first. But she soon explained that. You might as well know this now, Butler. She's a very sick woman, almost an invalid. She's got some kind of respiratory ailment. She's aged and wasted."

"Is she under treatment?" I felt like an actor reciting lines.

"She takes medication, but apparently there's nothing much they can do. Anyway, she told me that she came to Jordan City to spend some time with her daughter while she had the strength."

"Where is she living, Waldo?"

"She never told me. I think it's someplace in Spencer's Falls, because we used to meet over thee. The fact that she wouldn't even tell me where she was living gives you an idea of how terrified she is of her husband."

"You don't mean Philip Clayborne?"

"Hell no! This is the man she married years after she divorced Clayborne. She didn't know much about him when she married him, and he turned out to be a racketeer, a dope peddler. When Eleanor found out, she tried to leave him, but he caught her and gave her a terrible beating. The man's psychotic. So she bided her time and later turned him into the federal narcotics agents. He got three years, but he swore to kill her when he got out. She did her best to hide from him. She went to New York, changed her name, and got a job.

207

She even met an older man with money who wanted to marry her. Then she got sick, and while she was in the hospital, she learned that her husband had traced her to New York. Her wealthy boyfriend managed to get her out of the city. She spent part of the year in Florida, then came out here. She was certain she'd covered her tracks, but this maniac knew about Natalie. He called her a few weeks ago, pretending he was a friend of Eleanor's and asked Natalie for her address. Of course Eleanor had warned her never to tell anyone, but Natalie was fooled enough to let it slip that she had seen Eleanor."

"How did you learn about this phone call?" I asked.

He looked annoyed that I had interrupted him. "Eleanor told me last Sunday. Natalie had told her about the call. But how was Eleanor to know that this psychotic would come here and kill Natalie while trying to make her reveal her mother's whereabouts? It practically destroyed Eleanor. She felt responsible."

"But she still asked you not to reveal her presence to the police," I said.

"I told you she was deathly afraid of this man," he said.

"What's this character's name?" I asked.

"Frank Nogay. Duke is his nickname."

I almost laughed in his face. It read like the latest TV melodrama, the story of a once lovely girl whose life is shattered by this kill-crazy ex-con "Duke" Nogay, starring Joan Crawford and Richard Widmark.

"Waldo, if Eleanor came here to hide out and to be near Natalie, why did she get in touch with you at all? Did she ask you for money?"

Waldo shook his head. "The man in New York sends her money. No, she wanted to ask my forgiveness for what she destroyed between us years ago. I didn't tell you the other night exactly what she did to end our romance."

"Let me guess," I said. "She gave you a painting of herself as a whore."

His head jerked, but he wasn't even curious about how I had learned this. "Yes, it was a cruel act, a violent act. Now she knows that she did it like that because she was prostituting herself for the money, choosing the Harvard boy because of his million bucks.

Would you believe that I saved that painting for years? My second wife burned it. She knew it still meant something to me."

At that moment I felt that my position with Waldo was like that of a surgeon performing a delicate operation. "Tell me about your meetings with Eleanor," I said. "How did you get in touch with her?"

"I didn't. She called me when she felt well enough to have a meeting. We usually met in the Emporium in Spencer's Falls. That's the movie. It's a converted opera house, and they still have the old boxes along the side that you can reserve. You can talk there without disturbing anyone, and those boxes are very dark. She's terribly self-conscious about her appearance with me. She always wears dark glasses and a coat with a high collar. Remember, I knew her when she was young and beautiful."

"Do you mean that you never got a look at her face?"

"Oh, I saw her. One warm night she took her coat off, and they turned the house lights on at the end of the feature just as I turned to speak to her. It gave me a shock. She's badly wrinkled around the eyes and mouth, and she has an ugly scar on her face from the time her husband beat her."

"Let's get back to last night. Did she ask you to meet her at the movie?"

"No, last night's meeting was scheduled for three A.M., too late for the Emporium. We were supposed to meet at one of the picnic shelters in the state park. We met there once before. The park is closed at night, but there's a place where you can drive around one of the gates."

"When did she make the date?" I asked.

"Yesterday. She knew I would be upset about the janitor's indictment, and she wanted me to help her plan a way to prove his innocence."

"But without implicating her," I said.

"You're absolutely wrong! She said that if there was no other way, she would go to the police herself. We were going to talk about it last night."

"But she didn't show up."

"No. The longer I waited the more worried I got. And the more I nipped on my bottle. I fell asleep. It's been a rough week for me, Butler, keeping a secret like this. Trying to weigh her trust in me

209

against the necessity of bringing this murderer to justice. When you said you weren't the one who broke into my house, I decided it was Nogay, that he had connected with Eleanor somehow."

"When you had her on the phone yesterday, did you ask her about the blackmail business I mentioned the other night?" I asked.

"Yes! It was a shock to Eleanor, just as it was to me. She said that it could only be true if Natalie bribed the killer with that material, to make him leave Eleanor alone."

I considered this as a possibility for about ten seconds. It didn't fit the facts. But how to persuade Waldo that his fallen angel was really a witch, when I couldn't explain to myself why she would go to such lengths to dupe him? Oh, I could imagine the two of them together. Waldo paying court to this frail, broken creature, captivated by the drama and intrigue, while she unfolded her take of sin and suffering, a story of riches to rags, in the atmosphere of perpetual illusions, and American movie theatre. Yes, I could justify Waldo's participation, but not Eleanor's. Not that I minded an image of Eleanor as a woman grown prematurely old and embittered. But I rejected the portrait of an Eleanor frail and contrite. Unless I was totally wrong, she had cold-bloodedly masterminded the scheme to blackmail Philip Clayborne.

I studied him for a moment. I didn't believe it was possible to shock him out of this delusion that seemed to have doped all his senses, but I decided to try by telling him about Arthur King's murder. Before I could begin, I heard the distinct sound of a footstep on the front porch.

Waldo cocked his head. He said in a hoarse whisper, "If you've betrayed me, Butler, I swear you'll live to regret it."

Just as I got to my feet the front door was kicked open violently. Casey's big deputy Humpty barged into the room with a gun in his hand and a grin on his face. "Just freeze it right there, gents," he said. A second deputy glided in behind him. "Clyde, put the cuffs on the beard. Butler, the least you could of done was wait and pump the story out of this professor where Casey could hear it. You trying to hog all the credit?"

Waldo's nerves were too frayed to stand for it. He bellowed and lurched from his chair as if her were going for my throat. The deputy named Clyde grabbed his left arm. Waldo swung a terrific roundhouse that cracked against Clyde's jaw and knocked him over

210

the coffee table. Waldo was coming for me again when Humpty hit him in the stomach with his fist. Holding his gun hand fastidiously to one side, Humpty brought up the same fist to meet Waldo's face as it jerked forward. It sounded like a cleaver hitting meat. Waldo staggered against the wall. Humpty holstered the gun and stepped in to him again. I didn't relish breaking my knuckles on the big man, so I snatched the leather billyclub from Humpty's hip pocket and cracked him smartly behind the ear.

Humpty sat down heavily in Waldo's chair and spit a chew of tobacco on the floor. I moved close, watching his hands, the billyclub at the ready.

"Drop it or I'll your goddam head off!" This was Clyde, who had pulled himself to his knees and yanked his pistol out. I didn't like the jerky look in his eyes, so I dropped the club. Waldo was braced against the wall, vomiting."

Humpty's face was very pink. "Put the handcuffs on the beard, Clyde."

"What about this other joker?" Clyde panted.

"Take his gun," Humpty said.

Clyde walked up to me and ripped the Luger out of my holster. There was pink froth on his mouth where Waldo had hit him, and he had the tense, ecstatic look of a man who would joyfully empty his gun into anything that moved. "Why don't you slug this joker, Hump, for getting out of line?" Clyde said.

Humpty heaved himself to his feet and stood with his face about a foot from mine. His breath smelled like molasses. "Naw, we wouldn't want to bruise this cowboy. He might have a date tonight. Now take the professor outside, plowboy."

Clyde took Waldo to the squad car, and Humpty escorted me to the Mercury. To my surprise, he directed me to drive to Jordan City, not King's apartment.

"How did you know where I was?" I asked Humpty.

"A little birdie told us," he said. "A plump little pigeon."

Chapter 17
***

Humpty's pigeon turned out to be Nancy Brewer. When we entered Quartz's office in the old schoolhouse, she was sitting on the battered studio couch, as immobile as a choir girl, her eyes like shiny black beetles impaled in cotton. Paul McIntosh was perched beside her, Jack Casey was behind the big desk, and Quartz was in a chair beside the desk.

"Welcome to the latecomers," Casey said. "Looks like not all parties came willingly. Let's have a report, Deputy."

Humpty leaned over the desk and began talking to Casey in a low voice. Quartz moved back, as if to give them privacy, and I drifted over beside him. Paul got up and moved toward Waldo, but the deputy named Clyde waved him off.

"The girl showed up on her bicycle just after Casey got there," Quartz said. "She had some notes King had left with her, giving several reasons why Waldo might be the Clayborne girl's murderer. Jack figured you were over there making an arrest, so he sent Humpty to bring you both in."

"The girl looks like she's in shock," I said.

"She folded up when Jack showed her the body. Did you do that to Waldo?"

"That's Humpty's handiwork," I said.

"You were gone an hour. Did you get anything out of him?"

"Let's not have secrets, gentlemen!" Casey said, turning toward us. "Mr. Butler, you sit on that bench over there in the corner, all by your lonesome. Consider yourself in temporary custody. Humpty, you keep an eye on him."

Quartz took a quick step toward the desk. "Jack, don't start throwing your weight around. If you're making an accusation, then state it clearly."

Casey got to his feet. His slender body swayed and his back was curved in a way that reminded me of a cobra. "I'll make this much clear to you, Constable. I'm going to run this little circus in my own way, without interference from you or your hotshot assistant. Are we understood?"

Quartz didn't have a chance to reply. Paul McIntosh slammed his hand on Casey's desk. "Damn it, Jack, no one challenges the fact that you're in charge. But for God's sake, show some consideration. That girl should be under medical care. And Mr. Mason's hurt. Take his handcuffs off and let me clean him up."

Casey gave him a mock bow. "Editor, you're absolutely right. You have my permission to get the girl out of here. Humpty, uncuff the professor and let him soak the blood out of his beard. You, Willinger, didn't you say you wanted to slip up to the college and break the bad news to the authorities? This would be a good time. Surely they're out of bed by now."

Quartz hesitated, then departed on his errand, and for the next hour and a half I cooled my heels in the most remote corner of the room. McIntosh called a doctor for Nancy Brewer, then helped Waldo into the washroom. A deputy came in and held a whispered conference with Casey. The doctor from the infirmary appeared, and Paul talked Casey into letting him examine Waldo's face. Then the doctor escorted Nancy from the room.

At this point I signaled Humpty that I wanted to use the washroom. He made me wait until he inspected it. As soon as I entered I hooked the door, turned on the spigots, and took a roll of adhesive tape from the medicine chest. Slipping Clayborne's derringer from my pocket, I peeled my left sock down and taped the gun into the hollow behind my ankle bone. It hardly showed with the sock back in place. Then I went through my pockets, removing the poem, the blackmail letters, and the check from Clayborne. I sealed the papers in a piece of plastic from my wallet, and taped the package under the sink.

When I returned to the room, Waldo Mason was sitting across the desk from Casey, his chin on his chest. Casey was interrogating him. Waldo had very little to say, but this didn't seem to offend the sheriff at all. Then, to my surprise, Casey suggested to Paul that he drive Waldo home. Humpty didn't like it, nor was he cheered up by Casey's next order, that he and Clyde wait outside. Now there were only the two of us in the room.

Casey strolled to the coffee pot, poured two cups full, and placed them on his desk. "Come on over, Butler. It's time we had our little showdown."

213

I crossed to the chair across the desk from him, and for several minutes Casey watched me with his chin propped on his thumbs, his elbows on the desk.

Finally he said, "I'm going to ask you some questions, Butler, and you better give me the right answers. If you don't, I'm going to rack you. I can stick you for obstructing justice and for assaulting an officer, just for openers. I can guarantee you six months in the workhouse, and maybe a year and a day over to Columbus."

He looked like he meant business. I said nothing.

"Here's the first question: Exactly what did Clayborne hire you to do?"

"You're misinformed, Jack. Clayborne never bought the idea that the janitor killed his daughter. It's that simple. I've been humoring the man."

"That's a workhouse answer, son," Casey said. "Here's number two." He threw a big glossy photo on the desk. "Identify this man for me."

It was a morgue shot of Swanson. Something slithered through the underbrush of my mind. "He looks familiar, but I can't quite place him."

"That's strike two, Butler. Three and you're out. Here it is. Why did you send this King fellow out to the Stagecoach Inn last night?"

"Suppose you tell me, Jack. You've obviously already figured it out to your own satisfaction. Why should I confuse you?"

He put the photo away and leaned back in his chair. "You four-flushers are all alike. You all peg me as a hick cop with hog fat for brains. Look at this mess. Another dead student. A dead bodyguard to a millionaire. And a four-flusher on the make. A bunch of pieces that don't add up. But I'm going to fool you boy. I'm going to add them up anyway."

"Go ahead, Jack. I haven't had a good laugh since you indicted Ewing."

Casey showed me his teeth. "Let's try this on for size: Daddy Clayborne came to town last Monday with blood in his eye. Him and his bodyguard paid me a visit, remember? So when I got this picture from Sheriff Cunningham yesterday, I made this boy right away. I did some checking with the desk clerks at the Cavendish, and they tell me that you and Swanson were seen in the lobby on Monday.

You had a nice long visit Daddy. He was an angry man, burning for revenge, and I think you helped fire him up with the notion that the janitor was innocent. So he hired you to get the goods on the real killer. He assigned the bodyguard to help you, to handle chores you didn't have the stomach for."

"You ought to write for TV, Jack. You have quite an imagination."

"I've got the facts to support it, Butler. On Thursday Daddy came back to town, and you and him have another meeting. You're hardly at the door and he calls his boy Swanson at the Slumber Haven. That call's on the hotel record. My guess is that you sold Daddy the idea that King killed his daughter, and Daddy sent Swanson to nail King. But the boy was too sharp. King killed Swanson."

"You'll have to prove that, Jack."

"A cinch. Swanson was killed with two slugs from a .45, and I found a .45 automatic in King's desk this morning with two rounds gone from the magazine. I can almost promise you that the slugs came from that gun."

There had been no gun in King's desk when I searched it at three-thirty, so the killer had planted it there when he brought King home. "Tell me more, Jack."

"Beginning to pinch a little, is it? Okay, Swanson got killed Thursday night. Someone took his body back to the Slumber Haven and cleaned him of all identification. Maybe King did it, but I think you did. Whichever, you and Daddy had a meeting about it yesterday, just after you were seen with the King boy in the Tug and Maul. You conned the boy into going out to the Stagecoach Inn last night. The Brewer girl will swear to that. Why? I think you were setting him up for Daddy. Because Daddy left the Cavendish around eleven last night and didn't get home until two A.M. But King ruined the plan by hanging around the Stagecoach until two. So you and Daddy had to have another meeting. You stayed until three. Now here it gets tricky. The coroner estimates that King died at three-thirty. My hunch is that he had grown suspicious of you. He tailed you to the Cavendish. After you left, he went up to have a talk with Daddy."

He wouldn't have put it just that way unless he could back it up. "Jack, I'll bet you found King's station wagon on the parking lot at the Cavendish."

"That's where we found it, boy. There's blood all over the back, and the steering wheel's wiped clean. That's always the mark of an amateur."

I thought about it for a moment. "There's one thing I don't understand. Why don't you have me down as King's murderer?"

"I did, until we found that wagon. You wouldn't have tried to stick Daddy with the wagon like that. Once he was accused, you would be a dead duck."

Given the facts at Casey's disposal, it was a credible piece of deduction.

I said, "Jack, I compliment you on your logic, but you're wrong. King didn't kill Swanson, and Clayborne certainly didn't kill King."

"You're going to make me sore in a minute," Casey said. "Why do you think I told you all this? To hear you deny it?"

I didn't have to think about that. "You're dead without a witness," I said. "Arrest Clayborne with a flimsy case like this, and when his lawyers get done you won't be able to get a job as scoutmaster."

"All right!" he growled. "So I need a witness. I'll make you a deal about your part in it. I don't care if he bought you. We can say that you came to me when he braced you with his mad-dog scheme for revenge, and I assigned you to go along with him. We'll say you tried to stop Swanson when he was ordered to kill King, but you were too late. I'll even go that far."

It was pretty sophisticated police procedure for a country cop. "It's an attractive offer, Jack. But it didn't happen the way say it happened."

"Okay, buster!" He snapped out of the chair, crossed the room to the door, and barked a command. The deputy Clyde followed him back into the room.

"Take this piece of trash over to the Falls and lock him up," Casey said.

"My pleasure, Jack," Clyde said. "On your feet, joker and give me your hands behind your back." He was rough snapping the cuffs on me.

"Just a minute," Casey said. He moved close to me. "This Clayborne might not be as tough a nut as you think, Butler. He might crack when I show him this photo of Swanson and tell him you're ready to rat on him. He might even see the advantage of sticking you with the murder rap. You think about it."

My chief concern on the ride to Spencer's Falls was that Clayborne might panic under pressure. I didn't like the memory of how he had turned to mush when I accused him the night before. The fact that I now knew why he had been so vulnerable didn't help matters. That only made me desperate to talk with him.

They locked me in a cell on the second floor of the Parson County jail without fanfare. Clyde made me empty my pockets and frisked me, but didn't find the derringer. The cell was small, with newly whitewashed concrete walls that gave off an odor of Lysol.

It was nearly eleven o'clock when they brought me in. An hour later the turnkey appeared with lunch on a metal tray. I took only coffee, smoked a stogie with it, then stretched out on the bunk and went to sleep. It was the first decent rest I'd had in three days.

At six o'clock I was awakened by someone rapping the bars with a nightstick. It was Clyde. "Rise and shine, cowboy. You must live right. You're sprung."

I got up, crossed to the sink, splashed my face with cold water, and dried on a towel that smelled of creosote. "Where's Casey?" I asked.

"Your guess is as good as mine," Clyde said. He unlocked the door and moved down the hall to the door that led to the turnkey's office.

"Who authorized you to release me?" I asked.

Clyde chuckled. "You want it in writing? You're sprung, free as the air."

"How about my Luger?" I said.

"Why, surely. We don't want you going out into the cold, cruel world all naked." He got the gun from the desk and handed it to me.

I removed the clip, checked the action, reloaded, and put it in my holster. "Aren't you going to drive me back?" I asked.

"Naw, I got to mind the store. Take the bus. It's only two bits."

But I took a cab instead, and twenty minutes later I was crossing the lobby of the Hotel Cavendish. The desk clerk flinched when he saw me. As the tiny elevator labored upward, I experienced a dread for this meeting as strong as the odor of rotten meat.

Clayborne was a long time answering the door. When it finally opened, he was wearing a silk bathrobe, trousers and slippers, and a soft towel around his neck. His face was freshly shaved and his expression on the smug side. "Oh, it's you. Come in. I was given to understand that you had run afoul of the law. They said you were ready to throw me to the wolves, to perjure yourself to accuse me of murder. Of course, I didn't believe them. How about a drink?"

"I appreciate the vote of confidence," I said. "Yes, I'd like a drink." I walked past him into the bedroom, looked around, and returned.

"What was that for?" Clayborne asked. "Did you think they were still here?"

"You and I are going to chat," I said. "And I don't want to be overheard." I couldn't keep the gravel out of my voice, but he ignored it.

"Of course we'll chat," he said. "Where do we begin?"

"How did you talk Casey out of his quaint little notion?" I asked.

He gave a hearty laugh and handed me a drink. "Did you think that rustic Laurel and Hardy act would intimidate me?" Those two were dull compared to some of the men I've matched wits with. I almost hated to shatter the sheriff's illusions. He was convinced that I came here to kill that boy, Arthur King."

The Tycoon was back in the saddle. "How did you convince him otherwise?"

He gave an airy wave of his hand. "I told him about the blackmail. I saw that it was the only thing that would explain my presence here to his satisfaction. I'm surprised you didn't tell him about it."

"That wasn't my decision to make," I said.

"So you went to jail instead. The man or honor, even in the breach."

The mockery in his voice struck me as bravado. "I'm surprised Casey believed you about the blackmail. I thought I had all the documents."

"Mr. Butler, it's a basic rule of business to make photostatic copies of all documents. They're in my briefcase over there, along

218

with a carbon of the withdrawal slip for one hundred thousand dollars. The sum impressed Mr. Casey."

"How did you explain Swanson?"

He sobered a little. "I'll admit the sheriff took me by surprise with that. But I explained that I left him here, unbeknownst to you, to get a line on the blackmailer. I was appropriately shocked to learn of his death."

"I'm sure you were." I took a long pull at my drink. "By the way, what did you tell Casey you were being blackmailed for? You didn't use the old Yale-boy story, did you?"

The smiled melted off his face, and he watched me carefully as he answered. "No, I told him it was a family scandal Natalie had recorded, and that he could verify the theft of the tape with Pritchett. He appeared to believe me."

"That's because you tell your stories so convincingly," I said. "Take the Yale-boy story, for example. For a man in your position to tell a hired hand like me that he has engaged in a homosexual act, and to do it with all the proper gestures of shame and remorse, that alone adds a certain purity to the story."

Clayborne made a gesture of distaste. "Do we have to go through all your doubts again? I thought we covered that ground pretty thoroughly last night."

"No, this is new business," I said. "Last night I didn't know what was on the tape." I got up and made myself another drink, a strong one.

He uncrossed his legs and put his glass down. His profile was as sharp as an axe. "Of course you knew what was on the tape last night. I told you what was on it."

I had to clear my throat. "You didn't hear me. Now I know what's really on the tape. And it's not the Yale-boy story."

He raised himself an inch. I could almost read his mind. He had to consider the possibility that I found the tape and played it. From his eyes I could tell when he rejected this idea. "You're not making sense," he said.

Suddenly I was angry. Or maybe I needed that emotion in order to tell it. "Oh, it's an old dodge, Clayborne, confessing to a shocking crime to conceal a worse one. Not only that, there was just enough truth in what you told me to account for your guilt and fear. I'm sure the setting was your house on Cape Cod in the summer of 1957. No

219

doubt the state of mind you described for yourself was accurate. You were soured on women, gorged with wine and sun. And the temptation was sexual, all right. But you didn't have an affair with any Yale boy. You had an affair with your daughter, Natalie. 'Incest' is the word."

"You're crazy!" he said hoarsely. "Only a sick mind would even—"

Now it came easier. "You had to set her up for it. Maybe she was cool to the idea at first. So you got clever. You told her it was okay because you weren't her real father. She wouldn't be hard to convince, with Eleanor's reputation. Once she believed you, all the moral barriers were removed for her."

"God damn you! You broke your word. You've played the tape."

"Nuts to you, Mr. Clayborne. No, I haven't heard the tape. I put this together from scraps early this morning, just after I found King's body. The funny thing is, I might still have rejected the idea if the killer hadn't tried to get cute with a copy of *Hamlet*."

Clayborne opened and closed his hands, as if he lusted to hold a weapon. A note of horror made his voice husky. "You're in with them! They've bribed you with some of the blackmail money. You Judas. You whore! You—"

I threw my drink in his face, ice cubes and all. It was pure reflex, my reaction to his hysteria. He must have inhaled some of the Scotch, for he spent a good two minutes choking and fighting for breath, wiping his face with the towel pulled from around his neck. I stood over him.

"You grubby peasant," I said. "You could have prevented two murders if you had told me the truth on Monday. At least you could have told me that your ex-wife was part of the conspiracy to blackmail you."

He peered at me from behind the towel. "How could I have known that?"

I resisted the impulse to shake him by the scruff of the neck. "You had to know it on Monday for the same reasons I know it now." I sat on the edge of my chair and lit a stogie to calm myself. "Once you knew Natalie had made the tape and baited you to come out here, you had to draw certain conclusions. The big one was that she had somehow learned that you had lied when you told her you weren't her real father. That finally gives us the reason why she

220

despised you. But what convinced her? Remember, it was important for her to go on believing you weren't her father. She had to live with what happened that summer, too. The reason she came to Jordan was to find her father. So who persuaded her that you had lied? There's only one other person in the world whose word she would accept. It had to be Eleanor."

"I didn't draw that conclusion," Clayborne said. "I swear it."

"No? Then let's move on to the letter from your old housekeeper that the blackmailer sent you. Once I knew it wasn't a letter about a romp with a Yale boy, I knew it wasn't addressed to Natalie. Who would Mrs. McPherson write to about something so dreadful? The one person who, in her mind, deserved to know? Again, it had to be Eleanor. And you knew it."

"You're wrong. Oh, I considered the possibility, but I rejected it for two reasons. Mrs. McPherson would have written to Eleanor five years ago, and Eleanor would have used it to smear me long before this. Also, that would mean that Eleanor and Natalie had teamed up to blackmail me, that Eleanor had killed her. That's too fantastic. No, I decided that Natalie got Mrs. McPherson to write the letter as corroboration to her own story."

"Then you're a fool," I said. "Yes, Eleanor had the letter five years ago, but she knew it wasn't any good by itself. Not against a man of your stature. So she bided her time. She came here to Jordan, say early last fall, and made contact with one of her old lovers. Somehow she sold him on the blackmail scheme. His job was to befriend Natalie, win her confidence, and get her story on tape. Eleanor stayed in the background. But they ran into a snag. In Natalie's eyes, any older man who showed her attention was a candidate for fatherhood, especially if he admitted that he had been close to Eleanor in years gone by. No doubt she accused him of being her father. Eleanor and the man confer. They unravel the bill of goods you sold Natalie, and they see how it will benefit them once they convince her of your deception. Let's say our man tells Natalie that he can get in touch with Eleanor, that he proves he's not her father with a phone call. Natalie talks with Eleanor on the phone, and is persuaded. Imagine what a shock it must have been for her. She had found her father, only to lose him again. In a way, it was similar to what happened to her on Cape Cod that summer. She had a strong attachment with an older man, and suddenly all the moral barriers were gone. It must have been easy for this charming older gent to exploit the situation. I think they became lovers. In fact, I know it."

"Then why did he kill her?" Clayborne asked.

"Natalie discovered that Eleanor was running the whole scheme behind the scenes. That must have been purgatory for her. Again she was used as a substitute for Eleanor, a pawn for Eleanor. So she probably decided to smear you on her own. Remember, the money didn't really interest her, except as a nest egg for her and her lover. Revenge on you was her motive. She could have that without the lover. On Saturday night our man went up to talk her out of it. She refused. So he killed her."

It had grown dark as we talked, and I got up to turn on a lamp.

"Don't!" Clayborne said from the depths of the sofa. "No light, please."

I returned to my seat, and for some minutes he was quiet except for blowing his nose and pouring himself another drink.

Then he spoke in a low voice, "Let me try to explain what happened."

"I don't want to hear about it," I said.

"Please listen! You have to realize that it was on that same beach at the Cape that I fell in love with Eleanor when she was sixteen. She came home from school with my sister that summer. She was beautiful, a vision, and by the end—"

"Shut up about it!"

He coughed over his drink. "All right, I've done the worst thing a man can do. On top of that, I'm responsible for Natalie's death. Have you any idea what it's done to me? It's driving me mad. Now I suppose you'll expose me."

"Not me. I told you the other day that I won't judge you for your sins."

He was silent for a while. Then he said, "What'll you do now?"

"I've got a few ideas," I said.

Just then the phone rang. It was on the desk behind me, and when he didn't move after three rings, I picked up the receiver and said hello.

"Butler, I'm glad I found you. This is Waldo Mason. Listen, I behaved like an idiot this morning. My nerves were shot. I thought you had betrayed me."

"No harm done," I said. "You didn't mention our lady friend to the sheriff, I gather."

"No, of course not. And when he didn't mention her name, I realized that you'd been telling the truth. But listen, that's why I called. I've just been talking with Eleanor. She wants to see you. She can explain what happened last night with that boy, King. She's very upset about it, but she's willing to meet you here at my place. She's on her way now. Will you come?"

"Yes," I said. He hung up.

"That was business," I said to Clayborne. "I need your car."

"Take it. The keys are on the desk. Take anything you want."

I paused at the door. "Don't do anything foolish."

"I haven't got the guts."

On the way down in the elevator I asked myself the question I should have asked Waldo: How did he know to call me at the Cavendish? After I had climbed into the open convertible, I took the Luger out, pumped a round into the chamber, and slid it under my belt.

The shortest route to Waldo's house was over the road that led past Eddie Bell's. The night was cool and moonless. I made the turn, feeling very exposed in the open car. But I didn't expect any trouble while I was on the road. That was my first mistake. My second was that I didn't react intelligently to the police car. I responded as a good citizen would. It appeared behind me out of nowhere, siren blaring, red dome light spinning, and I pulled over as soon as I found a wide shoulder. It crossed my mind that Casey had turned up something new to charge me with.

Yet I was as cautious as the situation permitted. The patrol car parked a few feet behind me, and at once the headlight went on, swung around, and settled on my head. The doors to the patrol car opened, but they stayed behind the lights. I eased the Luger from my belt ever so slowly.

"Don't do it, friend! Put both hands on the sun visor. And they better be clean." The voice was vaguely familiar. I put my hands on the sun visor.

Then I heard boots on the macadam. But before they reached me, someone jerked open the right hand door of the car and slammed a double-barreled shotgun into my side. At the same time he gave out with a Dixie battle cry that lifted the hair on the back of my neck. I

223

had only to turn my head to look into the grinning face of the Kentucky mountain boy named Charlie.

Just then the voice that went with the boots said behind me, "You was told you had a date tonight." Now I recognized the voice: it belonged to LeRoy, the ox. I had the presence to drop my forearm over the old wound on my head just before he hit me on the right side. It didn't even hurt much. It was like seeing a white phosphorous shell go off in the night, so bright that it hurts your eyes, so near that the chemicals burn your nostrils, and you are grateful for the darkness when it fades.

Chapter 18
***

I was never totally unconscious. It was the kind of blow that paralyzes the nervous system, but leaves your senses functioning at about ten percent of capacity. Just enough to hallucinate with. By that I mean that the control center was out of order, allowing grotesque images to shuttle through my mind like floats in a Halloween parade.

Finally I tuned in on the conversation between Charlie and LeRoy. LeRoy was driving. I was bellied over the drive shaft on the floor of the back seat, with my hands tied behind me. Charlie was sitting with his feet on my rump and the stock of his shotgun on my spine. They had put the top up on the convertible, and we were going very fast over smooth roads.

"No, a thousand ain't enough," Charlie said. "Not even with this new Olds for a bonus. I'll lay you odds Willie is holding out on us. He rakes in the jack, and we do the dirty work."

"Hell, this ain't work, this is pleasure," LeRoy said. "Not for you, maybe. But it is for me and Charlie. This stud owes me for three teeth. And wait'll Cash sees him. He'll froth at the mouth."

"Nell's the one. She swore to leave a scar for every hair on Cash's head."

"Nell can wait her turn," LeRoy said. "I don't want him stuck like a hog before I get my licks in. I want this stud to sweat blood through his pores."

"Willie said not to mess around," Charlie said.

"Screw Willie. You think this stud will get loose, once we get him on our own stomping grounds?"

"Not this stud," Charlie said. And he slammed the butt of the shotgun into my back. It jerked a groan from me.

"That's it, tune him up," LeRoy said. "Let's hear that G string again."

But I faded out. When I came to again, we were crossing a bridge. I could tell by the hum of the tires on the metal grill. Before long we turned off on a dirt road. It got rougher, but LeRoy pushed the Olds hard, bouncing over rocks and potholes. Finally he slowed down and the car lurched violently as he drove through a stream. A minute later he began leaning on the horn, and soon he skidded to a stop. A dog began to bark, then a second one, a hoarse, frantic yelping. LeRoy got out of the car and shouted at the dogs. At once the clamor subsided, to be replaced by a high, eager whining.

Charlie climbed out over my feet, and again I was lifted like a suitcase by a grip on the back of my belt. It was LeRoy. He carried me across the yard, my head bumped steps, and we entered a room that smelled of hot bread and stale grease. The others trooped in behind us. Rough hands jerked me into a chair, a metal handle creaked, and cold water hit me in the face. I opened my eyes.

LeRoy was grinning at me with the half of his mouth that worked. Two of his front teeth were missing and a third was broken off near the gums. "How-do, Mr. Butler. Welcome to Kentucky. We don't get many visitors out thisaway, so don't mind if our manners are a little on the rough side."

Cash and Charlie laughed. Cash's left arm was taped to his body under a big sweater. The woman standing between them wasn't even smiling. She was as wide as LeRoy, wearing tight jeans over fat thighs and a man's flannel shirt. Her hair was the color of butter, tied with a ribbon in the back. Her mouth was small, and she had a rusty birthmark on her cheek the size of a silver dollar. Her eyes had about as much expression as two blue marbles in a fish bowl.

"So this is the stick that done all the damage," she said. "He don't look like much to me. You boys ought to be ashamed of yourselves."

"Well, he suckered us, Nell," LeRoy said. "He clobbered me from behind."

"You was playing with that chippy, the way Cash tells it," Nell said.

The scar on LeRoy's cheek turned red. "If these worthless brothers of yours were worth a tinker's damn, he wouldn't have licked us."

"Don't listen to him, Nell," Charlie said. "Who saved your hide, LeRoy, when he had you laid out like a side of beef?"

"Cut it out!" Nell said. She hadn't taken her eyes off me. "Stand him up."

"What for?" LeRoy asked.

"Just stand him up!"

They pulled me up to my feet and Nell moved so close I could smell her dinner. "So you're the stallion." She put a hand on my chest and ran it around to my back. "Sweet-talk me, honey, and maybe I'll keep around for a house pet."

The men laughed uncomfortably.

Nell moved closer, bumping me with her big breasts. Then she seized the lapels of my coat with both hands, shifted her weight, and gave me a terrific kick in the groin with her knee. The pain darted up to my throat. She got out of the way, and I hit the floor hard on my side, spewing Clayborne's Scotch.

Nell said, "Maybe he was a stallion. Now he's a gelding."

It drove Cash crazy. Screaming obscenities, he kicked me twice in the back, snatched a shovel from the coal bucket, and went for my head. LeRoy grabbed him and squeezed until Cash began to whimper from the pain in his shoulder.

"Damn it, Nell!" LeRoy said. "You want this halfwit to kill him?"

Nell was panting. "Set him up again. See how tough he is now."

"All right, but he's my meat, and don't you forget it. You ruin him for me, and by God I'll take a two-by-four to you."

They dragged me back up on the chair. Cash was on a bench, cradling his taped arm with his good one. I was still curled up, barely able to get my breath. It felt as if Cash has cracked some ribs.

"Give him a drink of corn," Charlie said. "That'll cure what ails him."

"Good idea," LeRoy said. He crossed the room and returned with a tin cup. Seizing my hair with one hand, he tilted my head back and poured my mouth full. I gagged it down. It burned like horseradish and filled my eyes with tears. But after a moment I could breathe if I didn't go too deep.

"You call this meat?" Nell said. "He looks as tame as an egg-sucking hound."

"Naw, he's tricky," LeRoy said. "He can scrap. If it was daylight, I'd turn him loose in the barnyard and give you a show."

I laughed in his face. I poured into it all the scorn and noise I could muster. It sounded a little mad, even to me, and Charlie jerked his shotgun up. I said, "Nell, this big slob couldn't whip a crippled old woman. I beat him the last time without even working up a sweat."

227

The scar in LeRoy's cheek turned as crimson as a fresh welt. He flung the cup aside, but Nell collided with him roughly, blocking him from me. "Not with his hands tied, Roy. You just said you didn't want him ruint."

Nell smiled for the first time, and gold glittered in her mouth. "You think we're all dim-witted like Cash?" she said to me. "You're baiting Roy so we'll turn you loose to fight. Then you'll run off in the dark."

"We could pen him in the barnyard, like LeRoy said," Charlie offered. "We got three sets of car lights to turn on him. Have us a midnight show."

"I'm game," LeRoy said. "Car lights suit me."

"But they don't suit me," Nell said. "Can't you see what this smart aleck wants? Out there in the dark he'd have a chance to fox us. If he got over that fence, we'd wind up shooting each other. Oh, he's a cool one. You just heard him brag on how cool he is. He didn't work up a sweat when he whipped LeRoy."

"Jesus, trust a woman to make a damn box social out of a simple thing like killing a man," LeRoy said. "What are you trying to cook up?"

"Well he's such a cool feller," Nell said. "And the poor boy wants to fight so bad. S'pose we keep him on ice till daylight. Then you can turn him loose in the barnyard with no worries. How does that strike you, LeRoy?"

"I don't like keeping him overnight," LeRoy said.

Charlie laughed. "I do believe you're scared of him, big man."

But LeRoy was watching Nell. "Where you going to keep him?"

"In the spring house," Nell said. "Where else would you keep such a cool feller? And he ain't about to bust out of there."

"Hell, that place is knee deep in water, ain't it?"

"I didn't say you had to sleep there," Nell said. "Just this monkey."

LeRoy began to laugh. "On ice, you said? That's downright cruel. Oh, you're a hard woman, Nellie Mae. Damned if you ain't."

"Take his shoes and coat off," Nell said. "We don't want the poor boy sweating hisself to death."

Charlie knelt before me and ripped the shoes off my feet. "His coat won't come off with his hands tied," he said.

228

"Hell, that's no problem." Nell took a knife from a drawer, went behind my chair, and literally cut the coat off my back. Then she stood in front of me. "I ought to nick you up a little, just to give the rats something to chew on," she said. "But then you wouldn't be much use in the morning, would you?"

"I won't be much good anyway, if you don't cut my hands free," I said.

"That's what we call tough titty around here," she said. "You said LeRoy couldn't beat a cripple. Now you get to prove it."

She turned and brayed some orders. Cash got a big flashlight, and the other two heaved me to my feet. Nell led the way outside, where the two dogs began yelping again. One of them was part mastiff, a big yellow dog with a deep chest. The other was a calico hound with a torn ear. We went around the house and took a path the led between steep banks, steadily downhill, to a thick wooden door set into the side of a steep hill. It was locked with a two-by-four fitted into iron brackets. Nell removed the beam and opened the door.

I felt the icy damp air as they hauled me over the doorframe. Two stone steps led down to a solid stone floor over which water lazily drifted. The water flowed from a natural spring in the corner, where a trough had been chipped from the stone. The room was roughly ten feet square, with stone walls on three sides and a stone roof.

"How about tying the bastard's legs?" Charlie said.

"Naw, he'd be stiff as a board come morning," LeRoy said. "It'd be like stomping a sack of coal."

"Ain't we brave all of a sudden," Nell said. "Should I cut his hands loose?"

"Go ahead," LeRoy said. "Give the stud a break."

"No, I was just teasing, honey," Nell said. "I want him crippled. I want to see him live up to his brag. One side, Cash!"

With that she gave me a tremendous shove down the steps. For a sickening moment I thought I might land on my head, but I caught my balance enough to land on both knees instead, burning them on the stone beneath the water.

"Sweet dreams, honeybunch," Nell said, and they were still laughing when the beam fell into place outside.

The darkness was absolute, and the water felt as if it trickled from a glacier locked inside the mountain from the last ice age. The sweat on my back was already chilled. Lurching to my feet, I waded back to the stone steps and sat down. I was low on fuel for eight hours of exposure in this tomb. My last meal had been a light supper with Quartz yesterday evening. Already I could feel the tingling sensation in my feet, a memento from a mild case of frostbite acquired in Korea. My hands were growing numb.

So my first task was to get my hands in front of me, where I could work on the knots. Fortunately, Charlie hadn't overlapped my wrists. He had crisscrossed the rope from wrist to wrist. The result was something like handcuffs, and it was a good snug job. First, I strained to get as much slack as possible between my hands. Then I made like a contortionist on the steps, working the bound hands over my rump. The strain on my shoulder sockets was terrific, but I made it.

Tentatively, I explored the knots with my tongue and teeth. The rope was thicker than clothesline and not nearly so flexible. The knots, soaked with water, felt hard as iron. My belt buckle was too flimsy to be of use, and they had cleaned out my pockets.

The next order of business was to make the derringer more accessible. I peeled the sock down, and I must have spent twenty minutes searching for the end of the tape that held the gun in place. There was no sensitivity in the ends of my fingers. Finally I scraped the end of the tape free, unrolled about half of it, then ripped the derringer from my ankle. I tucked it into my side pocket. It isn't much gun unless you are either accurate or lucky in your shooting, and I was worried that by morning I wouldn't be able to cock it. But the bite of the metal on my thigh made me feel foolishly optimistic.

My next step was to inspect the spring house. I waded to the corner where the water spilled out of the stone trough, dipped my hands in and felt the smooth sides and bottom. Then I moved to the wall where the water seeped back into the ground. I raked out the muck and sifted it. All I found was a rusted lid from a Mason jar and a hambone picked clean.

By then the cold was getting to me. So I returned to the steps and put in twenty minutes of calisthenics. I did deep-knee bends and waist bends. I bicycled and ran in place. I massaged my feet. Then I got on my back, jammed a foot into the stirrup formed by the rope between my wrists, and worked my hands with the pressure off. Then I rested. Then I did it again.

That was my schedule for the rest of the night. I exercised to keep the blood moving, then I rested so I could exercise some more. Happily I'd had that sleep in Casey's jail, and all things considered I was in pretty good shape. My groin was sore but bearable. My head hurt only when I sang. Brother, did I sing. Everything from *"Ol' Man River"* to *"The Battle Hymn of the Republic."*

During my rest periods I became curiously detached, free of all sensation, vacillating between euphoria and anxiety. Thoughts drifted through my mind sluggishly with only enough of each exposed to satisfy my forty-watt curiosity. This lethargy began to worry me, so I forced myself to concentrate on the case. I went over it a piece at a time, from the theft of Natalie Clayborne's tape to my last talk with Waldo. No scene was too trivial to replay, and in my icy cell, submerged in the darkness, I seemed to have total recall. I don't know how many hours I worked at it (they had taken my watch), but finally I glimpsed the murderer's face. Bless Natalie, she had done a better job than we knew.

I rose to begin my exercise again. And someone stealthily lifted the bar on the door not three feet from me.

It seemed too soon for them to come for me, but maybe I had miscalculated the time. The only way to hide from anyone coming in was to enter the water and stand against the wall. I did just that. I dug the derringer from my pocket and held it concealed in my hand.

The door creaked on rusty hinges. The beam from the flashlight danced on the steps, then across the water to the wall. "Hey, you! You better get over against that wall, before I cut loose with this shotgun." It was Cash.

He had the door for a shield, so I waded across the room and stood in the light. "That's a good little lamb," Cash said. He came into the room.

"Where are the others, Cash?" I asked. The light blinded me completely. It was a disadvantage I hadn't even thought about.

"Never you mind! I ain't nearly as bad off as they make out. Last night they drank up a storm, hardly let me have a drop. But all the time I was studying on you. You're my meat as much as Roy's."

I felt a congestion in my chest. If he really had a shotgun, I was a dead man. "Nell and LeRoy will skin you alive for this," I said.

"Naw, I studied on that, too. Nell wants a cripple for the fight. That's what I'm fixing to give her. Hey, how'd you get them hands in front of you?"

I told him I had worked them over my feet.

"Well, if that ain't slick. Okay, slick, just you turn around and face the wall. I'm going to bust one of your arms at the elbow. You hold still and it'll go like kindling. It won't hurt nearly as much as my shoulder did."

He had put the light down on the stone step, but I still couldn't see his weapon. I turned to the wall. Without the glare, my vision was better.

"That's a good little lamb," Cash said, stepping into the water.

I cocked both hammers of the derringer and found the first trigger. Cash splashed to within five feet of me, his shadow enormous on the wall. I turned and fired point-blank. He yelled with surprise, but not pain. The bullet had gone into the white pick handle he held across his chest. He yelled and drew the club back with his good arm and I shot him just under the right eye. The impact jerked his head back, and his body followed. He made a big splash on the floor. Flinging the derringer aside, I knelt beside Cash and searched his pockets. He didn't even have a penknife.

So I crossed the room, snatched up the flashlight, and slammed the door open. The air was warm and sweet, a boon to my lungs. I stumbled up the path between the banks and stopped, dousing the light. A few stars were visible, but an edge of the sky was pasty white on the horizon. After the total darkness of the cave, I could see objects with great clarity. I was in a small valley. The house was to my right, the yellow Olds parked in front of it. To my left were several ramshackle buildings, a black pickup truck, a new Ford sedan and, about eighty yards up the valley, a barn with a sagging roof.

There was no sound from the house. I circled it cautiously and flashed the light inside the Olds. No keys. I inspected the pickup and Ford with the same bad luck. There was a warm breeze blowing through the hollow, which I had ignored until, suddenly, a dog howled from the other side of the house with the deep belligerent roar of discovery. The sound shriveled my stomach. Then the second dog joined in, this one a deep bass growl punctuated by yelping. The dogs flung themselves against their kennel. Instantly a light went on in the house.

232

I damn near panicked. My impulse was to head for the tall timber, straight up the valley. But I wouldn't get half a mile with those dogs on my trail. So I trotted for the barn. I reached it and stepped inside just as someone bellowed at the dogs. I smelled hay and cow manure, and heard a chain rattle on a feed box. I trembled a little with exultation. To a farmer, a barn is not a bad place in which to make a stand.

I flashed the light around. On the left was a row of stalls, two of them occupied by cows stoically masticating their cud. At the end of the barn stood an old hay rake. On the right was the ladder to the hayloft and three rooms with closed doors. I moved to inspect the rooms. The first was the harness room, festooned with leather. The second was the granary. The third was a tool room, containing plowpoints, scythes, pitchforks, and a litter of old wooden rakes. But the tool that caught my attention was a corn cutter, a machete with a two-foot blade, bracketed to the wall between two nails. I grabbed it, embedded the point in the wooden floor, and began sawing the rope on my wrists. I didn't realize how I was grinning until my face began to hurt. I was peeling the fragments of ropes free when the dogs began to bay as if they'd gone berserk. Someone had gone out to the kennel. I still had a few minutes.

Plucking the corn cutter free, I selected a four-pronged pitchfork and returned to the granary. There I laid my weapons aside, removed my ruined shirt, and rubbed my chest and arms briskly with an old feed sack. There was an old mackinaw hanging on the wall, and I put it on. Then I flashed my light into the bins until I found one half full of wheat. The grain was cold to the touch, but the flavor of the first mouthful was nutty and rich. I was spitting chaff from a third helping when I heard the shouts of rage. They had found Cash. A minute later the dogs began again, a fierce exultant hue and cry. No doubt they had given the dogs my shoes to smell.

So I went out into the barn proper. A hay rake is a piece of equipment usually pulled by a team, with steel wheels, a metal seat for the operator, and roughly fifty curved steel prongs mounted on a tractable bar. The prongs of this one were locked high off the floor, the points towards the door I had entered. Picking up the tongue, I pushed the rake the length of the barn, until the prongs were against the big doors, and set hand brake. If they tried to enter that way, they would have to come over this obstacle. I swiftly reconnoitered the

233

first floor. There were two other entrances, one behind the stalls that led to the barnyard, and a small square door at ground level through which they shoveled out manure. Both doors were fastened by metal hooks from the inside. To help confuse the issue, I tied one of the cows to the door behind the stalls. Then I climbed the ladder to the hayloft. Loose hay was stacked to one side, and near the ladder hole were a dozen bales of straw. I went to the front of the loft and looked through the wide crack.

Charlie had both dogs on leashes, a shotgun tucked under his arm, moving steadily up the path toward the barn. LeRoy and Nell followed. She carried a rifle and LeRoy had a .45 automatic in his hand. When the dogs jerked Charlie into the barnyard, he knelt and slipped the leash on the yellow dog. The dog ran straight to the door beneath me and flung himself against it, bellowing furiously.

I eased back to where the bales of straw were stacked and began heaving bales down the ladder hole. After the ninth one, I descended in the moiling dust and stacked the bales into a crude fort, three bales high, from the ladder to the stall area. I had just finished when LeRoy called out to me.

"You might as well chuck it, Butler. We found your pop gun, so it won't cost us nothing to come in and blast you out of there. You hear me?"

I said nothing. Someone furtively rattled the door behind the stalls. That would be Charlie. After a moment the big front doors opened simultaneously, and LeRoy cursed the hay rake. Through a chink in my fort, I saw him standing in front of the barn, holding Charlie's shotgun. The light came only halfway into the barn. LeRoy barked a command, and the yellow mastiff came into view and began wiggling under the hay rake. He was through in an instant, and his claws rattled on the boards as he came for me. I backed to the wall, crouched low, holding the pitchfork like an M-1 with a bayonet. The big dog didn't even hesitate at the barrier. With a triumphant cry he left the floor as if catapulted. I had one quick look at the smooth, silken muscles of his chest, and I rammed the fork home just as he cleared the top. I felt the shock of his momentum in the sockets of both arms, and the pitchfork was snatched from my hands. He rolled off the straw fort, impaled, yelping with pain. I quickly ducked into the tool room. The shotgun boomed twice, and the heavy shot sprayed the corner like hailstones. The yellow dog was scrabbling on the floor, roaring and snapping at the pitchfork embedded in him. The rifle cracked and he was quiet.

Then things began to happen very fast.

LeRoy went berserk, probably over the dog, grabbed the rake prongs in both hands, and tried to drag the rake out of the barn. Then I saw a knife blade scraping for the hook of the manure door in the corner behind the stalls. I turned on the square flashlight and placed it in the corner outside the tool room, with beam on the small door. I was back inside the tool room when the door opened. Charlie fired the .45 five times at the light before he hit it. I expected him to come in then, because that was his best move. But he kicked the door shut, and next I heard him working on the other door, the one I had tied the cow to. LeRoy was still wrestling with the rake, cursing.

On hands and knees, I scrabbled behind the straw fort to the manure door. I reached it just as Charlie opened the other door and dragged the cow halfway out. She bawled at the indignity. I risked a look out the manure door. Charlie stood ten yards away, his back to me, and as I watched he stuck the automatic in his hip pocket and jerked a knife from a sheath to cut the cow free.

I dipped my shoulder through the small doorway, pulled my legs through, and went after him with the corn cutter. He heard my bare feet slap the mud, but when he turned what he saw made him decide he had to have the gun. His hand moved like a snake striking, but before he got the barrel up I chopped the machete with both hands into the bone and muscle where his neck and shoulder joined. It drove him to his knees. He groaned like a man lifting a tremendous weight. I jerked him forward onto his face, picked up the .45, and clipped him hard on the head. The cow watched it all with bovine indifference.

I checked the automatic. There was at least one bullet in it, because the receiver always locks to the rear on the final round. I moved the few feet to the corner of the barn. LeRoy had dragged the rake clear and was standing there loading the shotgun. I didn't see Nell. But as soon as I stepped clear of the barn and steadied the barrel of the .45 on the top of a fence, she snapped a shot at me from the wagon shed across from the barn. The slug hit a board five feet above me. Ignoring it, I shot LeRoy twice in the chest while he was trying to close the shotgun. The muzzle velocity of a .45 is tremendous. Big as he was, the slugs fairly jerked him off his feet and slammed him onto his back. I ducked behind the barn as Nell fired again.

My .45 was empty, the slide locked to the rear. I searched Charlie, found plenty of shotgun shells but no. 45 ammo. I went back into the barn and circled to the foot of the ladder. I had a good view of the wagon shed, and after a moment I spotted her yellow head in the bed of an old truck parked there. Apparently she didn't know my gun was empty. So she didn't dare approach the barn, and I couldn't go out and pick up LeRoy's loaded shotgun.

After another half hour, she must have decided that her position was untenable. She slipped over the side of the truck, very nimble for her size, and out the back of the wagon shed. Moving quickly to a better vantage point, I saw her dart to the corncrib. She was making for the house. It seemed a stupid move until I realized that she was after keys to one of the cars. She no longer liked the odds.

I could have let her go and been done with it. But the idea of her driving blithely off burned in me like another dose of their white lightning. I went into the tool room, snatched a rope from a peg, and made a loop out of it as I moved to the front of the barn. The next time she darted, I dove outside, slipped the noose over LeRoy's leg, and scrambled back to safety. I don't think she even saw me. Then I began to drag the big man into the barn. He was at the threshold when Nell fired, splintering wood up near the doorway. But I was deep in the barn, and soon I had him at my feet. The first thing I found was a full clip for the .45, and I reloaded. Then I found my wallet in his hip pocket and, mixed with his change, the keys to Clayborne's Olds.

I went out the stall door past Charlie, circled the rear of the barn, and trotted through a growth of sumac and elderberry until I was close to the Ford. Nell came out of the house cautiously, the rifle at port arms, her purse hanging on a strap from her shoulder. She was watching the front of the barn. Then she began to run, like a fat boy in full football regalia, her cheeks bouncing. As soon as she passed the black pickup, I fired a round into the ground in front of her. She flailed to a stop, flung the rifle from her and jerked her arms up.

"No more! I give up!"

I came out of the brush, walked up to her, and kicked her feet out from under her. She yelped when she hit the ground, and began to shake like blubber. "Don't hit me! You already killed off my men. Ain't that enough?"

Then I knew why I didn't want her to get away. "Who's Willie, Nell?"

She shook her head. "I don't know any Willie."

I picked up the rifle by the barrel and slapped her face smartly with the flat of the stock. "Who's Willie, Nell?"

She shook her head to clear it. "All right, he's the one they call Humpty, the deputy over to Spencer's Falls. He's LeRoy's cousin."

"All right, on your feet."

She got up slowly. "What are you fixing to do with me?"

It was in my mind to lock her in the spring house, but suddenly I had no stomach for it. I made her stand there while I opened the hoods of the Ford and the pickup and ripped out all the wires I could reach. "Let's go into the house, Nell. I want my shoes and my gun."

"Your gun's in my purse," she said. "Your shoes are on the porch."

I carried the purse a few feet from her, opened it, and dumped the contents on the ground. The Luger was the largest object among what appeared to be five pounds of costume jewelry. A unique shade of green caught my eye, and from the tangled junk I extricated the turquoise and silver bracelet they had taken from Linda Thorpe when they robbed the Stagecoach. I returned to Nell.

"Have you got a phone in the house?"

"No. I swear to God."

"All right. Don't you move until I'm gone."

She nodded dumbly. I flung her rifle deep into the brush, walked down to the porch, slipped the shoes on my feet, and climbed into the Olds. When I backed up to turn, she was still standing there, holding her face with her hands.

The clock on the dashboard informed me that it was just seven A.M.

237

Chapter 19
***

I didn't get back to Jordan City until nine in the morning. After I crossed the river, I stopped at a roadside diner for a breakfast of ham and eggs. The waitress was skittish with me, and when I returned to the car I took a good look at my face in the rearview mirror.

Mud and chaff had dried in my hair, my eyes looked hot, my mouth dry and taut, I sported a two-day stubble, and there were flecks of blood on my face like huge freckles. No wonder I had scared the waitress.

I tried to call Quartz twice before I reached Jordan City. Both times I let the phone in his cottage ring ten times before I gave up. After the second time, I put a call through to his office. Jack Casey answered the phone.

Raising my voice an octave, I said prissily, "This is Dean Collins at the college. It's urgent that I get in touch with Constable Willinger."

"Willinger's in the infirmary," Casey said. "But he can't have visitors for a while. You're speaking to the county sheriff. Can I help you?"

"No, this was a personal matter. I trust the constable isn't seriously ill."

"Serious enough. He got slugged last night. Skull fracture, the doc says."

"How terrible! Well, thank you very much." I hung up.

I entered Jordan City by a back road that ran behind the Cavendish Hotel and parallel to the Carthage Pike. It started to rain, a light drizzle that could last all day. I parked the Olds in the lot at the railroad station, walked two blocks in the rain, then up an alley to the back door of Quartz's cottage. I entered, locked the door, and made a tour of inspection.

There was a broken lamp on the living-room floor, and Quartz's bedroom was torn up a little, but otherwise the cottage looked the same. Naturally Quartz's clipboard was gone. Then I went into the shower. I must have stayed there fifteen minutes, through two shampoos, a thorough scrubbing, and a long soak. Then I shaved meticulously.

In my room I put on the last suit of clothes in my closet. I wore a polo shirt under the jacket. I field-stripped the Luger and LeRoy's .45 on the bed, cleaned and oiled both weapons, and reassembled them. Since I was fresh out of shoulder holsters, I tucked the Luger into the front of my belt. Slipping on a raincoat, I dropped the .45 into the right-hand pocket. I stopped in the living room, poured a double shot of Jack Daniels, and drank it neat.

The ten-o'clock church bells were tolling when I stepped outside. One of Casey's prowl cars was parked in front of the constable's office. There was a deputy in it, sprawled low on the seat, his cap over his eyes. I walked past the car, mounted the steps, then waited to see if the deputy was faking. He didn't move. So I crossed the porch and entered just as Jack Casey was pouring himself a cup of coffee. There was nobody else in the room.

"Good morning, Jack, long time no see." I snapped the spring lock on the door behind me and showed him the .45 automatic.

Jack spilled coffee onto his bare hand, but it didn't make him drop the cup. He lowered both pot and cup to the desk slowly. Then he wiped the burned hand with a paper napkin. "So the prodigal returns. Where you been, son? And what's the cannon for? You're not sore because I locked you up yesterday?"

"No, I figured you owed me that. But I'm sore as hell about that little barbecue your boys set me up for in Kentucky last night." Only the desk separated us now. The muzzle of the .45 was level with his belt buckle.

"You'll have to translate that into English for me," Jack said.

"Let's begin with your boy Humpty, Jack. Where is he?"

He flexed the thumb he had scalded. He let it irk him. "I don't see what that is any of your business! You can't come in here waving a—"

I grabbed his Sam Browne belt and fistful of shirt and jerked him across the desk. He caught himself on his elbows, and I laid the muzzle of the .45 into the point of his chin, not gently. "Jack, I killed three men this morning to keep this appointment, and my blood is up. Your boy Humpty set me up last night for those three corncobs your police force has been trying to find for a month. So answer my questions or I'll blow your goddamn head off." I cocked it.

I felt him swallow. Our faces were only a foot apart, and after a few seconds he must have seen in my face what the waitress had

239

seen. The difference was that Jack recognized it. "My mistake," he said. "Humpty got a call about an hour ago and took off on a personal errand."

"Where'd he go on this errand?" I asked.

"Spencer's Falls. He let on like it was a woman in trouble."

"Where'd Humpty work before he worked for you?"

Again he swallowed. "Some years back he went to a town up north and got on the police force up there. Then he got into trouble, and they canned him. So he came back to his old stomping grounds, and I hired him."

"What was the name of the town up north?"

"Steubenville, Ohio."

"Now I have to know about you, Jack. Talk turkey to me."

For a few seconds he didn't comprehend. Then he did, and I felt him bristle. "I didn't have any part in setting you up. But if Humpty did what you said, you have my word that he will pay the full penalty for it."

"Did you give the order to let me out of jail yesterday?"

"Yes. I couldn't hold you after Clayborne told his blackmail story. Hump placed the call. I had to run over to Carthage on that Swanson killing."

I released him and sat down in a chair. There was a small red circle imprinted on his chin. Jack stayed in place for a moment. "The first time I saw you I called you an amateur in this business. That was a mistake, wasn't it?"

"Yes, but your big mistake was the cheap case you made against that janitor. Sorry about the gun. But I had to know whether you were bought or just lazy."

Casey eased back into his chair. He raised his hand, then dropped it. He wanted to rub his chin, but he didn't for the same reason professional baseball players won't rub when they're hit by a pitched ball: simple pride. "I really believed the janitor killed the girl until yesterday. The blackmail story cast considerable doubt on it. You should have told me about the blackmail, Butler."

"You wouldn't have listened," I said. "You needed two more murders to cast that doubt."

"Maybe so." Then he asked a good cop question. "Was it just revenge that made you so popular with that Kentucky trash?"

"No, they were paid for their work. Humpty paid them, and somebody's been paying Humpty right along."

"It began to smell that way," he said. "You mind if I make one call?"

"Go ahead."

He dialed a number, talked for a few minutes, then hung up. "That was Humpty's landlady. She said he busted in there a while ago, made a phone call, then packed a suitcase and lit out. I'm afraid we're up a creek, son."

"Maybe not. Jack, would you be willing to forget my bad manners and team up with me? Unless I'm wrong, I can promise you the murderer, the one person who committed all three. I think we can still nail Humpty, too. What do you say?"

He thought about it, a lean, hard man with humiliation smoldering in his eyes. "Why don't you do it yourself?" he said.

"I can't cut it alone. I need your help, and, believe me, I'm not trying to steal your thunder. The credit—"

"God damn your soul!" he said. "Do you think I care about credit now? If I was that wrong about the janitor and Humpty, I'll eat my crow. But don't talk about credit like a fruity scoutmaster."

"My blunder," I said.

He sighed. "Okay, I'll back your play, Butler. But you better be right."

"Call Eddie Bell's house," I said. "If he's home, tell him you want to see him later about the King murder. Be casual. But I don't think he's home."

I lit up a stogie and smoked while he dialed and talked.

"That was Bell's wife," Casey said. "She said Eddie drove downtown to get the Sunday paper about ten minutes ago."

"He did like hell," I said. "He went to meet Humpty at the Stagecoach, to give him enough money to travel far and fast."

"But why the Stagecoach?" Casey asked. "He could meet him anyplace."

"Two reasons. Eddie wouldn't keep that kind of money at the house. The banks are still closed today, but the Saturday night receipts are in the Stagecoach safe. And since the Stagecoach is closed today, it would be a safe place to meet."

"Then we better move," Casey said. "Maybe his wife lied about the ten minutes."

"We'll take my car," I said. "Have your deputy follow us, but no sirens."

"No, we don't want to spook them, do we?" Casey said.

I brought the Mercury around while he talked to his deputy On the way to the Stagecoach, I gave Jack a summary of my battle with the mountain boys.

When I finished, Casey said, "You should have shot the woman, or else locked her up. She must have been the one who called Humpty."

"Yeah, I got careless," I said. "But then I don't often kill three men before breakfast anymore. Now tell me about Quartz."

"Not much to tell. He searched all over for you last night. I talked to him twice on the phone. Then about three A.M. I got a call from this lady friend of yours, Linda Thorpe. Quartz had got her so fired up, she left work to help look for you. She found Quartz at his place, out cold. They had him in the infirmary by the time I got to Jordan. That Thorpe woman was fit to be tied. Does she know you got home safe?"

"Business before pleasure," I said. "Here's the Stagecoach."

I drove past the parking lot and turned into the service driveway, which curved around to a loading platform behind the kitchen. When I saw two cars parked behind the building, I pulled into a slot beside the garage rack.

"You called this one right," Casey said. "That's Hump's car."

"They're probably in Eddie's office," I said. "Do you know the layout?"

"Yeah, I had a good look around after that big robbery a few weeks back. Bell's office has two entrances. One near the kitchen, and one from the club."

"You cover the door from the kitchen, and let me circle around through the club," I said. "I'll greet our friends, then you come in."

"Suits me. Watch that fat boy. He can shoot."

We got out of the car and walked thirty yards in the rain to the back door. It was covered with a sheet of black steel, decorated with a padlock as big as your fist, which was hanging open on its hasp. There was also a spring lock on the door. This one was locked, but Casey snicked the bolt back with a tool very much like one locked in the trunk of my Mercury. We entered the kitchen as silently as a pair of thieves. It was a long rectangle, and at the end of the room we

242

halted before a door with a porthole in it. Across the hall was Eddie's office. The door was closed, but there was a hairline of yellow light along its bottom. Casey held the kitchen door open wide enough for me to slip into the hall. It ran to the front of the building and opened into the lobby where Linda greeted the members. Here I shed my raincoat. I left the .45 in the pocket and took the Luger from my belt. Then I cat-footed into the club room.

The place was dimly lighted by tiny red bulbs. It had a sweet and sour odor, as if the perfume from all the gaiety and spicy stories and boozy illusions had turned bitter without nourishment. The door from the club to Eddie's office was ajar, throwing a funnel of light on the red carpet. A murmur of voices grew louder as I approached the office. Through the crack on the hinged side of the door I saw Eddie behind his desk, talking earnestly to someone out of my field of vision. Eddie was tapping a sheaf of money on the blotter for emphasis.

The door behind which Casey waited was directly across the room from me. I took a deep breath, let it half out, and stepped into the room with the gun leveled. Humpty was sitting in profile to me across the desk from Eddie. He wore a dun-colored raincoat as big as a pup tent, and on his lap he held a fawn-colored Western-style hat. Eddie stopped in midsentence when he saw me, but it was Humpty who moved, bolting to his feet so fast that his hat went flying.

"Go ahead, Humpty," I said. "Join your cousin LeRoy in hell."

He flushed to the color of raw meat. Eddie merely looked a little sad. I moved ten feet closer. A floor safe in the corner stood half open. There was a metal cashbox on the desk, and Eddie flicked the sheaf of money into it with a movement that reminded me of his deft hands. I wondered where Casey was.

"On your feet, Eddie," I said. "Both of you put your hands behind your neck."

"Don't do it, Willie," Eddie said. "Just stand there and breathe. Butler, this situation deserves talk. I mean money talk, negotiation." There was nothing slow about his speech now. It was crisp, staccato.

"No sale, pimp. I never make deals with hoods who order me dead." He winced at the "pimp." After all, he had worked hard to improve his image and social standing.

"Don't let's be emotional about it, Butler. Hell, you're no cop. When I say money, I mean the whole bundle. You get the hundred

G's, the tape, all of it." He kept doing tricky things with his hands, like a magician setting you up. He fingered his tie, dug wax from his ear, fondled his cuff links.

"You're right about one thing, Eddie. I'm not a cop. I'd rather kill you than take you in. So scratch your gun out, and let's get done with it."

His hands paused, two hairy spiders on the edge of the desk. "Don't kid me, Butler. You wouldn't pay a hundred thousand bucks for a cheap thrill. Besides, you put in a hard night. Your wrists are raw, your eyes look bad and your hand's shaking. You must have turned squeamish down in the country. You didn't have the nerve to shoot the woman."

He was good. He was so damn good, in fact, that I decided to shoot him in the shoulder just to shut him up. But just then I felt a draught of cool air and a gun boom behind me. The noise was like a howitzer in the small office. Humpty yelled and toppled like a tree, but I didn't watch him land. Eddie's hand darted into the top drawer of his desk. I fired into the blotter and he snatched his hand out as if it had touched fire. It was empty. He jerked upright and slapped his hands on top of his head and blinked at me.

"What kept you, Jack?" I said.

"The damn door was locked," he said. "Funny we didn't think of that. I like to never got it open with that gizmo. You didn't heed my warning. Fat boy was fixing to draw on you. He's with that cowboy draw."

"I told you I couldn't cut it alone. Where'd you shoot him?"

"I broke his goddamn knee for him. Here, put these cuffs on Bell. I've got an extra pair for this tub of guts."

I cuffed Eddie's hands behind his back, frisked him, and put him on a chair against the wall. By then Humpty was lying on his back, his hands cuffed in front, and blood seeped from his leg onto the rug. "Let's have a drink," Casey said. "This kind of work always gives me a thirst."

"Name your brand," I said. "We've got a bar at our disposal."

"Any good bourbon will do," Casey said. "You might see if my deputy's out front while you're about it. Tell him to call in for an ambulance."

The deputy was pounding on the front door when I reached it. I gave him the message, assured him the ambulance wasn't for Casey, and picked up glasses and a fifth of Jack Daniels on my way back to Eddie's office. Casey poured three fingers of the bourbon and drank it off as if it were tea.

"Now let's talk," he said. "I'll work in the blind up to a point, but now I'm starved for facts. I gather these two were behind that so-called robbery of this dump. Bell ordered it, and lard-belly sent his kinfolk to pull it off. I'm even bright enough to guess that the robbery was a dodge. They were really out to lay Quartz up. Then these two would have Jordan City to themselves."

"I don't understand, Jack."

He grinned. "Hump there coaxed me to assign him to cover Jordan City after Quartz was laid up. That was before we heard you were coming in. I would've done it, too. I trusted that fat boy. How'd these two get so thick?"

"Eddie used to be in the rackets in Steubenville. They probably worked together on some cute little blackmail deals up there. Eddie's wife was a hooker, and Eddie used to shake down some of her clients with photos he took of them with Madge. Humpty was probably his muscle. But you can't be greedy in the rackets. When the big boys got wind of it, they booted Eddie out. That's probably about the same time Humpty got canned from the force." I nosed around in Eddie's safe until I was satisfied that neither the blackmail money nor the tape was there. I wasn't surprised. I thought I knew where they were.

Casey poured himself another drink. "But if blackmail was this runt's game, why'd he kill the Clayborne girl?"

"Eddie didn't kill the girl," I said. "Eddie didn't kill anyone. He was chairman of the board in the blackmail scheme. There are two other people involved. One is Philip Clayborne's ex-wife, Eleanor Sheridan. The other partner is one of Eleanor's old flames from when she was a student at Jordan College. You see, Eleanor had the dirt on her husband, but she didn't have the stuff to make him pay off. Only the daughter could furnish her with that. You might say that Natalie was an eye witness to her father's crime."

Eddie Bell snickered to himself.

"From the way you're telling this," Jack said, "I'm beginning to think that I'm not going to learn the details of this scandal."

"We'll talk about it later, Jack. The point is that Natalie would never willingly have given her mother the dirt she needed. That's

245

where the old flame came in. He had to win the girl's confidence and get her to put it on tape."

"So he killed her," Casey said. "But why?"

"Because she learned that her mother was behind the scheme," I said. "Natalie was in love with this man. She thought the money was for them to make a life together. But as soon as she learned that her mother was involved, she knew where the money was going. She meant to ruin the blackmail scheme by using the dirt against her father. So the old flame had to kill her."

"But this character you call the 'old flame' would have to split with Eddie, wouldn't he?" Casey said.

"No, the old flame didn't know about Eddie," I said. "I know that for a fact. He thought it was just him and Eleanor. But Eddie and Eleanor were using him as a tool. He wasn't likely to give them away, after he killed three people."

"My, my," Casey said. "Such a den of thieves. How about this runt's wife, the hooker? Was she in on it?"

"Madge had to know about the blackmail plan. Whether she knew who the old flame was, I can't say. Maybe Eddie and Eleanor planned to dump Madge later."

Eddie snickered again and spoke for the first time. "Not for a crazy old hag like this Sheridan broad," he said. "She's a sick woman, strictly booby-hatch material. She drove me nuts, the way she snuck around to play footsie with Waldo Mason, mooning about the past."

"But what about the rest of it?" Casey said. "Did Butler call it right?"

"Screw you," Eddie said, and he stared at the rug.

"Oh, that's a sweet sound," Casey said. He eased off the desk and took a shiny black billyclub from his hip pocket.

I stepped forward and touched him on the arm. "Not now, Jack. You've got plenty to stick him with if Humpty talks, even without the blackmail rap. You and I had better pick up the murderer before he starts running."

"All right," Jack said. "And don't you worry about Humpty talking. He'll talk a blue streak. He'll talk if I have to shoot his other kneecap off and hang him by his thumbs."

"Maybe we'd better put a tourniquet on that leg," I said.

246

"We'll let Deputy Sturgill do that," Casey said. "We better scoot, so you can introduce me to this murderer. From the smug way you talk, I gather you know his name."

"Oh, I know his name," I said. "But I won't have to introduce you."

"Is that a fact?" he said.

It was still raining—little gray slugs against the light green maple trees—when I unlocked the front door of the *Jordan City News* with Jack Casey's skeleton key. Easing the door open a few inches, I raised my hand and trapped the bell that announced arrivals when no one was manning the front desk. I doubted that Paul would have heard the bell anyway, if he was absorbed in the work his wife had said he was doing. Casey had made the call from the constable's office, and I had listened on the extension.

"I'm sorry, Sheriff, but Paul's not home," she had said. "He's down at the shop melting his lead. It's a chore he often does on Sunday."

I heard the roar of some kind of furnace even before I reached the door at the back of the shop. I opened the door an inch and put my eye to the crack. The furnace was really a cast-iron stove, round and squat, with a loud gas jet. A round depression in the top of the stove held a cast-iron spoon the size of a small dishpan. The spoon was full of molten lead. Paul, wearing an asbestos mask and huge gloves, lifted the spoon carefully by its long handle, and poured the lead into a series of molds on the floor. Then he replaced the spoon on the stove and filled it with chunks of broken type from a wooden box. It was the last batch.

I closed the door quietly and walked back to his office. The two dirty windows afforded only a thin gray light from the sodden day outside. One corner was especially dark, so I shoved a chair over there, lit a stogie, and sat down to wait. After a moment, I got up and crossed to Paul's rolltop desk and turned his lamp on. Several items for next week's edition were impaled on a long steel spike on the desk. I leafed through them without reading a word, turned off the lamp, and went back to my corner. It was just noon. My stogie tasted like it had been cured over sulphur.

Ten minutes later Paul entered the office, went straight to his desk, turned on the lamp, and sat down in his chair. Leaning forward, he rummaged in the desk until he found a pint bottle of whiskey, which he uncorked and tilted up for a drink. Then his chair creaked as he stiffened and sniffed the air. He had smelled my stogie.

"Hello, Paul!" I said, booming it out.

He bolted clumsily from the chair and peered into my corner. "Who is it?"

"It's Morgan Butler. You remember me, Paul."

He was silent for a full minute. I couldn't see his face clearly because his back was to the lamp. "Of course I remember you. What a thing to say! But you gave me a start. I thought I locked the door. How long have you been here?" He reached back and jerked the cord that turned on the overhead light.

"Maybe ten minutes," I said. "I saw you melting your lead back there, so I thought I'd wait here. I didn't think you'd mind."

"No. Certainly not." Paul discovered the bottle in his hand. He looked at it sheepishly. "You caught me imbibing. On Sunday, too. How about a snort against the chill?"

"No, thanks." I got up and moved to the easychair that faced his desk.

Paul settled into his swivel chair and put the bottle on the desk. A hard gust of wind drove rain against the windowpanes like a handful of buckshot. "What brings you out on such a rotten day?" he asked. "Anything new on Quartz?"

"I haven't seen Quartz," I said. "I came to keep a promise I made to you. I told you I'd give you a scoop on this case as soon as I had the murderer pegged. Remember?"

He said softly, "So you know who the murderer is. Are you certain?"

"Absolutely. Aren't you going to put some paper in the typewriter?"

Paul glanced at the old Underwood. "Why don't you give me the gist of it first? Am I to understand that you haven't told the story to anyone else?"

"I had to tell Jack Casey," I said. "It really staggered Old Jack."

"But he believed you? You convinced him?"

"Oh, yes. No trouble there." Suddenly I felt awkward, inhibited by some memory of his wife. My chest felt as hard as a glazed cinder. But I thought of Natalie and Arthur King, and I said, "Let's

248

stop fencing, Paul. I would have had you cold last Monday, but too many people in this case lied to me."

Paul lifted his shaggy eyebrows in an effort to convey incredulity. "Did I hear you right? Are you calling me a murderer?"

"You killed all three of them, Paul. Natalie Clayborne. A man named Swanson, the night you tried to kill me. And Arthur King. That's quite a week's work for any killer."

He shook his head. "You've made some kind of terrible mistake, Butler."

"Please, Paul. Do I have to open you like a can of tomatoes? Should I start with that clue Natalie prepared under your nose that Saturday night? Remember the Dostoyevsky novel? She marked three pages, four, thirty, and thirty-nine. The first two numbers identify you clearly, and the third marries you to Eleanor Sheridan. Natalie did a good job under pressure. You know what the 'four' means. You even referred to yourself as one of the 'ink-stained wretches of the fourth estate' that day we drove back from the inquest. The 'thirty' is the tag all journalists use to end their stories. I haven't seen it in years, but there are plenty of samples on that spike on your desk. The trouble with Natalie's clue was that she expected it to be matched to a poem she mailed to Arthur King. But King kept the poem a secret, and I decided that the set of numbers had to be a date. Of course you know the poem I mean, the one she titled 'Coronation.' Very romantic little piece. I imagine Natalie watched you melt your lead more than once. Vulcan at the hearth. She called it a 'mawkish stew.' That poor, miserable girl loved you, Paul."

A nerve in his cheek jumped like a trout striking. "Surely you don't call this evidence," he said. "It's garbage. You can't prove anything with it."

Suddenly I was furious, far more angry than I had been at any time last night or this morning. I had to take a deep breath before I could speak. "Oh, the evidence is there, Paul, now that Casey knows where to look. I'm sure he'll be able to connect you with Eleanor Sheridan, back when you were an idealistic young Marxist and she was the campus whore."

"You filthy pig!" he said through his teeth.

"Hurts, does it? Well, maybe Casey won't have to go that far back. He'll likely turn up a witness who saw you and Natalie together. You probably met her right here, played daddy to her on the

249

couch over there. Yes, we know all about the incest, Paul. Casey also has the gun to work with, the one you left in King's desk. Those service .45's can be traced. The army keeps good records. Also, you killed King here in your office. I'm sure you cleaned up the blood, but a good man will find traces. Oh, Casey will find the evidence. But he doesn't need it, Paul. He can convict you on testimony."

He croaked, "That's impossible. What do you mean?"

"You thought you and Eleanor planned the whole thing, but you were her dupe from the beginning, Paul. She and Eddie Bell planned this blackmail scheme. Eddie was the pro behind the scenes."

"I don't believe it," Paul said. "You're trying to trap me."

"No, Paul. Three of Eddie's hoods are dead, a fourth is in the hospital, and Eddie is in Casey's jail. Remember, Eddie's been through the mill. He knows you committed those murders, and he'll tell it all to save his own skin. Odd how your instinct about him was accurate. You must have sensed the threat."

"How do you know she wasn't using him?" Paul said.

"Because Eddie knew about you, but you didn't know about Eddie."

Paul clapped his hands and rubbed the heels together hard, like an old man working up some friction for warmth. "You're wrong about my being Eleanor's dupe. She had her reasons for not telling me about him. You don't even know her. A clod like you could never appreciate a relationship like ours." Then he jerked his tortured eyes towards me. "What did Eddie tell you about her?"

"The same thing Waldo told us, with minor modifications," I said. "That she's sick, withered, practically a recluse. And quite mad."

He stopped rubbing his hands and wiped them absently on his coat. "Yes, she's sick, but she can be made well again. We were going to use the money to make her well. Clayborne owed her that, and more." His voice had gained in resonance, and now he looked at me calmly, sweat dripping from his chin.

"Don't try to justify yourself to me, Paul. Save that for the jury. I am curious about a couple of things, though. How did you know where I was the night you killed Swanson by mistake? Who sent you to Metterman's house?"

"That was a piece of luck," he said. "Or at least I thought it was luck until you told me Bell was involved. You see, I had planned to

250

kill you that night. I had decided you were dangerous to us. I planned
to go to the Stagecoach and visit Bell just to give myself an alibi. I
had my gun in my car. I intended to call you at midnight, persuade
you to meet me in a certain place, then I planned to slip away, do the
job, and get back in less than twenty minutes. But while I was talking
to Bell, he had a call from Madge about this housebreaker. She told
him you had gone to Metterman's. I know a shortcut to the Old
Sawmill Road from the Stagecoach. It bypasses Jordan City a mile
north of town. I drove to Metterman's in fifteen minutes."

A soft place in my mind quivered with awe at what he was doing.
"Answer me another question, Paul. How did you know King was
coming here on Friday night?"

"I didn't," he said. "That was another piece of luck. I left Waldo
at two A.M. We'd guzzled quite a few beers, and I took a walk to
clear my head. I saw a light in my shop. I came in from the alley and
caught him."

"That adds up to an awful lot of luck," I said. "Especially when
you add to it the luck you had with the janitor on the first killing."

"That wasn't all luck," Paul said. "I knew about Ewing and his
rag collection. Natalie had told me that the girls suspected him. I was
still in her room that night when he fired the furnace. I was looking
for the carbon of that damn poem. It occurred to me in a flash what a
fine suspect he would make. I took the blue girdle from Natalie's
drawer and wrote 'harlot' on it with lipstick. I drove straight to
Ewing's trailer and planted it. He almost caught me." Now his face
had the feverish look of a man scheming for survival. And the sad
part of it all was that it wasn't his survival he was scheming for.

He couldn't keep the zeal from his voice when he spoke. "I'll bet
that pimp Eddie Bell couldn't tell you where Eleanor lives."

"I didn't ask," I said. "And he didn't volunteer the information."

"Because he doesn't know," Paul said. "Eleanor might have used
him, but she would never trust him completely. She doesn't like to
appear in public, and she has a good hiding place. I'm the only one
who knows where she lives."

"Oh, I think we can flush the old crone out without much
trouble," I said.

"No! Wait, listen to me. I want to make a deal with you."

"You're hardly in a bargaining position, Paul."

251

"Yes, I am. You still have to convict me. And I know enough law to know that all that talk about evidence is bluff. You think the .45 can be traced? You're wrong. It was never checked out to me. You might find blood here, but it would only be a blood type. And you can stuff Eddie Bell's testimony. Do you think a jury will believe a gangster's word against mine in this country? With a good lawyer, the odds are very much in my favor. But I'm willing to make a deal. I'll write a full confession to all three murders—on the condition that you leave Eleanor Sheridan out of it completely. After all, she hasn't really committed any crime. You said yourself that Eddie planned the blackmail scheme. He sent those hoods after you. And I committed the murders. Eleanor's only crime is her obsession with the idea of punishing Clayborne. And did you ever know a man who deserved punishment more? So what do you say? Is it a deal?"

Now I knew what jumped in his voice, what gleamed in his eyes, what juices fed his emotions. It was the holy ecstasy of martyrdom, the romantic's last refuge.

I raised my voice. "Casey! You willing to consider such a deal?"

"Not hardly," Jack Casey said from the doorway behind me. "I'm greedy now. I want all these slick operators to pay through the nose. How do, Paul."

Paul didn't even look at him. His hot face was focused on me.

"But Paul hasn't finished describing his deal, Jack," I said. "Paul's willing to withhold all testimony about the blackmail business as part of the package. He'll have to, to keep Eleanor out of it. I'm sure Eddie will go along. That means I can fulfill my contract to Clayborne. His scandal won't be exposed."

Jack walked into the room and stood beside me. "You're not making sense. As I understand it, this Sheridan snail is the lady with all the marbles. She picked up the blackmail money, right? She's got the dirty tape, right? What's to prevent her from bleeding Clayborne until the fellow turns white?"

"That's his problem," I said. "If this sick old hag tries to blackmail him again, he'll have to negotiate on his own. But I seriously doubt that Eleanor will have the courage to do it, now that we know she's behind it."

"You're right!" Paul said. "She'll consider herself lucky to get out of this with the money. It's nothing to Clayborne, but she needs it. She's all alone."

"What do you say, Jack?" I asked. "Paul has a point about his confession. We damn near need it for a conviction. And even if we had the Sheridan woman, how could we convict her when neither of these fellows will testify against her?"

"I don't like it," Casey growled. "But I'm willing to buy it. You're the one who has to make his peace with Clayborne. I hope he decides not to pay you."

"That's my problem, Jack. Yours is the prisoner here. If I were you, I'd have him write the confession now, and I would have it signed and witnessed with Paul's lawyer present." I got to my feet.

"Where you going?" Jack said. "I want you to stay and read what he writes. I want to be sure it's all there."

"Like you said, I have to make my peace with Clayborne. I think you can trust Paul to do a thorough job. He'll start with how he and Natalie became lovers, and how angry he got when she threatened to spurn him."

"Yes, that's the way I'll write it," Paul said. "Thanks, Butler."

"Go to hell, buster," I said.

I went outside and hiked down to the Mercury. On the way I thought of something I forgot to tell Casey, that he had better keep a very close watch on his prisoner if he expected to bring him to trial. Martyrdom loses its zest if you begin to think about sitting on death row for six months while all the appeals are made. But I didn't give a damn about that either.

Chapter 20
***

An hour later I made myself a double Scotch from Linda Thorpe's liquor cabinet. I had earned it. My work was done, and I was entitled to all the comforts. I carried the drink to the black leather sofa and stretched out. Linda wasn't at home, but I had good reason to believe that she would return soon.

I heard her car even before I finished the Scotch. She drove in fast, her tires squealed when she stopped, and her heels were brisk on the walk. The door opened and she flicked a switch that turned on three lamps. Her bag clashed on a chair, and she was halfway across the room when I sat up.

"Hello, beautiful lady."

Immobilized, she seemed to glitter with tension. She was wearing emerald-green stretch pants and a pale-green sweater. She had dumped her coat with the bag. "Dear God, you're alive," she said in a hoarse voice. "I thought they'd killed you."

"You thought who had killed me?"

Now she was functioning again. She moved quickly around the sofa. "Hold me, Butler. Please hold me."

I rose as she collided with m, and I held her. "You thought who had killed me?" Her face was against my shoulder and I stroked her hair.

"I don't know. The murderer, I guess. When you disappeared last night, I thought the worst had happened. I spent a hellish night."

"I went on a little trip," I said. "Sorry you had a bad night."

She shivered in my arms. "Please fix me a drink, darling."

I lowered her to the sofa and went to the liquor cabinet. I spoke cheerfully, "I've been waiting for over an hour. Where have you been?"

"With Madge Bell. She's worried about Eddie. He drove out to the Stagecoach on an errand this morning and hasn't come home. She can't get him on the phone, and he's long overdue. She's afraid he's had an accident."

I returned with two drinks and sat down beside her. "I'm surprised you left her alone if she's upset."

Linda took a long drink of her Scotch. Then she moved closer to me and placed a hand on my shoulder. Her smile was intimate, a caress. "Oh, you know Madge. She's so insecure, so prone to hysteria. Eddie's a careful driver. He probably stopped someplace for a drink."

"Maybe he's got a lady friend stashed away in the neighborhood," I said.

"Eddie? I seriously doubt it. You have a dirty mind, Mr. Butler."

"Oh, I don't know. It would explain a lot of things. Madge's hysteria. Her fling with Metterman, her invitation to romp with me. Maybe she's really worried that someday he'll take off with this lady friend."

"That would take money," Linda said. "And I happen to know they count every cent Eddie makes." Now her smiled looked just a little artificial.

"Yeah, I guess that wrecks my little theory. A man would need a bundle of money to take off and make a new life for himself."

Her nails tightened on my arm. "Say, Butler. How did you get in here without a key? And why didn't I see your car out front?"

"My car's around back in your carport," I said. "And I came in through the door from the port, which you so carelessly left unlocked."

The lie about the door had made mincemeat of her insides. But her composure was superb. She put her drink down carefully, hugged herself with a delicious little shiver, and said, "This weather has chilled the whole house. Why don't we have a fire, Butler? There are logs and kindling in the basement, if you don't mind playing boy scout."

"In a minute," I said. "First, I want to give you a present." I took the turquoise bracelet from my pocket and dangled it before her.

It had a hypnotic effect. She sat absolutely still for a moment, then she took it and looked at me with an expression of wonderment.

"I should warn you that it's a very expensive bracelet," I said.

She shook her head slowly. "Don't be silly. I told you it wasn't worth more than twenty dollars. But how on earth—"

"You don't understand," I said. "That bracelet has increased in value since the last time you saw it. I killed three men to get it back for you. That's a lot of blood, not to mention the risk involved to me. Offhand, I'd say you owe me an even hundred thousand dollars."

Her spine stiffened. "That's a pretty sick job, Butler." She gave a dry, husky laugh. "That's quite a debt." Then she grew artful. Stroking my hand with her fingertips, she lowered her eyes and voice. "I were as bold as I'd like to be with you, I'd tell you you'd have to take it out in trade."

"That won't be necessary. I've already collected. I wouldn't want to make you into more of a whore than you already are, just to pay off a debt."

She jerked back as if I had spit on her. "What's the matter with you? How did you collect?"

"I'll save you some wear and tear on your nervous system. You can stop trying to trick me out of the room so you can run back to the sculptor's studio and see if Eddie took your money. I took it. I suppose you thought it was clever to hide your loot inside that plastic model of a nude, but that was just as obvious as your friend McIntosh trying to fool me with a copy of *Hamlet*. Oh, I also took that tape your daughter made. The masquerade is over, Eleanor."

She shook her head doggedly. "Butler, if someone planted money in my—"

I hit her hard in the mouth with the back of my fist. She caught herself with a hand flung behind her. Blood oozed from a corner of her mouth.

"That wasn't for lying," I said. "That was for setting me up last night for Eddie's hillbillies. I'll admit that call to Waldo was an inspired move. The poor sap really thought you were ready to come out into the open."

"Butler, listen, someone's deceived you about me—"

"Oh, for Christ's sake." I grabbed the front of her sweater, jerked her face down on the sofa, and swept the hair from the back of her neck. "You're Eleanor Sheridan, honey, and you've got the scar to prove it. That's the big one in cosmetic surgery, the complete overhaul. I knew an actress in San Francisco who shed fifteen years with that one." I jerked her face into profile. "Of course it wasn't just youth you were after. You had some other work done, too. You had him tilt the eyes a little. And the nose is changed, 'rhinoplasty' I think they call it. You probably had sandpaper surgery around the mouth, and you had him pump up that nice elastic bosom. I think they're using silicone jelly now, a great improvement over the old paraffin injections. Then, with the dyed hair and the tinted contact

256

lenses, you were a new woman. The real touch was having that mole removed from your belly. But then, in your line of work, you were as likely to be recognized by your belly as your face."

She lay there with her eyes closed, no longer resisting me. I got up and went to the bar with a sensation that I was leaking some valuable substance from every pore. My hand shook as I poured the drink. It wasn't merely that she had worked her sorcery on me, enchanted me, duped me. She had also distorted reality for me, drawn from me feelings of tenderness, joy, respect, eased in some mystical way the ancient terror of isolation. So my emotions about her were snarled, painful to cut away.

I didn't return to my seat on the sofa. I sat on the black leather chair across the coffee table from her. Propping my feet up, I drank and waited.

Presently she sat up, snatched the hair from her face with the heel of one hand, and gave me a bold look, a wry smile through swollen lips. "So the masquerade's over," she said. "I suppose Eddie and Paul are in jail?"

"That's the size of it."

"And you've got a nice cell reserved for me?"

"No, your playmates were loyal to you," I said. "They both told the same fairy tale about the sick, neurotic old woman in hiding. It's a story you worked hard to make credible, by setting Waldo up as a respectable witness. So it has to be the story they were coached to tell if anything went wrong."

She seemed not to comprehend for a moment. Then she said, "Yes, that was the plan. But if they told it that way, how did you know me? I thought—"

"Oh, you had me fooled all the way," I said. "I'll give you credit for that. You're the best I've ever seen. And I think I know why. You've perfected the whore's talent to a fine art. You have the ability to discover quickly what a man most desires in a woman, and to become that woman completely. You even boasted about the gift that evening you told me how you fulfilled the fantasies of the members at the Stagecoach. Remember? It's a career you probably launched at puberty."

"I wasn't quite that precocious," she said. Now there was a hint of zest in her voice, a subtle improvement in her posture.

257

"Quite a repertoire," I said. "I know what you were for me. And Waldo described the disguise you wore for him. I'll bet you enjoyed playing the tragic role, special makeup and all. Let's see, McIntosh shouldn't have been hard. A slightly tarnished image of that blithe spirit who scalded him when he was young. But now you could also offer him a grand adventure, direct action against the enemy. Not just Clayborne personally, but the rich, capitalist, the evildoer. And you were to be the prize. That was the big flaw in Paul's story. He's not the type to risk everything to pay an ugly old woman's doctor bills. Natalie knew he needed a grand passion to free him from his chains. She even wrote a poem about it. But you were Paul's grand passion."

"But Natalie's murder was never a part of it!" she said. "Paul did that on his own. The idiot let Natalie find out I was involved, and he killed her to keep her from destroying the plan. I would have given up everything to have prevented that. Believe me, Butler."

"You wouldn't have given up the money. Eddie wouldn't have allowed it."

"Eddie would have done anything I told him to do," she said.

"So you had him bamboozled, too. Let's see, for Eddie you were the opposite of Madge. A lady of breeding, embarrassed by your own appetites, girlishly shocked by Eddie's expertise. Yes, all those years you spent in the social register were Eddie's downfall. Hardly worth your talents."

"You keep harping on that, Butler. But in spite of my so-called talent, you found me out. Would you mind telling me how?"

The bitterness I felt about her informed me that this was just another pitch, an appeal to my vanity. But there was a certain fascination in seeing it through. "I wondered about you as soon as I read the blackmail note left at the Esso station. It told Clayborne to fire me. But I was supposed to be dead, remember? You were the only person who knew I had survived Paul's gun that night. You must have called Eddie after I called you, so he could rewrite the note. Also, you were Paul's alibi for the Swanson killing. Oh, he tried to get you off the hook with a story of how he overheard Madge's call to Eddie. But Madge didn't call Eddie, she called you. You sent Paul on his errand."

"Why wouldn't Eddie have sent him?" she asked.

"No dice. Paul didn't know Eddie was in on it. The third item has to do with Arthur King. Paul didn't just stumble on King in his

258

office, as he said. You overheard King's phone call to me around one-thirty that night, just after you got back with the money. You called Paul and told him King went to his office."

I waited for her to deny that one. She merely shrugged.

I went on. "I even backtracked to that first Sunday in Quartz's cottage, when I came back from investigating the stolen tapes. That gift for Quartz was a pretext. You were there to find out what we intended to do about the tapes. Then, when Natalie began to get out of hand during the week, you and Eddie smelled trouble. So you picked me up that night with the story about the bracelet. Not to mention that quaint little drama casting you as the devoted wife to the struggling writer in Mexico. Then, after Paul killed Natalie, and I began nosing around, it was easy to set me up for those hoods on Monday night."

She was watching me with rapt expression. "Most of that story about Mexico was true," she said. "Howard Thorpe was real. I loved that man, and if he hadn't died, none of this would have happened. It was too cruel."

I ignored her. "One reason you fooled me was the rough treatment the hoods gave you the night they ambushed us. I don't think that was in the script. They got out of hand. But they weren't the most stable boys around."

"All right, that's enough!" she said. "I'd like a drink. Do you mind?"

"Go ahead." Her gestures were almost jaunty as she moved to the bar and made the drink. When she was settled again, I said, "Now, answer me a question."

"I thought you knew everything," she said.

"Not quite. Why did you people sic Madge on Metterman?"

She laughed dryly. "That was a fluke. Carl saw me on the Bells' patio in a bikini that first hot Sunday. He offered to paint me, and he made a remark that led me to think he recognized me. Madge had to find out if he had."

"A chore she accepted with enthusiasm. Answer me another one. Didn't you and Eddie plan to dump Madge eventually? I know you planned to dump Paul."

She drank, wincing as the alcohol burned her cut mouth. "Yes, dumping Madge was part of the original plan. But I changed my mind about Eddie this week. I did it because of something else that wasn't in the script. You see, I was supposed to charm you, but I wasn't told to sleep with you."

"Don't tell me that was spontaneous combustion," I said.

"It was, whether you believe me or not. You made me feel feminine again. You purged me of a black loathing that has festered in me for years. Don't you see what I am? I've always been able to dominate men and manipulate them. It's the way I respond to men who attract me. And as soon as I become the dominant one, I despise them. Maybe it is a sickness. But the only cure is a man I can't dominate, like you. And Howard. Oh, I adored Howard. The years with him were the happiest of my life. I scrubbed for him, wore rags for him. When he died, I went crazy, much worse than I told you the other night. I drank tequila from dirty glasses in cheap Mexican cafes. I became a tourist attraction, the mad blonde *gringo* woman in the red serape. Eddie and Madge found me like that. They brought me out of it, and this blackmail plan was part of the therapy. It gave form to my rage. Then you came along. You jolted me, made me ashamed of it. Don't you remember how it was with us?"

I grinned at her while I lit a stogie. "You never stop working, do you?"

Her head drooped forward. "I don't blame you. Why should you believe me? But after Thursday night I couldn't go away with Eddie. I told him. I hoped you would take me to your farm, and I would make you love me."

"Sure, that's why you set me up for Eddie's hoods last night," I said.

"Butler, I swear to God, they were only supposed to rough you up a little, just enough to get you out of the way for a while. Eddie promised me faithfully. But he must have been jealous."

I shook my head in awe. "You black-hearted witch. Don't you think I know what made you hot for me those two times? Think about it. On both occasions I had just missed getting killed. You know what a man's like after that, and you wanted the thrill. Of course I didn't know you were aware of my close call that second time, so you were very convincing."

"No, you're wrong. I swear it wasn't like that."

"It would be a pretty hard relationship to sustain," I said. "Every time I wanted to turn you on, I'd have to go tangle with a killer."

"Don't, Butler. Please."

"You're even jazzed up right now, aren't you? You must be. This morning I killed like a madman. I'm still burning with it. You don't want to waste it, do you? Come on, witch. You must have a few tricks left in your bag."

She paled, and her eyes widened with horror. "If you really believe I am that kind of monster, then why don't you kill me?"

I managed a hard little laugh. "Not me, Linda. You'll get all the punishment you can handle before very long. And I imagine it will fit the crime."

"You don't mean prison. What do you mean?"

"Think about it. Who have you damaged the most with this caper?"

Her swollen lips uttered the word so softly I barely heard it, "Philip."

I nodded. "Add it up. You killed his daughter in such a way that he has to share the guilt for her murder. Not only that, but you've done irreparable damage to the rather delicate mechanism that makes Philip Clayborne function. You have smeared his image of himself with the slime of his corruption."

"To hell with him!" she said. "He brought it on himself."

"No, Linda. As long as his crime was a secret, he could color it to suit his purpose. He could call it a moment's weakness, a privilege granted to royalty. But you have exposed it, and now he has to view himself as the rest of us do, as the thief of Natalie's innocence, the man responsible for her murder. This Clayborne is the kind who mourns long and deep. I've seen him wallowing in his guilt."

"Do you think that bothers me?"

"It should. Because the day will come when Mr. Clayborne will have to have his vengeance. He has all that money and power, and that cancer of hatred and guilt eating at him. All you have is that pretty mask the nice surgeon made for you. There's not a corner of this earth where you can hide from him, once he decides to send someone after you. Then you won't even have the pretty face any longer."

Fear made her look pasty. She wet her lips. "Does he know me as Linda Thorpe?" she asked.

"No, that'll be my contribution." I patted the side pocket. "I've got a few pictures I lifted from the album in your bedroom."

She shook her head quickly. "No, Butler. You wouldn't do that. No matter how much you hate me, you have too much decency to do that."

"Don't use the word 'decency' to me, woman. You and your crew destroyed a decent girl, whose only crime was that she was your daughter. You killed a young man who might have written some decent poetry one day. Between us, the word has no meaning."

"Don't you see that you're trying to justify doing it, with all this talk? But you won't do it, Butler. You're not capable of such a thing."

"Just you watch me do it, sweetheart." I got up and walked out of the house. She made no move to stop me. She was right about the talk, but she was wrong about the other. I did, and I felt good about it afterward.

Chapter 21
***

There is more salvation in timothy hay and field corn than in all the churches in Christendom. You should cut the hay on a mowing machine, behind the rumps of a glossy team of blacks. Let the hay cure in the sun for two days, then turn it with a pitchfork and give it another day. You rake it into windrows with a hay rake, shoulder high to a tall man, and the real fun begins. You go down the windrows after the dew has lifted, your partner aloft in the wagon, and you fork and lift the hay to him in fifty-pound loads. You're awkward at first, but you find the rhythm, pacing yourself, sweating pleasantly, throwing up a green cloud of chaff with every forkful. You feel it first in your wrists, then in the small of your back, then in the shoulders. As the stack on the wagon mounts, you heave with greater gusto, until you are literally pitching your load. Then you sweat. It trickles down your neck, dances in golden drops on your eyebrows, runs into your shoes. You begin to feel that your stomach muscles are shredding. Your partner, if he is merciful, will declare the wagon loaded. Then you get to ride to the barn to unload it.

Field corn is another matter altogether. For one thing, it is solitary work. You harness one of the blacks to a five-point cultivator, tie the ends of the lines together, drape them over one shoulder and under the other, then you dig the points in and go down the long row as close to the corn as you dare. You heave your shoulders to guide the black, control the cultivator with your hands, ripping out weeds and churning dirt over the roots of the corn. When the steel points hit rocks, your hands sting. Occasionally you stop at the end of a row to give the horse a blow. But mostly you walk, mile after mile, tuned to the sound of the earth ripping, the chatter of sparrows looting grubworms from the furrows behind you, the music of the singletree and the harness.

I spent all of April and May in the fields, and I worked a twelve-hour day. In April my partner, Johnny Bass, and I harvested twelve acres of timothy hay and eight of alfalfa, replaced a hundred rotten fence posts with locust posts cut from our own woods, and trimmed and sprayed the orchard. Late in May I started on the cornfield, alternating the horses before and after lunch. Johnny started painting the barn. Each evening we met at the house at seven, showered, cooked and ate together, and I was in bed by ten at the latest.

Quartz Willinger arrived in May for a few weeks of convalescence in the sun. I eased up on the work, returning to the house early each evening so that Quartz and I could sit on the veranda and talk before dinner. He was pale, thin, and very subdued after a month in the hospital with a fractured skull. Quartz brought the news that Paul McIntosh had hanged himself in the Parson County jail two days before his trial was scheduled to begin.

One evening while we were sitting on the veranda, he told me that he had abandoned the idea of running for sheriff of Parson County. He was content with his constable's job, and his pension from the government. He left the farm tanned, heavier by five pounds, but still very subdued. I promptly returned to the old work schedule. There are a lot of miles to cultivate in fifteen acres.

Early in June Johnny Bass left on his vacation, driving west to visit his family near the Teton mountains. A week later I came in from the field for lunch to find an old station wagon parked in the driveway. Although I recognized it, I went on to stable and water the horse before going to the house.

Judy McIntosh rose from a wicker chair on the veranda as I mounted the steps. She was smartly dressed in a blue linen suit with a white blouse, and her hair was beautifully groomed. The overall effect was of poise and pride, the triumph of breeding over adversity. But when I got closer I saw the shadows under the eyes, the fingernails bitten to the quick, the brittleness in the smile."

"Hello, Morgan Butler," she said.

"Hello, Judy. I'd almost given you up. Please sit down."

She sat stiffly, her hands in her lap. "I didn't intend to come at all, but Quartz is very persuasive. Anyway, Jordan City is not the most pleasant place for me right now. I suppose I should be grateful for the opportunity to get away for a day."

She was talking too much. I said, "Why don't we start with a cool drink? Then I'll scrape up some lunch. Let's move inside."

She nodded, rose gracefully, and swept past me into the house. My living room is not quite the size of a tennis court, but it gives that impression because the side that faces our wooded acres to the north is all glass. With the old high ceiling, the original stone fireplace and

264

the furniture, heavy early-American pieces scrounged at country auctions, the room has both space and solidity.

I made Judy a drink and left her long enough to shower and slip into fresh slacks and a shirt. When I returned to the room she was holding the empty glass on her lap, looking out at the woods as if her eyes surveyed a winter landscape. I made two drinks and sat down on a chair beside her.

Without preamble, she said, "Do you want to know who's been nice? Waldo Mason. He's come to the house several times, to mow the lawn, run errands, to take the boys off my hands for the afternoon. He's very formal, but nice."

"Where are the boys now?" I asked.

"They're with Paul's parents in Pennsylvania. I kept them in school until the end of the term. Danny took it pretty well, but the youngest, Bobby, he suffered. Paul's parents are good people, and the boys need the change. In fact, I had the extravagant idea for a while that I would take the boys back to England, permanently. Suddenly, after all these years, I've gotten awfully homesick for England—that tight little isle."

"Why not go back?" I said.

"Didn't I say it was an extravagant idea? I couldn't begin to afford it. We don't own the house, and the money I'll get for the paper will barely cover outstanding debts. Paul didn't have much insurance, but it'll tide us over until I get settled in another town and find a job. You can see why it has to be a respectable job. I have to make it up to the boys. How can they be expected to reconcile themselves to this rotten business?"

I watched while she drained her glass. "I might ask the same thing about you," I said.

She twisted her mouth into a grimace. "Oh, I have an advantage over the boys," she said. "I have a treatise on the subject, a chronicle of the crime. In fact, that's what really made me decide to come up here. You deserve to read it."

"Lady, you lost me at the first turn," I said. "What chronicle is this?"

She took a deep breath. "Paul wrote a private confession to me during those weeks in jail," she said. "It's very different from the version they made public, that tale of the dirty old man who seduced and killed the innocent coed. This private confession tells all about

265

the Sheridan woman and the blackmail business. Oh, I don't mean he tried to justify himself. But he reveals his motives, his demons, if you like." She opened her purse and took a thick envelope from it.

I accepted the envelope and put it on the table between us. "I'll read it later. Now, how about another drink?"

She nodded, handing me the glass, and when I returned with the drink, her gaze was on the envelope. She said, "It's the story of a man who became secretly horrified at the insignificance of his life. He used to think that Jordan and the college were a kind of Athens. But in recent years he decided that the college wasn't much different from Standard Oil. The professors were as concerned about security, status and money as any businessman. There was no dedication, no suffering for a cause. Nothing but vanity and greed." A tear stuck in the oil of her makeup like a drop of wax.

"Will you please stop? I promise to read it."

"I'm sorry." She stood up abruptly, staggered, and caught herself with a hand on the chair. "Oh, dear. I'm afraid I'm a little light."

"Maybe you'd better lie down, while I do the galley work," I said.

She moved to the sofa. "Remember, you haven't told me yet why you wanted to see me. Quartz said it was very important."

"All in good time," I said. "Here, put a cushion behind your back. Take your shoes off if you like." On the way out of the room, I drew the light drapes over the picture window, which gave an effect of twilight in the room.

I didn't put much effort into the lunch. When I returned to the living room twenty minutes later, Judy was sound asleep on the sofa. I covered her with an afghan, tracked the heavy drapes over the window, and went back to the kitchen. I took Paul's private confession with me.

Judy slept for eight hours. During that time I read Paul's chronicle through twice, fed and watered the stock, milked the one cow we keep, and laid the groundwork for a nourishing dinner. Except for certain details, Paul's confession didn't reveal much that I hadn't already surmised.

Eleanor Sheridan had done a good job on him in thirty-nine. Paul devoted nearly two pages of his confession to a description of how he brooded and suffered after she married Clayborne. But later I saw why this suffering had to be believed. He claimed that he killed

266

Natalie in a delirium of madness. Sleeping with her had been very like sleeping with Eleanor at the same age. He was reliving that passion of his youth with the daughter, and the fulfillment of it was going to be the mother, Linda Thorpe. And when Natalie threatened to destroy the blackmail scheme, it was to Paul like a reenactment of the young Eleanor spurning him again for Clayborne. In one sense, this was a genuine fear. If he didn't get the hundred thousand, he couldn't have Linda/Eleanor, so Natalie, the young Eleanor reincarnated, was depriving him of Eleanor again.

At nine o'clock I heard Judy go upstairs to the guest room. I had pinned a note to the lamp beside the sofa, suggesting that a shower before dinner might prove refreshing, and giving directions about the guest room. When she entered the kitchen a half hour later, I saw by her face that she had already decided not to apologize for the long sleep. Her face was pink from the shower, and her eyes looked sane. "Can I help?" she asked.

"Just tell me how you like your steak."

She crossed the room and looked at the meat. "Seared and bloody," she said. "You'd better hurry. I'm so famished, I could eat it like that."

The table was set, the baked potatoes were ready, and within five minutes we were seated in the dining alcove. She did justice to the meal, and as soon as I had poured the coffee, she said, "Now are you ready to tell me why you wanted to see me?"

I looked at her for a moment. "Yes, but I want to put this in the form of a proposition. After I tell you, you'll have to make an important decision. I want you to promise not to give me the decision until tomorrow night."

"What a queer thing to suggest. Besides, I hadn't planned to stay. I didn't bring extra clothes with me."

"There are some casual clothes upstairs that will fit you, Levis, shirts, even sneakers. Believe me, this is important, for your sons as well as you."

She sipped her coffee, tilting her head a little. "You've intrigued me. All right, I promise. I can't imagine what it is, but you have my word."

"Good. Now let me ramble a moment. I've read Paul's confession, and that gives you most of the background. As for the rest, well, Natalie Clayborne once described the whole mess as a concoction of greed and lust. That's as good a description as any. Well, the greed and lust have had their day, and the guilty are getting their punishment in one way or the other. To hell with the guilty, as far as I'm concerned, but I see no reason why the innocent should be punished."

"And my boys and I are the innocent, is that it?"

"That's it. Now hear me out. You probably don't know that I took a sideline job in this case, to get Philip Clayborne's blackmail tape for him at a price. Well, I got it back and collected my fee. In the process I happened to get my hands on something which I didn't return to Clayborne, the hundred thousand dollars he had already paid in blackmail. In fact, I let Clayborne believe that his ex-wife had escaped with the money, for reasons of my own. I want you to take that hundred thousand for you and the boys. It's tax-free, and it's yours with no strings. Take the boys to England, invest the money, pay for their education, and live decently."

Her expression was trapped between shock and wry amusement. "Who do you think you are?" she said, and there was pain in her voice. "To go around handing out punishment and favors like some kind of czar? Who are you to make these judgments about people's lives?" She wrenched herself up out of the seat, banging the table with a hip, and went out of the kitchen with her arms folded.

I gave her five minutes, then followed her into the living room and poured us both a brandy in large glasses. She was sitting near the fireplace, staring into the cold, empty hearth. She accepted the brandy, and said suddenly, "No one should have the power to make another person feel so vulnerable."

"I shouldn't have been so clumsy about it," I said.

She laughed dryly. "Dear Mr. Butler, how can you be subtle with a hundred thousand dollars? Is it against the rules to ask a question or two?"

"No, go ahead."

"What will you do with the money if I refuse it?"

I didn't hesitate. "I'll give it to the college. They took a beating from all this. They got a bad press."

"Why not keep it for yourself?"

"Ah, that would be against the rules. I make it a point never to profit more from a job than the fee agreed upon beforehand. It keeps me from temptation. And from slothfulness. That's one of the seven deadly sins, isn't it?"

"So morality rears its ugly head at last. You fascinate me, Mr. Butler. And what was your fee for this job, if I may ask?"

"Six thousand dollars," I said.

"That's quite a sum for a week's work. But at least you earned it, according to your code. You'll spend it with a clear conscience. But how am I going to spend this other money? Don't you see what you're asking? You want me to live off the profit from murder and blackmail, just to make my lot a little easier."

"A very noble little speech," I said. "But that's not the real reason why the money is repulsive to you."

"No? Then what is the real reason?"

"First of all, you're too intelligent to believe that the money has some kind of stigma on it. It's just money, coin of the realm. You might argue that it rightfully belongs to Philip Clayborne, but I throw that out on the grounds that he was a big contributor to that concoction I described in the kitchen. A man ought to pay for his vices, and for him this is getting off cheap."

She thought about it for a moment, then flashed me a tense smile. "You still haven't told me why the money is repulsive to me."

"Because you don't think you're worth it," I said. "Paul fixed you so that you don't think you're worth much at all. Hell, I read that confession. You described it yourself as the story of a man who became horrified at the insignificance of his life. He committed the worst crime in the book to escape from you and that life. That's not only rejection, that's judgment. You weren't just scorned, you were vilified, humiliated."

"That's enough!" She was as rigid as a mannequin.

"Not yet, it isn't," I said. "Now you're getting ready to live according to that maniac's judgment of you. You'll slink off into a corner someplace, take a menial job, pinch pennies so the boys can have a little meat on their plates, all in the name of respectability. But you'll know that the real reason is because he's convinced you that you don't deserve any better."

Her mouth was a garish, crooked line against the waxy sheen of her face. "All right, you've had your say. Can't you have the decency to leave me alone? I'll be here tomorrow. I gave my word, didn't I?"

I said goodnight and went upstairs to bed.

269

The next morning I cultivated corn from seven in the morning until noon, starting with the sun a pale-yellow disc above the ears of the strong black, and stopping when it was directly overhead, as yellow as molten brass. I unhooked the cultivator, swung astride the big horse, and jogged him down to the barnyard. When I entered the kitchen through the back door, Judy was stirring batter in a bowl before the stove.

"Good timing, Mr. Butler," she said. "Give me ten minutes."

I used the shower in the basement, as is our custom when we return from the field, and I put on a clean shirt for the occasion. As I began to eat, I noticed that she was dressed in the same clothes she had arrived in yesterday. I asked if she had failed to find the clothes I had told her about.

She carefully put her knife and fork down. Her gaze was calm, her complexion richer than I had ever seen it. "It isn't that," she said. "But there isn't any point in my staying until dinner now. I've decided to accept the money. I'll admit that what you said last night has something to do with it. I know I'm better than he made me feel. But there's another reason, a purely selfish one. I can't refuse this chance to go back to England. Just thinking about it gives me a lift. So I'll take the money, tainted or not, deserved or not. That means there's no reason for me to stay on."

"You're welcome to stay, anyway. For a week, if you'd like."

A new luster came into her eyes. "I know the invitation is sincere, and I am grateful. But I won't stay because I feel like an intruder here. You're alone, and there's some purpose in it. I can almost feel it. Maybe I wasn't the only one brutalized by what happened. You got a little smashed up, too, didn't you? I don't mean just the physical punishment."

"Yes, I got a little smashed up." It was an apt phrase.

She nodded. "But you're home now, and you're working it out alone, which is the only way. That's why I have to go home. Not for the boys. I need the comfort, so I can work it out alone."

She left that afternoon with the money. An hour later, walk-in rhythm with the horse, the plow points deep in the earth, oiled with sweat, I was aware of the comfort she had mentioned. It was more intense than yesterday, because she had taken the money.

David Anthony was a pen named used by author **William Dale Smith** (1929-1986). He wrote *'A Multitude of Men'* and *'Naked in December'* under his real name; as David Anthony he penned *'The Organization'*, and *'Blood on the Harvest Moon'*. In 1979 he was nominated for the Edgar Allan Poe award for Best Original Paperback for *'Stud Game'*.

In addition to writing novels, he was a farmer, a crane operator in the open hearth of a steel mill, a newspaperman, as well as a staff writer for General Hospital. He also served in Korea as a Staff Sergeant in the U.S. Marine Corps.

Original theatrical poster for 'The Midnight Man'